Jill Sorenson's family moved from a small town in Kansas to a suburb of San Diego when she was twelve. In the past twenty years, she hasn't lost her appreciation for sunny weather, her fascination with the Pacific Ocean, or her love for Southern California culture. She still lives in San Diego with her husband, Chris, and their two children. Jill is happily working on her next novel.

She is the author of *Crash into Me*, *Set the Dark on Fire* and *The Edge of Night*, all available from *Rouge Suspense*.

KU-415-577

Also by Jill Sorenson:

Crash into Me
Set the Dark on Fire
The Edge of Night

JILL SORENSON

SET THE
DARK ON FIRE

ROUGE
SUSPENSE

1 3 5 7 9 10 8 6 4 2

First published in the United States in 2009 by Bantam Dell
A Division of Random House, Inc. New York

Published in the UK in 2012 by *Rouge*, an imprint of Ebury Publishing
A Random House Group Company

Copyright © 2009 by Jill Sorenson

Jill Sorenson has asserted her right to be identified as the author of this
Work in accordance with the Copyright, Designs and Patents Act 1988

This novel is a work of fiction. Names and characters are the product
of the author's imagination and any resemblance to actual persons,
living or dead, is entirely coincidental.

All rights reserved. No part of this publication may be reproduced, stored
in a retrieval system, or transmitted in any form or by any means,
electronic, mechanical, photocopying, recording or otherwise, without
the prior permission of the copyright owner

The Random House Group Limited Reg. No. 954009

Addresses for companies within the Random House Group can be
found at: www.randomhouse.co.uk

A CIP catalogue record for this book is available from the British Library

Penguin Random House is committed to a sustainable future for
our business, our readers and our planet. This book is made from
Forest Stewardship Council® certified paper.

Printed and bound in Great Britain by Clays Ltd, Elcograf S.p.A.

ISBN   9780091949136

To buy books by your favourite authors and register for offers visit:
www.randomhouse.co.uk
www.rougeromance.co.uk

For Chris

Acknowledgments

Many wonderful people helped make *Set the Dark on Fire* possible.

Thanks to Shauna Summers, Jessica Sebor, and Vincent La Scala at Random House. Working with this team has been a dream come true. Extra thanks to the art department for the hottest cover ever.

I'd also like to thank Dr. Sean Bush, emergency physician and venom specialist featured in Animal Planet's *Venom ER*, for his generosity and patience in answering my questions about rattlesnake bite treatment.

Thanks to Rob Schmidt, a freelance writer and contributor of social commentary columns at *NewspaperRock*, for sharing his expertise on Native American culture.

Special thanks to my husband, Chris, an avid rock collector and enthusiastic admirer of cultural artifacts. While I was conceptualizing this project, he showed me photographs of the fertility stones in one of his grandmother's books, Manfred Knaak's *The Forgotten Artist:Indians of Anza-Borrego and Their Rock Art*. Those pictures inspired one of my favorite scenes.

1

Shay opened her eyes with a low moan. Her ears were ringing, her mouth was dry, and her head pounded with every heartbeat. From the blurry-edged space beside the bed, the telephone continued to shrill.

She blinked until the numbers on the digital clock came into focus: 4:52 A.M.

Reaching out, she fumbled for the receiver. "Hello?" she croaked, rolling onto her back and squeezing her eyes shut as a wave of nausea lapped over her. Her voice sounded like crushed gravel.

Another voice, one that was far more pleasant, low-pitched and even-toned, drifted into her ear, awakening a new level of consciousness. "This is Sheriff Meza with the Tenaja Falls Police Department. May I speak with Shay Phillips, please?"

He paused between her first and last name, as if reading it from a piece of paper. Although he was a complete stranger, he spoke with assurance and authority, like a man who was accustomed to getting what he wanted.

Something about his voice made her toes curl up under the covers.

Her headache throbbed and receded, throbbed and receded. Then the meaning of his words penetrated the fog surrounding her brain. "What?" she said, bolting upright.

"May I speak with . . ."

Barely listening, she dragged her tired body out of bed and stumbled across the room. All knees and elbows in the best of circumstances, she was extra-clumsy after a rare night of overindulgence. She hadn't felt this wrecked since her twenty-first birthday.

Five years ago exactly.

The room shifted, sending her careening into a set of dresser drawers, and she caught her hip on the edge. A bolt of agony shimmied down her leg, but she ignored it, lurching out into the hallway, toward the extra bedroom.

The door that loomed before her was littered with graffiti. A collage of crass bumper stickers, CD album covers, and website graphics ate up every inch of available space. Most of the images were angry and some of the words were profane, but Shay drew the line at pornography. If her little brother wanted to look at naked women, he could refer to the material stuffed under his mattress like a normal teenage boy.

At eye level, a magazine clipping featuring an airborne skateboarder urged her to "Get Bent." Beyond the door, she could hear music, not loud enough to melt eardrums, so he was probably asleep.

She rapped her knuckles against it. "Dylan?"

"Do I have the wrong number?" Sheriff Meza asked.

"Hang on," she said into the phone, twisting the doorknob. A few months ago he'd locked the door and climbed out the window, leaving the music blaring to throw her off. Since then, she'd removed the lock, but she hadn't entered his room uninvited.

She didn't want to walk in on him . . . doing anything.

Dylan was home, to her relief. To her chagrin, he wasn't asleep, nor was he alone. Angel Martinez, her next-door neighbor's dark-haired, wild-eyed daughter, was underneath him, digging her fingernails into his naked back.

The phone fell from her hand, landing with an audible thud on the worn carpet.

Dylan hadn't heard it ring, and he hadn't heard her knock, but he heard that. Looking over his shoulder, he fixed her with a murderous glare. "Get out."

Too horrified to do otherwise, she pulled the door shut and closed her eyes with a wince, trying to dispel the image. It registered, somewhat belatedly, that this was her house and she was in charge. Dylan was underage, and so was Angel, as far as she knew.

"I'm going to open this door again in two minutes," she warned, raising her voice. "Two minutes!"

Her head swelled with pain, making her dizzy. At her feet, Sheriff Meza was silent.

She picked up the phone. "This is Shay Phillips. Sorry about that."

"No problem," he replied smoothly. "I wouldn't have called so early, but we have a wildlife situation, and I was given your name."

She frowned, trying to focus on the conversation

instead of what was going on behind Dylan's bedroom door. Local law enforcement contacted her on occasion, if a mountain lion had been spotted in the area, but that wasn't the kind of news she needed to get out of bed for. This was rural Southern California. Mountain lions lived here.

"This is a lion situation?" she interpreted.

"Yes. I was hoping you could offer your expertise."

"How?"

"Well, there's been a fatality."

Her jaw dropped. "A *human* fatality?"

"Yes."

"Oh my God," she said. Mountain lion sightings were infrequent, attacks extremely rare, and fatalities . . . a person was more likely to be struck by lightning. "Are you sure?"

"No," he admitted. "I'd like for you to take a look at the scene."

She swallowed sickly. This hangover was going to get a whole lot worse before it got better. "Of course," she said anyway, her pulse racing. "Where is it?"

"On the outskirts of town. Kind of hard to get to. If you don't mind, I'll pick you up and take you there myself."

"Okay. Let me give you my address."

"I already have it," he said. "I can be there in about ten minutes."

Rubbing her aching temple, she groaned a reluctant agreement.

"See you then," he said, and hung up.

Shay pulled the receiver away from her ear and stared at it in disbelief. Was any of this really happening? She got a flash of how she must look standing outside her brother's room in her underwear, half-drunk, half-asleep.

No wonder the kid had issues.

Shaking her head, which felt too heavy for her shoulders, she stalked back into her own room and returned the phone to its cradle. After tugging on a pair of jeans, she ducked into the bathroom and turned on the fluorescent light.

Upon seeing her reflection, she grimaced. Even blurry, it was bad. Puffy eyelids, raccoon eyes, pale lips. Freckles everywhere. She'd tried to wash off her makeup last night, but the attempt hadn't been very successful.

"Damned waterproof mascara," she grumbled, leaning over the sink to splash her face again. Feeling dehydrated, she drank several mouthfuls of water from her cupped hands. Her stomach lurched in protest.

When it settled, she straightened, studying the woman in the mirror. "I will never drink again," she muttered, lifting a hand to her tangled hair.

It was a promise she'd made more than once, especially in her college days, because she'd never had a head for alcohol. Since coming home to Tenaja Falls she'd had few opportunities to engage in this kind of foolishness. Stepping back into her role as Dylan's caretaker, managing the run-down house her parents had abandoned, and working hard to put food on the table hadn't left her a lot of time to cut loose.

Trying to comb her hair only amplified her headache. Abandoning the effort, she tied it back, brushed her teeth, and called it good.

This was not going to be an "I feel pretty" day.

She sat at the foot of the bed to pull on thick socks and the scuffed hiking boots she used for work. Grabbing one of Dylan's old sweatshirts, a faded black hoodie, she walked back out into the hallway, squaring her shoulders for another confrontation.

She had at least five minutes left before the sheriff came.

Outside her brother's door, she took a deep breath and raised her hand to knock. Before she got a chance, Dylan wrenched it open. He stood there blocking the doorway, trying to look as menacing as possible, which would have worked better for him if he'd been wearing a shirt.

Her brother wasn't exactly a beanpole, but at seventeen, and six-two, he'd yet to grow into his height. He was all raw bones and sharp edges, as skinny as she'd been at that age. Shay's heart ached for him, for what she knew he was going through.

She crossed her arms over her chest. "Can I come in?"

In lieu of a response, he shoved the door against the wall and threw himself down on the unmade bed. Tucking his hands behind his head, he scowled up at the ceiling, waiting for his punishment.

Shay didn't know where to begin. She looked around her, as if the answer might be hidden amidst piles of schoolbooks and dirty clothes. Like his choice of artwork on the bedroom door, she didn't hassle him about how he kept his room. He did his own laundry, and judging by the amount of time he spent in the shower, he was the cleanest boy in the neighborhood.

Angel Martinez was gone, having crawled out the

window she came in, presumably. Shay sank into the only chair in the room. "How old is she?"

His blue eyes flew to hers in surprise. He must have expected her to talk at him, not to him. "Eighteen," he said.

She was too tired to feel relief. "I don't see her at the bus stop anymore. Did she graduate?"

He shifted on the bed. "No. Her dad makes her stay home."

Shay figured Fernando Martinez needed all the help he could get. His wife had run off a few years ago, leaving him to raise their five children on his own. Speaking of which . . . "Are you using protection?"

His mouth thinned with annoyance. "I would have, but we didn't get that far." He glared at her. "You ruin everything."

Despite her headache, she smiled.

"Where are you going?"

Tension twisted inside her empty stomach, reminding her that she should try to eat something before she left. "The new sheriff called. I guess there's been some kind of freak accident. A lion attack."

His brows lifted. "Really? Cool."

"Someone's dead. Not cool."

He studied her appearance. "You look like crap."

"Yes," she agreed with a sigh, and stood to leave.

"That's it? I'm not in trouble?"

"I don't know," she said, too weary to decide. In a few months he'd be eighteen, and she found herself perpetuating the old double standard. If he were a girl, she'd handle things differently, but he wasn't. If they were closer, she'd ask him if Angel was his girlfriend, or if he was in love with her. But they weren't.

Since Mom died, their relationship had been strained.

She might not like the answers to those questions anyway, or know how to deal with his responses. Was it acceptable for him to have a girl in his room as long as they were "in love"? Jesus, that sounded ridiculous, even to her.

The doorbell rang, signaling the shift from one grueling situation to another.

She closed her eyes, wishing she could go back to bed. Or better yet, go back in time and say no to that last drink.

"Do you want me to answer it while you fix yourself up?" Dylan asked.

Selflessness wasn't usually in his repertoire, so she was surprised by the offer. "Thanks," she said wryly, "but I think I'm beyond repair." Resisting the urge to ruffle his hair, something he hadn't let her do since kindergarten, she left the room.

In the kitchen, she grabbed a Coke and a couple of saltine crackers, pocketed her keys, and went out to face an abominable day. The instant she saw the man on her doorstep, Shay knew the interlude with Dylan had been its highlight. How cruel was fate! To throw her in front of a man who looked this good, when she looked this bad.

Few men towered over her, but he did. Even fewer made a bland uniform look like a million bucks, and he did that, too. Although the star on his breast pocket proclaimed his status, he was younger and more handsome than any sheriff ought to be. His hair was short and black as pitch, his skin was dark against the collar of his shirt, and his arms were sinewy with lean muscle. Unlike the state troopers and sheriff's deputies she saw on occasion, he wore no gun holster or CB radio at his waist, just a plain leather belt and army green trousers.

He was a tall, cool drink of water.

Moistening her lips, she let her gaze wander a leisurely path back up to his face. His jaw was shadowed by a day's growth of beard and his brown eyes were somber, reminding her of his business here.

With a jolt, Shay realized she was staring, and he wasn't flattered by her attention. She blinked a few times, trying to snap out of her lustful stupor.

"Miss Phillips?"

Ah, that voice. Carefully modulated and unerringly polite. Somehow she got the impression he'd rather chew on nails than converse with her. "Shay," she corrected, offering him her hand.

"Luke Meza," he said, accepting the handshake but releasing it sooner than he had to. Although his touch could only be called perfunctory, at best, a shiver of awareness passed through her. "Are you ready?"

She nodded.

His truck was parked along the gravel road in front of her house, and as she followed him down the cracked cement walkway she was struck again by how surreal the situation was. The sun had just begun to climb over the rock-covered hills in the east, and the first rays of dawn peeked through the cloud cover, casting the world in an eerie yellow light.

"You're tripping," she muttered to herself as she

made her way around to the passenger's side. "Try not to puke on his front seat."

The Ford pickup was desert issue, pale green, with the Tenaja Falls Sheriff's Department insignia painted on the door. The logo matched a round patch on Luke Meza's shirtsleeve. Trying to be more subtle, she studied him from beneath lowered lashes as he got behind the wheel. In a town as small as Tenaja, newcomers were always remarked upon, but he'd only been here a few days. So the only thing she knew about him was that he'd been appointed to the position after the previous sheriff had suffered a heart attack, and would serve until the townspeople elected one of their own to do the job.

"So you're the interim sheriff," she said. *Way to state the obvious, Shay.*

Giving her a curt nod, he started the engine and put the truck into gear.

He had nice hands, she noted, remembering the feel of his palm against hers. They weren't chafed from years of manual labor, like most of the men's around here, but they weren't soft, either. "Where are you from?"

"Las Vegas."

Sin City. Hmm. "Are you going back there?" He might be young, and an outsider to boot, but she figured he had a good shot at staying on as sheriff if he wanted to.

By the way he glanced across the cab, she decided he understood the implications of her question. "No," he said shortly, and didn't elaborate.

The strong, silent type. Check.

They traveled along the main drag for a few minutes before he turned on an unmarked dirt road south of town. It led to an undesignated off-highway-vehicle area, a cross-section of 4x4 trails local teens and other hell-raisers used as a racetrack.

With no conversation to distract her, Shay concentrated on not throwing up. Being jounced around inside the cab of the pickup didn't help. She reached into her pocket, took out a cracker, and started chewing. It tasted like sawdust. Shuddering, she choked down the pasty mouthful and popped the tab on her Coke. The instant the sickly sweet, overcarbonated soft drink hit the back of her throat, she remembered something bad.

Something very, very bad.

Last night, after drinking wine with dinner and beer at the bar, her crazy girlfriends had ordered a round of mixed drinks. Rum and Cokes.

A hot wave of nausea washed over her, causing beads of sweat to break out on her forehead. When they went over a bump, syrupy brown liquid sloshed over the rim of the can, dripping from her hand and soaking into her jeans. Setting the Coke aside, she removed her sweatshirt and rolled down the passenger window.

The sheriff finally gave her his full attention. She must have looked a little green, because he asked, "Are you going to be sick?"

"I don't think so," she said, hoping it was true. Really, she had a stomach like a steel trap. What went down did not come up. Usually.

Her tummy lurched, threatening to make her a liar.

She put her face out the window and gulped cool, early-morning air.

With a muttered curse, he pulled over.

Luke's initial impression of Shay was that she was beautiful. His second, from the way she fidgeted in the passenger seat and acted sort of spacey, was that she was on drugs.

Now he figured she just had a killer hangover.

Her disheveled appearance and unsteady gait didn't inspire much professional confidence, but it did spark his prurient interest. With her messed-up hair and smoky eyes, she looked like she'd been up all night giving some lucky guy the ride of his life.

He rubbed a hand over his face, wishing the Department of Fish and Game had recommended someone older, more reliable, and more experienced.

Getting out of the truck, he rummaged around in the cab for a fresh bottle of water and some paper towels. She was standing with her back to him a few feet from the dirt road, bent forward, her hands resting on her knees.

Not interested in watching her decorate the bushes, he leaned his forearms against the hood on the driver's side and stared out at their surroundings. There was nothing but barrel cactus, rock-strewn dirt, and sagebrush as far as the eye could see.

It could be worse, he supposed. He could be back on the beat, waiting for a drunken vagrant to vomit on the Strip.

He'd seen too many used-up party girls in Vegas to

find humor in Shay's predicament, but he'd over-indulged a time or two when he was her age, so he could sympathize. She was probably barely out of college, and hadn't learned her limit.

Although Luke didn't consider the situation amusing, he had to admit it was pretty ironic. He'd come to Tenaja Falls to avoid trouble, but here he was, neck-deep in it, on his way to a crime scene with a woman who couldn't walk a straight line.

When he glanced over at her again, she was crouched down farther, elbows planted on her slim thighs, head in her hands. The position wasn't deliberately provocative, and there was no doubt in his mind that she was truly ill, but this time it didn't deter him from looking.

Her hair was an improbable shade of blond, dark ash mixed with platinum, twisted in an untidy knot atop her head. Even in disarray, it looked thick and shiny and soft to the touch. Some obsessive-compulsive part of him wanted to take it down and comb his fingers through the tangles. He stifled the urge by imagining it would smell like cigarettes.

Her clothes were just as wild as her hair. Faded jeans, snug in all the right places. A thin white tank top that did nothing to disguise her subtle curves or the lacy black bra she wore underneath. One strap hung off her shoulder, an invitation to touch.

His fingertips itched to slide it back into place.

She had a tattoo on the nape of her neck, a tiny cat's paw with four little scratches. Wondering if she liked to be kissed there, he let his gaze trail down to her lower back. Between the waistband of her low-rise jeans and the hem of her tank top, a creamy expanse of skin was visible, lovingly detailed by curling ribbons of ink.

He'd bet his badge she liked to be kissed there, too.

His pulse quickened at the thought, but he shoved it aside. His mind had no business going that direction. She was way too young for him, and not everything about her appearance was seductive. Her well-worn hiking boots were sensible and the hooded sweatshirt she'd been wearing earlier covered her from neck to midthigh.

Maybe he should give her the benefit of the doubt.

Abruptly, she straightened. "Is that water?"

He jerked his gaze from the back of her jeans a split second too late. "Yeah," he said gruffly, stepping forward to hand her the bottle.

"Thanks." Tilting it to her lips, she downed a couple of ounces, her pale throat working as she swallowed. She looked like she wanted more, but she didn't push her luck. Neither did she take the paper towels he offered. "False alarm," she said, managing a weak smile. "I think I'm okay now."

Luke wasn't convinced, but he didn't have time to find another wildlife expert. "Are you sure?" he asked anyway. "I can try to get someone else."

"No. This is my territory. My responsibility."

Evaluating her sincerity, and her level of sobriety, he looked into her eyes. They were mildly bloodshot, her pupils tiny amidst a sea of dark blue. She was calm and lucid and quite lovely in the early-morning light.

Managing a careless shrug, he climbed back into the truck, waiting for her signal before he started the engine.

"Is it bad?" she asked after they'd been on the road a few more minutes.

"Yes." He'd seen worse but she probably hadn't.

"Are you going to tell me anything about it before we get there?"

"I would prefer that you draw your own conclusions."

"Is the victim . . ." her lips trembled ". . . a child?"

"No," he answered, voice grim. "A woman."

"Who?"

"She hasn't been positively identified," he hedged, keeping his attention on the road. Switching to a safer topic, he said, "I don't have much experience with wildlife. Why don't you give me a rundown on mountain lion behavior?" He cast a speculative glance her direction. "If you're up to it."

"Lions are notoriously shy. Usually they avoid humans at all costs."

"What about a mother protecting cubs?"

"It's a possibility," she admitted. "Bears will, but they tend to be more aggressive. They also like people food, which leads them into populated areas. A transient lion might skirt past suburban neighborhoods and go after livestock, even a family pet. Lions prefer deer, but if they get hungry enough, they will eat almost any prey that becomes available."

"Including humans?"

She hesitated. "Yes. In the cases I've studied, I believe hunger was the motivation for the attack." Her eyes met his. "Again, this is an extremely rare situation. Only five or six fatal incidents have occurred in California over the past two hundred years." Her tone was defensive. "Dog attacks are far more frequent."

Luke was sure what he'd seen couldn't have been done by a dog, but he didn't say that. He was also pleasantly surprised that she seemed to know her stuff, but he didn't comment on that, either. "Are there bears around here?"

"No. A black bear could wander this far, in theory, but I've never seen bear sign, and I've hiked every inch of this wilderness."

He fell into silence as they rounded the next bend, hoping he hadn't imagined the flinty determination in her eyes when she spoke of her responsibility to the land. She'd need it, along with nerves of steel and a cast-iron stomach, when she saw what lay ahead.

2

He brought her to the Graveyard.

It was a flat stretch of land, grassy and desolate, broken up by a single oak tree and a congregation of large, slate-colored rocks. They looked more like the humped backs of whales than headstones, and as far as Shay knew, no one had ever been buried here. Rumor had it the place was haunted by the spirits of dead Indians, and that it had been an execution site where horse thieves were hung. Teenagers called it the Graveyard because they'd been gathering here to tell ghost stories, and to mourn their losses, for decades.

Whenever a local kid got killed doing something stupid like drunk driving (which happened with alarming frequency around these parts) his friends got together at the Graveyard to have a party in his honor. Some came to grieve, some to drink, some to socialize. It was a popular hangout even when no one had died. High school boys flocked to the location, hoping a spooky setting and a bonfire would encourage their girlfriends to get cozy.

More than just memories had been laid to rest here.

Shay didn't believe any of the old stories, but she had to admit she'd been caught up in the ambience once or twice. Before she left for college, she'd given her virginity to Jesse Ryan beneath the hanging tree on a hot summer night.

She closed her tired eyes, picturing Jesse's face in her mind, wishing he'd been a little less handsome and a lot more sincere. Together they'd burned fast and bright, an old flame that rekindled from time to time, especially when she was feeling weak or self-destructive.

If there was anything positive about the morning so far, Shay thought, it was that she hadn't woken up in bed with Jesse.

She opened her eyes to see a lone officer at the side of the road. He was standing guard next to his police cruiser, his barrel chest all puffed up with importance. Shay had known Garrett Snell since they were kids. He was a bully and a blowhard and she didn't envy Luke Meza for having him as his only deputy.

Luke parked beside Garrett's cruiser, got out of the vehicle, and started off toward the Graveyard. She had to hurry to keep up with his long-legged stride, an experience she was not accustomed to. When he stopped suddenly, she almost crashed into his back.

"Just look," Luke said, holding up one hand. "Don't touch anything. Watch where you step. And don't talk until you're finished."

Feeling peevish, she stared back at him in silence.

"Do you understand?"

"Of course. I'm hungover, not stupid."

A ghost of a smile touched his lips. Then it was gone, as if she'd imagined it, and he took her by the elbow, walking her toward the circle of stones like a suitor leading a debutante. When she saw what was beyond the rock border, she was thankful for his support.

At first glance, the woman on the ground resembled a sleeping child curled up on one side. She was slim and small of stature, barely five feet tall, but the lines on her face and curves of her body showed her true age.

Shay recognized her, and like most of Tenaja's residents, she knew the woman hadn't been a child for quite some time. They weren't friends, and they never would have been, but that didn't make her any easier to look at.

Her long dark hair was matted with blood, partially obscuring the fatal wound on the nape of her neck. Mountain lions often attacked from behind, severing the spine, and she hadn't been spared this indignity. Deep scratches covered her hands, her shoulders, her exposed arms, her face. She'd fought. Her clothing hung in blood-soaked tatters from her petite frame. Flies and ants swarmed around her, lighting in and out of her open mouth.

Shay grimaced, covering her eyes with one hand and turning away from the gruesome sight. Her cheek met the hard wall of Luke's chest, and even in her tumultuous state she noticed how rigid he held himself.

To Shay's surprise, her response to the corpse was more emotional than physical. Her headache was still there, like a dull roar, and she was sicker than ever, but what she was most aware of wasn't her own discomfort or Luke's chest or even the woman lying dead before her. For a fleeting moment, the present receded, and she was sixteen again, standing in the barn behind the house, catching her first glimpse of death.

Gasping, she banished the image, relegating it to the dark, faraway corner of her mind where it belonged. Then she was staring up at Luke Meza, not the rafters in the barn, and he was gripping her upper arms as if he thought she might faint.

She risked another glance at the victim. This time, her brain worked to compartmentalize the elements of her reaction. Fear and horror went into one box, empathy into another, allowing her to analyze the subject with clinical detachment.

This was not a woman. It was a kill. Lion sign. Nothing more, nothing less.

"Okay now?" he asked, sensing a change in her demeanor.

"Yes."

When he released her, she gave the remains a closer study, measuring the size of the tooth marks with her eyes, noting the distance between the scratch lines. A part of her was proud of her composure, another ashamed of her inability to feel.

Remembering his instructions, she took a step back and considered her surroundings. There was no question that a lion, and a large one, probably a male, was responsible for this attack. But what had he been doing here, of all places?

The Graveyard looked the same as always. Low-lying rocks, the perfect height for lounging, were evenly spaced around the smoldering embers of last night's bonfire. Crushed aluminum cans and cigarette butts littered the soft dirt. In the close, quiet distance, grass-covered hills swayed with the gentle morning breeze.

Saying nothing, she examined the ground near the body. Her brow furrowed in concentration as she walked in a wide circle around the site, searching for any other evidence of the lion's presence.

"Well?" Luke asked when she returned to his side.

"It was a lion."

"But?"

"He wasn't here."

Although her words didn't make any sense, he acted like they did. "How do you know?"

"First of all, this is the last place a lion would bring a kill. Signs of humans are everywhere. Lions have an excellent sense of smell, and avoid fire."

He nodded. "What else?"

"Lions attack by stealth or ambush. If he followed her here, or was lying in wait—where's the blood?"

He didn't have to look to know there was no pool beneath the body. "Maybe he drank it."

"Sure, but some spilled onto her clothes. Why not on the ground as well?" Following that train of thought, she continued, "Even if he attacked her somewhere else, and dragged her from there, he would have chosen a more secluded place. That grass is high enough." She lifted her chin toward the adjacent hills. "It would provide better cover."

"So you're saying it's possible that he dragged her here, just not typical lion behavior."

"Right."

He played devil's advocate. "Attacking humans isn't typical, either."

"Yes, but there's another problem with your scenario."

"What's that?"

"No drag marks."

Looking out at the horizon, he swore softly. "Do you know who she is? The man who reported the body gave a name, but I'd like a confirmation."

"Didn't Garrett tell you?"

"No."

She sighed, wondering if the deputy was too lily-livered to take a good look, didn't want to admit his connection to the victim, or was just refusing to be helpful on principle. Garrett wasn't qualified to run for sheriff, so maybe he resented Luke Meza. "It's Yesenia Montes."

"Garrett knows her?"

"Every man in town knows her. Except you, I guess."

"She gets around?"

"And then some."

His dark gaze narrowed on Garrett for a moment, then came back to her. "Have you seen her with anyone in particular lately?"

She felt the color drain from her face. "You don't think—"

"The body was moved somehow," he interrupted, "and I don't suppose a lion floated her over here on a cloud. There's a term we use for circumstances like these."

"What's that?"

"Foul play."

Feeling weak-kneed, she lowered herself to sit on a nearby rock. Her stomach churned with renewed nausea. "I saw her at the bar last night," she whispered.

"With who?"

"Jesse Ryan," she said, putting her head in her hands.

Shay spent another hour searching for lion signs, scouring every inch of terrain. During that task, which required both patience and concentration, she couldn't find a single track, nor could she come up with a plausible explanation for the discrepancy.

The county coroner took the body to the morgue for an autopsy, and until he made a ruling concerning the cause of death, Luke said he had to consider it a homicide. Accordingly, he spent a lot of time taking pictures with a digital camera, recording everything from the position of the body to shoe prints and tire markings.

Then he started collecting evidence.

As a deputy, a crime scene investigator, and a man, Garrett Snell was pretty much worthless, so Shay asked Luke if she could help. He countered by suggesting she let Garrett drive her home. Both offers were politely refused.

With nothing left to do until she heard from her supervisor at the Department of Fish and Game, Shay curled up on the passenger seat of Luke's government-issue pickup and fell asleep. She dozed on and off, plagued by strange dreams. An indeterminable time later, Luke laid a warm hand on her bare shoulder, startling her awake.

She jumped at his touch, instantly alert. Her hands were curled up beneath her head, buried in the sweatshirt she'd been using as a pillow. As she straightened

she cataloged her condition. Her headache had faded.
She felt better.

"Mike Shepherd wants you to call him back."

Groaning, she massaged her eyes. They refocused on
Luke, who was standing at the driver's side door, extending his cell phone toward her. Not ready to talk to
her boss, she merely took the phone from him and
rested it in her lap.

His gaze followed her hand. It lingered there for a
moment then wandered up to the shoulder he'd just
touched.

Shay felt her bra strap slip down her bare arm.
Damned ill-fitting thing.

Across the cab, their eyes met. Her heartbeat kicked
up, throbbing hard and heavy against her ribs. Her fingers tightened around his cell phone.

"Just let me know when you're done," he muttered,
pushing away from the door.

After his back was turned, she let out a deep breath,
resisting the urge to fan herself. Had it gotten hot in the
cab of the truck, or was it just him? While she'd slept,
the morning sun had come out in full force, blazing
through the front windshield. Her can of Coke was sitting in the cup holder where she'd left it, getting warm.

No longer nauseous, she drank every drop.

Luke wasn't an easy man to read, but the look on his
face just now had been clear enough. It was the same
expression she wore when she saw leftover chocolate
cake in the refrigerator.

Disgusted with herself for wanting it.

She didn't know whether to feel flattered or insulted.
Confused by his reaction, she stared at the phone in her

lap. It looked harmless enough now. A moment ago its placement had seemed disturbingly erotic, an object he'd held to his mouth resting between her thighs. Was she just imagining that he'd thought so, too?

Trying to dismiss the exchange as post-hangover hormones, she flipped open his cell phone and scrolled down to recent calls. Mike's number was at the top of the list. Hoping Luke hadn't said anything to her boss about her "illness," she pushed Send.

"Mike Shepherd," he answered.

"It's Shay."

"Tell me what you've got."

Feeling way out of her league, she told him what little she knew, assuming he would think she was either blind or inept.

"Meza said he didn't see any sign either," was his only remark.

"Are you coming out?"

"I can't. Teri's in Sacramento, and I have the girls."

"What about Jeff?"

"I haven't been able to reach him."

Shay experienced a twinge of panic. She knew as well as anyone else in the field what procedure to follow when a wild animal threatened or attacked humans. The Department of Fish and Game's response to this kind of situation was to shoot on sight. She just hadn't expected to be the one to pull the trigger.

"I checked the GPS," he continued. "Sign or no sign, one of our collared lions was in the area at approximately 2:00 A.M. I triangulated his position to the exact coordinates of the attack. Now he's holed up at Queen's Den."

Her grip on the phone tightened. "Who?"

"Hamlet."

"Oh, no," she whispered, squeezing her eyes shut.

"Shay, I know he's special to you," Mike said, his voice pained. "I was there when we found him. It kills me to ask you to do this."

"Then don't."

He was silent for a moment. "The sheriff says his deputy has some experience with long-distance targets."

A flash of anger surged through her, replacing sorrow. Garrett had been a sharpshooter during his tour of duty in Iraq, and she didn't doubt he could get the job done. He might also enjoy doing it. "No," she said from between clenched teeth. "Deputy Snell is not going anywhere near my lion."

Mike sighed.

"I'll take care of it," she said, sniffling. "I want it done right."

"At least let Meza go with you."

"He volunteered?"

"Well, yeah. He doesn't want another incident any more than you do. And you know you can't go alone."

"Fine," she said, trying to get used to the idea. It was hardly the first unpalatable task she'd had to perform. "Fine," she repeated, feeling the hot sting of tears anyway.

Luke finished processing the scene for traces. In Vegas, he'd have had a team of investigators to collect evidence, but Tenaja Falls didn't have the resources, or the corresponding crime rate, to justify such expenditures.

When he checked in on Shay, she was wiping tears from her face with the sleeve of her sweatshirt. He rested his forearms on the open window jamb, trying to avoid the forced intimacy wrought by the close confines of the vehicle. He didn't want to get caught up in her drama, or to repeat the mistake of looking too deeply into her sultry blue eyes.

"So what's it going to be?" he asked.

Her lips twisted a little at his brusque treatment. "I need to get some stuff at headquarters before we go. My GPS tracker. The long-range rifle."

He felt his jaw tighten with annoyance. Deputy Snell wasn't his favorite person, but Luke would rather go shoot a lion with him than an emotionally unstable female. Not that he knew anything about hunting. "What about Garrett?"

She looked over his shoulder, assessing Deputy Snell's less-than-svelte physique. "He'd slow us down."

"How far is it?"

"Five miles, uphill."

She was right. Garrett got short-winded traversing the parking lot. Mike Shepherd better not have been lying when he claimed Shay Phillips could "track like an Indian and shoot like a white man." "Give me a minute," he said. Walking away from her, he instructed Garrett to take the trace evidence down to the sheriff's office and catalog it.

Not that Luke really expected him to comply.

In the three days Luke had been acting as interim sheriff, Garrett Snell had called in sick, dozed at his desk, driven around aimlessly in his cruiser, and camped out in a booth at the local café. Luke suspected he took kickbacks from the casino for looking the other way when its patrons violated the speed limit. He may have been involved in some even darker dealings.

Luke didn't really care one way or another. Garrett was a problem for his successor; Luke had more than enough on his plate right now.

Removing all thoughts of the troublesome deputy from his mind, he went back to the truck and got behind the wheel. Shay Phillips didn't smell like cigarettes, he couldn't help but notice. More like sun-warmed skin and sleepy woman and something faintly herbal, like wildflowers or handmade soap. In the short time she'd occupied the cab of his pickup she seemed to have transformed it into her own cozy personal space.

Determined to steel himself against her allure, and ignore her tantalizing scent, he drove on in silence, doing a good job of blocking her out. Until her stomach growled.

"Are you hungry?" he asked.

Shrugging, she hugged her sweatshirt to her chest in a forlorn, childlike gesture.

Luke didn't have much of an appetite, but if they were going to hike, they needed to eat. She'd probably been too sick to hold anything down earlier, and he'd been working almost eight hours without a meal himself.

"I'll stop by the café on the way out of town," he decided. He didn't need her getting weak or dehydrated on top of everything else.

Bighorn Café was one of two restaurants along Tenaja's main drag. The other was Esparza's Mexican

Food. Luke had patronized both and suffered no ill effects.

In addition to these establishments and a couple of fast food joints, the sleepy little burg boasted an auto repair shop, a hardware store, and a grocer's market. On the way out to the interstate, there was also a Super 8 motel, dueling gas stations, and a funeral parlor.

From what he could gather, Tenaja Falls was a convenient place to stop if your car broke down or ran out of gas. While visiting here, you could eat, sleep, or die.

After the frenetic pace of Las Vegas, Luke should have found Tenaja Falls restful and quaint. He didn't.

He parked outside the café and held the door for Shay on the way in. She arched a brow at him when he chose a booth, but he figured only truckers sat at the counter. When Betty Louis, the proprietor, came to take their order, he realized the error of his ways.

The town was even smaller than he thought.

"Howdy, Sheriff," she said. Betty was a tall woman, broad-shouldered and sturdy, with fading blond hair and sharp blue eyes. Yesterday she'd asked him if he was married, where he was from, and if he had a girl waiting for him back there, so he already knew she was an insatiable gossip. Or worse, a matchmaker.

"Looks like you had a nice time at the party last night," Betty said, giving Shay a sly wink. She had a full carafe of coffee in one hand and a bandage on the other, as if she'd burned herself in the kitchen.

Cooking accidents and nosiness. Hazards of the trade.

"No," Shay said, darting a glance at him. Although he was in uniform and on official business, Betty was implying that he and Shay had spent the night together. "I mean yes, the party was . . ."

Betty smiled, delighted to watch her stammer.

"Just bring me the special," Shay said with a glare, handing back her menu.

"Same for you, Sheriff?" When he nodded, Betty filled both their mugs from her carafe. "And all the coffee you can drink, on the house."

Luke took a sip of coffee, which was nothing fancy but tasted a lot better than the swill at the station. Out of habit, he'd chosen a booth in the corner, and from that vantage point, he could see both exits while keeping an eye on his pickup through the fine coat of dust on the windows.

Bighorn Café was like a hundred other roadside diners in a hundred other podunk towns. From its worn vinyl booths and chipped Formica tabletops to its old-fashioned cash register and laminated menus, everything was outdated.

On the wall behind the counter, a single dollar bill had been framed.

"Sorry," Shay said when Betty was out of earshot. "I would have told her we were working together, but I thought you might want to keep things quiet."

"I do," he admitted. "At least until the coroner releases a report."

She hunched her shoulders a little, as if trying to make herself smaller, and wrapped her hands around the steaming mug. "I've been thinking it could have been kids. Maybe they found her on the dunes and took her to the Graveyard. They didn't report the body because they'd been out after curfew, drinking and driving or whatever, so they brought her to a place where she was sure to be discovered."

He'd thought of that, too. It was far-fetched, but possible.

"Or migrant workers," she ventured. "We've got plenty of those around here. In the country illegally, afraid to call the police, that sort of thing."

She seemed to be awaiting his response, so he said, "You may be right."

"I mean, this is Tenaja Falls, not Las Vegas. The circumstances are strange, but people just don't . . . off one another around here."

He made a noncommittal murmur, sipping coffee. Unless he could prove the scene had been staged, there wouldn't be much to investigate. "When a body has been moved or tampered with, procedure dictates we assume a homicide has occurred. Burial in an unmarked grave, for instance. That usually doesn't happen when a person dies of natural causes."

"Were you a homicide investigator in Vegas?"

"No. I was on a task force for organized crime."

Luke was saved from her next question—what brought him to Tenaja—when Betty laid down hot, heaping plates. Eggs, bacon, hash browns, toast. It was typical small town fare, and even he could take comfort in that simplicity.

Shay picked up her fork and dug in, so she must have been feeling better. She ate with economical efficiency, apparently not interested in starving herself skinny or affecting dainty mannerisms. Her unselfconsciousness amused him until she noticed him watching her.

She looked from her plate, which was almost empty, to his. Something like hurt darkened her eyes, and he understood the reason for it. She thought he found her provincial. And of course, he did.

Setting her fork aside, she picked up her coffee mug and drank from it, daring him to comment on her appetite. He wisely refrained. Nor could he think of any way to smooth things over, or understand why he wanted to.

His attention was drawn away from her a moment later when a cocky-looking young man came through the front door. Luke evaluated him the way he did everyone, with an instinctive assessment of height, weight, age, and attitude. His dark hair was slicked back, his Levi's were rolled up at the cuffs, and his plain white T-shirt fit him more snugly than current fashion dictated. He moved like a man who could handle himself in a fight but wasn't expecting one, and as he looked in their direction, his surly mouth went slack.

One glance at Shay, who had grown tense in the seat across from Luke, revealed the young man's identity. Well, well. It was the infamous Jesse Ryan.

Jesse must have come to the same conclusion as Betty, which Luke found even more ridiculous the second time around. On-duty police officers weren't supposed to parade around with female conquests. But maybe any man with Shay Phillips was considered guilty by association.

"Excuse me," she said, sliding out of the booth and retreating to the ladies' room.

Jesse's eyes followed Shay until she disappeared. When they returned to him, narrowing with animosity,

Luke amended his impression of the local Lothario. Maybe Jesse *was* spoiling for a fight.

Shay had told him that Jesse lived above the auto shop down the street. What she'd left unsaid was the relationship between them. Jesse stared after her like she was his unclaimed possession.

"You want a booth, Jesse?" Betty asked, because he was just standing there.

Jesse mumbled something about not being hungry anymore and went outside. Leaning his back against the building, he took a pack of smokes out of his pocket, struck a match on the heel of his black motorcycle boot, and lit one up.

He looked just like James Dean.

Luke threw a couple of bills on the table and rose to his feet, walking outside to grant the younger man's unspoken invitation.

Against the brick wall, Jesse continued to smoke, feigning indifference.

"Jesse Ryan?"

"Yeah."

"I'm Sheriff Meza."

His expressive eyebrows rose. "So?"

"Can you answer a few questions about Yesenia Montes?"

Those words seemed to penetrate his cool façade. "What about her?" he asked, meeting Luke's gaze for the first time.

"Did you leave the Round-Up with her last night?"

Jesse opened his mouth to say no, but at that moment, Shay came through the double glass doors. Luke couldn't have timed it better. Standing in front of them, she moistened her lips in a nervous, provocative gesture both of them were intensely aware of.

"Go wait in the truck," he said. Although she didn't appear pleased by his tone, she complied, so the gamble had paid off.

Jesse threw his cigarette butt on the ground and crushed it under his boot heel. He didn't like the way Luke talked to Shay either, and Luke enjoyed needling him a bit more than he should have. He'd been a young, jealous fool himself, once upon a time, and knew from experience that it was always better to be the cause of envy than the source.

"I left with her," Jesse muttered.

"Where did you go?"

"We walked to my place." He indicated Tenaja Auto, a few doors down.

"What time?"

He shrugged, leaning his back against the brick siding. "A little after midnight, I guess. She bummed a cigarette. I went on up." He paused for emphasis. "Alone."

"Why didn't she stay?"

"I didn't invite her to."

"Why not?"

He looked past Luke's shoulder, to where Shay was sitting in the truck. "She wasn't the one I wanted."

3

Dark Canyon State Preserve, where Shay did her field research, was a mixed chaparral and live oak woodland a few miles west of Tenaja. Its northern border skirted the edge of the Los Coyotes Indian Reservation, the Anza-Borrego Desert stretched far and wide to the east, and to the south, there was only Mexico.

Mountain lions inhabited all of those areas. According to Mike Shepherd, the one they were after was on the preserve.

Dark Canyon was in the rain shadow of Palomar Mountain, so what few storm fronts rolled in from the coast rarely climbed past the summit. Tenaja Falls and its environs received more uninterrupted sunshine than the beach. The canyon was situated between the mountains and another low-lying ridge, so it also got plenty of shade, and Deep Creek ran through the center, so it had water, too. A break from the relentless heat and a little extra moisture gave the land a fresh, verdant look the rest of the area lacked.

It was a pleasant place to hike, picturesque and

invigorating. Shay would have enjoyed herself if she were alone, unfettered by a job she didn't want to do and a man she didn't want to be with.

She set a grueling pace, wanting to test Luke's city-boy limits and punish him for the way he'd looked at her in the diner.

Shay had grown up dirt poor, right here in Tenaja Falls. She may have a college degree and a career that supported her family, but she was only one step away from white trash, and she resented Luke Meza for making her feel like it.

Unfortunately, he didn't have any difficulty keeping up with her. She was sweating like mad and dizzy from exertion, while he'd yet to utter a single complaint. Exercise and a good meal were the best cures for a hangover, in her opinion, and she felt better for having both, but she needed a break.

Conceding her defeat, she slowed to a stop, resting her back against a smooth sycamore. Taking small sips of water from her pack, she closed her eyes and concentrated on regulating her breathing.

When she was cooled down enough to speak, she focused her attention on him.

He was leaning against a tree, sweating as much as she was, if not more. The sight would have pleased her except that he also looked fit and virile and alarmingly sexy.

"Are you trying to kill me?" he panted.

She chuckled weakly. "You should have said something."

He only shook his head, telling her he'd been too

proud to do so. "Didn't you hear me whimpering a mile back?"

Laughing, she let her eyes fall closed again, blocking out his appealing smile and dark visage. She found him very attractive, and that was a damned shame. It hadn't escaped her notice that he considered Tenaja Falls a roadblock on his path to bigger and better things.

Shay, on the other hand, was here for the long haul. She was fond of the familial atmosphere and she loved this land like a mother. If Luke Meza thought she was small town, well, maybe he was right. However common, she was proud of her heritage, and however sordid, she wasn't ashamed of her past.

Sighing, she adjusted her gun strap, which felt like it was burning a diagonal mark across her chest. His smile faded as his eyes followed her movements, reminding her that it wasn't necessary for them to have similar interests.

They didn't even have to like each other.

Shay wished she'd dressed with a little more care this morning, because it was hot. In mid-April, the weather was usually cool, especially in the higher elevations, but today a Santa Ana wind was blowing, bringing an increased fire hazard and warm, dry conditions.

Her sweatshirt had been abandoned in the truck, leaving her clad in a thin cotton tank top. The black lace push-up bra she was wearing underneath had gone great with the satin camisole from last night, but it was hardly appropriate for hiking.

The sheriff must have thought so, too, because he tore his gaze away from her chest. "How much farther?"

With trembling hands, she took the GPS tracker out

of her pack to double-check Hamlet's location. He was still near the top of the ridge, probably sleeping in a shady nook, awaiting sunset. "Only another half mile."

She'd explained how the tracking system worked when they'd dropped by base headquarters, a small stucco building where she compiled research and studied wildlife data. It was there that she'd nursed an eight-week-old lion cub back to health after his mother had been killed by local ranchers. The cub had been reintroduced to the wild when they'd found a surrogate mother lion and added him to her litter.

To Shay's amazement, Hamlet had not only lived, he'd thrived.

It had been a risky experiment, but a young lion couldn't survive on his own until he was several years old, and prolonged contact with humans would only reduce his chances.

Shay had been careful not to treat him like a pet during the time they'd spent together. To do so would have been dangerous for both of them. But he'd been irresistibly cute! Maybe she'd spoken too softly, touched him too lovingly.

Had she done something to assuage his fear of humans? Did he remember her still?

Over the past five years, she'd seen Hamlet on a regular basis. After he'd survived into adulthood, Shay and her fellow research biologists had collared him with the GPS device. He'd been tracked and tranquilized for routine checkups. Just last year, she'd cleaned his teeth.

And now she would kill him.

"We'll have to go slower as we get closer, and move

as quietly as possible," she said. "If he spooks, we'll never catch up to him."

"Why don't you use dogs?"

Mountain lions could be treed fairly easily. In California, it was illegal to hunt lions for sport, but in other parts of the country the practice was widespread. And unfair to both animals, in her opinion. "Hunting dogs are a risk to the lions, and vice versa. Besides, this is a wildlife preserve. Wild animals avoid places domestic animals have been."

He studied her face, then her rifle, and she knew he was wondering if she had the heart to shoot it. "How big is this lion?" he asked warily.

"Almost two hundred pounds at his last weigh-in."

Before they'd set out, Luke had put on his gun belt. Now he placed his hand on the holster, eyeing the trail ahead of them with some trepidation.

Shay wanted to smile, because his Ruger 9mm was no match for Hamlet. Luke was probably good with his weapon, but it was designed for close range. If Hamlet got within fifty yards of them, he could move faster than any man's hand.

She approved of his caution, however. A person would have to be stupid not to be afraid of a lion Hamlet's size. That was why she was glad Garrett hadn't come along. "I know the area pretty well," she said, to calm herself as well as him. Emotional baggage or not, this was nerve-wracking business. "His mother used to live here. There's a low hill directly across from the den we can use for cover. From there it's an easy shot."

He grunted at her oversimplification. "How many times have you done this?"

"Killed a lion? Never. But I've tracked and tranq'd plenty." Taking another gulp of water, she bolstered her courage. "Ready?" She wiped the sweat from her forehead. "I want to get this over with."

Queen's Den wasn't so much a cave as a sheltered rock outcropping with enough brush to hide the comings and goings of its inhabitants. Hamlet had been born and first captured at this place; now his life had truly come full circle.

Shay would much rather have tranquilized him and let the veterinary scientists at UC Davis handle a more humane euthanasia, but that was against policy. Several years ago, two victims were attacked by the same lion on the same day. The incident was unprecedented, but it created a scandal within the Department of Fish and Game. The warden was accused of dragging his feet, and the "shoot to kill" solution implemented afterward was very much a political maneuver.

It was up to her to make Hamlet's passing as peaceful as possible.

Peering across a grassy, sun-drenched clearing, Shay attached the scope and lined up her shot. She was lying on her belly along the slope of the hill, ants crawling up her arms, pebbles digging into her elbows. A strand of hair fell into her eyes. She blew it out of her face.

"Okay," she whispered, signaling Luke.

He had the stronger arm, so he threw the lure. The fist-sized balloon of deer blood exploded on impact, splattering a cluster of rocks below the den. Flattening himself next to her on the slope, he cupped his hands over his ears and waited.

Her heart roared with trepidation. Sweat stung her eyes.

For a long moment, she thought Hamlet wasn't going to come out. A sated lion didn't always answer the call of the lure, and it would be too risky to go in after him.

Then she saw him, moving stealthily, so low to the ground he was almost crawling. She couldn't pull the trigger too early or he would bolt, but her body was taut as a wire, her finger screaming to flex.

Wait for it, she told herself. *Just wait for it.*

Hamlet had excellent eyesight, but he didn't see them. Lifting his nose in the air, he didn't smell them either, for they were downwind. He only caught the scent of the lure, and walked right into its heady trap.

He came out into the clearing, muscles rippling beneath his tawny coat. Her heart jumped into her throat. He was immense. A healthy male in his prime, two hundred pounds of pure, unadulterated power.

He could close the gap between them in about fifteen seconds.

Beside her, Luke's attention was rapt. Intuition told her he was sharing this experience with her, feeling the same conflict she was. They were in awe of the lion's presence, exhilarated to be in such an intense, dangerous situation, and disturbed that a magnificent animal had to die this way.

Blood thundering in her ears, she lined him up in the crosshairs, stroking her finger over the trigger, waiting for the perfect opportunity . . .

And when she had it, she took the shot. Straight through the heart.

Hamlet fell like a titan.

Stumbling forward, he lost his footing and collapsed in a boneless heap. He didn't get up. It had been quick and easy and virtually painless, just how Shay wanted it, but she wasn't proud or satisfied or even numb.

She was devastated.

Rolling away from the rifle, she clenched her hands into fists and pressed them to her stomach, trying not to sob.

Luke tore his gaze from Hamlet's lifeless form. "What happened?" he asked, instantly alert. Taking her by the wrists, he pulled her hands away from her body, searching for injuries. "Are you hurt?"

She shook her head, unable to speak. Unable to breathe.

His hold on her wrists loosened. Her lungs expanded and contracted, releasing her from panic's grip.

"What's wrong?" he asked, gentling his voice.

She closed her eyes, seeing the cub Hamlet had once been. Batting at dragonflies, leaping through foxtails. Falling asleep in the cradle of her arms, just like her brother, Dylan, had done so many times, so many years ago. "I bottle-fed him," she whispered, feeling like a fool.

"Who?"

"Hamlet."

He looked around in confusion. "The lion?" he said, his tone incredulous. "You bottle-fed that beast?"

She laughed so she wouldn't cry. "He was just a baby then."

His expression softened as he checked on Hamlet, making sure he was still down. Rather than reproaching her for the misplaced compassion, he rubbed his thumb over the bones in her wrist and let her hands go.

"You're some crack shot," he said admiringly, and she burst into tears.

They waited at a safe distance for the helicopter to land.

Luke felt the strange urge to comfort her while two men from UC Davis rolled Hamlet into a body bag and hefted him aboard the craft. Although Shay had remained stone-faced, for the most part, at the sight of a dead woman, she'd fallen apart after the lion went down.

He'd also been shaken by the incident. Judging by what he'd seen this morning, getting mauled by a lion was a horrible way to die, and when he'd caught his first glimpse of Hamlet creeping across the meadow, he'd been damned scared. He wasn't comfortable putting his life in a stranger's hands, let alone a tree-hugging Barbie who'd been partying all night, but her trigger finger hadn't wavered and her aim was true.

Gazing upon the lion's prone form, with Shay weeping silently beside him, he'd felt his own measure of sadness. Unlike humans, animals killed without malice. Luke's ancestors would have mourned the loss of this rogue lion's spirit.

The helicopter would take Hamlet all the way to UC Davis for analysis. His coat bore no trace of blood, but Shay said all cats were fastidious. Either way, forensics would tell the tale. His teeth, claws, fur, and stomach contents would be tested for human tissue.

She waved at the pilots as they lifted off, her expression sober. When the noise faded and the wind from the rotor died down, she surprised him by taking his hand.

And just like that, the mood changed. One moment he was lost in contemplation, a thousand miles away, the next he was right there beside her, having a very physical, very inappropriate response to the feel of her palm sliding against his.

"Thanks," she said, nibbling on her lower lip.

She had a lush mouth, ripe for kissing, and if she didn't know the effect it had on men, she was a fool.

Luke had to force himself not to jerk his hand from hers. His reaction was immediate and visceral. He wanted her. Her face was smudged with dirt and her tank top damp from sweat, but he wanted her. Wanted to press her down to the ground and make her dirtier, pull off her top and make her sweatier.

"What are you thanking me for?"

She blinked her wet-lashed eyes. "For not being like Garrett."

"What's Garrett like?" he asked, although he knew.

Proving she wasn't a fool, she pulled away from him. "Never mind," she said, picking up her rifle and adjusting her pack.

For a moment, he was sorry he'd been so abrupt. Her doelike innocence might be feigned, but her love for animals was genuine and her shooting skills were impeccable. Maybe lust had tainted his perception, changing a simple gesture of gratitude into what seemed like a blatant come-on.

Luke wasn't a trusting soul, for good reason. He'd been blindsided before.

Whatever her intention, he couldn't afford to be distracted by her. The bond they'd forged over the course of the morning had caught him off guard. Yeah, he felt an instant connection to her, an almost irresistible sexual pull, but he wasn't going to act on it. He didn't need any extra complications right now. Her relationship with Jesse Ryan, a suspect, was more than enough incentive to keep his distance.

They headed back down the canyon in silence. It seemed as though several days had passed since Luke was woken up by the emergency telephone system at the station. Having no interest in securing permanent lodgings in Tenaja Falls, he'd been bunking at the firehouse like a vagabond. He had plenty to do before he called it a day, including interviewing the man who'd reported the body and talking to the coroner about the autopsy.

He wouldn't have believed it was only midafternoon if the sun wasn't beating down on the top of his head.

Being from Vegas, the heat didn't bother him, and although he was no outdoorsman, he found his surroundings remarkably peaceful. The vegetation was green, the air was fresh, and the nearby brook bubbled pleasantly. He also enjoyed a strenuous workout, and Shay Phillips could hike her curvy little butt off.

When she stopped midstride, he almost lost his footing. "I'll catch up with you in a minute," she said, skirting around him.

He waited while she ducked behind some bushes.

"I have to pee, Meza." She fiddled with the tab of her jeans. "Give a girl some privacy."

"Oh. Right." Turning on his heel, he went on ahead without her.

He hadn't gone far before he realized he had no idea where he was. She'd been following a trail of some fashion, but damned if he could see it. The ground beneath him was strewn with oak leaves, and there was no discernible path. Gnarled tree trunks loomed close, their sharp-edged branches reaching out to snag at his clothing. When the underbrush began to snarl around his feet, he had to admit he'd made a wrong turn.

It was embarrassing, really. He hadn't been on his own for five minutes, and he was already lost.

Looking around the shady glen he was standing in for a familiar landmark, he noticed a rock wall he didn't remember passing. It was cracked and moss-covered, seeping with moisture. At the base, behind a waist-high bush, one of the fissures widened to a good-sized hole.

If he wasn't mistaken, it was some kind of cave.

His heart rate kicked up, blood surging with adrenaline. He squinted into the dark confines, almost certain he could see something in there.

Something . . . wriggling.

The sound of leaves crackling behind him made the hairs on the back of his neck stand up in awareness. He put his hand on his gun, wondering if Yesenia Montes had been given a similar warning before the lion pounced.

Shay had expected Luke to walk a few feet down the trail and wait for her there, so she was surprised when she couldn't find him. Tracking his footsteps, she realized he'd wandered off in the wrong direction.

Smothering a smile, she followed his obvious path through the thick sagebrush. When she heard a surprised shout, she started running, panic flooding her system.

He was on the other side of an enormous oak, back pressed against a flat rock formation, pointing his 9mm handgun at a ferocious, menacing, terrifying . . .

Skunk.

"Don't shoot it," she cried out, holding a hand over her heart. She was weak with relief, giddy from too little sleep and too much stress, all of her emotions on edge. Apparently, the skunk had startled him, and she couldn't help but laugh at the picture he made.

He cast a withering glance in her direction. "I wasn't going to," he said, holstering his weapon.

With Shay standing behind the female skunk, trapping her in, and Luke blocking the front of her den, the protective mama did what nature deemed appropriate. Turning around, she raised her tail.

"Oh, no," she gasped. She tried to tell him not to move, but she couldn't quite get the words out.

When he sidestepped, the spray hit him full-on, with absolute precision.

Shay clapped a hand over her mouth, snorting with laughter. Taking affront, the mother skunk whirled around and sprayed again, coating Shay in the most noxious substance on earth. With a final twitch of her tail, she darted past Luke into the shelter of her den.

Shay's amusement cut off like a switch. The stench was overwhelming; she couldn't breathe, let alone laugh.

"Come on," she choked, gesturing for him to follow.

Crashing through the brush, she made her way toward the water, trying to see through stinging eyes.

She dropped her gear at the edge of Deep Creek, shed her boots and socks, and jumped in. Luke did the same, wading in after her.

The water brought instantaneous relief.

Ducking her head under, she scrubbed at her face and arms, hoping the smell wouldn't linger on her skin. She'd known dogs who'd been skunked, and with or without tomato juice, sometimes their fur carried the scent for weeks.

After a vigorous washing, she felt brave enough to look at him.

"That was your fault," he accused. He was glowering, waist-deep in icy cold water, soaked to the skin.

"My fault?" she sputtered. "You pulled a gun on a skunk!"

The corner of his mouth quirked up. "If you hadn't shown up and started laughing, it wouldn't have sprayed."

She smiled back at him, admitting her guilt. Then, cocking her head to one side, she said, "I don't know about that. You were tromping around by her babies, way off the beaten path."

"Beaten path," he scoffed.

The pool they were standing in was one of many along Deep Creek. It was a pretty area, sun-dappled and bright, surrounded by cattails and purple larkspur. The water wasn't deep, but it was clear and fresh, fortified by snowmelt from Palomar Mountain, and so cold it made her teeth chatter. Even on a hot day it wasn't the place to take a leisurely dip, but she found herself wanting to linger. When Luke Meza let his guard down, he was good company.

She lifted her arm to her nose and sniffed. Either she'd washed off the scent, or she was suffering from olfactory fatigue. "Is it gone?"

He eyed her warily. "I don't know."

Shay was about to ask him to smell her when she noticed him averting his gaze. She looked down, realizing that her tank top had been rendered see-through, putting her black lace push-up bra on intimate display. Embarrassed, because the lingerie was designed to accentuate curves that didn't exist, she waded out of the water and pulled her tank top over her head.

"Our clothes will dry faster this way," she said, wringing out her top and spreading it over a flat rock in the sun. They still had another hour to hike before they hit civilization, if Tenaja proper could be called such, and walking in wet fabric was miserable.

When he took off his own shirt, she felt her jaw go slack. He may be tall and lean, but the man had muscles. Nice ones. His chest was smooth and taut, there were lateral ridges along his rib cage, and his stomach looked as flat and tight as a drum.

She shivered, wondering how all those muscles would feel against her fingertips. Her lips. Her nipples. The tips of her breasts tingled at the thought. The hard little nubs were already threatening to burst through the lace of her bra.

Flushing, she turned her back to him, lamenting her "look at me!" nipples and barely-there breasts. At the zipper of her jeans, she hesitated, considering her skimpy underwear. It had been chosen as part of her "girls' night out" ensemble, like her bra, and was an insubstantial swatch of pale pink. It couldn't be helped, so she shucked out of her jeans, squeezed as much water from the well-worn denim as she could, and hung them up to dry on a tree branch.

He was looking again, she discovered, and this time he wasn't so quick to avert his eyes when she caught him. Crossing her arms over her chest, she decided turnabout was fair play. "Keep going, Sheriff," she said, gesturing for him to continue undressing. "It's not like I've never seen a man in his shorts before."

"I'm sure you have," he said, dropping a pointed glance at her wet panties.

She stifled the urge to cover herself there, too. "Your underwear can't be any more revealing than mine," she added, giving him a tight smile.

He didn't dispute that, but when he came out of the water he removed his pants slowly, obviously not pleased by the role reversal. As it so happened, she was wrong. His boxer shorts were white, soaked through, and left absolutely nothing to the imagination.

He didn't appear to be suffering unduly from the cold, and she felt her entire body flush with heat. Cheeks flaming, she turned away from him, wishing she hadn't looked.

Feeling like a ninny, and a drowned rat, she scrambled onto a large, sun-warmed rock by the edge of the pool. Lying down on her back, she fanned her wet hair out behind her. Despite the tension humming in the air and the grim duties they'd performed that day, Shay found herself savoring the moment. The afternoon sun felt glorious on her bare skin and the icy dunk had revived her senses, making her more aware of her body, of the damp fabric against her tingling flesh and the soft caress of the breeze.

She let her eyes drift shut, not opening them even when he settled in beside her. "This has been the worst day ever," she murmured. It was an offhand comment, for she had experienced far worse days, one in particular that made today seem like a cakewalk, but she didn't want to talk about that. She never talked about that.

On the scale of bad days, however, it ranked pretty high. She'd woken up with the mother of all hangovers, examined a dead body, and been forced to kill an animal she loved. Getting skunked was just the icing on the cake.

Happy birthday, baby.

She snuck another glance at Luke, wondering how old he was. At first glance, she'd have guessed him to be about thirty, but now she wasn't so sure. He was calm and deliberate, with none of the bravado she associated with younger men. Whatever his age, he was in prime condition, hard and well muscled, his face as fine as his physique.

She squirmed, self-conscious about her soft tummy and flat chest. Next to him she couldn't help but feel awkward. Her skin was too pale, her hair a tangled mess. Here she was, half-naked with a good-looking man, and she hadn't shaved her legs all week.

"So what's with you and Jesse Ryan?"

"Jesse Ryan?" she parroted. He'd never been further from her mind.

"He's your boyfriend, right?"

"No. Not since we were kids."

He gave her a look that said she was still a kid, which was insulting.

"We went steady in high school," she clarified, her pulse kicking up a notch. "Almost ten years ago." She may be younger than Luke, but she wasn't a kid. She hadn't been since Dylan was born, maybe even earlier.

Was Luke wondering if she was available?

"It didn't bother you that he left the bar with another woman?" he asked.

Shay's ego deflated like a popped balloon. He wasn't interested in her—he was investigating. "It bothers me to see him self-destruct," she admitted quietly.

"Was Yesenia Montes dangerous to a man's health?"

She threw an arm over her eyes, blocking out the sun. "She was poison, but that's not what I meant. He's married."

"Really." His tone was flat, indicating he knew that already.

"I mean, he's separated," she corrected, then cringed at what she'd given away. She and Jesse may have broken up after graduation, but they'd dated off and on all throughout college, and slept together more than once since he'd said his vows.

This was perhaps the only aspect of her life she was ashamed of, and like hard alcohol, she'd sworn off Jesse Ryan many times.

Luke didn't miss the nuance. "Is that so?" he asked, studying her face.

She looked away. "His wife and daughter live on the other side of town."

"How old is his daughter?"

Her stomach twisted with regret. "Six months."

"And how long have they been separated?"

"Three years."

Of course, this information cast Jesse in a terrible light, exactly where he deserved to be. He'd been bouncing back and forth between women since puberty. Shay hadn't spoken to him since she'd found out Tamara was pregnant. She didn't miss his lying, cheating ways, but she *did* miss his friendship. Jesse Ryan was a charming ne'er-do-well, the mischievous boy who refused to grow up, the life of every party.

In retrospect, she'd used him as an escape from her depressing family situation. But playtime was over. She'd matured, and moved on.

If only Jesse would do the same.

"He said he didn't go home with Yesenia last night. Do you believe that?"

She shrugged. "She's not his usual type."

"Why not?"

"His standards may be low, but hers were nonexistent."

"Was she a prostitute?"

"People said that."

"Who went to her?"

Shading her face with one hand, she said, "You'll have to find that out on your own, Sheriff."

Satisfied with her answers, he rested his head back against the rock and threw one arm over his eyes. Apparently, the interview had concluded.

Shay lay back and closed her eyes also, irritated by his nonchalance. It didn't seem fair that she be interrogated when he'd revealed nothing of himself. "Have you ever been married?" she asked, posing the first question that came to mind.

"No." His tone suggested he didn't care for the topic.

She pressed on, undeterred. "Do you have a girl-friend back in Vegas?"

"No."

"Don't you like women?"

He shifted beside her, lifting the arm that was covering his face. Too late, she realized how provocative her question sounded. She could feel the heat of his gaze all over her body. Her nipples tightened, pebbling against the lace of her bra, and a beat pulsed between her legs. The sun was shining on the front of her panties, soaking them in warmth, and the sensation was so pleasurable she had to smother a moan.

She wanted to squeeze her legs together to ease the ache.

Instead, she sat up. Desperate to find something else to focus on, she reached out and plucked a green sprig from the plant next to her. "This is white sage," she said inanely, because he was still watching her. "Cowboys used it for deodorant." Like a moron, she rubbed the tiny leaves against her armpit to demonstrate.

His eyes darkened and his nostrils flared.

It was a pleasant fragrance, she supposed. Better than skunk anyway. "Do you want some?" Twisting off another sprig, she held it out to him, moistening her dry lips.

He moved so fast she gasped. Ignoring the sage, he took her upper arms in his hands, pressing the full length of his body against hers. When the hard wall of his chest met her lace-covered breasts, the sprig of sage fell from her hand, forgotten. "Do you always get what you ask for?" he said, his eyes on her mouth.

He was breathing hard, and she could feel tension in his pectoral muscles and the tautness of his abdomen. More to the point, she could feel the exciting proof of his arousal, nudging the sweet spot between her legs.

"Yes," she said, brushing her lips over his, answering the question his body was asking rather than the one his mouth had posed.

He let her go as quickly as he'd grabbed her, denying them both.

Muttering a curse, he stalked over to the tree branch where his pants were hanging and proceeded to put them on. In his condition, the damp fabric must have been twice as unforgiving, because he had some trouble with the zipper.

While she sat there, feeling confused and dejected, he wrestled into his shirt and strapped on his gun belt.

Then she finally understood. The signs had been right there in front of her face all day, but she hadn't seen them. Now the answer to that question she'd asked was as clear as tracks in the snow: Luke Meza liked women, all right. He just didn't like her.

4

The hike back to Luke's pickup really sucked. Shay was hungry, tired, and uncomfortable. Each step she took was an agony of damp, form-fitting denim. The adrenaline that had been driving her since sunup fled, leaving her running on empty.

Every few moments a fresh wave of humiliation washed over her. She wanted nothing more than to stop and rest, to collapse in a pathetic little heap, to curl up in a ball and wrap her arms around her head.

Instead she straightened her shoulders and lengthened her stride. On the downhill grade, she went faster than she should, and was pleased to hear him stumble a few times in an effort to keep up with her, sending a spray of loose pebbles down the trail.

What had possessed her to throw herself at him? Even at her lowest, loneliest moments, she'd never come on to a stranger. She'd never had a one night stand. She'd never picked up a guy at a bar and gone home with him.

So why had she acted like such a desperate slut after

one touch from Luke Meza? God! He hadn't even kissed her.

Clenching her hands into fists, she rounded the last bend to the clearing where his truck was parked, torn between wanting to punch him and wanting to punch herself.

"I need to talk to your neighbor," he said as he got behind the steering wheel. He consulted a small wire-bound notebook that had been resting on the dash. "Fernando Martinez?"

Frowning, she pulled on her seat belt. "Why?"

"He found the body."

"Oh."

He gave her an assessing glance. "You're State Parks, right?"

She nodded, catching his drift. A lot of park employees were also trained peace officers, assigned to serve and protect the people as well as the land, but Shay was a field biologist, not a ranger. Dark Canyon State Preserve didn't get many visitors, and she had no law enforcement experience. Nor did she want any.

The last thing she felt like doing was spending more time with Luke, extending what had already been an excruciating, exhausting, embarrassing day.

"I really shouldn't do a drop-in interview alone," he said.

Sighing, she furrowed a hand through her drying hair. It was hanging loose down her back, keeping her shirt damp and her neck cool. At early evening, the Santa Ana winds were still blowing, warming the night air.

Although she wanted to refuse, she'd engaged in

enough unprofessional behavior today. "What do I have to do?"

"Nothing, really. Just come along and let me do the talking."

"Fine," she muttered, annoyed with his ability to focus. After what had transpired between them, she felt painfully self-conscious. How could he act so unaffected?

With Hamlet gone, the immediate threat had been taken care of, but the work had only just begun. Weeks of study would be dedicated to sorting through the particulars of the attack. If Shay could discover a reason for the lion's behavior, she would do her damnedest to prevent another tragedy from occurring.

Because Hamlet had been her baby, her lion, her research experiment, Shay felt as though she had Yesenia Montes's blood on her hands. Maybe Fernando had seen something she hadn't, a track she'd overlooked, a detail she'd missed. The sooner they talked to him the better, because once word got out about Yesenia's death, rumors would fly.

There were no secrets in Tenaja Falls.

Fernando Martinez lived a quarter of a mile down the road from Shay. Like hers, and most of the residences on Calle Remolino, his was a ranch-style adobe, flat-roofed and low to the ground. In the summer, when temperatures soared above 100 degrees on a regular basis, this type of building stayed relatively cool.

As Luke parked his truck in Fernando's driveway, two brown-skinned boys came flying around the side of the house wielding super-soaker squirt guns. Smiling at their antics, Shay pulled on her sweatshirt before she exited the vehicle.

She knew the boys' names, if not which was which. Fernando had two kids in grade school, another teenager besides Angel, and the sweetest little curly-haired kindergartener you'd ever seen. Shay had often wondered what kind of mother would leave so many children behind, especially one so young.

She'd often wondered how her own mother could have done the same, but never came up with a satisfying answer to that question, either.

"Dad!" the taller boy yelled in the direction of the screen door, lowering his water gun. His younger brother took that as an invitation to soak his T-shirt, and they were off, laughing and chasing each other through the lengthening shadows.

Angel opened the door, a harried expression on her pretty face. Her long black hair was caught up in a ratty-looking ponytail. Unlike Shay's, this style appeared deliberate. She also had circles under her eyes, a half-dozen rings in her ears, and a metal-studded leather bracelet around her wrist.

No wonder Dylan had a crush on her.

Clinging like a vine to Angel's jean-clad legs, there was a small girl with chocolate-colored curls. Her eyes widened when she saw Luke's badge.

"Hi there," he said, looking down at the little girl. "What's your name?"

Too shy to answer, she hid behind her older sister.

"I'm Sheriff Meza," he offered politely.

Angel stared at him in mute defiance, her hand on

the doorknob, as if she was thinking about barring him entry.

"Do you know Miss Phillips?"

"Yes," Angel said, nodding at Shay.

"Can we speak with your father?"

When panic crossed over Angel's features, Shay realized the girl thought this visit was regarding her late-night tryst. Fernando must not have told his daughter about the gruesome discovery he'd made this morning.

"It's not about Dylan," Shay said to reassure her.

Luke arched a questioning glance in Shay's direction, and Angel relaxed immediately. "Come on in," she said, putting her hand on the top of her sister's head to guide her forward. "He's just out back." Angel led them past a family room that looked well used and through a kitchen that smelled of good things to eat. There were chopped vegetables on the countertop and simmering pots on the stove.

Shay's stomach rumbled.

Angel opened the screen door leading to the backyard, gesturing for them to go on without her.

Fernando was tossing feed to a group of chickens in a small coop. He was a strong man, wiry and compact, with a face that showed plenty of wear and tear. Over the past three years, since Maria left, he'd aged a decade.

When he saw them he straightened too quickly, then grimaced and placed a hand on his lower back, a telling gesture. Despite his weariness, and the lines around his eyes, he was handsome. Hard and handsome and, like a lot of Tenaja's men, old before his time.

She'd known him for most of her life, but Fernando

greeted Luke first, showing deference to his rank. After introductions were exchanged, Fernando invited them both to sit in a couple of green plastic chairs around a matching table on the back patio.

Luke took out his notebook and pen. "Tell me what you remember about this morning," he requested, "beginning with the time you woke up and ending with the phone call you made to emergency services."

Fernando paused, collecting his thoughts. Although his kids spoke English without a trace of an accent, Fernando struggled with the language. "I woke well before sunrise," he said. "It was dark. I clean my rifle and go out to hunt."

Luke's brows rose. "What's in season?"

"Rabbit is always . . ." He made a gesture with his hands, like a bunny hop, then turned them palms-up, empty. "But not today."

She waited for Luke to ask Fernando if he had a license, or if he knew hunting any kind of game was illegal on county property, but he didn't.

"I went to Graveyard, as kids say. I look for bottles and cans to recycle."

"Did you find any?"

He frowned. "I did not notice. When I drive close, I see . . ."

"What?"

"Her. Yesenia. On the ground."

"You recognized her."

He considered his response. "Not at first. I just thought she was a girl in trouble. Maybe drink too much. Or go with boys . . ." He trailed off, shaking his head. "Then I get close, see her face. Torn clothes.

Marks on neck." He rubbed the back of his own neck with a wince. "I went home to call right away."

"How close did you get?"

Fernando gave an approximate indication, widening his arms.

"You didn't touch her?"

"No. Nothing to do. She was already dead."

"How did you know?"

He thought about it. "Her chest was not moving. Head . . . turned funny."

Luke was silent for a moment. "Did you see anyone else this morning? Driving on the road, or in the area?"

"I passed a few cars on the main drag. No one near the Graveyard. No one for miles."

Luke slanted a glance at Shay. "Anything you want to ask?"

"Fernando, you're a hunter," she said, leaning forward. "Did you notice anything unusual at the Graveyard?"

"*Sí,*" he said. "No tracks. No blood."

"What do you think killed her?"

"*Un león,*" he replied immediately.

"Did you see one?"

"No. I have never seen one."

Shay sighed. The locals would be whispering about vampires and *chupacabras.* She turned to Luke, not sure what else to ask.

"You said you recognized Yesenia," Luke continued. "How well do you know her?"

Fernando shifted in his chair, uncomfortable for the first time since the interview began.

"*La conóces . . . o la sábes?*" Luke asked.

Shay felt heat rise to her face, and not just because

Luke was asking Fernando if he knew Yesenia in the biblical sense. By posing the question in Spanish, he was cutting her out of the conversation, dismissing her as if she weren't there, and insulting her by assuming she wouldn't understand. He was wrong. Not only did she catch his meaning, she discovered something new about him: he was not a native speaker of Spanish.

His pronunciation was a little too . . . hard. Spanish speakers tended to soften some consonants and drop others altogether.

"I didn't know her very well," Fernando replied in the same language, choosing to ignore Luke's insinuation. "But where are my manners?" he said with a smile. "Would either of you like something to drink? There is cold cerveza inside."

Shay shuddered and Luke declined, standing and thanking Fernando for his time. When they passed through the kitchen once again, she inhaled deeply, wishing such a feast would be waiting at her house.

Instead she'd be met by a sink full of dirty dishes and an empty fridge.

She said good-bye to Angel with a conflicted heart, hoping Dylan wasn't serious about her. Angel seemed like a nice girl, but she represented the kind of complication her brother didn't need. Dylan was rebellious, abrasive, and smart as a whip. Shay wanted him to go to college more than she'd ever wanted anything for herself. As much as she loved Tenaja and respected its blue collar men, she wanted better for her brother than a lifetime of backbreaking manual labor under the hot desert sun.

As they walked toward Luke's pickup, Shay shoved

her hands deep into the pockets of her sweatshirt, feeling the heaviness of damp denim against her legs and the weight of the world on her shoulders.

She settled into the passenger side, not bothering with her seat belt, and studied Luke with open interest. He could be of European heritage, she supposed, but with his dark coloring, and a name like Meza, she'd figured differently.

"What?" he asked, surprising her. She'd have sworn he could pull off stone-faced silence for any length of time.

"You speak Spanish like a white man."

He narrowed his eyes at her. It was a stupid thing to say, impulsive and presumptuous, but what the hell. She was curious, and he didn't like her anyway. "I'm Luiseño," he said, turning his attention back to the road.

"Really?" Her interest was piqued further. The Luiseño tribe, named by the founding fathers of the San Luis Rey Mission, was one of the twenty-six registered tribes in the area. San Diego had a more diverse Indian population than any other place in the United States. "Where were you born?"

"Pala."

Shay was stunned. Pala Reservation was only thirty miles from Tenaja, and one of the poorest communities in the county. Luke Meza wasn't a well-to-do city boy from the lights of Las Vegas. He was local. Not only local, but Native.

He'd probably grown up with less than she had. Now he thought he was too good for her, and that rankled her hard.

"Who's Dylan?" he asked, rolling to a stop in front of her house. "You mentioned that name to Fernando's daughter."

"He's my younger brother," she said, glancing toward the door.

"He lives with you?"

"Yes."

He followed her gaze, assessing the single car in the driveway, rusted basketball hoop above the garage door, and sadly neglected front lawn. "Where're your folks?"

The question shouldn't have caught her off guard, but no one in Tenaja Falls ever asked about her parents. They already knew. "Gone," she said shortly.

He nodded, looking down the road instead of at her face.

She supposed that was his way of saying good-bye, and it left a lot to be desired. "I can't say it's been a pleasure," she muttered, getting out of his truck.

"I can't, either," he replied, his eyes licking down her body once more before he slammed the truck into gear and drove away.

Eager to put some distance between them, Luke was driving too fast along the bumpy dirt road, leaving a cloud of dust in his wake.

He knew he'd done the right thing, but he cursed himself for having the presence of mind to say no when she'd been soft and pliant underneath him, granting him free use of that sweet-looking mouth and luscious body.

He groaned, picturing her pert little breasts, encased

in the sexiest scrap of black lace he'd ever laid eyes on, and those pale pink panties, clinging to her ass like wet tissue.

He could have kissed her. Hell, he was almost certain she'd have let him strip off her panties and bury himself in her right there on that sun-warmed rock. He was hard all over again just thinking about it.

His hands curled around the steering wheel until his knuckles went white.

Perhaps it was a poor excuse for the intensity of his physical reaction, but he'd been too long without a woman. Sin City had a way of making a man feel dirty, inside and out, and the last few months in Vegas had really taken their toll. He'd seen enough bachelorettes, strippers, and whores to last him a lifetime.

So why was he panting after this small town bad girl?

Shay was easy on the eyes, to be sure, and she was probably easy in bed, but women like her were hard on men. And Luke had never been into casual sex.

He'd never been tempted to throw down his bone in the great outdoors either, but when the opportunity presented itself, he'd been so goddamned ready. He was still ready. For some reason, her earthy sensuality triggered this utterly primal, embarrassingly powerful, "me Tarzan, you Jane" response.

He couldn't stop thinking about her wet panties.

Shifting in his seat, he leaned back and eased off on the gas. If he took the turns any faster, he'd end up in the ditch.

He should have gone ahead and given her what she'd been asking for. Never mind that he was on duty. Never mind that until he heard from the county medical examiner, he was supposed to be investigating a possible homicide. Never mind that if the autopsy report indicated wrongful death, he might have to consider Shay Phillips a suspect, along with her "rebel without a clue" boyfriend and gun-toting next door neighbor.

"Goddamn it," he muttered, hitting his palm against the steering wheel.

Garrett Snell had told him all about Fernando Martinez this morning. Apparently, the man had caught his wife in bed with another *hombre* a few years back, and according to Garrett, Fernando ran them both out of town with a shotgun.

The quiet, unassuming father of five he'd met a few moments ago didn't quite match up to Deputy Snell's colorful description of him. Luke didn't know who to believe, but his deputy was as shady as they came. He might have to add Garrett's name to the list of suspects.

Cursing his luck, which had taken a turn for the worse in Vegas a few months ago and gone downhill from there, Luke reached into the glove compartment for his cell phone. As he leaned toward the passenger seat, he got a whiff of Shay Phillips' sweet herbal scent. His upholstery would probably smell like her for days.

Gritting his teeth, he checked his messages. Two missed calls and no bars. Damned hillbilly town had the least reliable cell phone service this side of the border.

This interim sheriff position was turning out to be a real bitch.

Luke hoped the ME would be able to make an unequivocal decision regarding cause of death, to reconstruct the last moments of Yesenia Montes's life in a way that explained every unanswered question, and to rule out foul play.

Maybe he was mistaken about the body being moved postmortem, and wrong to think the scene had been staged. Maybe, just this once, good had prevailed over evil, and the most innocent explanation would turn out to be the right one.

The county medical examiner was long gone, so he had to deal with Barry Snell, the funeral home director. In addition to being Garrett's father, Barry was the mayor of Tenaja Falls and its coroner when no suspicious circumstances were evident. Having already been introduced to him, Luke knew that unlike his son, Barry had an upbeat temperament and perpetual smile. Luke wasn't sure which man he trusted less.

"Official ruling is accidental death," Barry said as he opened the door to the morgue's side entrance, his gentle grin belying the seriousness of his words. Luke wondered if Barry was capable of a suitably grim expression. "But Dr. Hoyt remarked upon a few anomalies."

Luke followed him to the autopsy room. "Like what?"

"Take a look," Barry said, ushering him inside.

Luke had seen his share of dead bodies, mostly drunks and vagrants, old men who had succumbed to illness, drug and alcohol abuse, or the elements. He wasn't a homicide detective, however, and the only time he'd been in this particular situation, standing over the corpse of a young woman in a morgue, he'd been identifying her body.

The memory was painful, to say the least, and

carried with it a thousand regrets. Though he'd tried to, he hadn't been able to save her. Leticia Nuñez had been another casualty of Vegas, the city that chewed up beautiful women and spit them out.

Luke pushed the disturbing recollection aside, because the victim before him deserved his full attention. He vowed not to fail her, too.

Yesenia Montes was lying on her stomach on a stainless steel table, her head turned to the side, sightless eyes staring forward. Under the light of the high-powered lamp above her, he could see a number of broad, vertical lines on her naked back, shoulders, and buttocks.

"They're lividity marks," Barry explained, thumbing through a three-ring binder.

Luke was no forensic expert, but he knew such marks were common postmortem artifacts. A body often bore signs of whatever it had been resting against, or upon, in the moments or hours after death.

Stepping forward, he studied the darkened bands of flesh. They were widely spaced and evenly distributed, obviously not a result of the lion's attack or caused by the soft dirt she'd been stretched out on. He frowned, guessing such marks couldn't be found anywhere in nature, and feeling as though he should recognize their origin.

"What else?" he asked, his pulse accelerating.

Barry gave a good-natured shrug. "The doctor said he'd never viewed a victim of a lion before, but the wounds were consistent with what he'd researched. Trauma to the spinal cord and cardiac arrest were the primary causes of death."

"Hmm," Luke replied, wondering about the lack of blood.

"Says here the lion had a broken tooth," Barry added, flashing his own pearly whites.

"Really?"

"One of the punctures left less of an impression than the others," he said, closing the binder. "Dr. Hoyt made a dentistry mold."

"What about DNA?"

"He took a sample from the bite area, in case there was saliva. And several swabs from . . ." He cleared his throat. "Other places."

Luke glanced at the body on the table. With so many cuts and scrapes on her battered form, it was difficult to determine whether the woman had also been the victim of sexual assault in the days or hours before her death. Noting the pink stains on Barry's rounded cheeks, Luke decided to discuss that possibility with the medical examiner. "When will Dr. Hoyt be available for a phone consultation?"

"Tomorrow morning."

Luke sighed and rubbed his tired eyes. There was one more thing he had to do before he went off duty, and it was the worst job imaginable. "Who's her next of kin?"

Her house was unnaturally dark, quiet, and empty.

It was also stiflingly hot, so Shay made the rounds, opening the windows in her bedroom, the bathroom, and the kitchen, pushing aside the sliding glass door in the living room and turning on the ceiling fan overhead. They had an air conditioner, one that worked, but now that the temperature outside had dropped there was no reason to turn it on. By midnight, if she left the windows open, the house would be cold.

As predicted, a pile of dirty dishes littered the kitchen sink. A plastic milk jug, sans milk, sat out on the cream-colored tile countertop. The red leather purse she'd been carrying last night was upended next to an open pizza box on the coffee table in front of the TV, proof that Dylan had fended for himself.

He'd left her a single dollar bill and one solitary slice.

Upon sight of congealed cheese, red pepper flakes, and grease spots on cardboard, her stomach should have rebelled. It didn't. Sighing, she sank onto the couch, picked up the cold slice of pizza, and took a bite. It wasn't half-bad.

Having anticipated her little brother's presence, and an inevitable discussion about Angel Martinez, she should have been relieved he wasn't there. Instead she pictured Yesenia Montes's battered, bitten body and felt a trickle of unease. Dylan hadn't left a note, but that was nothing new. She was lucky he hadn't taken her car.

Normally Shay appreciated solitude. She worked alone a lot and enjoyed her own company. Her friends were few but constant, her social calendar steady, if uninspired, and her love life . . . well, her love life had always been hit or miss. More miss than hit, but who was counting? She had her friends. She had her career. And she had Dylan.

Except that she didn't have Dylan anymore. She hadn't had him in a long time. Her mother's death had torn them both apart, and he'd met the tragedy the way boys do, with defiant glares and sullen silence. Shay, on the other hand, had waged a teenage girl's rebellion, falling in with the wrong crowd and staying out all night.

If her father had stepped up as head of the family during that tumultuous time, maybe things would have been different. But her daddy had never been much of a provider, emotionally or financially. Hank Phillips was a restless dreamer who refused to be tied down by mortgages or material things. While Shay went to community college, they'd survived on welfare checks, food stamps, and the grace of God.

Shay managed to graduate at the top of her class despite these hardships, and when she'd been offered a scholarship to Cal Poly, she'd jumped at the chance to escape her dysfunctional home life. In some ways, she'd sacrificed Dylan to save herself.

Since then her brother had been distant. By age ten, he'd mastered the art of apathy. She'd given him space, thinking he was missing their mother, having growing pains, and grieving in his own way.

As soon as she came home from college, their father took off again. Dylan hadn't shown any reaction to his departure.

They hadn't seen Hank in almost five years now. Every so often they got a postcard from Tucson, Albuquerque, or Saskatchewan. The sporadic correspondence was a poor substitute for a father who hadn't been much of a parent when he *had* been around.

She wasn't sure who'd had the more unconventional upbringing, her or Dylan. Shay had been raised almost solely by her mother, Lilah, a tenderhearted flower child no more equipped for reality, or the trials of parenthood, than her freewheeling husband. She'd been too soft, too emotional, too ethereal for this world.

For all her faults, Shay had loved her mother desperately, and been loved by her the same way.

Feeling a lump in her throat. Shay swallowed her sudden sentimentality along with the last bite of pizza. Directly across from her, next to the boxy old TV set, three half-deflated helium balloons were hovering above the carpet, their shiny, crinkly surfaces rustling under the whir of the ceiling fan.

Happy birthday.

5

Dylan made his way down Calle Remolino with his hands thrust deep in his pockets and his head hanging low.

At just past 10:00 P.M., late by Tenaja standards, the street was deserted. The only sound was the almost indiscernible crunch of his sneakers on hard-packed gravel, and for the thousandth time, he wished he had an iPod.

He was tired from the long walk and an intense pickup game. Every Saturday night a motley mix of locals, some white, some Indian, played against the only rival team, a group of Mexicans who were short, quick, and ruthless. There had been a few minor scuffles, but that was to be expected, because from the high school cafeteria to the b-ball court, Indians and Mexicans were always feuding.

As far as Dylan could tell, the two heritages had a lot of similarities, so he wasn't sure what the beef was. Mexico was part of North America, and the culture was, by definition, a mixture of Native and European. Dylan figured most Mexicans had as much Indian blood as the guys on the reservation.

Even so, they seemed to hate each other.

Tenaja Falls was kind of backward that way. A lot of the white kids, who enjoyed a slight majority at Palomar High School, stuck together and acted superior to everyone else. It was lame, but there wasn't much else to do in this buttfuck town but drink and fight.

He could see his house in the distance, and knew Shay was home because the lights were on in the living room. Instead of going inside, he decided to keep walking. His pulse accelerated and his mouth went dry at the thought of seeing Angel again.

If she'd returned any of his calls, he'd have dropped the pickup game and asked her out in a heartbeat. She hadn't, and he was pretty sure he knew why.

Dylan couldn't believe his stupid sister had busted in on them this morning. Of all the lousy luck. Shay hardly ever came into his room. Not only that, she'd been out boozing it up with her friends the night before, and she couldn't handle her liquor worth shit. He'd expected her to sleep in late.

His only chance to get laid in the past seventeen years, and she'd totally ruined it.

He didn't fool himself into thinking Angel would be up for a repeat performance. At eighteen, she was an elusive older woman, ten times better looking than he was, and way out of his league. She'd also made it clear she didn't consider him boyfriend material, and as far as he knew, she didn't sleep around. Damn it.

She'd probably only let him kiss her out of gratitude.

Last night had been totally out of control. By the time they got to his door, it was already late, and they were both tired, but he'd invited her inside anyway. To his surprise, she accepted. They started talking about music, and although he'd never had a girl in his room before, let alone a really hot one with a knockout body, he felt comfortable with her. Which had been cool, because he'd always been tongue-tied around her before.

It was the bane of his existence. He had a 4.0 GPA. All of his classes were college prep, advanced placement, or honors. But when he tried to talk to girls, his brain shut off and his mouth went numb.

Cursing himself, and his sister for interrupting the most exciting moment of his life, he continued walking, even though he knew Angel didn't want him, and that he would probably never drum up the nerve to talk to her again.

Like most of the houses on Calle Remolino, hers was quiet and dark. The Martinezes used to have a dog, a mangy old shepherd mix with a menacing bark and a mouthful of sharp teeth, but when he died, they hadn't replaced him. Angel's dad had a hard enough time feeding his kids.

Feeling like a stalker, and a fool, he walked along the side of the house, wondering which bedroom was hers, hoping Fernando wouldn't come out with a loaded shotgun. He was about to turn around and head home when he noticed the muted glow from the kitchen window.

He stepped forward, drawn to the light.

Angel was inside, standing at the sink, her back to him. Apron strings were tied loosely around her waist, and her ponytail, sooty black in the fluorescent light, was curled over one shoulder. She was washing dishes.

He froze, struck by a powerful recollection of another time he'd spied on her without her knowing.

Her brother, Juan Carlos, was a year younger than Dylan, and he'd always been an enterprising little bastard. Right now he was in juvenile hall for selling an assortment of drugs out of his locker at Palomar High. When Dylan was thirteen, he'd paid Juan Carlos five bucks for the opportunity to watch Angel take a shower.

His gut clenched with guilt and longing, because he remembered the incident in achingly vivid detail.

After pocketing the cash, Juan Carlos had taken him to his dad's workshop, a small outbuilding next to the main house. The bathroom window was visible through the shop's dusty windowpane. Juan Carlos instructed him to stand on the worktable, and from that vantage point, Dylan could see into the shower stall.

A few minutes later, Angel had come in, taken off her robe, and stood under the shower spray in her bare naked glory.

He was floored by the sight. He'd looked at dirty magazines before, of course, but this was different. She was real. While he stared, transfixed, she'd turned and let the water cascade down her slender back. By the time she started shampooing her hair, he was painfully aroused. With his eyes peeled and his mouth slack, he'd watched soapy rivulets course down her belly and into the dark triangle between her thighs.

Juan Carlos must have decided upon seeing Dylan's reaction that pimping out a peep show of his sister was wrong because he let out a feral growl and tackled him. They landed in a heap of arms and legs on the shop's dirt floor, and Dylan, too stunned to fight back, didn't even begin to defend himself until Juan Carlos blood-ied his nose.

"It was your idea," he protested when Juan Carlos let up on him.

"*Cochino,*" Juan Carlos shot back, spitting on the dirt. "I changed my mind."

Dylan groaned and stayed where he was on the floor, unable to move, unable to think. Incredibly, the furious attack hadn't eased the pressure in his groin.

"*Sácate, cabrón,*" Juan Carlos said, standing him up and pushing him out the door.

Walking was difficult, for the clutch of desire refused to release him. Blood was dripping from his nose but he hardly felt it. He couldn't see anything but wet skin. He couldn't think of anything but hot sex.

He got as far away as he could manage, into the copse of trees near his house, and jerked open the fly of his pants. A couple of awkward strokes and he was con-vulsing with pleasure, sinking to his knees and gasping for air. It was kind of like dying, he supposed. And so compelling an act . . . that when he'd recovered well enough to catch his breath, he immediately chose to die again.

Now, four years later, he was an expert in self-gratification. But he still felt awkward around Angel Martinez, the sight of her still made him breathless, and the prospect of seeing her naked again still had the power to bring him to his knees.

Angel finished drying the dishes and hung up her apron with an exhausted yawn. She hadn't slept at all last night, and Saturdays were always rough. The amount of housework this family generated was astronomical.

Rubbing her tired eyes, she left the kitchen via the back door and rounded the side of the house, anticipating nothing more adventurous than a full night's sleep.

Her thoughts scattered as a man came out of nowhere, clamping his arm around her waist and securing his hand over her mouth. Her first instinct was to scream, but she couldn't draw breath. When she tasted the salty skin of his palm, she bit down hard, sinking her nails into his forearm and kicking out with her legs at the same time.

"Ow!" he said, releasing her.

Angel whirled around, to see Dylan Phillips standing in the shadows. "*Hijo de puta,*" she gasped, holding her hand over her galloping heart. "Are you *loco*?"

"Sorry," he said with a wince, cradling his injured palm. "I didn't mean to scare you. I was afraid you would see me and scream."

"Haven't you ever heard of knocking?"

When he made no reply, she realized he'd had no intention of approaching her back door. He'd been hanging around in the dark, spying on her.

For a genius, he acted pretty dumb sometimes.

"Come on," she said, walking toward her bedroom door. Last year, when she turned eighteen, her dad had converted his dusty old workshop into a studio for her. It still didn't have electricity, but it boasted other luxurious amenities, such as a private bathroom with running water and a door that locked.

Inside, she lit the kerosene lamp before she turned to face him.

"Is this your room now?" he asked.

"Yeah."

"Cool."

She scanned the contents of her bedroom, wondering if he was being sarcastic. The place was sparsely furnished, cramped, and rustic, but it was hers. Her jail. Her only sanctuary. "Is your hand bleeding?" she asked, dragging her gaze back to him.

Frowning, he rubbed a thumb over the wound on his palm. "Nah. You didn't break the skin. I think it'll bruise, though. It hurts like a mother."

"Sorry."

"No, it was my fault. I didn't mean to remind you of what happened last night." Even in the meager light, she noticed the flush that stole over his cheekbones. "At the Graveyard, I mean. Not in my room."

He wasn't smooth, but he was chivalrous. He'd proven that much the night before. "Why did you come here?" she asked, annoyed with herself for finding him so appealing.

"You forgot to take the CD when you left." Shrugging out of his backpack, he rummaged around for it. "Here."

She took the disc from him reluctantly. Before last night, she'd never have considered hooking up with him. He'd always been her little brother's friend, the skinny kid whose hair stuck up all over the place, the nerdy boy next door.

Since Angel had dropped out of high school, he'd changed. He'd grown about six inches taller, for one.

He was still skinny, but now he had a lot of lean muscle under those baggy clothes. He was still nerdy, with his thrift store T-shirts and serious blue eyes, but these days he made quirky look hot. His hair still stuck up in the middle, but even that flaw worked in his favor. He had this new punk rock haircut, short on the sides and spiky on top.

The biggest difference was in his demeanor. He'd always been mischievous, and he'd often been angry. Now that he'd matured, he'd learned how to guard his emotions more effectively, but he was still troubled.

He fairly smoldered with pent-up rage.

With his edgy new look, pretty blue eyes, and fuck-you attitude, Dylan Phillips wasn't just hot. He was dangerous.

She studied him from beneath lowered lashes, thinking it was too bad she wasn't in the market for a boyfriend. Because after a few basic instructions, he'd been an exceptional kisser. He had great instincts. And good hands.

"Dylan," she said, sitting down on the edge of her bed and urging him to take a seat beside her. The eager expression on his face told her everything she needed to know. "I don't want there to be any confusion, because of last night. I know I said one thing and did another, but after what happened, I guess I felt . . . indebted to you."

He was silent for a moment. "Is that how you always repay your debts?"

She flushed. Sometimes she liked him better when he was at a loss for words. "Of course not. It's just that you've always been more like—"

"A friend?"

"A kid brother," she corrected, pulling no punches.

His eyes darkened. "I'm not a kid."

She couldn't help but remember the way he'd touched her last night, the weight of his body on hers, and the delicious friction of his nylon basketball shorts as he moved against her. "No," she agreed, swallowing dryly.

"Are you seeing someone else?" he demanded.

"No."

"Then I don't see why we can't—"

"Sleep together on the down-low?"

"I never said that," he murmured, less angry with her than she wanted him to be. "I'd be happy just to kiss." His gaze, which was usually trained on her face, refreshingly enough, dropped to the apex of her thighs. "On the down-low. Or wherever else."

Her belly warmed at his insinuation. She was tempted to pull him over her and let him have another go. Taking a deep breath, she reminded herself that boys always thought kissing led to sex, no matter what they said. Her only other intimate encounter had been with a major fumbler, and she wasn't in any hurry to make that mistake again. Nor was she knowledgeable enough to think she could tutor a virgin.

Sometimes it was better to be cruel than kind.

"Look, Dylan, you're a great guy," she began, implementing a classic brush-off technique, "and I'm sure you'll make some other girl very happy. But I'm not looking for a boyfriend right now. Even if I were, I'd choose someone older . . ." she had to force herself to continue, knowing this part would sting, ". . . and more experienced."

His eyes dulled with disappointment. She knew that in his short life, he'd been let down too many times. Well, so had she.

"Right," he said, pulling his backpack on as he stood. He may be young, and easily bruised, but he'd never been dense. "Tell Juan Carlos I said hi, will you?"

"Of course," she said, smiling too brightly.

He paused on his way out, and she held her breath, afraid he would be so selfless as to extend her his friendship. *If you ever just want to talk . . .* he'd say, and her façade would crumble.

Fortunately for her, pride won out over nobility, and he left without another word.

Dylan kicked an aluminum can out of his way as he headed back down the gravel road, moonlight and self-loathing his only companions.

He would never understand women.

His own mother had been diaphanous and distant, a pale, pretty mystery. He'd given up trying to figure her out, or even capture her attention, at a very young age. She'd rarely ventured from the confines of her room or the safety of her daydreams. When faced with harsh reality, she only retreated further.

He hadn't even been able to count on her in an emergency. When he was seven, he'd fallen from a tree in the backyard and broken his arm. He'd run to her bedroom, screaming, his arm hanging at an odd angle by his side. She'd patted him on the head and told him an obscure fairy tale. They didn't have phone service at the time, because she'd forgotten to pay the bill, and he hurt too much to walk down to the Martinez place.

He remembered sitting on the front step for what seemed like hours, snot-nosed and teary-eyed, until Shay came home from school.

His sister had mothered him more than Lilah over the years, but now they were more like strangers than siblings. Shay said she cared about him, but she spent most of her time at work. She said she was proud of him, but she paid more attention to him when he was in trouble. She was pleased by his grades and she came to his big games, but they never talked about anything important. It was like they were stuck in limbo, refusing to discuss the past, unable to relate to each other in the present, and afraid to speculate on the future.

Shay was the closest person in the world to him, but he still found her impossible to read. Why didn't women just say what they meant?

Although Dylan could solve the most complicated quadratic equations, he couldn't figure out, for the life of him, what Angel Martinez was thinking.

She said she was sorry he'd fought with Chad over her, and then brushed her lips over his abraded knuckles like what he'd done had turned her on. She said she didn't want a boyfriend, but when he kissed her, she kissed him back. She told him not to take off any of her clothes, but she hadn't been shy about helping him out of his.

She said he was like a kid brother to her, but she'd moaned and dug her fingernails into his shoulders when he'd moved against her.

That last part had been exquisite. He'd stripped down to his basketball shorts and she'd been soft and pliant beneath him, mouth open, legs spread. A few more minutes and he probably would have embarrassed himself.

If Angel didn't like him, not even a little bit, why had she let him do that? Had she been toying with him, getting him all revved up for fun?

Maybe his friends were right. Maybe she was a tease.

In her bedroom just now, she'd been giving him the same sultry looks as last night, and he'd been almost certain she wanted him to kiss her again. Then she'd torn his heart out of his chest and stomped on it. And although she smiled at him before he walked away, he could have sworn she was about to cry.

Like she was the one who was devastated instead of him.

"What the fuck?" he muttered as he approached his driveway. The house was dark now, so Shay was probably asleep. Good. This morning she'd been too rushed to give him a talk about the birds and the bees, but he knew one was coming.

Jesus. She'd probably show him an educational video. *Lions in Love*, or some shit.

Groaning, he rubbed his hand over his face. His dad was a total loser, almost as bad as his mom, but he hadn't shirked out on all of his duties as a parent. The day Dylan came home with blood on his face from the fight with Juan Carlos, the old man sat him down for a talk. Dylan spilled the whole story, including the part about watching Angel in the shower and his powerful experience in the oak trees after.

Rather than reprimanding Dylan for being a Peeping Tom, his dad had smiled and clapped him on the back. Along with a bunch of outdated sex advice, he'd given Dylan a stack of old *Playboys* and told him to have at it.

Not all of his dad's pointers were worthless, now that he thought about it.

Hank Phillips was a "make love not war" kind of guy, and Dylan rolled his eyes when his dad talked too much hippie crap, but he did say one thing that stuck: don't force it. He'd stressed that women's bodies were gifts, not prizes. *Hers to give, not yours to take.*

Which was one of the main reasons Dylan had intervened when Travis and Chad had been hassling Angel last night.

Scowling, because his friends were idiots, he used his key to unlock the front door and went straight to his bedroom. Normally he raided the fridge as soon as he came home, but tonight he wasn't hungry. He shed his outer clothes and climbed into bed, vowing to put Angel Martinez out of his mind for good.

It wasn't like there weren't any other pretty girls in Tenaja Falls.

He liked Jennie Heinz a lot. She had a great body and decent taste in music. So what if she giggled over her bad grades and bragged about getting stoned? No one was perfect. And, let's face it, he wasn't that interested in her brain.

Dylan decided he would try to talk to her on Monday. But it was Angel's face he pictured, not Jennie's, in the vulnerable moment before he drifted off to sleep.

6

Luke's fourth day as interim sheriff started out much the same as the previous three. He hadn't slept well in his jailhouse-style digs at the firehouse. A couple of wet-behind-the-ears Explorer Scouts made runny eggs, muddy coffee, and a lot of superfluous noise.

It was clear that the firefighters-in-training didn't mean any harm, but if Luke heard any more questions about Vegas or jokes about showgirls, he'd lose it. Had he ever been that young and stupid? He couldn't remember.

By the time Luke got to the station Deputy Snell was already there, sitting at his desk reading the newspaper. Even more surprising, Luke smelled fresh coffee, a better blend than the stuff he'd choked down earlier.

Luke was instantly wary. "Who made this?" he asked, gesturing with the carafe.

Garrett didn't look up. "Me."

Figuring it couldn't be any worse than the muck at the firehouse, Luke poured himself a cup and retreated to the safety of his office. He and Garrett hadn't engaged in a lot of "getting to know you" chitchat, and that suited Luke just fine.

He had a lot of work to do, none of which he trusted Garrett with. Picturing the look of devastation on Liliana Montes's face when he broke the bad news, Luke picked up the phone to call the medical examiner. Accident or not, he had a mystery to solve. Moving a dead body wasn't as stiff a crime as murder, but it was damned peculiar.

Dr. Hoyt's receptionist put him right through. "Sheriff Meza?" he inquired, his accent vaguely . . . Transylvanian. "What can I do for you?"

Luke flipped through the autopsy photos he'd taken himself and printed out last night. "I have a few questions if you have the time."

"Of course."

"As far as the marks on her back . . . well, I'm no expert, but a lot of people out here drive trucks." This morning, he'd glanced into the corrugated bed of his pickup and a lightbulb had gone off inside his head. "Could she have been lying on a bed liner?"

"I'm almost certain she was," Dr. Hoyt admitted. "But I've only seen marks like that once before, so I can't be positive."

"How long would it take to make them? I've got witnesses who saw her alive at midnight." He consulted a copy of the preliminary report. "You've estimated time of death between 1:00 and 2:00 A.M."

"Lividity sets in quickly. She could have visible markings after an hour or less of resting in one place."

"Is there a medical explanation for the lack of

blood? There was a small amount on her clothing, but none at the scene."

"Yes. In this case, death was instantaneous. When the heart stops beating, blood stops pumping. She probably never knew what hit her."

Luke leaned back in his chair and looked up at the ceiling, as if more answers might be written there. "Is there any possibility she was killed by something other than a lion?"

"No," Dr. Hoyt said. "The amount of pressure needed to sever a spinal cord is immense. The size of the bite, depth of penetration, the space between punctures . . ." He trailed off. "Even with a piece of specialized equipment, these things cannot be duplicated."

"Haven't you seen *Shark Week*?" Luke countered, only half-joking. "They made a set of robotic jaws that could bite through steel."

Dr. Hoyt's laugh reminded Luke of the Count from *Sesame Street*. "Yes, well, you speak of technology that does not exist, with regards to predatory cats. And the cost of such machinery would be prohibitive. A million-dollar hoax, if you will."

"She was moved," Luke said quietly, any trace of humor gone.

"Indeed she was, Sheriff. But unless you can find a mountain lion with criminal intent, she was not murdered."

"What about sexual assault? The mortician said you took DNA samples."

"Only as a matter of procedure. I found no evidence of rape, although she'd had intercourse, possibly with more than one partner, within twenty-four hours of the attack. The swabs from the wounds on the neck will be analyzed and compared with the sample from the lion at UC Davis to make a positive ID. The others will be filed."

Luke thanked him for his time and hung up, unable to shake the feeling that all was not what it seemed.

Deciding it was time for another hunting expedition, he pushed away from his desk. Like a lion stalking prey, he strode out of his office and zeroed in on Garrett. If he wasn't mistaken, his deputy had spiffed up his work area and his appearance. Other than a few folded sections of the Sunday paper, the surface of his desk was clear. His uniform was neatly pressed and Luke could count the comb lines in his slick black hair.

Garrett Snell was not a handsome man, with his considerable bulk and gloomy, deep-set eyes, but he had a distinct presence. He reminded Luke of a carnival ringmaster. There was a flair about him, as if he were performing, rather than being.

It also occurred to Luke that Deputy Snell wanted to make a better impression today than he had before, and Luke thought he knew why.

He pulled up a chair in front of Garrett's desk and stretched out his legs. When the deputy merely shot him a questioning glance over the top of his newspaper, Luke made a show of studying his fingernails. Two could play at this game. "How long have you been involved with Yesenia?"

Garrett's reaction was quite genuine, for once. His forehead turned red and his nostrils flared. "Who says I was?"

Luke manufactured a bored look. "Come on, Garrett. You pretended not to know her."

"I didn't get close enough to make a positive ID."

He made an impatient gesture, waving away Garrett's denials. "I don't care what you do off duty. I'm only asking because the medical examiner took DNA samples and I don't want any surprises."

Garrett blinked several times, as if he were calculating the probability of getting caught. "My wife just had a baby," he muttered, unable to meet Luke's eyes. "I went with Yesenia to take the edge off."

"When?"

"A week ago."

Luke nodded pleasantly, stifling the urge to sink his fist into Garrett's doughy face. Funny, his deputy had been less repulsive as a liar than he was as a cheat, and Luke regretted having delved into his slimy personal business. "Have you ever investigated a homicide?"

Garrett's mouth fell open. "No."

"Me, either."

"You don't think—"

"Nah. But why would anyone move her body?"

Something sparked in Garrett's sunken eyes, a hint of intelligence Luke hadn't realized was there. He decided to overlook the fact that his deputy was a disloyal creep. Devious minds were often great investigative tools.

"They're building a new casino on Los Coyotes," Garrett said.

"The Indian reservation?"

"Yeah. No offense, but those guys don't like a lot of

interference from the outside. And a body found on federal land always brings in the FBI."

Luke squinted at Garrett, wondering if he should be offended. Shay Phillips had mentioned kids and illegal aliens. Now Indians were being thrown under the bus. "What does the casino have to do with anything?"

Garrett's face became animated. "Well, there's been this big controversy over environmental regulations. Something about wildlife and seasonal pools. The builders are supposed to be following codes, but if they don't, the tribal leaders have the funds to pay off inspectors. And plenty of reasons not to want the feds poking around on the reservation, looking into their business practices."

Ah, irony. His people had once been known for championing environmental causes. Luke couldn't fault anyone for making a buck, and in California, Indian Gaming was making a lot of them, but he was so weary of cash, corruption, and casinos.

Still, Garrett's idea was plausible. For a person to tamper with evidence, and open themselves up to a murder charge, there had to be a lot at stake.

"Okay," he said, collecting his thoughts. He'd go over and visit the boys at Los Coyotes himself. Meanwhile, he wanted to ask Shay who else had been at the bar that night. A thrill raced through him at the thought of seeing her again, and it had nothing to do with investigative fervor. "The autopsy report hasn't been released, but the media will be calling. Just say that we're investigating the accident, refer them to the Department of Fish and Game, and make no comment."

The light in Garrett's eyes dulled. "Sure," he said, flapping his newspaper.

Pleased by the exchange, Luke went back to his office. Before he spoke to Shay, he wanted to check up on Hamlet, so he rifled through the files on his desk until he found the number for the lab at UC Davis. A postgraduate student named Dr. Brenna answered. He sounded about fourteen.

"Did that lion have a broken tooth?" Luke asked.

Dr. Brenna made a lot of fumbling noises. "No sir. All of his teeth were intact." More papers rustled. "Preliminary tests are negative for human blood or tissue. We found two partially digested rabbits among the stomach contents." He cleared his throat. "Are you sure you shot the right lion?"

Luke sat up straight in his chair. "Didn't he have a satellite tag?"

"Yessir. Subject 122, otherwise known as Dark Canyon's Hamlet. According to the GPS, he was in the general vicinity of the victim. But these tests don't add up."

"Run them again," Luke ordered, although he wasn't sure he had the authority to make such a request.

"We have, sir. Three times over. I need to notify the Department of Fish and Game, because it looks like your man-eater is still on the loose."

Shay woke up late, stretching her arms over her head. Remembering the miserable birthday she'd had the day before, she buried her face in the pillow and groaned.

She'd love to drift back to sleep, or laze about in bed

for a few more minutes, but memories of her forward behavior with Luke Meza assaulted her, stripping her continence and making her squirm with discomfort.

Kicking off the blankets with more force than was necessary, she climbed out of bed. Dylan had left early this morning for basketball practice, as usual. Normally she used the quiet time to catch up on reading or indulge in a leisurely bubble bath, but having been away all day yesterday, she had a pile of housework waiting for her.

Rubbing her eyes, she bypassed the dirty dishes in the kitchen sink and headed straight for the coffee-maker. After a few bolstering cups, and a hearty breakfast, her spirits revived. She wasn't the type to mope about, especially over a man. Concern for Dylan and sorrow over Hamlet were understandable, but getting all twisted up in knots because of one momentary lapse of reason with Luke was an exercise in futility.

So what if he didn't like her? This wasn't junior high. They probably wouldn't have to work together very often, and he'd move on soon enough. He was only an interim sheriff after all. No more important, or irreplaceable, than your average, everyday temp.

Welcoming the distraction of mindless chores, Shay turned on the portable radio as she tidied up the kitchen and living room. While she waited for a load of laundry to dry, she decided to treat herself to some basic upkeep. Last night she'd showered before bed, but she'd been too tired to shave her legs. Maybe it was vain, but it stuck in her craw that Luke Meza had seen her at her worst, with wet clothes, tangled hair, and stubbly legs.

Humming along with the music, she carried a couple of buckets of warm water out to the old washtub on the back porch. Shaving in a tub outside wasn't quite as relaxing as a long bubble bath, but it held a simple, rustic appeal. Shay's mother had often scrubbed her down outdoors, weather permitting, and it was shaping up to be a fine morning. Not too hot, the perfect mix of wind and sun.

After grabbing a towel, her razor, and some all-natural soap, she settled into a chair on the patio and sank her feet into the tub of warm water, shivering with pleasure.

She'd only finished one leg when the doorbell rang. Muttering a string of mild curses, she hopped up to answer it, forgetting her towel on the porch and dripping a trail of water across the living room.

It was Luke.

Shay stifled a gasp of dismay and did quick inventory of her appearance. Dylan's ratty old boxers were too short, barely peeking out from under the hem of her roomy blue T-shirt. Raising a hand to her hair, she was relieved to find it brushed and clean, tied back from her face in a simple ponytail.

It could have been worse, she supposed. After yesterday, anything was an improvement.

Luke looked even better than she remembered, which didn't seem fair or even possible. His jaw was smooth and chiseled, his uniform military crisp. "Hi," he said.

"Hi," she said back, feeling soapy water drip between her toes.

"Is this a bad time?"

Shay's heart skipped, and she had to remind herself that this was the man who'd treated her like leftover cake. "It's fine," she said, stepping aside to let him in.

When she didn't offer him a seat, they stared at each other for a long, awkward moment. He looked away first. "Whose birthday was it?" he asked, his eyes resting on the deflating balloons she hadn't the heart to throw away yet.

"Mine."

"When?"

"Yesterday."

He knew better than to say something lame like *happy birthday*. Instead he asked, "How old are you?"

"Twenty-six."

His mouth curled at the edge, as if he found her age amusing.

"How about you?"

His manner turned gruff. "I'm thirty-six."

"Why, you old man," she said, rolling her eyes. "Try not to break a hip." Refusing to let his unexpected visit throw her, she went back outside, sat down, and picked up her razor. The water wouldn't stay warm forever. And he wasn't interested anyway.

Maybe he thought he was too old for her, or that she was too white trash for him, but that didn't stop him from following her out. It didn't prevent him from taking a seat opposite her on the patio, or from watching as she propped one foot on the rim of the tub, lathered up, and resumed shaving.

"Friday night," he began, clearing his throat, "you were celebrating?"

She ran the blade over soap-slick skin. "Mm-hmm."

"With whom?"

"My girlfriends."

He took out his notepad to write.

"Monica Reyes and Lori Snell," she supplied with a sigh. "Why? What did the medical examiner say?"

"Official ruling is an accident. Definitely a lion."

Shay nodded. The wounds were impossible to mistake, but it was reassuring to get professional confirmation.

"That doesn't mean I don't have anything to investigate," he explained. "Your people will conduct their own inquiries, I'm sure, but I'd like to find out what Yesenia Montes was doing that night. Where she went. How she ended up at the Graveyard."

"Did you talk to her mother?"

His expression became shuttered. "Yes."

Shay's heart went out to him. Mrs. Montes must have been destroyed by the news, and she'd have hated being the one to break it to her.

"Lori Snell," he said, looking down at his notepad. "Is that Garrett's wife?"

"The one and only," she replied, returning her attention to her soapy leg.

"Who else was there?"

Moving the blade over her bended knee, she named a few names. Good old boys and regulars, mostly. Guys she'd known since grade school, like Jesse Ryan.

"Did Yesenia talk to anyone besides Jesse?"

"Probably," she admitted. "I didn't notice."

"Tell me what happened at closing time."

She swished the blade around in the water. "After last

call, which is midnight in Tenaja Falls, everyone started to leave. Yesenia walked away with Jesse."

"How did that make you feel?"

"It made me feel like drinking some more," she said flippantly. "Lori had to get home to her baby, but I went over to Monica's. She only lives a few blocks away from the Round-Up. I was there until about 2 A.M. Then I called a cab."

"You went home?"

"Yep."

"Alone?"

Shay froze, razor in hand. Did he really think she'd go home with a guy on Friday night and come on to him Saturday afternoon?

"You didn't see Jesse again? Or Yesenia?"

She let out a slow breath. "No. But the cab ride was kind of a blur, if you know what I mean."

He was quiet for a moment while she finished shaving. She'd never been more acutely aware of a man's eyes on her body, and it was all she could do to keep her hand steady.

"I didn't come here just to ask questions," he said finally.

She nicked herself. "Ouch!"

"Would you put that thing down for a minute?"

Glaring at him, she set aside her razor and sluiced water over her legs, clearing away the suds. Her heart was racing now, anticipating his next words, but she picked up her towel casually and dabbed at the tiny cut on her inner thigh.

"Did you hurt yourself?"

She imagined him kissing it better and felt her

tummy jump. "No." She looked up at him, blood rushing through her veins, waiting for him to speak. He stared back at her in silence. Just like the previous day, on that sun-dappled rock at the bank of Deep Creek, the rest of the world seemed to fall away, leaving only the two of them.

The tension between them was as thick as steam.

Then Dylan crashed through the front door at his usual breakneck pace, destroying the ambience. He was almost on top of them before he realized she had company. Stopping in his tracks, he stood there in the doorway, six feet two inches of pure angst, a basketball lodged under one skinny arm. His T-shirt was sweaty and his hair was damp.

"What the fuck is this?" he said, summing up the situation in an instant. "I'm not allowed to have Angel in my room, but you can bring home random dudes whenever you want?"

Shay's mouth dropped open. Not only had she never said he couldn't have Angel over, at a reasonable hour, she'd never brought home a man, random or otherwise. "Dylan, this is the new *sheriff*," she hissed, mortified by her brother's behavior.

Dylan scowled at the star adorning Luke's front shirt pocket. He hadn't been a fan of the old sheriff.

"We're working together," Shay explained, wondering why Luke didn't stand and introduce himself. "A woman was killed by a mountain lion yesterday. Remember?"

"Yeah, I remember," he said, looking from the washtub to Luke's face. Although Dylan had a lot to learn about the human condition, as a hormonal teenager, he was well acquainted with lust. "But I'm not stupid. You're taking a bath in front of him."

Shay curled her toes up in the tub self-consciously.

"He's right," Luke interjected at last. "Your brother understands the way a man thinks even if you don't. It was inappropriate of me to watch you."

Dylan relaxed his stance, mollified to have been told he was right *and* promoted to man status. Somehow, Luke had also made Shay seem innocent of any wrongdoing, which they both knew wasn't true. She understood very well what he'd been thinking, and hadn't been above taunting him with a glimpse of what he'd passed up.

Shay felt her cheeks burn. Having her brother walk in while she was flaunting herself in front of Luke was so embarrassing! What had gotten into her?

"You play?" Luke asked, nodding at Dylan's basketball.

Dylan shrugged, reassessing Luke as a fellow baller. "Yeah. You?"

"All four years at UNLV."

Dylan's face lit up. "Really? They have a good team. Were you first string?"

"Nah. Third."

"You see any court time?"

"Nope."

Her brother nodded eagerly, impressed all the same, and they started talking about UNLV players, playoffs, and plays. It never failed to amaze her that Dylan seemed to remember every shot from every game he'd ever watched, but Luke was right there with him, discussing the merits of a three-pointer from a final eight over five years ago.

It was the longest, and least contentious, conversation she'd seen Dylan have with an adult in ages. Watching his animated gestures and avid expression, Shay felt her heart twist. Dylan had known Luke five minutes and already connected with him better than her.

Dangerously close to tears, she busied herself by dumping the tub over the edge of the patio and gathering up her supplies.

"I still have to talk to you," Luke said before she slipped away.

She cleared her throat. "Fine. I just need to, um, get a drink of water." Knowing she was being inhospitable, she left without offering Luke anything. Because a lively debate had ensued over Shaq's abysmal free-throw, he probably didn't notice.

By the time Luke and Dylan returned from the wide world of sports, and gravitated back inside the house, Shay had pulled herself together. She'd also gathered a basket of clean laundry to fold. Propping it on one hip, she stood in the hall, waiting for them to move out of her way. Dylan was tall, but Luke was taller, broader of shoulder, and more heavily muscled. The two of them took up an uncomfortable amount of space.

Shay gave her brother a pointed stare.

"I guess I'll hit the shower," Dylan muttered, taking the hint. He turned to walk away then stopped short, seeming to remember his manners. "Nice meeting you, uh . . ."

"Luke," he said, shaking Dylan's hand.

Her little brother took off in his usual fashion, doing

some air basketball moves down the hall before he disappeared from sight.

Giving Luke a wide berth, Shay made a beeline for the living room couch. He remained standing while she sat and separated socks from T-shirts. After they heard the shower turn on, Luke said, "He seems like a good kid."

She nodded because it would be disloyal to disagree. But since the beginning of the school year, Dylan had been suspended for fighting and ordered to take conflict resolution classes for arguing with a teacher. He'd also been arrested twice, with charges ranging from destroying county property to being out after curfew.

Her brother wasn't a good kid. He was difficult, defiant, and absolutely brilliant. If he could get rid of the chip on his shoulder, he'd be a star, but his behavior had been getting worse for years, and Shay didn't know how to help him.

She'd failed him in so many ways.

Not meeting Luke's eyes, she folded one of her everyday bras, an athletic racer-back style with an A-cup, wishing he would say his piece and leave.

"That lion," he began. "He wasn't the right one."

Her hands stilled. "What?"

"Hamlet. He didn't do it."

She felt the blood drain from her face. "How do you know?"

"Tests at Davis came back negative for human issue."

"No," she gasped, pressing her fist to her stomach. "That can't be."

"The medical examiner said the lion who perpetrated the attack had a broken tooth. Hamlet didn't. Right?"

"I cleaned his teeth myself while he was under sedation a year ago," she murmured. "At that time, they were all intact."

"We made a mistake."

"No," she protested. "According to GPS, Hamlet was at the Graveyard."

"Yes, but Yesenia wasn't killed there. How unusual would it be for a lion passing by to investigate a corpse? Perhaps he only got close enough to recognize the scent. The scientists who performed the autopsy said his stomach contents indicated he'd eaten recently."

She looked up at him, feeling bleak. "Then it was all for nothing. I killed him for nothing."

"I'm sorry," he said, and appeared to really mean it.

Sadness for the loss closed in on her, blurring the edges of her vision. That goddamned "track and kill" policy! If she'd used a tranquilizer gun instead of a rifle, this would never have happened. She wouldn't have another unnecessary death on her hands.

"Shit," she whispered, brushing her tears away angrily. She hated that he was seeing her like this. Every time she thought she'd shown him her worst, she sank a bit lower.

"My top priority right now is public safety. I need to know if there's another collared lion in the area, and I could use your expertise."

Her ingrained sense of responsibility took over, reaching out like a lifeline, giving her something to focus on besides grief. She twisted her hands together, thinking, and realized she was holding a pair of lacy thong panties. Shoving them back in the laundry pile, she hopped up from the couch and started pacing the living room. "Male lions are extremely territorial," she said. "They don't often cross paths."

"You're sure it was a male?"

"Relatively sure. The size of the claw marks indicated a very large lion. Males also tend to roam more. As far as GPS goes, no other collared lion was within fifty miles of Tenaja that night, according to the monitors."

"Are all of the lions in the area collared?"

"No. GPS is expensive. And Dark Canyon is a wildlife corridor, so without tracks, finding the culprit may be difficult."

"What's a wildlife corridor?"

"Kind of like a natural highway. The canyon links the Santa Ana Mountains to the Anza-Borrego Desert, two vast habitats. Lots of animals use it to go back and forth."

He let out a frustrated breath. "So what do we do?"

She stopped pacing and turned to him. "We set a trap."

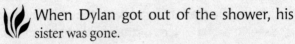 When Dylan got out of the shower, his sister was gone.

No big surprise there.

She was usually absent, working too many hours at Dark Canyon and hiking around the godforsaken wilderness all the time. That was fine by him. He didn't need a babysitter. He'd been taking care of himself most of his life.

At least she left a note. And her car. The old Subaru was still in the garage, so she must have gone with the sheriff.

Luke seemed like an okay guy, but Dylan didn't like the way he'd been staring at Shay when he walked in. Sure, he'd seen men check her out before. It happened all the time. Chad was particularly crude about it, but even he waited until her eyes were averted.

There was nothing furtive, or polite, about the way the sheriff had been looking at her, and Dylan knew damned well he wasn't thinking about *work* while he did it.

Scowling, he examined the contents of the fridge. It was still empty. There wasn't even any milk for cereal.

Shay usually went grocery shopping during the weekends, and sometimes she made him breakfast on Sunday morning. Most days he fended for himself, but when she did cook, it was good. His stomach rumbled at the thought of buttermilk pancakes and sausage links.

There were eggs, and even he knew how to scramble, so he heated up a frying pan and cracked about a half dozen into it, listening to the sizzle. He couldn't remember the last time he and Shay had eaten a meal together.

Maybe after he left for college, she'd hook up with the sheriff and start a new family without him.

He tried to convince himself that the idea didn't bother him, but it did. Everybody knew she'd had an affair with Jesse Ryan, and that bothered him, too. Jesse had been stringing her along for years, two-timing her, his wife, and whoever else he had on the side.

Why did women go for guys like that? Dylan couldn't get any girls to notice him, but a shiftless dirtbag like Jesse Ryan had more chicks than he could handle.

Shaking his head, he turned off the burner and took the entire pan of eggs over to the kitchen table, shoveling forkfuls directly into his mouth. Before he was finished, he heard the rumble of a souped-up car engine.

Chad Pinter's Chevy Nova.

"Fuck," he muttered, dumping the mostly empty pan in the sink. His knuckles were still bruised from their last meeting. Now he also had a crescent-shaped bite mark, compliments of Angel Martinez, between his thumb and his forefinger.

Dylan enjoyed a brawl every now and again, but he'd had enough excitement this weekend. Besides, Chad outweighed him by at least fifty pounds, and probably wouldn't be willing to let him off again so easily.

He outlined his choices. Pretending he wasn't home sounded good. Telling Chad to get bent sounded better. Opting for the middle road, he went ahead and answered the door when Chad knocked, hoping his muscle-bound friend hadn't come for blood.

When Dylan saw the purple half moon beneath Chad's left eye, and the apologetic expression on his handsome face, he felt some of his anger fade.

He also experienced a surge of pride, because Chad deserved the shiner, and damned if it wasn't a good one. Although he wanted to gloat and grin, he just mumbled, "What's up," and jerked his chin toward the living room.

Dylan sat on the couch. Chad took the only chair.

"Is your sister home?" Chad asked.

"No."

They usually listened to music or played video games when Chad came over, but Dylan made no move to turn on either. He was willing to hear Chad out, not to go on as though nothing had happened.

Dylan also knew what he was risking. Chad was popular and influential; Dylan wasn't. Chad could make his final months at Palomar High hell. Even so, Dylan waited in silence for him to speak, studying his wavy brown hair and broad shoulders, the well-arranged features and dark, thickly lashed eyes that made all the girls swoon.

After some more fidgeting and procrastinating,

Chad cleared his throat. "It got pretty crazy the other night."

Dylan leaned his head back against the couch, unimpressed. "Yeah."

"Look, dude, we both said some things we didn't mean—"

"I meant everything I said."

Chad appeared startled. He'd probably thought Dylan was going to roll over quicker than this. "Okay. Fine. I said some things I didn't mean. About your mom."

Dylan felt a coil of rage unfurl inside him, and he was no longer interested in talking. One word about his mother, and his hand constricted into a fist.

"You gave me a black eye," Chad pointed out, obviously thinking they were even.

"You left me and Angel out on the dunes," Dylan countered in a cold voice. "Miles from town."

Chad couldn't offer an excuse for that. Instead, he looked for a bright side. "Did she give you any play?"

Dylan rose to his feet. "Get out."

Chad stood also, emitting a harsh laugh. "Are you seriously going to let a little trick like that come between us?"

Dylan pressed his fist into the palm of his other hand in an attempt to keep it from flying toward Chad's face. "Get. The fuck. Out."

Chad came closer, deliberately taunting him. "You really don't know, do you?"

His eyes narrowed. "Know what?"

"Angel is a cheap slut, dude. Why do you think I didn't mind when Travis tried to get on her? She gives it up to anyone."

Dylan found himself searching Chad's face for signs of deception, and saw none. "Like who?"

He smiled a dark, humorless smile. "Me."

Dylan's vision blurred with anger. He didn't want to know any more details; he wanted to drag Chad out into the front yard and kick him until he vomited blood. "When?" he asked, trying to control his rage.

"A couple months ago," Chad said, reaching out to massage Dylan's shoulder in a way that was hardly relaxing. "But don't waste your time. She wasn't any good."

Chad always bragged about his conquests, but he'd never said anything about Angel. Why? "You encouraged Travis," Dylan said from between clenched teeth, knocking Chad's hand away. "You told him to hold her down."

"She was loving every minute of it," he boasted, no longer smiling.

"No," Dylan said with complete assurance. Angel may have been with Chad, at one point or another, but she hadn't wanted Travis. She'd kicked and screamed and fought like a wildcat when he tried to force his mouth over hers.

"Are you mad because I threw you both out of the car?" Chad asked softly, getting in his face. "Or because you never got your turn?"

Dylan shoved him backward, his heart pounding with adrenaline and his muscles poised for action. When Chad didn't tackle him, Dylan went to the front door. "You're a pig and so is Travis," he said, throwing it open. "Now get the fuck out."

Chad's lips tightened, making him appear more like a petulant child than a boy on the cusp of manhood.

"You're nothing without me, bro. You're like a ghost at Palomar High."

It was true, and the words stung. Dylan lifted his chin, refusing to let it show. "Have fun in summer school." He may have been invisible, especially to girls, but Chad didn't have a snowball's chance in hell of passing Algebra without his help.

Chad slammed his fist against the door, puncturing the cheap wood. Dylan waited for him to make the next move, his pulse racing with trepidation, but the hot-headed quarterback didn't take the exchange any further.

Swearing under his breath, he left.

Dylan watched as the Nova roared to life, peeling out of the driveway and spitting gravel across the parched front lawn.

Angel pulled the last load of laundry from the washing machine, humming an unnamed tune as she carried the basket outside into the morning sunshine.

On a day like today, clothes dried faster on the line, which was good, because the dryer quit last week. It couldn't keep up with her brothers, who'd never met a mud puddle they didn't like, or her little sister, who loved to change clothes and play dress-up.

Her dad had taken all of her siblings to the movie theater in Chula Vista, so Angel had several hours to herself, a rarity on a Sunday. After she finished the laundry, she knew she should try to get some studying done. Since Yoli started kindergarten, Angel had been taking correspondence classes to complete her GED.

She was no whiz kid like Dylan Phillips, and with only two years of high school under her belt, she had a lot of catching up to do before she felt confident she could pass the equivalency exam.

What she really wanted to do, rather than hit the books, was pull her acoustic guitar out of the closet and flesh out the melody that had been flirting with the back of her mind for the past few days. Enticed by the prospect of spending some quality time with her 12-string, she made haste as she hung up the sheets.

In addition to trying on and discarding every item in her closet on a regular basis, Yoli had taken to wetting the bed lately.

Angel smiled grimly around the clothespin in her mouth. She disliked the extra work, but appreciated the fact that she no longer shared a bed with her sister.

When a shadow appeared on the other side of the sheet, showing the outline of a man, taller than her brothers or her father, she stumbled back a step. Her legs got tangled up with the laundry basket and she went down hard, landing on her butt in the dirt.

Dylan Phillips towered over her. The sun behind his head and the sudden tears in her eyes made it difficult for her to read his expression.

"Did you fuck Chad Pinter?"

A surge of anger replaced her fear. After a question like that, she didn't need to see his eyes to know his mood. She glanced toward the house, wishing her father, and his shotgun, were home. "That's none of your business," she said, rising to her feet. He didn't offer to help her up, and she was certain now that she'd made the right decision in spurning him.

Of course, he took her response as an admission. "You—you said you weren't looking for a boyfriend," he sputtered.

She dusted off her stinging backside. "I'm not."

"You said you wanted someone older," he continued, incredulous. "He's younger and more immature than I am!"

"Yes," she agreed, shuddering.

Dylan closed the distance between them, taking her upper arms in his hands. His fingertips burned into her bare skin as his blue eyes searched hers. "Did he . . ." His throat worked convulsively. "Did he force you?"

Her emotions welled up, too close to the surface. She felt the absurd longing to rest her head against his chest and cry. Denying herself, and him, she held her body stiff in his arms. "No," she said, her tone bitter. "I knew what I was doing."

And she had.

She'd known exactly what she was doing the night she accepted a ride from Chad, and she understood what he expected from her in return. He suggested they park at the Graveyard, and she accepted, knowing just what he wanted.

He'd been taking sips from a pint-size bottle of whisky, and so had she, but neither of them were drunk. She wished she had been.

It was Christmas, and Mamá hadn't sent any gifts, or a single card, or bothered to make one simple phone call.

Angel held herself together throughout the festivities, putting on a smile for her siblings, waiting until everyone else went to bed to call her mother. The conversation had been brief, but devastating. A baby wailed in the background. Angel's new sister.

She hadn't even known her mother was pregnant.

Angel remembered running down Calle Remolino in her best dress, tears streaming down her face, breath puffing out in the cold night air. When Chad pulled up in his Chevy Nova, she'd jumped at the chance to go somewhere else. Do something else. *Feel* something else.

At the Graveyard, he didn't even have to make the first move. She was the one who had slid her hand along the nape of his neck and brought his lips to hers. And although she hadn't liked the way he'd kissed her, shoving his tongue too far into her mouth, or the way he'd touched her, with rough, fumbling hands, she'd encouraged him. Desperate for it to be over, she'd torn at his clothes. When he moved away from her to put on a condom, she'd almost lost her nerve. Then he was stretching out on top of her again, pushing into her, hurting her.

She'd cried out and shoved at his shoulders, changing her mind in an instant, but he'd merely held her arms over her head and continued. Tears had rolled down her cheeks, and she'd prayed for him to finish quickly, but she'd ceased struggling and she hadn't said no.

She never told him no.

"He didn't force me," she said, blinking up at Dylan. To her embarrassment, her face was wet again. Using jerky motions, she wiped her cheeks with the back of her hand.

He must have believed her, because he let her go.

"He's a clod," he said in a low voice. "He's proud of it. He always brags about how fast he is. Like it's a race. And he never treats the girl with respect afterward."

Angel crossed her arms over her chest and looked down at the ground. If she'd known that, would she have climbed in his car that day? Probably.

Chad had seemed surprised when he noticed the blood. He must not have realized she was a virgin, not even by the way she'd reacted. He'd looked somewhat chagrined, but he hadn't apologized, and he hadn't asked her any questions. Perhaps he was worried she would tell her father how he'd treated her, because he offered to call her. Instead of her phone number, she'd given him a look of pure disgust.

The next time she saw him, at the Graveyard on Friday night, she'd wanted to crawl under a rock and hide. Instead, she was put in the awful position of having to accept another ride in his car. Drunk and belligerent, he came on to her, expecting more of what he'd already had. She told him it would happen again over her dead body.

Maybe that was why he'd goaded Travis into making a play for her. If Dylan hadn't been there, she might have had to fight them both off.

"How could you—" He broke off, shoving a hand through his short hair. "He's such an asshole!"

She stared at him stonily. "And you've been friends with him for years."

"Not anymore," he protested, putting space between them. As if he thought her dirty. "Unlike you, I have some standards."

Indignation burned through her. "Sure you do. You

hang out with Chad, not because you think it will get you girls, but because he has so many great qualities. Right? And you invited me into your room Friday night to listen to music, not because you wanted to find out if I was like my mother."

A flush crept up his neck. "I never wanted to find out . . ." He paused, for that statement would have been blatantly untrue. "I never thought you were like—" He stopped and swore, having backed himself into a corner there, too.

"Let me save you the trouble," she said, advancing on him, shoving at his chest. "I'm a slut, just like Chad said. Just like my mother. If you hadn't interfered, I'd have shown Travis a real good time. Hell, I'd have serviced all three of you. At the same time! Now, aren't you sorry you missed out on that action?"

He didn't know what to say to that, or how to react. He just stood there, a pained, bewildered expression on his face.

Angel didn't need his jealousy, his judgment, or his confusion. She didn't even want his friendship. Not anymore. "Go home, Dylan," she said with a sigh, her anger leaving as quickly as it came. "Go home and grow up."

His eyes darkened at her words, but he made no reply. Showing an impressive amount of control for a boy his age, he only gave a curt nod and walked away.

Dylan returned home in a foul mood, turned the stereo on full blast, and dumped the contents of his backpack out on the middle of the bed. Ears ringing soothingly, mind numbing from heavy metal anesthesia, he reached into the corner of his closet and brought out his stuff.

Shay would freak out if she knew what he kept in here. But she didn't know. If there was anything good about his sister, it was that she didn't snoop. She didn't come into his room, or rifle through his personal belongings, or interrogate him about where he'd been.

She didn't care.

Well, she cared about his grades, because they were his ticket out of this shithole town, and she cared about his game, for the same reason.

Scowling, he shoved the contraband items into his backpack, knowing he couldn't have another run-in with the law. He couldn't wait to get out of Tenaja Falls, but if he didn't do something to release the tension inside him, he was going to explode.

He couldn't believe Angel had slept with Chad.

It wasn't that he'd expected her to be innocent. She'd dated Tony Duran for years, and although Tony was quiet and religious and stuff, everyone assumed they'd done it. Angel's age, and her experience, was actually part of her appeal. Dylan would have no idea how to handle a virgin. The idea of hurting a girl, especially *that* way, made him cringe.

And he liked the way Angel had taken charge in his bedroom.

The first time he kissed her, she'd laughed. That made him mad, so he gripped her upper arms and kissed her again, with more enthusiasm. She stopped laughing, but she also broke the contact, putting her hands on his chest and holding him at bay.

"Like this," she'd said, brushing her lips over his, very softly.

It was nice, and although he'd wanted to crush his mouth over hers and French kiss like they did in movies, he forced himself to relax and let her call the shots. It was a good choice, because she moved her hand to the nape of his neck, threaded her fingers through his short hair, and kept kissing him.

That had really turned him on. He went motionless, afraid he would do something wrong and she would stop. To his amazement, she continued, teasing him with small licks and—oh, God—little nibbles.

Then a lightbulb had gone off inside his head. She was kissing him the way she wanted *him* to kiss *her*.

Curbing his natural inclination to be overeager, he slid his arm around her waist and leaned forward, kissing her back, using a lighter touch.

She made a low murmur of approval. He deepened the kiss, and she pressed closer, and . . . things got pretty heated after that.

He stared at the surface of his bed, picturing them there together, torturing himself by wondering if she'd responded the same way with Chad. A series of disturbing sexual images flashed through his mind, and he couldn't help but consider the logistics of a scenario in which Angel serviced all three of them.

Stomach churning with nausea, he zipped up his backpack and strode out into the hall, grabbing his sister's keys from the hook before he headed out the door.

8

Luke was having a hard time keeping his eyes off Shay Phillips.

As he drove the now-familiar road toward Dark Canyon State Preserve, the object of his inconvenient desire sitting passenger beside him, he analyzed her appeal.

He had to admit his initial impression of her hadn't been completely accurate. She wasn't just a party girl from the wrong side of the tracks or a kitty-loving bimbo with a biology degree. She was smart, dedicated, and responsible. Other than a night of mild debauchery for her birthday (and who could begrudge her that?) she seemed to have a quiet life. And she was doing an admirable job of raising her brother single-handedly.

If she had a lot of boyfriends, so what? He knew plenty of guys who played the field and didn't get slammed for it. She was young and beautiful and sexy as hell. He could understand why she wasn't in any hurry to settle down.

What he couldn't figure out was why his gut

clenched with longing every time he looked at her. Or why, for the life of him, he couldn't stop looking. He was like a gawking schoolboy in her presence, and not only was it embarrassing, it was completely out of character for him. Slavering over a woman just because she was hot and available wasn't his style. He'd had plenty of opportunities to indulge in casual encounters and no-strings sex in Las Vegas.

Why did he want that now when he never had before?

Okay, so she smelled good. Maybe pheromones were responsible for his uncontrollable physical reaction. And she looked good. He'd seen more beautiful women, but something about her made his senses go haywire.

Being able to picture her in wet lingerie didn't help.

He cast a surreptitious glance her way, afraid she would guess what he was thinking. She was looking out the window, lost in her own world. A strand of blond hair blew across her face, lingering on her lips before she brushed it away.

Luke forced his gaze back to the road. As lovely as the sight of her near-naked form had been at the pond yesterday, it was her armpit, of all things, that had driven him over the edge. He'd been doing a passable job of controlling himself. The ice cold water had helped. But when she'd rubbed that herbal stuff under her arm, he'd been struck by the ridiculous urge to lick her there like a snow cone, and his entire body had gone rigid.

It was crazy! He'd never ogled a woman's armpit before, let alone fantasized about making out with it.

After thirty years in Vegas, he should have been anesthetized to sex, but one day with Shay Phillips had him panting like a teenager.

This morning he'd been no more successful at curbing his wayward thoughts. Watching a woman shave her legs was kind of a turn-on, he supposed, when the woman had legs like hers. Pale and silky-looking, miles long, a symphony of skin. He'd seen one soapy rivulet run down the inside of her thigh and wanted to follow its path with his tongue. From there, his mind had taken the natural progression, and he'd been down on his knees before her, mentally, when her little brother walked in.

He'd had to start a conversation about basketball to give himself time to recover.

Of course, she'd known exactly what she was doing. A woman didn't frolic about half-naked or caress her slippery-smooth, soap-slick legs in front of a man unless she wanted to work him up into a lather.

The last thing he needed was to get involved with someone like her right now. She wasn't his type. She wasn't even his *age*.

Besides, he'd come here to lay low, not to get laid.

Tenaja Falls was supposed to be a kind of sabbatical for him, an opportunity to pick up the pieces of his career and reshape his outlook on life. Things had gone south in Vegas, personally and professionally. The casino kingpins he'd been investigating had won the battle. They'd almost taken him out for good.

A near-death experience tended to change a man, encourage him to reevaluate his priorities and consider what had almost slipped from his grasp.

Instead of discovering what was most important to him, Luke had come up empty-handed. He loved his family, but they all had their own lives, peripheral to his. His stepsister, Lauren, had a child of her own and another on the way. His intense focus on work had left him with few friends outside of law enforcement, and even fewer relationships with women.

He wasn't sure what he was searching for, but he didn't think he'd find it in a struggling town, a temporary job, or a meaningless fling.

"So where should we set this trap?" he asked, trying to refocus. They were on their way to preserve headquarters to pick up supplies. She'd run the plan by Mike Shepherd, her boss, with one caveat: no lethal force. Today, they'd take tranquilizer guns instead of rifles. If the mission was successful, Mike would send air support, and Shay would run tests on the sedated animal at HQ herself.

"The best place might be near the tenajas on Los Coyotes."

"Tenajas?" he said, glancing at her.

"You don't know what it means?"

"Should I?"

"It's an Indian word."

He felt his lips curve into a humorless smile. "And we Indians all speak the same language, right?"

"I know you don't," she insisted, frowning at his sarcasm. "But you said you're Luiseño. The people of Los Coyotes are Cahuilla. Both are descendants of Shoshoni, and the languages have a Uto-Aztecan base. Lots of the words are similar."

He arched a brow at her and she blushed. Was she

embarrassed about being educated? "Well, I've never heard it," he admitted. "What does it mean?"

"Tenajas are seasonal pools. Natural rock basins that fill with water after a period of rain. They usually form along streambeds that are dry in summer."

Hadn't Garrett said something about seasonal pools? "Are they protected?"

"They're supposed to be, because so many animals use them as a water supply, but state and federal laws vary. The Cahuilla have been better about preserving the habitat than most Californians, until recently."

"What happened?"

"The casino craze." She cast him an uncertain look. "Not that I have anything against gambling. Or self-reliance. But with new roads, land development, in-creased traffic . . ." She sighed. "The impact on local wildlife will be significant."

"You would prefer the people languish in poverty?"

"No." She threaded her fingers though her ponytail, a contemplative expression on her pretty face. Before leaving her house, she'd changed into a brown tank top and tan pants. The sedate colors didn't suit her, but a full night's rest did, because she looked even better than she had yesterday. And so achingly young, with her fresh-scrubbed skin, unpainted lips, and freckled cheeks, that he felt like a lecher for wanting her. "There is no easy solution."

"So where are these tenajas? Five miles uphill?"

"Not quite that far," she said with a laugh, dropping a glance at his thighs. "Why? Are you sore?"

Experiencing an ache that had nothing to do with

hiking, he grunted a noncommittal response. "I'll have to talk with tribal police before we head out."

"That goes without saying," she murmured, looking out the window. "You can't set foot on Los Coyotes without their permission."

They made a brief stop at Dark Canyon, loading up the tranquilizer guns, camouflage mesh, drinking water, and energy bars. To her pack, Shay added something that looked like a bullhorn. It made a sound like a dying deer, she explained. Like the blood lure they'd used before, the horn was sure to attract carnivores, even those from miles away.

As he drove along the dirt road toward the reservation, Luke began to sweat. It was only midmorning, getting hotter by the minute, and he wasn't looking forward to the remainder of the day. This job as interim sheriff wasn't much better than paid leave. It was supposed to be a cakewalk, not a lion hunt.

To top it off, he didn't expect a warm reception at Los Coyotes. The Cahuilla and Luiseño may have had a common heritage, and a similar language, but like many neighboring tribes, they also had a history of strife. It wasn't easy to ingratiate yourself with men whose grandfathers had warred with your grandfathers.

And reservation politics had never been his forte.

The guard at the gated entrance waved them on, and as Luke made his way down the gravel road that served as Los Coyotes' main drag, he was struck by a wave of nostalgia. So much about it was familiar, but it didn't feel like home. He'd been born on a reservation just like this, and sent back to visit every summer until he turned eighteen.

That place had never felt like home, either.

The houses here were modest, adobe-style, one-story, tile-roofed. Some had busted windows, covered with tar paper. Others had piles of rubble on the lawn. Chunks of concrete, broken-down appliances, and twisted lengths of rebar waited to be hauled away.

Like in Tenaja Falls, and Pala, his hometown, children and dogs roamed free.

There were signs of hardship, of disorganization and disillusionment, but there were also hints of prosperity. New trucks sat alongside rusted jalopies. On Sunday, men were working on household projects, evidence that they were not only gainfully employed, but spending part of their paychecks to better their living conditions. The casino wasn't even open for business yet, and people were already benefiting.

Not all of the townsmen were involved in industrious pursuits, of course. It was shy of noon, early for drinking, but if Los Coyotes was anything like Pala, more than a couple of cold ones had already been cracked.

Refusing to let himself drift into the past, Luke swallowed back the taste of bitterness as he pulled into the parking lot of a small stucco building that passed for the tribal police station. As soon as the truck rolled to a stop, Shay made a little sound of feminine surprise and jumped out, right into another man's arms.

He was about Jesse's age, ten years younger than Luke, and although he had sun-streaked brown hair and blue eyes, the darkness of his skin and the tribal police uniform he was wearing gave away his heritage.

"You get prettier every year," the guy said when he released her.

Shay laughed at the compliment, touching his arm. "Luke, this is Clay Trujillo," she said, introducing them. "Clay, this is Sheriff Meza."

Luke shook the other man's hand with reluctance, stifling the urge to tighten his grip and turn the introduction into a pissing contest. He hadn't felt this defensive since he was eighteen, but he hadn't been on a reservation since then, either.

He was proud of his culture, but not his past. As a kid who wasn't Indian enough for the streets of Pala or white enough for the Vegas suburbs, he'd engaged in more than his share of brawls. Too often, he'd felt as though he had to prove himself with his fists, to show his Native American blood by spilling it.

It had taken him a long time to learn how to walk away from a fight.

Clay Trujillo wasn't challenging him, but he was assessing him openly as they shook hands. Luke knew that unlike Shay, Clay recognized his heritage at a glance. He also met his gaze head-on, for they were of a similar height.

"I didn't know you were home from grad school," Shay said. "I would have invited you to my birthday party."

"I'm sorry I missed it," Clay replied. "I've only been back on the job a few days."

Luke waited impatiently while they exchanged news, laughing and touching each other with the ease and frequency of longtime acquaintances. Shay's eyes sparkled with affection and Clay's grin was wide with masculine appreciation. They looked like they belonged on a fucking toothpaste commercial.

He ground his own teeth together, tearing his gaze away.

It occurred to him that he was jealous, and he hadn't felt that way about a woman since Leticia. Disturbed by the comparison, he quashed his irrational response to the sight of Shay flirting with another man and gave her a pointed stare, reminding her of their business here.

Catching on immediately, she told Clay about the lion attack and requested permission to trespass on Los Coyotes.

"Let's go inside," Clay decided. "Granting a permit to hunt is just a formality, but the attack is something we should talk to the chief about."

Chief Mortero was sitting behind a polished oak desk, with his brother, Samson, at his side. They were short and round and unflappable, their dark hair going silver at the temples and their faces lined with age. Neither reacted to the news of the mauling, but appeared to absorb the information like a couple of stone sponges.

Luke doubted either of these men had been involved with Yesenia Montes, or transported her broken body off federal land to avoid dealing with the authorities. Even so, he asked a few questions about procedure and invited himself on a tour of the facilities. It wouldn't hurt to check out their official vehicles, or scout the area for trucks with bed liners.

The chief answered his questions, granted permission for the tour, and wrote up the hunting permit with very little fanfare. After exchanging a weighted glance with his brother, Samson said, "Deputy Trujillo will accompany you on the hunt."

"Of course," Clay interjected. "I'd be happy to come along."

It was the last thing Luke wanted, and Shay must have been able to read the reluctance in his body language, because she shook her head. "Actually, my plan will be easier to execute with fewer men. But thank you very much for the offer."

Luke realized that the elders were wary of him. He was an outsider, a man from a corrupt city and a hostile tribe, a man whose forefathers had stolen their horses. The Luiseño and Cahuilla had often been manipulated into battle with their white or Mexican "allies."

His Indian blood was no free pass here, or anywhere.

When Chief Mortero nodded his acceptance, Clay led them down the hall and through the station, explaining their technological capabilities and highlighting every available resource, showing off the new holding cell and recently remodeled garage.

Most of the information Clay shared should have been irrelevant to an interim sheriff, but Luke listened carefully, as if he were considering a partnership between their law enforcement teams instead of trying to rule them out as suspects.

Dylan shifted the weight of his backpack, which was considerably lighter than when he'd first broken into the deserted construction site, and kept moving.

He stuck close to the trailers, taking advantage of the

early-afternoon shadows. His sister's car was parked in a safe location, about a mile down the road, so he still had a distance to travel after he hopped the fence again.

When he rounded the last corner, he made two disturbing observations: the front gate was no longer closed, and he was no longer alone.

"Hey, you," someone behind him yelled, and he froze.

Judging by sound, the man who'd called out was at least fifty feet away. Dylan didn't bother to look. He was confident he could outrun just about anyone, but he couldn't outrun the two-ton pickup truck parked at the fence line. If the man followed, he would catch up with Dylan long before he made it to Shay's car.

Besides, running made him look guilty. Guiltier than he already was.

He squared his shoulders and turned around.

Oh, *fuck.*

The man striding toward him was one of the richest, most powerful, and most easily recognizable men in Tenaja Falls. With his ten-gallon cowboy hat, handlebar mustache, and stocky build, Bull Ryan had always reminded Dylan of Yosemite Sam.

Running was not an option, now that he'd shown his face, so he took a hesitant step forward. "Mr. Ryan?" He extended his hand. "I'm Dylan Phillips."

If Bull knew who he was, he didn't show it. He probably couldn't keep track of his son's girlfriends, much less their little brothers. "What d'ya want?"

"I'm looking for work."

"Don't work on Sundays," Bull said, opening the

door to one of the trailers and ducking inside. "Come back tomorrow."

He breathed a sigh of relief. Jesse Ryan's dad didn't know who he was, and unless he looked into his backpack, he would never know what he'd been doing here. But instead of walking away, Dylan followed Bull into the makeshift office. "I have school tomorrow," he said. "And basketball practice until three."

"Don't have much use for you, then. Quittin' time's at four."

There was only one chair, and Bull took it. Dylan had no choice but to remain standing. He was never sure how to act around men like this, brawny types who lived by their fists rather than their wits. Adopting a tough-guy attitude, he widened his stance and blanked his expression, because nobody had ever liked his smart-ass face. "I bet you don't leave at four," he said. "You probably got paperwork and stuff to do."

"So?"

"I could do cleanup," he said. "Put tools away. Whatever."

Bull didn't look very interested. "You free Saturdays?"

"Yessir."

The older man gave him another halfhearted once-over.

"I'll work for minimum wage," Dylan said in a rush, not sure why he was taking the ruse so far. He should have been happy to escape without getting arrested. "You can hire me on a temporary basis. If you're satisfied, I can work full time in the summer."

"Summers here are hell," Bull said bluntly. "No shade.

Never one drop of rain. A hundred fifteen degrees. You wouldn't last a half day."

Dylan just stared back at him in silence, thinking he could endure a lot more than anyone gave him credit for. He was so tired of being ignored, dismissed, and discounted. Or worse, treated like a brain, useless in all physical pursuits. Even the guys on the basketball team thought he was weird. Too cerebral. He approached the game as though the court was a mathematical grid, an infinite combination of probabilities, a series of lines and angles.

"What part of construction are you interested in?"

He didn't hesitate. "Demolition."

"Not much to tear down on this site," Bull commented.

"There's hills."

"Come again?"

"Those hills," he said, jerking his chin toward the window, indicating some rocky dunes a short distance away. "You need to get them out of the way, right? You could use explosives."

Bull stroked his long mustache, following his gaze. The method wasn't particularly revolutionary on a job this scale, so perhaps the option wasn't viable. Dylan knew there were environmental sanctions and cost issues to consider.

He just liked the idea of blowing shit up.

"Hmmph," Bull said, looking away from the window. "I need diggers. Graders. Guys who will shovel until their backs ache and their hands bleed."

Dylan turned his palms faceup. They were already

calloused from handling a basketball so much, but he wasn't so naïve as to think working at a construction site wouldn't affect his playing in a negative way.

"I can do that," he said, liking the idea of blood on his hands.

9

Dylan left the construction site with a spring in his step. The day was turning out better than he'd hoped. His experiments had gone well, he hadn't gotten caught, and the interaction between him and Bull Ryan was an unexpected bonus.

He was actually looking forward to starting his new job. Shay wouldn't approve, because she wanted him to focus on his grades and excel in sports, but the basketball season was wrapping up and the last few months of high school would be a breeze. Seniors couldn't concentrate for shit this time of year, and most teachers planned accordingly.

Before he reached Shay's car, the day took an abrupt turn for the worse. Garrett Snell's cruiser was inching down the dirt road, driving slowly to avoid kicking up dust. For a guy who never seemed to do any actual police work, Garrett managed to be everywhere at once.

"Motherfucker," Dylan said under his breath, quickening his pace. If he could get to the car, he might have a chance to stash his pack. Unfortunately, the deputy had already spotted him. He sped up, flashing his siren and jerking to a stop behind Shay's car.

Swearing, Dylan shrugged out of his backpack and fumbled for the keys in his pocket. Garrett moved at a deceptively lazy pace, but he was out of his car with time to spare, standing in Dylan's way and blocking his exit route.

"Why do you always hassle me?" he asked, exasperated.

Garrett stared at him, his black eyes flat. "Because you deserve it. Now drop the backpack and put your hands on the hood of the car."

Dylan's stomach pitched. "I didn't even do anything! You have no right—"

"I have every right," Garrett claimed. "Folks said they heard gunshots."

"Bullshit," he muttered under his breath. But Dylan wasn't stupid, so he cooperated, letting his backpack fall to the ground and placing his hands on the hood of the car. It was blazing hot.

"Spread your legs."

Dylan gritted his teeth and did as he was told. It wasn't the first time the deputy had patted him down, and he was pretty sure Garrett enjoyed it. Not because he liked boys, but because he liked humiliating him. His touch was swift and impersonal, brushing along the undersides of his arms and around his waist. When he dropped down to check Dylan's ankles, and moved up to the baggy crotch of his pants, Dylan couldn't take it anymore.

"Does your wife know you love balls?"

Garrett grunted at the insult and continued frisking

him. Dylan thought he was going to get away with the comment until Garrett brought his knee up and rammed him forcefully between the legs.

The pain was instantaneous, debilitating, excruciating. Dylan fell forward against the hood, letting out a pathetic, strangled sound. Agony spread through his lower abdomen, making him nauseous. He slid down the wheel well and collapsed in the dirt, curling up in the fetal position with his hand cradled between his legs. He was only vaguely aware of Garrett unzipping his backpack and rifling through its contents.

"Does your sister know what you've been up to?"

Dylan retched and spat on the dirt, ridding the bad taste from his mouth. "Fuck you," he moaned.

"You're going to blow your pecker off."

That prediction brought another round of nausea. He struggled not to vomit, not to cry. Bits of dirt and gravel cut into the side of his face, but it was a minor discomfort compared to the ache in his groin.

Instead of arresting him, or confiscating the stuff in his backpack, Garrett tossed it on the hood of Shay's car. "Don't come around here anymore."

Tears seeped out of his eyes. "Have to," he said from between clenched teeth. "I've got a job now."

Dylan felt Garrett's beady little eyes on him, relishing his pain, assessing his weaknesses. "Bull hired you? To do what, suck dicks?"

"No," he panted. "He said you took care of that for him."

He braced his body for another blow, waiting for Garrett to kick him in the stomach, or make him eat gravel. Nothing happened. Dylan knew he had a dirty mouth, and his inability to control it caused him no end of trouble. When he thought he could open his eyes without losing his lunch, he squinted up at Garrett in trepidation.

The deputy wasn't even looking at him. He was staring out past the construction site, toward Cahuilla Ridge. Where Shay had gone with the new sheriff. "Give your sister my regards," he said, and left him there, lying in the dirt.

Luke had been acting weird ever since they crossed the border into Los Coyotes. He was aloof with Clay and indifferent toward the elders. After the tour, he'd asked a few questions about trucks and custom bed liners, of all things, a few more about the new casino.

"When did you leave Pala?" she asked, forming the words as soon as they popped into her mind. They had a thirty minute drive before they reached the trailhead to the tenajas, so she might as well make conversation.

"A long time ago."

"How old were you?" she persisted.

"Three."

"So you moved to Vegas with your family?"

"My mother and I went."

"What happened to your father?"

"What happened to yours?" he returned.

She rested her head back against the seat, feeling weary. "He's a truck driver."

"Tenaja Falls has roads."

"Not ones he travels."

His hands relaxed on the steering wheel. "My dad stayed in Pala. They're divorced."

She could only guess he associated the reservation with whatever had gone wrong between his parents. It wasn't difficult to look around Los Coyotes, or Tenaja Falls, for that matter, and see only life's failures, hard luck and harder times. "You didn't come back to visit?"

"Every summer."

"How was it?"

"Not too good," he said, surprising her with honesty.

"What was he like?"

"Strict." After a short pause, he added, "Rigid."

"Hmm," she said, studying the way he held himself, ramrod-straight, and the military precision of his uniform. "I can't imagine that."

He leaned back in his seat, distancing himself from the comparison. "He also drank a lot. And he put me to work on his property. I guess he thought he'd make a man out of me."

"Did he?"

For a moment, she thought he was going to admit that being a man had nothing to do with physical labor. Instead he said, "Maybe. But I resented it, and I never got to know him very well." He glanced at her. "How well do you know Clay?"

"What a ham-handed segue," she murmured, brushing a stray wisp of hair off her forehead.

The corner of his mouth tipped up. "Do you go out with him?"

She wondered if he had any idea how proprietary he sounded. Although he must have a point to this line of questioning, one that had nothing to do with staking a claim on her, she felt her heart beat a little faster. "No."

"Why not?"

She shrugged, not wanting to explain the situation because it involved Jesse. Clay was Jesse's half brother and Shay would never come between them. She left that role to Jesse's wife, who had been Clay's girl once upon a time. Jesse had no compunction about lying to, cheating with, or stealing another man's woman. After Clay left for college, Jesse set his sights on Tamara, probably just to see if he could take her away from Clay.

Catching a female at a vulnerable moment was a Jesse Ryan specialty.

Family connections aside, Clay was younger than Shay and there had never been anything romantic between them. She couldn't help but notice he'd grown up tall and strong and very fine, but they were just friends.

Besides, Clay was in love with Tamara Ryan. Always had been, always would be.

"Why are you so interested in my dating habits?" she asked, batting her lashes. "If you want to ask me out, Sheriff, stop pussyfooting around and get on with it."

She'd been joking, of course, but his eyes dropped to her mouth as if she'd said something suggestive. That made her look at his mouth, and remember how his lips felt against hers yesterday, in the split second before he pulled away. She wondered what would have happened if he'd gone ahead and kissed her, if his tense mouth would have softened or stayed firm, if he'd have let his weight press down on her or held himself taut, if his hands would have gentled or moved fast and rough all over her arching, aching body.

He looked away first, turning his attention back to the road, leaving her bereft, empty, unsatisfied—again.

The tenajas were inaccessible by automobile, but one could get within a few miles by traversing a wickedly bumpy 4x4 trail. Luke's truck was well equipped to handle the ride and he didn't bother to take it easy on the shocks. Shay spent the remainder of the trip braced against the dashboard, trying to avoid being tossed about inside the cab.

When they reached the trailhead, she loaded up her pack and strapped on her tranquilizer gun in silence.

Tenaja Trail ran along the eastern edge of Los Coyotes, where Dark Canyon left off, and the two areas had similar habitats. Both were in the shadow of Palomar Mountain and reaped the benefits of fresh snowmelt. Deep Creek flowed year-round, although in late summer it petered down to a trickle, but Tenaja Creek, like the pools themselves, was seasonal. In April it had a steady flow; by October it would be dry as a bone.

In this drought-prone climate, water made all the difference. While Dark Canyon was mostly woodland, Los Coyotes was hilly chaparral, sagebrush and sumac as far as the eye could see. During wildfire season it was a 100,000-acre tinderbox.

Although the tenajas were evenly dispersed along the trail, Shay headed toward the summit. The brush there grew thick, with a number of rocky outcroppings and a couple of live oak trees. It wasn't an ideal location for a den, but it was a perfect spot for an ambush, as it afforded plenty of cover and enough open space to watch for an approach.

It was early afternoon by the time they reached the clearing near the summit, and the sun was blazing. Like yesterday, the Santa Anas were out in full force, blowing wind so hot and dry her sweat evaporated before it had a chance to cool her off. She drank more than half her water supply and watched to make sure Luke did the same.

Lions rarely hunted at this time of day, but it would take her at least an hour to set up, and by then the sun would be behind the mountain. Dusk came early around these parts.

She chose a shady spot beneath an immature oak tree to set up the "trap." It wasn't so much a trap as a hiding place. Her plan was to build a small shelter, cover it with the camouflage netting, sound the horn, and wait.

It wasn't rocket science, but if there was a hungry male holed up near the tenajas he would hear the deer distress call and come to investigate. Although lying in ambush among a cluster of rocks would have been even simpler, lions had excellent eyesight and she didn't want to take the chance of being seen. Besides, the shelter would provide both cover and shade.

After they'd gathered enough branches to make a basic dome-shaped structure, Luke started bothering her with questions. "Remind me why we can't use hunting dogs," he said, eyeing the hillside with trepidation.

"It's illegal."

"Even in this kind of circumstance?"

"What trail would they follow? They would need to

start from the point of the attack, and we don't know where it actually happened."

He swore under his breath. Unfazed, Shay continued bending branches for the shelter. "How many lions are around here?"

She shrugged. "We'll be lucky to attract one."

"And after you shoot, how long before he goes down?"

"A few minutes."

More cursing. "I'm all for conservation," he claimed, "but do we really need two-hundred-pound predators roaming the woods? I mean, shouldn't protecting humans be more important?"

Shay resisted the urge to roll her eyes. She'd heard this uninformed argument more times than she cared to. "Protecting our natural resources is essential for all living things, humans included. Mountain lions are a cascade species."

"What does that mean?"

"They're integral to the ecosystem. Removing them would have a cascade effect, endangering other animals and damaging the habitat. Without predators, prey run rampant and deplete resources. It's the same with sharks or any other dangerous animal. Eliminating the threat to 'protect' humans would be more harmful to us in the long run." She dusted off her hands and stood. "I should think you'd understand the lion's plight."

"Why's that?"

"We've invaded his turf, colonized his territory, and claimed his land for our own."

He gave her a wry smile. "Okay, earth girl, you made your point. Just don't expect me to start singing the praises of the striped skunk."

She smiled back at him, telling herself that the flutter in her tummy was nerves, not desire. Tracking a lion without GPS was dangerous, and the shelter a flimsy barricade if they were spotted, although a tranq'd lion would be more likely to flee than charge.

"So what made you choose this line of work?" he asked. "Why lions?"

"I've always liked wild animals," she said, making a few adjustments to the outside of the shelter. "But I would say they chose me."

"How?"

"Well, one day I was walking to class at Palomar College. The back parking lot is right next to a designated wilderness area, with a nature trail leading toward the campus. It was summer, so there were only a few classes in session, and very early in the morning. I was hurrying along and I dropped one of my books. When I bent to pick it up, I heard this hissing sound."

"What was it?"

"A bobcat. Probably a juvenile, not much bigger than a house cat. And only a couple of feet away."

"What did you do?"

She grinned at the memory. "I held out my hand and said, 'Here, kitty, kitty.'"

"You didn't."

"Oh, yes, I did. But I should have just stayed quiet and still, because he bolted as soon as I reached out."

He shook his head, chuckling at her moxie.

"After that, I knew what I wanted to do. It was a life-defining moment." She arched a glance at him. "Did you have one of those, when you decided to be a cop?"

"Yes," he said, sobering. "But mine isn't as nice to tell."

She waited for him to continue with undisguised interest.

He stared across the hills below them, far into the distance. "The last summer I spent with my father, we . . . argued. I was eighteen and thought I knew everything. He didn't like my attitude. I didn't like his. One night, he'd been drinking pretty heavily, and he grabbed me by the arm." Frowning, he studied his clenched fist. "I let him have it. Knocked him on his ass. He didn't get up."

She nodded, seeing the regret in his eyes.

"I called nine-one-one, because I was worried. By the time the tribal police got there, he was up and hollering for them to take me away. I spent my last night on the rez in jail. Took quite a few sucker punches that night, too."

"The tribal police beat you up?"

"Yes. I decided then that I was going to be a real cop. A good cop." His gaze met hers. "Better than them."

Her own tummy ached at the thought of him lying on the floor of a jail cell, beaten by men he should have been able to trust. "They're not all like that," she felt compelled to say. "The police on Los Coyotes aren't dirty."

Although he didn't argue with her, she knew he wouldn't take her word for it. He was clearly a man who made up his own mind about people, and that was admirable, as long as he didn't judge them based on his past.

Sighing, she looked at the shelter, surveying her handiwork. The camouflaged mesh was kind of obvious in the sunlight, but under the shade of the oak, the shelter passed for a waist-high bush. From inside, they would have a 360-degree view of the area. "Ready?" she asked, holding open the flap. "Get in."

Luke folded his lanky body into the shelter. Sitting down, he took up almost all the space. Shay frowned. She hadn't built it big enough. "Can't you, like, scrunch over?"

"Like, no, I can't," he said, mocking her speech.

It couldn't be helped, so she squeezed in beside him. They sat hip to hip, shoulder to shoulder, their heads almost touching. She had to bring her boots up to her bottom to close the front.

Twisting, she managed to get the deer horn out of her pack.

"Cover your ears," she warned before sounding it off. The noise was deafening, disturbing the quiet and piercing the still air, but what bothered her most was the raw agony of the cry. It sent chills down her spine.

"Jesus Christ," Luke whispered after the echo died away. "If that won't bring a lion I don't know what will."

Turning back-to-back, they waited, guns resting on bent knees, muzzles pointing opposite directions. The minutes ticked by. Nothing happened. Shay focused on the landscape, watching grass sway and shadows stretch. Insects buzzed. The interior of the shelter was dark, hot, and airless. She was intensely aware of the way her tank top clung to her, the heat of his body next to hers, the muscles shifting in his back.

She felt every heartbeat, every intake of breath.

An hour passed.

"Let's take a break and then sound the horn again," she said finally.

"Thank God," he said, engaging the safety and putting his weapon aside. "I'm dripping sweat."

"We can't go out."

"Why not?"

"A lion might come."

"I'm willing to take my chances."

She turned to face him. "Don't be such a baby. We can't leave the safety of the shelter and you know it." Rummaging through her pack, she took out her secret stash: an apple. Her elbow caught him in the cheek as she brought it to her mouth. "Sorry," she said, crunching loudly. "Do you want some?"

He scowled at her, touching his cheekbone.

Smiling, she held out the apple, turning it so he could take a bite from the unmarred section. For a moment, she thought he would decline, but then he reached out and wrapped his hand around her wrist, tilting the apple and sinking his teeth into the part of the fruit her mouth had already touched.

If he'd nipped at her belly, or placed his open mouth on her inner thigh, she'd have reacted the same way. Heat coursed through her, singing in her veins. She swallowed too soon, almost choking on bits of apple, and she had to drink several ounces of water to recover.

He took the apple from her hand and proceeded to finish it for her, his manner as cool as hers was flustered.

In her defense, the man had a sexy mouth. Strong white teeth. Chiseled jaw. Watching him eat an apple was like some kind of foreplay.

He smelled nice, too. And if he was sweating, well, so was she. Shay wasn't sure if her deodorant was working, but she could detect the faint scent of his, along with shaving soap and laundry detergent, starched collar and warm male skin.

"You smell too good," she accused.

"*I* smell too good?"

"Lions can detect human scents. Trackers know better than to go overboard on personal hygiene products."

"What are *you* wearing?"

Uh-oh. Shay fought the urge to lift her arm and do a sniff test. Was she stinky?

"You smell like flowers or herbs or something," he clarified.

"I do?"

"Yes, you do, so don't act like I'm the one who's fuming up the place. I'm not even wearing aftershave."

She bristled. "The only product I use is an all-natural deodorant. It doesn't smell like anything."

His eyes dropped to her bare arm, which was wedged against his, then returned to her face. "How does it taste?"

She moistened her lips. "How does it—what?"

"Never mind," he said, and lowered his mouth to hers.

10

Shay's first instinct was to pull away.

She may have been entertaining lustful fantasies about Luke's mouth, but that didn't mean she wanted it on her in real life. She wasn't willing to overlook the way he'd treated her yesterday. He'd had his chance with her and he'd blown it. *Blown* it.

He must have sensed her reluctance, because he lifted his hand to the nape of her neck, holding her in place. If he'd been a little more aggressive, she'd have pushed him off, but he merely brushed his lips over hers, using a light touch. At the same time, he did something to the back of her neck that sent shivers down her spine.

Her brain turned to mush and her body went boneless. Feeling like his puppet, she fought to keep her mouth clamped shut and her eyes wide open. Her lack of cooperation didn't deter him any; she felt his lips curve against hers as if her stubbornness amused him. Maybe he was one of those men who liked a girl to play hard to get.

Jesse certainly had.

Incensed by the idea, she opened her mouth to tell him off. His tongue dipped in, and all thoughts of Jesse Ryan fled.

He tasted as good as he looked, like hot man and Red Delicious—and boy, did he know how to kiss. He didn't move too fast or press too hard. He just took it slow and easy, kind of like he didn't care if it went any further. Only their lips were touching, his tongue tracing the rim of her mouth, his hand resting lightly on the back of her neck, but her entire body tingled with sensation. She imagined his fingertips stroking her nipples, or pressing against the sudden ache between her legs. Forgetting her protests, she leaned into him, wanting more.

He eased back.

Damn it.

Her body was throbbing with awareness, her mouth wet from his. She sucked in a tortured breath.

He stared at her parted lips. "I smell smoke."

"Smoke?" she repeated stupidly. They were generating a lot of heat, she supposed. One little kiss and she was about to go up in flames.

"As in fire."

Then she smelled it, too. Looking out across the grassy field to the sumac-covered hills in the distance, she saw it. Thick black smoke, roiling up to the sky.

Wildfire.

Gasping, she shoved aside the front flap of the shelter and scrambled out, dragging her pack along behind her. Luke winced as he rose from his cramped position.

Resisting the urge to panic, she strapped on her pack and studied the landscape, assessing the greatest opportunity for escape. She couldn't see the flames but knew they were just beyond the trail. Santa Ana winds blew west, away from the desert and toward the coast. They couldn't go uphill, and they couldn't go back the way they came. The best course of action would be to head for the tenajas and hope the fire didn't reach them first.

"This way," she said, grabbing his arm.

The streambed leading to the tenajas was in the direction of the smoke, so he balked. "Shouldn't we go the other way?"

"We can't outrun a fire by going uphill. It could overcome us in minutes."

He hesitated, instinct warring with logic.

"Trust me," she said, pulling him along.

The next few moments took on a surreal, dreamlike quality. The flames were approaching fast, eating up the thick underbrush and igniting dry branches, throwing sparks and black wind in every direction. The Santa Anas might be blowing west, but a large fire created its own weather, and this one was all over the place.

By the time they reached the streambed, the flames burned frighteningly close. If they didn't make it to the tenajas before the fire, they could take cover in the shallow creek, but with the heavy foliage along the bank, that would be a hot, dangerous option.

Knowing they were in serious trouble, she quickened the pace as much as she dared, hopping over boulders and trudging through the ankle-high water. Her boots became wet and heavy with mud. Branches struck her across the face.

She stumbled, losing her footing on the slippery rocks, and went down hard on one knee. Pain radiated through her, slamming all the way up to her hip. Luke crouched beside her. She could see flames reflected in his dark eyes.

"I'm okay," she said, struggling for breath.

"I'll carry you."

"No." Allowing him to help her up, she let him support her on one side and kept moving, ignoring the pain. The fire was advancing quickly now, jumping the creek, surrounding them. If they didn't hurry, a bum knee would be the least of her problems.

The largest pool was the closest, less than a quarter mile down the streambed. It took an eternity to get there. The force of the heat was intense, whipping at her clothes, burning her eyes and nose and lungs. Her skin felt raw from exposure. When they finally reached the edge of the falls, Shay didn't take off her boots or throw aside her pack before she jumped in, and Luke was right there beside her.

The water was cold. Shockingly, blessedly cold. And deep. The pool embraced her like a lover, inviting her stay a little longer, to sink down a little farther, to immerse herself in the safety of its sweet, dark depths.

Luke's arm snaked around her waist, jerking her up. They broke through the surface, panting, staring, wide-eyed. All around them, fire blazed.

"We'll die in here," he gasped, releasing her to tread water.

She wasn't sure they wouldn't, so she didn't respond. The flames roared. Hot ash rained down on top of the water, singeing and sizzling.

Cursing, Luke shrugged out of his pack. Mutely, she slipped hers off her shoulders and let him take it from her. She watched while he found a place under the water where his feet could touch, stared at him while he removed his uniform shirt, eyes blinking, mind blank. He made a tent with it and gestured for her to take shelter underneath. She did, holding on to his bare shoulders, feeling his strength.

"Are you all right?"

She nodded and buried her face in the hollow of his throat, tightening her grip on him, never wanting to let him go. She felt the need to cry but couldn't. He tucked his shirt around their heads and they stayed that way, shivering with cold and stunned into silence, until the danger passed.

When they came out from beneath his shirt, the world was black.

It wasn't yet dusk but clouds of smoke and heavy ash occluded the sun like a solar eclipse. The air was thick with the smell of burning sage, oak, and mesquite. Everywhere she looked she saw a blanket of ash. Charred branches and smoldering tree trunks were all that was left. An eerie gray light cast their shapes into stark relief like a photo negative.

In less than a week, green shoots would sprout from black soot, nature reinventing itself, but for now, the sky was dark and the landscape barren.

Shay shuddered in Luke's arms.

"Your lips are blue," he said, studying her cautiously.

She was cold. So was he. Beneath her fingertips, his shoulders were like chilled granite. Her own body felt limp, bloodless. When he released her, she thought she might float away.

"You're in shock," he accused.

Normally that kind of insult would have riled her up. Now the liveliest response she could muster was a yawn.

Muttering Dylan's favorite curse word, Luke put his shirt back on, leaving it unbuttoned, and treaded water, searching the perimeter of the pool for a way out. This particular tenaja was called the Devil's Cup, and it was basically a giant bowl of granite with smooth, high sides. After a lone explorer drowned here more than fifty years ago, hand- and footholds had been notched into the stone. Luke found them with no help from her. Then he dragged her over there and made her go up first.

Her wet fingers couldn't seem to find purchase on the slippery rock, and her legs were all but useless. "Hmm," she said. "Maybe we will die in here."

"I don't think so," he replied, sounding mad. Covering her hands with his, he forced her to get a grip. Literally. Then he gave her bottom a hard push and insinuated his shoulder underneath it, using his body to keep hers from sliding back down. It was awkward and undignified, but with Luke's help, Shay made it up.

He heaved himself over the edge as well, and they both lay there, panting from exertion.

After a few moments, she realized he was waiting for her lead. He didn't know where they were or how to get out of here. The fire wouldn't come back to a burned-out area, but that didn't mean they were in the clear. They were cold and wet, and dark was fast approaching.

"How's your knee?"

"I don't know," she said honestly. "My whole body is numb." Experimenting, she bent both legs, feeling a dull throb in the left one. She touched it and didn't find any broken bones or loose parts. It was only a little swollen. Maybe the cold water had helped.

"There's a cave near here," she said, her brain kicking back into gear. "I think I can make it that far."

His eyes narrowed. "A cave?"

"Not a lion cave," she said, stifling a hysterical giggle. "It's a sacred site, actually. Petroglyphs and stuff." There might be drinking water there, too. The site was little known and seldom visited, but Shay had stashed some supplies there herself six months ago. From the Santa Ana Mountains to the Anza-Borrego Desert, there was only this desolate, treacherous stretch of land, and hikers got lost in the area occasionally.

"Do you want to rest?" he asked.

"No. We need to get moving."

Nodding, he gathered up their packs. Shay put all of the essentials in one, the last of their drinking water, a first aid kit, and a couple of energy bars. The tranquilizer guns were wet and the cell phones out of range, but she added them anyway.

He took the pack away from her and helped her up. She tested her knee, putting weight on it gingerly. It didn't feel good, but it didn't buckle, either.

"I can carry you," he said again.

"No, you can't," she snapped. "I'm too heavy."

He frowned, perusing her body for evidence of heaviness. Or maybe he was just assessing her injury. "Let me look at your knee."

Grumbling, she sat down and drew up the leg of her pants. The wet fabric bunched around her knee, making tending to it impossible. Cheeks heating, she hobbled to her feet again, fumbling with her zipper and dropping her pants.

Shay was glad today's panties were a dark, unrevealing blue.

She wasn't seriously injured, just a bad scrape and the makings of a nasty bruise, but he examined her knee carefully, pressing gently here and there before applying some salve from the first aid kit and wrapping her up in an ace bandage. She remained standing, trying to ignore the fact that he was kneeling before her, his face just inches from her crotch.

When he was finally done, his gaze moved from her knee to her bikini briefs. He jerked away from her and straightened, his color darkening.

My, my. Luke Meza could blush.

Hiding a smile, Shay tried to drag her pants back up, almost losing her balance when the wet fabric refused to cooperate. Luke stepped in to offer his assistance, hands sliding all over her slippery skin.

"Did these shrink or something?" he had the nerve to ask.

She swatted his hands away and completed the task herself, her cheeks heating with embarrassment. Of course he wouldn't understand about wet clothes and extra curves. His butt was probably hard as a rock, like the rest of him.

With his uniform shirt hanging open, and his hair all wet and choppy, he was most enticingly disheveled.

His eyes met hers and shuttered instantly, hardening

into black chips of ice. "Ready?" he asked, throwing the pack over one shoulder.

She nodded, preparing herself for another long haul.

Her boots squished as she walked, growing heavier with every step, and her knee ached, but she soldiered on, leading him over scorched earth and smoldering embers, heading toward Cahuilla Ridge. Traveling so soon after a wildfire wasn't recommended, but the temperature was dropping fast and they needed to find shelter before nightfall.

She was aware of her wet clothes clinging to her and the pervasive silence, the fuzzy gray sunset and falling ash. It was as if the fire had sucked up every breath of air and ray of light, swallowing sound and muting color, leaving nothing but dark soot, charred black bits, and quiet.

Putting one foot in front of the other, she trudged on, relying heavily on her right leg. Anyone who followed their tracks would know by the uneven depressions her boots made that she was hurt. When the burned soil beneath her feet became sandy, she knew they were close.

Cahuilla Ridge was a rock exposure made of multi-layered sandstone, carved deep by wind and erosion, too barren to provide fuel for the wildfire. The area's only foliage, a cluster of fan palms, stood high and proud, untouched by flames. Nestled into the side of the ridge there was a small cave, tall enough to stand in and wide enough to move around. It wasn't a five-star resort, but it would serve as lodgings for the night. Native American couples had been using the place to perform sacred rituals for centuries.

Ascending the trail along the ridge proved more difficult than she'd anticipated. The pain in her knee was bearable so she didn't think it was responsible for her sluggish pace. She was shivering but didn't feel the cold, aware of her surroundings but unable to focus.

She was almost to the safety of the cave when the ground tilted beneath her feet. Gravity pulled her backward, into Luke's arms, and he caught her neatly, as if they'd choreographed the incident. "Hello there," she said, blinking up at him.

He looked mad, or maybe that was just his face.

"You could have fallen forward," he said from between clenched teeth. "Or to the side."

Shay didn't have to peek over the edge to know it was a long way down. She wanted to mumble something sarcastic about him being her knight in shining uniform, but her mouth wouldn't form the words.

"You're ice cold," he added, continuing to scold.

He wasn't, she noted, clinging to his shoulders. Despite the wet shirt, his skin was hot. She put her cold lips to his bare neck, seeking warmth.

He carried her the rest of the way. She was a tall woman and not exactly a featherweight, but he managed the task with impressive ease, as boasted. If she weren't so disoriented, she might have enjoyed the ride.

He set her down on the floor of the cave and immediately found the basket of supplies. On her last visit she'd brought a small stack of firewood, some food and water, and—bless her industrious little heart—a multicolored wool blanket in one of those airtight space bags. Getting her warm must be his first priority, so he spread the blanket out on the ground next to her. After shrugging out of his own wet shirt, he went to work on her clothes.

The way he undressed her was insultingly impersonal. His eyes were cold and his hands were hot. While he unlaced her boots and removed them, peeled off her pants and checked her knee, she lay there like a corpse, immobile but not indifferent. For some reason, tears stung at her eyes, and he saw them.

"Lift up your arms."

She did. He pulled the soggy tank top over her head. Beneath it she wore a plain white cotton bra, no underwire, no padding, no artifice. He didn't look. Rolling onto his side, he brought her body toward his, spoon-style, and pulled the blanket over both of them.

It occurred to Shay that her physical breakdown had some kind of emotional root, and she felt ashamed. Her reaction to her mother's death had been the same. Shock. Confusion. Despair. And a complete inability to articulate her feelings.

"Tell me about your mother," she whispered.

His body tensed, then relaxed. "She's not Luiseño."

"She's white?"

"Yes."

"I wouldn't have guessed that by looking."

"Thanks."

"It's not an insult. You must know you're handsome."

He shifted, uncomfortable with the subject. Shay didn't mind. Regardless of what had passed between them, before or after the fire, they were here and they were alive and she would ask whatever she pleased. "So you like her? Better than your dad?"

"Yes."

"What's your favorite thing about her?" she continued. "What do you miss the most, when you don't see her?"

It was a tough question, and he gave it the consideration it deserved. "Her smile, I guess. There are so many other things, but her smile . . . it's just, always there. She's always happy to see me, even if I was with her the day before."

Shay felt more tears coming, and she sniffed them back. "Have you ever told her that?"

"No."

"You should."

"I will."

She believed him and so she quieted, resting her cheek on his bicep. It was nice to be with someone who loved his mother, even if he didn't like her. "My mama had a beautiful smile."

"Did she look like you?"

"No. Dylan and I both take after Daddy. She was a redhead, all soft and delicate."

"You have her skin," he surmised.

"Yes," she said, thinking her mother had made pale and freckled look as sweet and fresh as a bowl of strawberry ice cream. Her mind skittered to the way her mother's face had been made up for the funeral, and back further, to an even darker place, to how she had looked, swollen and grotesque, in the short hours after death.

"What happened to her?"

Shay didn't talk about this—ever—but she found herself saying, "She hung herself in the barn behind the house," in a faraway voice, as if the incident had happened to some other mother, some other girl. "I found her."

He sucked in a sharp breath. "I'm sorry. I had no idea."

"The only good thing about it was that Dylan was away," she said, thinking back. "It was the middle of summer, and she'd sent him to camp. She'd also packed up all her things and put them in marked boxes. She'd planned so far ahead! I think she'd have made the funeral arrangements if it wouldn't have drawn suspicion."

"You couldn't have known," he said softly, reading her mind.

Logic told her those words were true, even if her heart said different. "I'm glad we didn't die," she murmured, changing the subject.

His arm tightened around her. Outside the cave, it was almost pitch black. In a few moments they wouldn't be able to see a thing.

"I hate to suggest this, but we should make a fire," she said. "For warmth, and light, and to keep away animals."

That got him moving. There was a circle of rocks near the mouth of the cave. He put a couple of small logs in the middle of it and found a book of matches. Then he frowned, as if he knew something was missing. "What about . . ."

"Kindling? There should be some palm fronds in that basket."

He rummaged around, going by feel in the deepening gloom. "You brought this stuff?"

"Yes."

"Have you stayed here before?"

"Not overnight."

She could tell by the way he proceeded that he didn't have much experience building fires, but she enjoyed his shirtless performance too much to offer any advice, and before long he had it going. While she lazed about, getting warm and cozy, he brought her water and they shared a tin of crackers and some beef jerky from her stash. They saved the last energy bar and a can of peaches for breakfast, although Shay could have eaten more.

Luke knew enough not to burn all the wood at once, so the fire was small and didn't give off much heat. He must be cold in wet trousers and no shirt, and she would have invited him under her blanket if she thought he would accept.

From the way he kept his distance, she knew he wouldn't. In fact, he looked prepared to stay up all night, holding vigil.

The fire did generate plenty of light, illuminating the dips and curves in the walls of the cave. Some of the natural rock features had been enhanced by human hands, and they drew Luke's attention. "What's this?" he asked, running his fingertips over a plump crevice.

She assumed he knew it was a petroglyph. Apparently, he didn't know what the rock carving represented. "It's a yoni," she explained. "A female fertility symbol."

Realizing he'd just been fondling a sacred stone vulva, he dropped his hand like it had been burned.

Shay smothered a laugh. "Cahuilla women used to rub it for good luck. They thought if they slept with their husbands after touching the shrine, a baby would come."

He stared at his fingertips in dismay.

"I don't think it works the same way for men," she said with a smile.

Wiping his hand against the fabric of his pants anyway, anxious to get rid of whatever fertility mojo he may have picked up, he said, "You should try to get some sleep."

Shay got his meaning, loud and clear: He didn't want to share a blanket with her. He didn't want to have sex with her. He didn't even want to *talk* to her.

Incensed, she sat up, clutching the blanket to her chest. "I didn't ask you to kiss me earlier."

He looked at her mouth, her bare shoulders, then away, into the darkness. "I know."

"I didn't even want you to."

At that, he shrugged, as if the subject was debatable. Or maybe just not interesting enough to warrant a verbal response.

She looked around for something to throw at his head, and came up empty. "I'm not going to jump on you if you lay down next to me, either," she said in a scathing tone. "Don't worry, your virtue is safe."

The corner of his mouth tipped up, but he didn't rise to the bait. Instead, he asked, "It's not fire season, is it?"

"What?"

"April isn't fire season."

"No," she said, feeling derailed. She'd wanted an argument, not a casual discussion about the weather. "But this is the desert. All a fire needs is dry fuel."

He nodded, staring out into the black night once again. "I should keep watch."

Understanding dawned. "You think someone set that fire deliberately? Knowing we were out here?"

"It came from the same direction we did."

"So does the wind."

"Then an arsonist could predict its path."

She was flabbergasted. "Who would do that? And why?"

"To keep us away from something. To protect someone. I don't know. Why would anyone move a dead body?"

She shook her head helplessly.

"Try to get some sleep," he repeated, more gently this time. "You'll need it if we're going to hike out of here tomorrow."

11

Dylan turned off the TV with a flick of his wrist and tossed the remote aside.

He was frustrated by the lack of information about the fire. Nothing that happened in Tenaja Falls ever rated a top story. The television crews in San Diego probably wouldn't care if the whole town burned down.

According to the brief news bite, a small fire had engulfed several thousand acres on the Los Coyotes Indian Reservation. Now fully contained, its origins were unknown.

So where the hell was Shay?

When he saw black smoke curling up through the air on his way home from the construction site, his first thought had been: Oh, shit. What if his extracurricular science project had started the fire? He'd chosen the construction site precisely because it was deserted. There was nothing out there but freshly leveled dirt, with nary a bush or tree in sight. He knew a spark could travel quite a distance on the wind, so he'd been meticulous.

And he'd covered his tracks.

He was getting more worried now, because Shay hadn't called, and he couldn't reach her cell phone. Cell service was usually unreliable, but his sister never was. She always let him know when she was going to be late.

"Goddamned cops," he muttered, blaming Luke for detaining her. His sister had been a little crazy when she was younger, but she'd never been irresponsible. And the sheriff had practically been drooling all over her this morning. If she encouraged him, Dylan figured Luke would be happy to serve her.

The new sheriff seemed like an okay guy, but Dylan hated Garrett Snell, and every other man who abused his power, with an alarming ferocity. Sulking, he imagined blowing the sheriff's station to smithereens.

The doorbell rang, interrupting his fantasies of mayhem.

He rose to his feet, the bag of ice that was resting in his lap falling to the floor with a squishy clink. Hobbling less than he had a few hours ago, he made his way to the front door, and opened it to Angel Martinez.

She jerked her hand away from her mouth, as if she'd been biting her fingernails and didn't want to get caught. In a plain black T-shirt and dark jeans, she looked fantastically beautiful. Her hair was pulled away from her face by a headband with a skull-and-crossbones design and a series of tiny silver hoops graced the curve of her ear.

"Hi," she said, a little breathlessly.

He leaned against the doorjamb. "Hi."

She looked down at her pointy-toed boots, and then back up at him. "Can we talk for a minute?"

His seventeen-year-old libido, ever frisky, revved up at her words.

"Sure," he said, stepping aside. Trying to walk as though he hadn't been kneed in the crotch earlier, he led her toward the living room. He sat on one side of the couch and she took the other. Both of them stared at the soggy ice pack resting on the worn carpet.

He didn't offer any explanation for it. "My sister's not home," he said when her eyes returned to his.

"Oh." After fiddling with some white threads at the knee of her worn jeans, she picked up one of the couch pillows and hugged it to her chest. Why did girls do that? "I just wanted to say I was sorry about the way things turned out. I should never have led you on."

Her apology made him feel like a real jerk. He'd stormed over to her house and accused her of having no standards. *He* should be apologizing to *her*. "You didn't—"

"Let me finish," she said. "Please."

He shrugged one shoulder, uncomfortable.

"One of the reasons I didn't want to . . . get involved with you . . . is because of what happened with Chad. I knew you'd be mad if you found out."

She was right, and he was ashamed of himself, not just for being predictable, but for disrespecting her. "I acted like a total jackass, and I'm sorry." He forced himself to meet her gaze. "It's none of my business who you go out with."

"Chad and I didn't even go out," she admitted, misery brimming in her dark eyes. "It was just . . . one of those things. A mistake I don't want to make again."

Dylan knew what she meant. She regretted what

she'd done with Chad, and she regretted what she'd done with him. The foolish hope he'd been entertaining since she walked through the door died a swift, painful death. Angel hadn't come to tell him she was wrong, or that she'd changed her mind. She didn't want a boyfriend. She didn't want *him*.

No one ever had.

Her eyes softened with sympathy as she read his disappointment, and he hated her for that. She nibbled on her lower lip, drawing his attention to it, and he hated himself, too, because he still wanted her.

"I don't think I ever thanked you for helping me fight off Travis."

His gaze lingered on her mouth. "You thanked me enough. Although I wouldn't mind getting thanked a little more."

It was meant to be an insult, but his delivery was off. Maybe because he was more eager than angry. Her lips looked glossy and ripe, as if she'd put some shiny girl-stuff on them, and her chest rose and fell in agitation. Or anticipation.

The ache in his groin returned with a vengeance, reminding him not to risk his heart. Too many of his important parts had been crushed lately. Besides, she'd made it clear she wasn't interested in being his girl, no matter how many fuck-me looks she gave him.

No meant no.

He pulled his attention from her lips and stared down at the melting ice at his feet, trying to channel cool energy.

"Did you hurt yourself?" she asked.

"I ran into Deputy Snell. He hurt me."

"Where?"

"Same place you hurt Travis."

She frowned at his lap. "Are you all right?"

"I will be," he said, his stomach muscles tightening. If she kept staring, his blue nylon basketball shorts wouldn't be able to conceal the proof of how well he was recovering. Everything seemed normal down there, if a bit tender, so he figured he was in better shape than Travis. His overzealous friend had screamed like a little girl when Angel kicked him. He'd also vomited, but that might have been from the beer.

"Come on," he said, standing. "I'll walk you home."

"You don't have to."

Ignoring that, he picked up the bag of ice water and took it to the sink, wishing it didn't seem like a metaphor for the cool-off between them. Why did he inspire lukewarm emotions? Everyone he'd ever been close to had disappeared too soon; every feeling of affection had melted away.

Angel couldn't think of anything to say as they walked down Calle Remolino, side by side, the gulf between them as wide as the Anza-Borrego Desert.

Since discovering that he liked girls in general, and her in particular, Dylan had been nervous around her. She'd always thought it was cute. Now it was she who felt tongue-tied when they were together, she who blushed every time he looked at her a certain way, and she who kept stealing furtive glances at his whipcord physique.

Qué loca!

This was Dylan Phillips, not Brad Pitt. He wasn't built. He wasn't suave. He wasn't even gorgeous.

Okay, so he was kind of hot, if you liked quirky white boys, and he had some muscles here and there. He'd be a real heartbreaker when he filled out, but right now he was just a trouble-seeking teenager, all angst and hormones.

She wasn't sure why she came to apologize. He'd acted like a jerk earlier and she'd given him a proper put-down. She supposed she felt guilty for encouraging him in his bedroom, and responsible for the rift between him and his lame friends.

He *had* fought with both of them to protect her.

She'd also known him her entire life and considered him a friend. The least she could do, before she left, was clear the air between them.

"Do you want to come in my room?" she asked when they arrived at her doorstep.

That eager, almost desperate expression flickered across his face, then his eyes became shuttered and it was gone. "Sure," he said anyway, probably just to be polite.

Feeling unsettled, she opened her door and turned on the lamp, bathing the room in a pale yellow light. With its small desk, large bed, and single armoire, the space was cozy, but cramped. And although it was clean, she was embarrassed by her Spartan quarters. Why had she invited him in?

"Do you play?" he asked, nodding toward the guitar case on the bed.

Maldiciónes. She'd forgotten to put it away. "Um. Yeah. A little."

"Cool," he said, sitting down next to it. The bed had once belonged to her parents, and it dominated the tiny room. His long, rangy body seemed well suited to the space, and her mind manufactured several inventive ways they could put it to good use. "Play something."

Angel looked everywhere but the bed. Which was hard to do, with him sitting on it. "Oh, no. I'm not that good and I haven't been practicing enough and you wouldn't like any of the songs I know . . ." She snuck another glance at him. He arched a brow.

Her choices were to stare at the wall or play her guitar, so she stopped stammering and picked up her acoustic. Like the armoire in the opposite corner, the guitar was an art piece, one of a kind, and hand-carved. Both were from Paracho, Mexico, famous for woodwork. Her mother's hometown.

She pulled the ladder-back chair away from her desk and sat facing him. The style of music she played differed greatly from the kind he preferred. She liked to listen to a wide range of genres, from punk to pop, and although she was especially fond of some of the furious noise Dylan favored, what she played was more forlorn than angry.

Too self-conscious to break into one of her originals, she decided on an older ballad by Shakira. The song was pensive and soulful, with a folksy sound she often tried to emulate. If the lyrics hit a little too close to home for comfort, at least they were in Spanish, so that felt safer.

Mis días sin ti son tan oscuros, tan largos, tan grises . . .

She stumbled through the first few verses, in which

the speaker describes how dark her days are without the one she loves. Her voice was pitchy and her fingers fumbled for the right chords, and then she just sort of . . . found her rhythm. Found herself.

It was always like this with music. She got lost in the melody, and the rest of the world faded away.

When she was finished, she let the last chord ring out and slowly came back down to earth. By the way Dylan was staring at her, she knew the song had been a poor choice. Foreign language aside, the emotion of the piece must have been written all over her face.

"That was beautiful," he said.

Her insides warmed as though she'd taken a sip of brandy. "I didn't write it," she said unnecessarily. Of course he wouldn't think she'd written such a lovely song. "It's called '*Moscas en la casa*.' That means 'Flies in the house.' "

He smiled. "I know. Everything sounds so much more poetic in Spanish."

"You understood the words?"

"All but *ahogándome en llanto*. Drowning in tires?"

It was her turn to smile. "Drowning in tears."

His look of confusion cleared. "Ah."

She shouldn't have been surprised that he knew Spanish. He was Dylan Phillips. He knew everything. He probably spoke her native language as well as she did. Now she felt completely exposed, as if she'd shown him a piece of her heart.

"Do you play an instrument?" she asked, scrutinizing him in return.

His brows rose. "Me? No."

"Why not?"

When his eyes darkened with sadness, she regretted the innocent question. Dylan may be gifted, but he was also wounded, and it was clear the subject disturbed him. "My mother played the violin," he said, which was explanation enough. "Her music was . . . strange. Sorrowful. Haunting." He swallowed visibly. "It was one of the only things she seemed to enjoy . . . near the end. I think playing kept her well, for a while. She wanted me to take it up, but I was too antsy. Too impatient."

Angel smiled, remembering how hyperactive he was as a little kid. Like his mind, his arms and legs had never stilled.

"Reading music was easy for me. That part I understood immediately. I just couldn't get my fingers to cooperate." He made a stiff claw with his right hand, as if trying to force it into a more elegant position. "I should have tried harder."

Her heart broke for him, for the boy he'd been. All of seven or eight years old when his mom died, and here he was, thinking he could have made a difference.

Angel had gone around that bend herself, many times. She and Dylan had a lot in common—none of it good.

"Now, a basketball," he continued, reshaping his hands around a phantom ball, "that always felt right."

Her tummy tingled as she imagined his hands on her rounded parts. Yes, she could certainly attest to the fact that his touch felt right.

Their eyes met and held. He dropped his gaze, and his hands. "Your voice is incredible."

"No," she protested. "It's all scratchy. Not appropriate for singing."

"That's what I like about it. It's unusual. Sexy."

The sensation in the pit of her stomach deepened into a dull ache. "I want to be a songwriter, actually."

"Really?" His eyes brightened with interest. "Play one of yours."

Qué horror! Why had she said that? "You don't want to hear—"

"I do," he said, wrapping his hand around the neck of her guitar. "Please."

Reluctant to deny him, after he'd just shared that painful memory of his mother, she reached into her desk drawer and found a crumpled piece of notebook paper. She knew the words by heart, but it comforted her to have something to look at besides Dylan's too interested, too earnest face.

Although she found Spanish easier to work with, and much more pleasing to the ear, "Deserted" was in English. The words just came to her that way, raw and edgy and unromantic. The harsher sound fit the dark subject matter, but her raspy voice softened it, made something layered and lovely out of the twisted, often ugly emotions inside her.

After the song ended, she flattened her palm over the strings of her guitar, silencing it, and glanced sideways at him, awaiting his reaction.

"You wrote that?" he asked, sounding impressed. "You should record it. Send it in to a radio station or something."

She laughed, shaking her head.

"I mean it," he insisted, grabbing the paper from the desk. "That part about the desert sky at night was awesome—"

Panicking, Angel tried to take the lyrics back, but he moved them out of her reach. "Don't read that," she warned, shoving her guitar back in the case hurriedly so she could attack him with both hands.

Thinking it was a game, and obviously enjoying the wrestling match, he stood and held the paper over his head. When he got a glimpse of the words on the page, he started laughing. "Do you write in code? This is indecipherable."

Shaken and humiliated, she let her hands fall away. It was too late.

Unlike her, Dylan was no dummy. The smile slipped off his face. "Oh," he said. "Oh, sorry. I didn't mean to—"

"It's okay, Dylan. I know I'm stupid."

"You are *not* stupid," he said, his brows slashing downward. "These lyrics are brilliant. You just need a little help with . . . spelling."

She tore the paper from his hands and shoved it in the desk drawer. What an awful joke she was. A songwriter who could barely write. Trying to prevent him from seeing the tears that were building in her eyes, threatening to spill down her face, she crossed her arms over her chest and looked down at the ground, blinking rapidly.

"You're not stupid," he repeated. "I go to high school, so I know stupid. You're twice as articulate as the kids there."

Sniffling, she swiped at the tears on her cheeks. "I don't even know what that means."

"It means that you express yourself well," he said, reaching out to put his hand on her upper arm. Her skin prickled with sensation, and when she looked up at him in confusion, his gaze cruised over her face like a caress. "It's a talent I can appreciate, because sometimes my tongue is as clumsy as my feet. Especially around you."

She stared back at him, moistening her lips. "Not always," she whispered.

Although she meant those words in a nonsexual way, his eyes darkened, and she knew the direction his mind went. And when he stepped forward, she knew the direction his mouth was going. Her palms flattened against his chest to ward him off, but when he touched his lips to hers, she stopped thinking about what she *should* do and starting doing what she wanted to do.

He didn't ease into the kiss slowly, like she'd taught him. Instead, he jumped straight into a full-on, open-mouthed, tongue-stroking kiss.

It was kind of scary how good it was, considering his lack of experience.

She stood on her tiptoes and threaded her hands through his hair, plastering her body to his and kissing him back with matching enthusiasm. Her breasts crushed against his chest and he made this sound, low in his throat, like a wounded animal. Before she knew it, her back was against the wall and his hands were on her butt, lifting her to him.

Uh-oh. This was happening way too fast. This wasn't supposed to be happening at all. "Wait," she gasped, tearing her mouth from his. "Stop."

"Sorry," he said, breathing heavily. "I'll go slower."

She knew he would promise anything to keep her in this position. Or to get her into an even more compromising one. "No," she said firmly, pushing at his chest. "I can't."

He let her down with a strangled groan.

"I can't see you anymore."

He gaped at her incredulously. She stared back at him in silence, her heart pounding, every muscle in her body taut with tension. When he saw that she was serious, his jaw hardened and the hot look in his eyes cooled. "Don't act like you didn't want me to kiss you," he said. "I'm not Travis. Or Chad."

His insinuation that she was a tease stung, but it strengthened her resolve. "I want a lot of things. That doesn't mean I should let you do me against the wall."

"I wasn't going to do you!" he sputtered. "You can tell me to stop anytime."

She regarded him with skepticism. "You want sex."

"So? I didn't think I was going to get it."

He was probably telling the truth, but it didn't matter. "I'm sorry," she said, opening her bedroom door and letting in the cool night air. A coyote howled in the near-distance, its plaintive cry sending a shiver down her spine. "Good-bye."

After he left, she wanted to lie down on her bed and indulge in a good, long cry. Instead, she took the bus schedules out of her desk drawer and studied them, wishing the idea of leaving didn't tear her apart inside.

12

In the dark, she was running. Behind her, she could hear labored breathing. Heavy footfalls and the rustle of tall grass.

The hanging tree loomed before her, dark branches against moonlit sky. She knew she was running toward it. But what was chasing her? A lion wouldn't have made a sound.

Fire exploded before her eyes like a cloudburst, illuminating the scene. On the ground in front of her, Hamlet crouched, mouth wet with blood.

She stopped and blinked and he was gone.

Everything was gone.

She stood alone in the quiet dark at the Graveyard, hands clenched at her sides, searching for her pursuer. She looked behind her warily. There was no one there.

A strange sound, one that was oddly familiar, whispered from above. The creak of wood. Swaying weight on a taut length of rope.

Fear crept up her spine, making the little hairs on the nape of her neck stand on end. Slowly, very slowly, she turned around.

Mama was there. Swinging. Her chin was down, tucked into her chest, a fall of wavy hair hiding her face.

Shay cried out, clapping her hand over her mouth.

Mama's head snapped up. Her eyes were wide open, dark as wine. "Don't look back," she said, lifting one slender white arm to point.

Of course, she looked. And saw only the glint of metal as she was struck.

She woke up, gasping for air, clutching the blanket to her throat. The ground was hard and her surroundings strange. The dark shape of a man wavered into focus. Instinctively, she covered her head and screamed.

"What is it?" Luke asked, taking her hands away from her face.

Shay stared up at him in blurry-eyed confusion. The fire had burned down low, but she could see him, all hard lines and sharp angles. She could feel him, rock solid and just as cold. "I had a nightmare," she said, moistening her lips.

"What about?"

"I don't remember."

He released her hands but didn't move away.

"You're freezing," she murmured, touching his shoulders. They were as if sculpted from ice. "Why didn't you get under the blanket with me?"

Every part of his body tensed further, including his mouth. He said nothing.

Shay pushed off the blanket and came to her feet, shivering as she added the last logs and the remaining palm fronds to the fire. It sparked up, blazing bright for a few moments then settling into a slow burn.

Luke watched her, motionless.

Already chilled, she returned to her place on the blanket. Not asking or inviting, she just pulled him close and covered both of them, wrapping her arms around him and pressing her face to his chest, trying to generate body heat.

"My knee," she whispered after a moment. "It would feel better if I, um, elevated it."

Without a word, he insinuated his leg between hers, lifting her knee over his hip and fitting into the notch of her thighs as naturally as any man had ever fit against a woman.

Shay shivered again, but not from the cold.

As the time passed, it became obvious that neither of them was suffering from the effects of the cold any longer. With the fire at his back, and her at his front, Luke warmed up nicely. His skin felt like heated marble beneath her palms. The night wind rustled through the palm trees and the burning logs crackled, and, under the blanket, things got downright toasty.

She was as close to him as a lover, and her body knew it. With her leg resting on his hip, her breasts touching his chest, and her arms around his neck, it was an explicit embrace. His hard thigh was snuggled right up to her crotch. Her lips were just inches from the pulse point in his throat. Through half-lidded eyes, she watched it throb.

He smelled smoky and musky and hot. Her mouth watered to taste him.

The remnants of her nightmare faded away, unable

to compete with the sensory overload she was experiencing here and now. Her body swelled with longing and her skin tingled for his touch. On some level, she knew he wanted nothing to do with her emotionally. He didn't even want to desire her physically. He seemed to think she was beneath him.

In that moment, it was exactly where she wanted to be.

Trembling, she leaned forward and placed her open mouth on his neck, touching her tongue to that pulsing vein, tasting the evidence of his desire. He drew in a sharp breath and tightened his hand around her upper arm, pushing her back.

At first she thought he was going to get up and leave her. She didn't have to look down to know he was aroused; she could feel the heat of him, see the proof in his glittering eyes and taut face. But unlike other men of her acquaintance, he didn't let his body govern his actions, and he'd walked away from her sporting an erection before.

She wasn't sure why he stayed, but when he threw back the blanket and feasted his eyes on her near-naked form, she knew he wasn't going to walk away. With the absence of his warmth and the rush of cool night air, she was aware of every inch of her skin, every part of her body. Her bra and underwear weren't quite dry, and neither were his wool-blend pants. She could feel the damp heat against her inner thigh.

His gaze raked over her like a caress.

She was conscious of his eyes on her mouth and her barely covered breasts, the slight curve of her tummy and not-so-slight curve of her hips. As always, her stiff nipples were tenting the thin cotton of her bra, begging for his touch. It was kind of embarrassing how prominent they were, considering the size of her breasts.

"Do your nipples ever relax?" he rasped, staring at them.

She moistened her lips, tasting the salt of his skin there. "Um . . . yes."

"When?"

"I'll let you know."

He smoothed his palm over the dip of her waist, and her entire body flexed. She clenched her hands into fists, fighting the urge to tilt her hips forward and ride his thigh. Avoiding her straining nipples, he traced the upper edge of her bra with his fingertip and paused at the tiny clasp between her breasts. Instead of releasing it, he moved on, dragging his thumb down her middle, burning a hot trail all the way to the front of her panties. When he reached the apex of her thighs, his eyes met hers, and her tummy jumped.

He may not have recognized a yoni when he saw one, but he knew his way around the real thing well enough. His fingertips grazed the plump lips of her sex and slid along the crease. She was so swollen and sensitive, if he used any more pressure, she would come.

And he hadn't even kissed her.

Shay realized she was lying there, acquiescent, letting him call the shots. She was enjoying what he was doing, of course, but she'd never been shy about being an active participant in sex. Stranger still, she didn't want foreplay. She wanted his tongue in her mouth and his body over hers. She wanted his penetration, his climax, his control.

With trembling hands, she reached up and undid the front clasp of her bra, exposing her breasts. His eyes darkened in the flickering light, but she wasn't done. Hooking her thumbs in the waistband of her panties, she pushed them down her hips and off her legs, moving carefully over her bandaged knee.

He swallowed convulsively, drinking in the sight of her naked body and appearing far from unaffected by the view. When she propped her knee back up on his hip, his eyes widened and his nostrils flared. He wrapped his hands around her waist and dipped his head to sample the wares, but she flattened her palms against his chest, denying him.

He frowned, disliking the shift in power.

Using a light touch, she raked her nails down his belly. His stomach muscles tightened and his jaw clenched. With one hand, she went to work on his belt buckle, anticipating his reaction.

Sure enough, he clamped his fingers around her wrist. "Not yet."

Ignoring his protest, she slid her other hand along the length of his arousal. His eyes lost focus and his grip went slack. Smiling at the predictable male weakness, she unzipped his fly and reached inside, finding only him.

Luke Meza was going commando? Sometime during the night, he must have laid his shorts out to dry.

He hissed out a breath as she wrapped her fingers around the heat of his erection, and she was unable to stifle her own tiny gasp. He felt . . . very impressive.

He looked down at himself in her hand, and she looked, too, experiencing a hot thrill at the thought of him inside her. His body was so beautiful, so rock hard and marble smooth, she wanted to lick every inch of him. In lieu of that, she wet the pad of her thumb and brushed it over the tip of his penis, making his body jerk, shocking him with her audacity.

She shocked herself, too. Active participant or not, it had never occurred to her to do anything like that before.

Groaning, he pulled her hands away from his groin and pushed them over her head, trapping her wrists as he lowered his mouth to hers. This kiss was nothing like the whisper-soft caress they'd shared before. It was a total possession.

He didn't linger on the seam of her lips, or take it slow and easy, or maintain a polite distance. He thrust his tongue inside her mouth and pinned her underneath him, rocking his hips against hers. Sparks of pleasure shot through her. She kissed him back with equal fervor, making urgent sounds in the back of her throat and curling her tongue around his.

His mouth was hot and his sex was hard and she was wet. The ridge of his erection slid up and down along her slippery cleft, creating a delicious friction. It was so good she almost couldn't stand it. At the same time, she wanted more. She wanted everything. She squirmed, trying to free her hands from his hold so she could take what she needed.

He lifted his head and stared down at her, breathing hard. "I don't have a condom."

Those words should have brought the progress to a grinding halt. In some corner of her mind, she knew this was madness. And yet, if he didn't come into her now, she would die. "I don't care," she heard herself say.

It was all the encouragement he needed. He shifted, releasing her wrists and positioning the blunt head of his erection at her body's opening. Panting, she splayed her hands over his shoulders and spread her legs wide, urging him on.

He pushed forward, using none of the delicacy he'd employed during their first kiss. Even so, the quick flash of pain startled her, because she was more than ready.

He stopped, feeling her tense. "Is it your knee?"

Knee? What knee? She bit down on her lower lip and shook her head.

Frowning, he moved his right hand down to her injured knee, lifting it higher. She felt him slide into her deeper and moaned. The muscles in his back bunched beneath her palms. He stroked his way back up her thigh, making her body twitch with pleasure, and settled his mouth on her left breast. He flicked his tongue over one aching nipple, then the other, leaving them both rosy and wet.

Shay gasped at the contrast between his hot mouth and the cool air, feeling as though she might fly apart. Moisture pooled between her legs, easing his way. With a low growl, he lifted his head and pushed forward again, filling her completely.

From there on out, separating one exquisite sensation from another became an impossible task. Every thrust made her moan, every drag made her shudder. Coherent thought was beyond her, but she did realize it had never been like this for her before. She'd always preferred kissing and touching to actual intercourse. What Luke was doing to her blew every other encounter she'd had out of the water.

Another wave of pleasure crashed over her, promising the ultimate rapture. She clung to his shoulders, scarcely able to believe how good it felt.

His body froze and he pulled back, trying to move away from her.

Sobbing a protest, she tightened her legs around him and sank her fingernails into his back, straining for completion. He couldn't leave her now, she was so close, and it had never happened this way for her before . . .

She cried out, falling over the edge. Her legs quivered and her back arched and her inner muscles squeezed him hard. He buried his face in her neck and groaned, his entire body quaking with the power of his own release.

Her very first thought, after the sensual fog lifted, was . . .

Oops.

Luke's initial reaction wasn't panic, but smug male satisfaction; his first instinct, not to flee, but to sleep.

He'd committed the stupidest, most irresponsible act of his life, and he wanted nothing more than to fall upon her and snore. If she hadn't tapped on his shoulder and told him to get off her, he would have done just that.

More clearheaded than he was, she left the cave to relieve herself. Like a horny, lunkheaded fool, he watched her go, admiring her shapely bottom as she disappeared into the moonlight and experiencing a second, equally idiotic reaction: renewed arousal. With his pants pushed down his thighs, he was aware of the night air on his rapidly cooling, still-damp body. His cock sprang up hard, ready to get warm again.

Then he heard her splashing water in the dark, washing away his semen, and reality came crashing down around him.

Sleeping with her was a mistake. Not taking the necessary precautions, a disaster.

What the hell was he thinking? He knew better than to have unprotected sex. He'd never been this reckless, not even when he was eighteen. Las Vegas was a great place to catch an STD, so Luke had always been careful, always responsible, and always polite.

Another thought occurred to him, one more frightening than the last. She had to be on some kind of birth control. Didn't she?

He scrambled to his feet and yanked his pants up his hips, working his zipper over his flagging erection. She came back into view, her eyes cool, unsurprised by what must have been an expression of dismay on his face.

Saying nothing, she searched the blanket for her underwear. Luke knew a moment of distraction, because her naked body was . . . achingly lovely.

He cleared his throat. "You're on birth control, right?"

"Wrong."

The air rushed out of his lungs. "Why didn't you tell me?"

"You didn't ask."

"I didn't ask?" he repeated, dumbfounded. "What the hell did you think I meant when I said I didn't have a condom?"

Her pretty mouth twisted with annoyance, but she made no reply.

"You let me come in you," he said, incredulous. "I was going to pull out, and you . . ." He trailed off, needing no explanation for why she'd held him close. Her orgasm had been explosive.

"I what? Forced you to stay in me?" Securing her bra and panties, she wrapped the blanket around her body like armor. "You're stronger than I am, Luke. If you wanted to pull away, you could have pulled away."

Luke clenched his hands into fists. He could still feel her nails digging furrows into his back, her long legs wrapped around him like a vice, and the delicious clasp of her body. Sure, he could have pulled away. He could have spilled on her soft little belly or on the ground, and in doing so completely ruined the moment for her.

She turned over, facing the cave wall and shutting him out.

A maelstrom of emotions raged inside him. He raked a hand through his hair and closed his eyes, cursing himself for a fool. He couldn't believe he'd been so careless. And he couldn't remember the last time he'd been so undone by a woman.

Actually, he could. He just didn't want to.

Living in Vegas had caused him to tire of hedonism early, and the seedy atmosphere had definitely affected his dealings with the opposite sex. In a town full of scantily clad women looking for a wild time, it was wise to exercise caution. Luke had been too staid, perhaps, but he'd never been a saint. The moment he laid eyes on Leticia Nuñez, he'd wanted her.

It was lust at first sight.

She'd been sitting at an outdoor café, sipping iced coffee and reading a book, her black hair in a sleek knot at the nape of her neck, a pair of square-framed glasses on her adorable nose. Her legs were crossed prettily, showcased by a slim pencil skirt, the fullness of her breasts apparent beneath a prim white blouse. The fantasy was carefully crafted, a sexy librarian no man could resist, and he'd fallen for it hook, line, and sinker.

God, she'd been beautiful. And he'd been criminally naïve.

Another image flashed into his mind, one far less pleasing to the eye. The last time he'd seen her, she'd been lying cold and dead on an examination table, her face almost as gray as the stainless steel beneath her, all of those curves he'd worshipped a distant memory, her body as sunken as her hollowed cheeks.

Would things have turned out differently if their relationship had been fueled by something less volatile than passion? He'd always thought so. And he'd never dated a woman based solely on sexual attraction again.

Until now. Although what he'd just done with Shay could hardly be called a date.

Stifling a groan, he sat down at the edge of the cave and watched the dawn creep over the horizon, as raw and pink as a fresh-knit scar. Using protection was his responsibility, and despite the miscommunication, he was angrier with himself than with her. He shouldn't have started touching her in the first place. He hadn't intended to take it so far.

Upon further deliberation, he'd taken advantage of her. She was in shock. She was injured. She was vulnerable. The post-coital interrogation hadn't been well done, either. Safe sex was a topic to be discussed before the deed, not after.

Luke was a man who was always accountable for his actions. He seldom acted on impulse and entertained very few regrets. But he'd done Shay a great disservice, from that inexplicable kiss in the camouflaged shelter to his startling lapse of judgment at the, ah, culmination of their encounter, and he owed her an apology.

Feeling nauseous at the prospect, he hazarded a glance at her. Unlike him, she appeared to be resting comfortably, unmolested by second thoughts. In the hazy dawn light, he could see the outline of her body beneath the blanket, the sweet curve of her waist and the enticing swell of her hip. Her hair was a mass of rumpled blond silk; the cat's paw on the back of her neck visible through the tangled strands.

Incredibly, he still wanted her.

He wanted to brush aside that soft hair and press his lips to her neck, to peel away the wool blanket and bury himself in her warmth. He'd made a mistake in sleeping with her, but Christ, what he would give to do it again. Really, he hadn't done a thorough job the first time. He'd barely whetted his appetite.

He forced his gaze away from her, focusing instead on the wall carvings above her head. Now the artwork mocked him with its blatancy, the lips of a woman's sex so obvious he felt like a damned fool.

Plagued by self-loathing, he lurched to his feet. What a place to slip up. The only time he'd failed to use protection in his entire life, and he was in a fucking fertility shrine.

With jerky, frustrated movements, he pulled on his shirt, which was no longer wet but reeked of smoke. His shorts and socks were also dry, so he put them back on, along with his damp boots. When he opened the pop-top on a small can of peaches, Shay stirred.

He shoved the can at her. "Here," he said, more gruffly than he'd intended.

She rubbed her puffy eyes but took the can and started eating peach slices with her bare hands, as raw and sensual and unaffected as ever.

"How's your knee?"

She swallowed a mouthful. "Better."

"Can you hike?"

Under the blanket, she stretched her legs. "I think so."

He rummaged through the pack, looking for his cell phone. It was still dead.

"Don't you want any?" she asked, clutching a piece of golden fruit between slippery fingers.

He thought about all the ways he'd wanted to touch her last night but hadn't. "No."

With a shrug, she finished the contents of the can, upending it and drinking the juice. "What about that last power bar?"

He tossed it at her. "It's yours."

Instead of eating it, she held the bar in her hand, a crease forming between her brows. He supposed she was planning to save it for later, which was a good idea.

They were miles from civilization, and he didn't want her getting weak or falling down on him again.

After a moment, he realized she was waiting for him to avert his eyes so she could get out from underneath the blanket. Was this the same woman who'd walked around buck naked in the moonlight? "Let me see your knee," he said.

Wearing a defiant expression, she stuck out her injured knee, keeping her torso demurely covered. He knelt down beside her and unwrapped the bandage, trying to ignore the way her skin felt and looked, like cream-colored silk against his dark hand.

She had a nasty purple bruise but the swelling was down. During his years at UNLV, Luke had ruptured his ACL, so he knew what a more serious injury looked like. "Good," he said, winding the bandage back up tight.

"Thanks, Doc," she said lightly. Her eyes burned into his, communicating something far less congenial than gratitude.

Jaw tightening, he stood and gave her his back, allowing her some privacy to get dressed. Feeling a pang that had nothing to do with hunger, he released a slow breath, knowing what he had to do. Putting it off would only prolong the inevitable.

"About last night . . ." he began, wincing at the tired old cliché.

"Don't *even*," she warned.

He looked over his shoulder. She was buttoning her pants. "Don't even what?"

"You know what," she said, wrestling her tank top over her head. "I don't want to hear your lame excuses."

"I was going to apologize."

"For what?"

"You were . . . hurt, and I shouldn't have . . . taken it so far."

Her eyes narrowed into dangerous slits.

Luke forged ahead, wanting to get it over with. "I also don't want there to be any misunderstandings. I'm not planning to stay on, in Tenaja Falls, so . . ."

She flipped her ponytail over her shoulder and put her hands on her hips, daring him to feel lucky enough to say more.

He knew he was screwing this up royally, but he didn't have any experience with letting a woman down easy after a one night stand. "Don't get me wrong, you're . . ." Beautiful, sexy, dynamite in bed. "Sweet," he said. "And it was . . ." He stared at the blanket on the floor, searching for a word to describe the most mind-blowing sex of his life. "Nice."

She gaped at him incredulously.

He suppressed the urge to duck and run for cover.

To his surprise, she didn't start throwing sharp objects at his head. She merely crossed her arms over her chest and arched a dark blond brow. "Honey, if you think what we did on that blanket was 'nice,' you must not have been paying very close attention." Stepping forward, she fingered the buttons on the front of his shirt. "And if you believe, even for a second, that I'm 'sweet,' you are so far out of touch with reality it's no wonder you can't tell the difference between a rock carving of a vagina and the real thing."

Luke felt heat creep up his neck. Although he hadn't

heard any complaints from her last night, he wasn't so deluded that he thought he'd knocked her socks off.

"Let's get another thing straight," she continued, "there are no misunderstandings between us. I never asked you to be my boyfriend. You've made it abundantly clear that you're not interested in filling the position." Her gaze dropped to the front of his pants, then reconnected with his. "So why don't you do us both a favor and keep your nightstick to yourself from now on, huh?"

"With pleasure," he growled, lying through his teeth. "And why don't *you* do us both a favor by keeping your clothes on and your . . ." he gestured angrily toward the carving behind her, ". . . *yoni* out of my face!"

"Fine," she said, glaring at him.

"Fine," he repeated, shrugging into the backpack. He should have been glad they'd come to an agreement.

Instead he felt like putting his fist through the cave wall.

13

Shay wanted to plant her fist in Luke's face.

If he hadn't acted like such a jerk after they slept together, she'd have apologized to him. She'd just had her period a few days ago, so they were probably safe, but she shouldn't have told him to go ahead, knowing he didn't have a condom. She also shouldn't have panted and moaned and clawed his back like a low-class hooker.

The sex hadn't been *that* great, she told herself huffily.

What had he called it? Nice.

Bastard.

Gritting her teeth, she loped along, careful not to rest too much weight on her injured leg. Her knee was better, but a long hike was always tough on tender muscles. Her other leg began to ache from overcompensating.

Much of the area they covered was burned and black. The fire had raged hot and fast, burning out as quickly as it started. Charred tree trunks peppered the hillside and a fine, light ash clung to the ground, rising in smoky wisps from their footprints. The wind was low and the air was clear and crisp, several degrees cooler than the days before.

When they came to the trailhead where Luke's truck was parked, the fire's origin was immediately clear. The grass on the opposite side was swaying in the breeze, untouched. His truck was also intact, to Shay's relief. She didn't want to walk anymore.

Clay Trujillo was standing there waiting for them, studying the black ground at the side of the dirt road. His white Ford Ranger was parked behind Luke's truck. "I was about to send a rescue team out to look for you guys," he called out.

"We're fine," Shay said. "Cell phones got wet."

Clay held out a bottle of fresh water for her, his blue eyes showing concern. "What happened?"

Shay accepted the water and took a long drink. "The fire came up near the summit," she said, catching her breath. "We had to take shelter in the Devil's Cup."

He let out a low whistle, acknowledging the close call. "Are you hurt?"

"Nah. A bump on the knee is all." She stared at the ground beneath her feet, toeing the charcoal-colored earth. "We stayed at the fertility cave."

"The fertility cave?" Clay laughed, his teeth making a brilliant contrast to his dark skin. "Let me know how that works out for you."

Shay felt her cheeks heat. Beside her, Luke was tense.

The smile slid off Clay's handsome face. "Because of the legend, you know. Folks say the shrine brings babies."

"We get it," Luke said.

Clay looked back and forth between them. "Right," he said, clearing his throat. "You two light up any cigarettes on your way out yesterday?"

"No," Luke answered, as humorless as ever.

"What about you, Shay? Smoking the loco weed?" He held an invisible roach up to his lips, sucking in air.

Clay was only joking, but Luke narrowed his eyes at her. "No," she said, giving him a dirty look. "Of course not."

"Do you think that's what started it?" Luke asked.

"Hard to say." Clay waved his hand at the grass-covered hill on the other side of Luke's truck. "A lit match would have done it."

"It was arson?"

Clay shrugged. "No chemicals, no incendiary device. No proof."

Shay glanced at Luke, feeling sick to her stomach. She wouldn't have believed the fire had been deliberately set if the evidence wasn't right there for the whole world to see, just a few hundred feet from Luke's truck.

Someone had it in for him.

"You making a lot of friends in town, Sheriff?" Clay asked.

A muscle in Luke's jaw ticked. "Tribal police are the only ones who knew where we were going."

Clay blanched at the implication, and Shay saw a glimpse of her boy-next-door buddy she'd never seen before. A hint of violence lurked behind those pretty blue eyes.

"Garrett knew," Shay said, jumping to Clay's defense.

Luke shot her a dark glare. It probably wasn't a sound

investigating tactic to rule out one suspect in front of another, but she'd known Clay her whole life. She'd known Garrett that long, too, so she understood what each man was capable of.

Clay relaxed his stance. "Garrett Snell?" He made a tsking sound. "He's some piece of work."

"What makes you say that?"

"He gambles. More than he can afford to lose."

When Luke glanced at her sideways, Shay gave a terse nod. She knew Garrett's addiction was a disease, but it was no excuse for him to treat his wife like crap. Before Lori got married, she and Shay had been inseparable. Their friendship had suffered since, because Garrett was a constant sore spot between them.

Luke and Clay walked along the edge of the burned area, burying the hatchet long enough to confer about the origin of the fire and speculate on the lack of distinct tire marks. When they came back to where Shay was standing, Clay gave her a thorough once-over. She must have appeared a little worse for wear, because he frowned and said, "I'll take you home. Or to the doctor, if you need it."

Startled by the offer, Shay looked at Luke. He stared back at her, eyes flat, expression closed, waiting for her decision. The two men stood side by side, of a similar height, broad shoulders almost touching.

Shay sighed. She'd had enough male posturing for the day, and it was only 8:00 A.M. "Whatever," she said, starting toward Clay's truck.

"Hang on," Luke said, reaching out to wrap his hand around her wrist.

Her heart, ever foolish, skipped a beat. She turned to face him.

"I need to stop by the Round-Up tonight. Talk to the regulars."

She pulled her hand from his grasp. "So?"

"I'd like for you to come with me."

Shay couldn't believe he had the nerve to ask. If Clay hadn't been there, she'd have told him to take a hike. Then again, no one at the Round-Up would talk to Luke if he went by himself, and she was obligated to help with his investigation.

That didn't mean she had to let him walk all over her. "Why don't you come, too, Clay?" she asked. "I'll buy you a drink."

"Sure thing, blondie," he said with a smirk, opening the passenger door for her. "I can pick you up at eight."

Luke's mouth made a thin, hard line. "See you then."

After he turned away from her, his spine ramrod straight, Shay climbed into Clay's Ranger and sat in silence while he drove down the hill.

Of course, Clay wouldn't let sleeping dogs lie. "What's between you and Meza?"

Shay tucked a strand of hair behind her ear. "Nothing. Why?"

"I thought he was going to start growling at me, like a dog guarding a bone."

"He's a little stiff," she acknowledged.

"A little?"

"He's from Vegas," she said, as if that explained his unfriendly personality. "And speaking of guard dogs, why were you being so protective? I didn't need a ride."

"I don't trust him," Clay said, looking in the rearview

mirror. "I thought maybe he tried to put the moves on you in the fertility cave."

Shay stared out the window, feeling her cheeks get hot.

"Is that why you asked me to come along tonight? Because if that guy's been acting like a creep, just say the word, and I'll—"

"You'll what? Trip and fall all over him?"

Clay smiled, amused by the joke at his expense. He wasn't the most coordinated fellow. "I throw a mean elbow," he boasted.

Shay smiled back at him. "He's not a creep."

"So he didn't try anything?"

She nibbled at her lower lip, trying to think of a plausible lie.

"He did," Clay surmised, "but you didn't mind." He turned his attention back to the road. "Jesse's going to flip out," he said, sounding pleased.

Shay realized she hadn't thought about her ex in what seemed like ages. It was funny how upset she'd been yesterday when Jesse saw her and Luke at the café. Now his opinion mattered about as much to her as a puff of smoke.

Speaking of smoke . . . "Jesse already saw us together at the Bighorn," she said. "You don't think . . . ?"

They exchanged a worried glance. For the first time since she'd entered the cab of the pickup, the mood between them was strained.

"No," Clay said. "He's still hung up on you, but he's not homicidal. And unless he was following you, how would he have known where you guys were going?"

Shay relaxed a little, resting her spine against the

back of the seat. Then it dawned on her that there was one other person who knew where she and Luke had been headed. Someone with a dysfunctional family background, a history of rebelling against authority, and a penchant for playing with fire.

Her little brother, Dylan.

Shay didn't think she needed to see a doctor, so she had Clay drop her off at home. Although she'd been working all weekend, she had duties at Dark Canyon that couldn't be put off another day. Her plan was to take a quick shower, grab some breakfast, and head out to the preserve.

As soon as she walked through the front door, she was confronted by another set of arduous responsibilities: Dylan was home.

He was sitting on the couch in the dim morning light. The TV wasn't on and there was no punk rock music blaring. The surface of the coffee table was clear.

"Why aren't you at school?" she asked, dreading his answer. Please God, not another suspension.

Dylan scowled, drumming his fingertips against his jean-clad thighs.

She put her hands on her hips. "Well?"

"I didn't go to school," he said with a glare, his voice gaining volume, "because I've been up all night worrying about you!"

"Oh." She sank into the armchair beside the couch, feeling the wind go out of her sails. "Sorry. My cell phone went out."

"I thought you burned to death."

Her stomach dropped. Had Dylan really been concerned, or had guilt kept him awake? "How did you hear about the fire?"

"It was on the news," he said, giving her a disgusted look, as if he knew what she was thinking. "And there was smoke all over the place."

Shay closed her eyes, her heart twisting in her chest. Last night, she hadn't thought of Dylan. She hadn't considered his feelings. Not once. "I'm sorry," she repeated, hating the inadequacy of those words.

"Never mind," he muttered, wiping his palms on his baggy jeans. "Just write me a note for school. I'm late enough as it is."

"I'll drop you off on my way to work," she said. So much for a meal and a shower. "But first we need to talk."

"Let's talk in the car. I can't miss calculus. In that class, I have to actually show up and pay attention to get an A."

Shay smiled ruefully. She hadn't been able to help Dylan with his math homework since the fifth grade. She was a mediocre sister, a bad role model, and a terrible guardian. "Fine," she said, getting up with a groan.

"What happened to you?"

"I hurt my knee."

"How bad?"

"Not that bad."

He grabbed the keys off the counter. "I'll drive."

She sighed, too weary to argue. The inside of her car wasn't an ideal setting for the discussion she had planned, but at least she'd have a captive audience. "So let's talk about Angel," she said, settling into the passenger seat.

"Let's not," he replied.

"Dylan—"

"Look, I know what you're going to say. I should be thinking about college, not girls. You don't want me to screw up my future. I'm not supposed to be drinking, or having sex, or hanging out at the Graveyard—"

"The Graveyard?"

"Yeah. And don't worry, Angel isn't my girlfriend, and I'll probably never come close to getting laid ever again. So thanks for interrupting."

Shay's head was spinning. "Back up a minute. When were you at the Graveyard?"

He sighed. "Friday night."

"Pull over," she said, bracing her hand on the dash. "Pull over!"

Slamming on the brakes, he jerked to a stop at the side of the road, sending a cloud of dust floating around them. "What's wrong?"

"The victim of the lion attack was at the Graveyard, Dylan. It was Yesenia Montes."

"Whoa," he said, raising his brows.

She grabbed his T-shirt. "You know her?"

He shook her off. "Not like that. Jeez."

"Tell me everything about the night at the Graveyard," she ordered. "Who you were with. What you were doing."

He wrapped his hands around the steering wheel, deliberating.

"Please. It's important."

"You promise you won't put me on restriction?"

"Yes," she said easily. She'd never been much of a disciplinarian.

"I was with Chad and Travis."

The wonder twins, Shay thought. They shared the same pea-sized brain.

"Chad filched a twelve-pack from the Qwik Mart and we took it to the Graveyard. Angel was there with another girl and some guy. I don't remember their names."

"What happened?"

"Angel's friend took off in her car with the guy. Angel thought she was coming right back for her, but it got late . . ."

"Then what?"

"Chad told her he would give her a ride home if she would, ah, do him a favor."

Shay didn't have to ask what Dylan meant. She knew the way Chad's disgusting little mind worked. "She agreed?"

"Of course not. But we couldn't just leave her there. She got in the backseat with Travis and I was riding up front with Chad. They were both pretty hammered."

"Oh, God," she moaned, not wanting to hear more.

"You promised I wouldn't get in trouble," he warned.

"I know," she said, waving her hand. "Just—go on."

"Well, Travis decided he should be the one to get the . . . favor from Angel. At first he was just teasing, but then he started getting aggressive."

"How?"

"Holding her down and trying to kiss her. Stuff like that."

Shay felt sick to her stomach. "Then what?"

"This whole time Chad was driving really crazy, so

everyone was kind of, you know, bouncing around inside the cab—"

"Weren't you wearing seat belts?" she asked, horrified.

"I took mine off when Travis started messing around with Angel. I finally got a grip on the back of his shirt and pulled him off her. She was kicking him and cursing up a storm in Spanish, which was pretty cool, 'cuz I'm in Spanish IV now and I understood most of it."

Shay covered her eyes, trying to block out the mental image.

"Meanwhile, Chad's trying to drive with one hand and fight me with the other. Travis is yelling at me for interfering, saying she's just a slut like her mother—"

Shay gasped.

"—and then they said some stuff about Mom."

"What?" she whispered.

His animated expression fell flat, just like that. "They called her Looney Lilah."

"Oh, Dylan," she said, her heart breaking for him. Not knowing what to say or do, she reached out to put her hand on his shoulder.

He held up a palm, warding off her touch. "Chad must have decided Angel was too much trouble because he stopped the car and kicked us both out."

"That bastard."

"Yeah."

"You walked all the way home?"

"We made it to the highway and Angel's friends picked us up."

Shay placed a hand over her pounding heart and took a calming breath. Stealing, drinking and driving, sexual assault . . . She'd had some wild nights in her youth, but nothing like that. She was shocked by the story and concerned for Dylan's welfare, but she was also proud of him for helping the girl next door.

On top of all that, Shay was ashamed of herself for suspecting her own brother of arson. She studied him from across the cab, wondering what he was thinking. With his dark blond hair and vivid blue eyes, he was the spitting image of their father. She and Dylan had been on their own for most of their lives, but sometimes she didn't think she knew him at all.

Every day, he drifted a little farther away.

Dylan squirmed under her perusal. "You don't believe me," he guessed. Like her, he always assumed the worst.

"I believe you," she said, saddened by their stunted relationship. "And I think Angel should report Travis."

"She doesn't want her father to shoot him."

"What if Travis attacks another girl? He might not get interrupted next time."

"I'm pretty sure he learned his lesson."

"Why's that?"

The corner of his mouth turned up. "She kicked him really hard in the balls. His mom had to take him to the ER the next morning. I talked to him yesterday."

"What about Chad? Has he called you?"

"He came by to apologize."

"What did you say?"

"Fuck off."

Shay smiled. "What time did you and Angel get home that night?"

"About two."

"And you didn't see Yesenia? You didn't see anyone else at the Graveyard?"

"Just the people I told you about," he said with a frown. "I guess we're lucky the lion didn't kill us instead of her."

She nodded, thinking Yesenia had been in the wrong place at the wrong time. But where, exactly, had she been?

"Go on," Shay said, gesturing for him to keep driving. By the time they reached Palomar High School, she was plagued by worries. Her brother was acting out in some of the same ways she had as a teenager. Hanging with the bad crowd, living on the edge, taking unnecessary risks.

What a mess she'd been after her mother's death. Ten years later and she still wasn't over it. Neither was Dylan, she suspected.

"You won't fight with Chad?" she asked as he pulled into the parking lot.

He shrugged.

Shay watched with growing panic as he got out of the car and tugged on his backpack. She stepped out also, meeting him in front of the bumper.

"Dylan," she began, holding on to his arm. Her heart was beating fast again, her pulse racing, throat dry. "You know I love you, right?"

For a second, his eyes widened with surprise, and she saw her own pain reflected there. Then it was gone, shuttered behind the walls he always put up between them. "Whatever you say," he muttered, and pulled away from her, just like he'd done a thousand times before.

14

Mike Shepherd was waiting for Luke when he came in to work that morning. Luke was late and it was Garrett's day off, so the sheriff's office was closed. About a dozen members of the press were camped outside the door anyway.

Mike didn't look happy.

The warden of San Diego County's Department of Fish and Game wasn't one of Luke's superiors, but he wasn't someone Luke wanted to piss off, either. Groaning, he weaved through the media vans and parked as close to the building as possible, shouldering past photographers and reporters with a firm "No comment."

Christ. The autopsy report hadn't even been released yet.

Fumbling with his keys, he unlocked the front door, letting Mike and himself in before he locked the press out.

"Nice uniform," Mike said drolly.

"Thanks," Luke muttered, smoothing his hand down the front of his T-shirt. Both of his summer-weight uniforms were dirty, so he didn't have much choice about the casual attire; one set smelled like smoke, the other stank of skunk.

"I heard you and Shay ran into some trouble yesterday."

"From who?"

"Clay Trujillo."

Luke had met Mike only once before, so he wasn't sure how much information to reveal about the ongoing investigation. Shepherd was Native American, not Luiseño or Cahuilla, but from one of the many other tribes local to the San Diego area. He was the kind of man Luke had always envied, able to move about freely between both worlds, respected by the Anglo community but maintaining that elusive reservation credibility.

Luke had never figured out how to walk that line.

During his summers on the rez, kids with light hair and blue eyes had taunted *him* about not being Indian enough. Kids who looked like Clay Trujillo, now that he thought about it.

Luke decided not to share his suspicions about tribal police or to mention his own deputy's shady dealings. Either way, he'd seem disloyal.

"The medical examiner called me yesterday when he couldn't reach you," Mike continued.

"What did he say?"

"Tests indicate the presence of more than one blood type on the samples taken from the victim's body."

"Human blood?"

"Yes."

Luke's mind swam with possibilities. Perhaps Yesenia had been assaulted in the hours or moments before the attack. Transfer of evidence was common in violent crimes. When one person hit another, he often picked up a little blood and left a little behind.

"DNA won't be back for weeks, but the doctor was able to determine blood type and the sex of the donor."

"Male?"

Mike shook his head. "Female."

Luke sank to a seat behind the desk in his office. "Hell."

Mike checked his appearance in the small mirror on the back of the door. From gleaming black ponytail to polished black boots, he was formidable. "The media won't leave without a sound bite, but I think it would be best to keep the . . . unsavory details quiet. When we catch the proper lion, no one will be the wiser."

Unless the animal struck again, Luke thought. "Have there been any incidences of a lion attacking multiple victims?"

Mike moved his gaze from the mirror, meeting Luke's eyes. "Unfortunately, yes. A few years ago a mountain lion took down two people in the same twenty-four-hour period, killing one and seriously injuring the other."

"Hell," Luke repeated, rubbing a hand over his tired face. He really, really wished he'd slept last night.

As far as keeping the details quiet, it was Luke's call. Failing to alert the press about a rogue lion might pose a threat to public safety. Then again, having a dozen gun-toting good ol' boys roaming the woods might be worse.

"What do you want to tell them?" Luke asked.

"Just that we have a lion in custody and are process-ing the evidence."

Luke threw open a desk drawer, searching for the uniform shirt he kept there and sorting through his mental list of suspects. None of them were female.

Jesse Ryan, the last known person to see Yesenia Montes alive, was a smoker with a motive for lighting the fire. And yet, Jesse didn't strike Luke as the violent, vindictive type. Guys like him coasted through life, playing it cool, manipulating women, and taking the easy way out. Sneaking around didn't gel with his bad-boy image.

Garrett Snell was sneaky, but he was smart. Driving out to Los Coyotes in broad daylight to burn down the place didn't seem in character for him, either. Besides, he'd been in the office all day yesterday. Hadn't he?

Clay Trujillo may have had the opportunity to start a fire, and if the movement of the body was tied up in reservation politics, he also had a motive, but he seemed genuinely fond of Shay. The arsonist wouldn't have been concerned with additional casualties.

Fernando Martinez found the body, so that auto-matically put him under suspicion. Other than the un-fortunate sequence of events leading to the dissolution of his marriage, Luke didn't think there was anything odd about him, though.

He found his extra shirt in the back of the desk drawer, still in the package. It was a generic tan button-down with front pockets and no rank patches, but with his star pinned to the breast pocket, he'd look official enough from the waist up.

"Let's get this over with," he said, pulling his T-shirt

over his head. He changed into the uniform shirt and tucked it in, his frustration increasing by the moment. His list of suspects was useless, he had no evidence that any crime had been committed, and the media was going to have a field day with this fatality.

If word got out about the lion mix-up, his career would be over.

Again.

"You're going out there?" Mike asked, surprised. He knew the circumstances of Luke's transfer.

"Yeah."

"Do you have a death wish?"

"It's not like I'm undercover here," he said, running a hand over his jaw, wishing he'd taken the time to shave. "The press has already seen me. What do you expect me to do, hide?"

Mike studied him anew. "It's your funeral," he said finally.

Luke disagreed, but he didn't bother to say so. His funeral had been in Vegas a few months ago. This place was more like hell.

After the press conference, Luke went with Mike Shepherd to the Graveyard and then revisited the burned-out area on Los Coyotes Indian Reservation. They didn't find any more clues, but Mike was able to set up security cameras at both locations in hopes that the perpetrator (or the lion) would come back to admire his handiwork.

Shay called while they were gone, leaving a message in a husky, emotional voice that made Luke's stomach clench and his pulse skyrocket. He'd been trying not to relive those stolen moments in the fertility cave, trying not to remember the feel of her body and the scent of her skin, to no avail.

After Mike left, Luke listened to the recording three more times, just to torture himself.

"My little brother told me he was at the Graveyard on Friday night with a couple of his friends. Chad Pinter and Travis Sanchez. I don't think they know anything about Yesenia." She paused, said, "This is Shay," and hung up.

Something about her forlorn tone, and the way she assumed he wouldn't recognize her voice, ripped him to shreds.

He wanted to throw the phone through the window. Instead he grabbed the receiver and called Garrett. "Tell me what you know about Dylan Phillips," he ordered when his deputy answered the phone.

"He's a punk."

"Why?"

"He's got a foul mouth and a bad attitude. I've arrested him a few times."

"What for?"

"Being out after curfew and, uh, starting a fire in the Dumpster behind the post office."

Interesting. No wonder Shay sounded upset. Luke looked down at the names on his list. "What about Chad Pinter and Travis Sanchez?"

"I don't know Sanchez, but Pinter's a troublemaker like Dylan Phillips. Drives a beat-up Chevy Nova like a bat out of hell."

A Chevy Nova was a car, not a pickup. It couldn't have made the marks he'd seen on Yesenia Montes's body. "I need you to come in," he decided. Luke had interviews to do, and bad help was better than none at all.

Garrett breathed heavily into the receiver, probably wanting to refuse. "I can be there in an hour," he muttered.

Luke didn't bother to thank him before he hung up. Frowning, he rifled through the papers on top of his desk, looking for the fax from the emergency room at Palomar Hospital. He'd requested the names of any patients from over the weekend on the off chance that whoever bled on Yesenia Montes had gone there for treatment.

Travis Sanchez was on the list.

Luke sighed, annoyed with the direction the investigation was taking. Every time he turned around it widened, and he had the feeling that the answers he was searching for were getting farther and farther away.

He took the autopsy pictures out of his top desk drawer and studied the dark, linear bruises, the dried blood, the marks on her neck. "Who moved you?" he murmured, brushing his fingertips over the surface of the photo.

Shay dropped by her house before heading out to Dark Canyon, deciding a meal and a hot shower were imperative. There was a message on her answering machine from Mike Shepherd, telling her not to worry about coming in to work.

He must have heard about her knee.

Feeling anxious, she called to leave Luke a message of her own, knowing Dylan would hate her for ratting him out. She'd promised not to ground him, but she'd never said she wouldn't tell anyone.

For once, Shay wasn't hungry, and the shower that should have relaxed her sore muscles only left her tied up in knots. Dry-eyed and damp-haired, she collapsed on top of her unmade bed and buried her head in the pillows, struck by the overwhelming urge to cry. Her relationship with Dylan was in shambles. She missed Jesse, although their "friends with benefits" arrangement had been sporadic and unsatisfying. Her connection to her father was tenuous, worn as thin as the postcards he'd sent.

Getting involved with Luke was just another recipe for heartache.

When the phone rang several hours later, she came awake with a start, surprised she'd drifted off. "Hello?" she mumbled into the receiver.

"Mrs. Phillips? This is Rose from Palomar High School."

Shay sat up in bed. What had Dylan done now?

"Sheriff Meza has asked to speak with your son—"

"My brother," she corrected. As many times as she'd been in there, the staff should have been able to remember their relationship correctly.

"Yes, of course, your brother. As his legal guardian, we need you to sign a release."

Shay blinked at the clock. It was afternoon already. "I'll be right there," she said, hanging up and swinging her legs over the edge of the bed.

Twenty minutes later, she was in the front office. Dylan, Travis, and Chad were sitting on a wooden bench in the waiting room, wearing identical expressions of affected discontent. Chad was also sporting a dark bruise under his left eye. When he saw her, he gave her a disgustingly thorough once-over. "Hey, Mrs. Phillips."

Shay wanted to sock him in the other eye. Unlike Rose, Chad knew damned well she wasn't married, and he liked to annoy her by pretending he thought she was Dylan's mom. Once she'd overheard him referring to her as a MILF. Needless to say, she wasn't flattered.

Rose, the receptionist, craned her neck to look over the top of the counter. "If you could just sign here," she said, tapping the sheet of paper with her fingernail.

From her vantage point, Shay could see Luke and Garrett standing with Principal Fischer in his office. She forced her gaze down to the form in front of her. "Can I be with him during questioning?"

"If you insist. The other parents didn't."

Shay signed it and turned to Dylan. "Do you want me to stay?"

He scowled. "Hell, no."

It was the answer she'd expected, but it still hurt. From Principal Fischer's office, a rumble of male laughter caught her attention. Logically, she knew the men hadn't been discussing her, but when she glanced their way, Garrett's deep-set eyes met hers.

He looked from her to Luke, who was engaged in conversation with Principal Fischer, and arched a brow.

Shay felt the blood drain from her face. Had Luke told Garrett about last night?

Luke turned his attention her way also, as if sensing

her discomfort, and Principal Fischer glanced over, too, reading the tension in the room.

Shay was aware of all eyes on her, scrutinizing, criticizing, judging. She hadn't given a thought to her appearance before she left, but now she regretted showing up in a state of dishabille. The brief shorts and T-shirt she'd been sleeping in were comfortable, but totally inappropriate for the occasion. She couldn't have felt more self-conscious if she'd been wearing a scarlet letter on her chest.

Tightening her grip on the handbag under her arm, she turned back to Dylan. "I'll see you after basketball practice."

Chad regarded Dylan with a self-satisfied smirk. "Why don't you kiss your mommy good-bye?"

Dylan answered in kind, suggesting Chad do something far more explicit with his own mother. A minor scuffle ensued, after which Principal Fischer threatened to suspend the next boy who moved, and Rose glowered at Shay, as if her moral ambiguity were responsible for Dylan's bad attitude.

Well, maybe it was.

Feeling tears burning in her eyes, clogging up the back of her throat, she fled the scene. She'd never been more aware of how every mistake she'd made in life, and she'd made a lot of them, affected her brother. God, she was such a screwup. She'd screwed him up, too.

The best she could do for Dylan now was to make sure he got out of Tenaja Falls, as far away from her as he could get.

———

Luke was struck by the absurd temptation to go after Shay, who was visibly shaken, and take her in his arms.

Of course, that would only solidify Garrett's assumptions. Luke's deputy knew they'd spent the night together, and although he hadn't said anything, his smarmy attitude spoke louder than words.

With some difficulty, Luke tore his gaze from Shay's retreating form, aware that every male in the room, Dylan excluded, was watching her butt jiggle as she hurried away.

Animals.

Luke gave Garrett a cold stare, daring him to make a sexist comment. He wisely refrained.

Principal Fischer cleared his throat. "You can use the meeting room," he said, ushering them into a small space with a long rectangular table.

Luke wanted to talk with Travis first. He was the smallest, the most nervous, and looked the most likely to cave under pressure. Hopefully, the other two wouldn't kill each other while they waited.

Luke hadn't interviewed a teenage boy in a while and he'd forgotten how tiresome it could be. Travis Sanchez stuttered, mumbled, lied, and evaded. Given three different tries, he told three different stories. A criminal mastermind he was not.

Annoyed, Luke dismissed him and called in Dylan. Yesterday the kid had been energetic and open, rattling off the most obscure basketball stats from memory and showing surprising insight into the sport. Today he radiated defiance from the top of his faux-hawk haircut to the frayed cuffs of his baggy jeans.

"Snell," he said, greeting Garrett with a sneer. He didn't acknowledge Luke at all.

For some reason, Luke was amused by his surly attitude. "Travis told us you kicked him in the balls," he said, getting right down to business.

Dylan's eyes flashed with anger. "Yeah," he said, obviously lying. "So?"

"Explain how you managed to blacken Chad's eye and deliver a below-the-belt hit on Travis at the same time."

Dylan cracked his knuckles. "What can I say? I'm dexterous."

Luke smothered a smile. "Were you in the front seat or the back?"

Knowing the feat couldn't be accomplished from either, he shrugged. Luke studied Dylan carefully, wondering what he was missing. Travis had claimed they didn't meet anyone else at the Graveyard, but Luke knew finding the opposite sex was priority numero uno for most teenage boys.

Luke was struck by a mental image of Fernando Martinez's eldest daughter. Hadn't Shay mentioned Dylan when she spoke to the girl? And yesterday, Dylan had complained about not being able to have someone in his room. He'd said a name.

Angel.

On Saturday morning, Luke had overheard Shay arguing with her brother. She'd gone to his room to check in on him and found . . .

"Angel Martinez," Luke said.

Dylan jumped a little. "What about her?"

"Was she sitting in the backseat with Travis?"

He narrowed his blue eyes. "Who told you that?"

"Travis," Luke invented. "He said she was all over him."

"That's a goddamned lie."

"So tell us the truth."

Dylan clammed up, refusing to be manipulated. Unlike Travis Sanchez, he was nobody's stooge. "We didn't see Yesenia Montes," he said finally, "and we didn't see any lions. If you want to find out what Angel was doing that night, you'll have to ask her."

"We'll do that," he said. "Thanks for your time."

Dylan stood up. "I can go?"

Luke leaned back in his chair. "Sure."

"Should I send in Chad?"

Luke nodded reluctantly, remembering the way the kid had spoken to Shay. Times like this, he wished he could play bad cop. Luke doubted he would get any new information out of Chad, and he'd rather staple the mouthy little bastard's lips together than hear him talk.

15

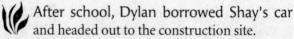 After school, Dylan borrowed Shay's car and headed out to the construction site.

To his surprise, she hadn't freaked out about his new job. She'd just gotten really quiet and looked kind of sad. "What are you going to do with the money?"

Buy drugs, he'd wanted to retort. "Save up for my own car," he said instead. "Yours sucks."

Her face took on a pinched look. She had dark smudges under her eyes and he knew she hadn't slept last night. Well, neither had he. "You're still planning on going to UCLA?"

He rolled his eyes. "Of course. You think I'd give up a choice scholarship to dig ditches?"

She stared at him as if he were a complete stranger, and she couldn't possibly predict what he would do next. "Dinner's at seven."

He took off, eager to escape her measured glances and long-suffering sighs. She was in another one of her weird moods, and he couldn't really blame her. Living in Tenaja Falls wasn't easy for a woman like her, but she was too stubborn to leave.

Sometimes he thought she cared more about this goddamned town than she cared about him.

People here liked to gossip, and there was always speculation about her love life. She was criticized for her affair with Jesse Ryan, envied for being young and pretty and unmarried. Her tough attitude and casual style didn't help matters. Once, he'd heard Chad's mom say it wasn't proper for her to go braless when there was a teenage boy in the house.

As if he were checking her out or something. *Gross.*

Scowling, he turned into the dirt lot just inside the front gate. Unlike yesterday, today the site was bustling with human activity. A newly poured flat of cement, probably for an outbuilding or security office, stretched across the lot. It covered a large area, but was nowhere near the size needed as a foundation for the casino.

They wouldn't be ready to lay down the main slab for a while.

Dylan felt a flutter of nerves. After a sleepless night, a shitty day at school, and a miserable run at basketball practice, what he really wanted to do was go home and go to bed. Because he couldn't call in sick his first day on the job, he straightened his shoulders and tried to look tough as he approached a group of men standing near Bull Ryan.

Bull gave Dylan a brief glance, nodded toward a short, dark-skinned man beside him, and continued shooting the breeze with his work crew.

The short man greeted Dylan with a warm handshake. "My name is Pedro. You are my new slave, no?"

He mumbled an affirmative.

Pedro laughed and led him toward a series of shallow black washtubs full of dingy water and jagged tools. "You clean these," he said, picking up a triangle-shaped piece of metal with a wooden handle. To demonstrate, he gave the tool a few quick swipes with a sponge and dropped it back into the water. "Don't bang them together or scratch the surfaces. If you damage them, I will fire you." He smiled, but it didn't take the edge off his words.

Dylan gulped.

"Ah . . . one more thing. *Mira las manos.*"

Dylan looked at Pedro's hands. They were cracked and dry, riddled with dozens of thin white scars. "Tools like these are used to smooth the surface of the concrete, and they are kept very sharp. Be careful."

"Do I need gloves?"

Pedro laughed again. "They would only fill with water and slow you down."

It took him an hour to get through the first tub. He didn't cut himself, but it was a near thing. The sun was blazing down on the back of his neck, he was dying of thirst, and he felt like crap. This job was already totally fucked.

Pedro returned and inspected his work. "You are very thorough," he said, nodding his approval. "But much too slow. Do the rest."

Dylan stared at the other tubs in disbelief. It would take him forever to finish. Resigning himself to an afternoon of agony, he went on to the next set of tools, trying to work fast and keep all of his fingers attached. It wasn't wise to let his mind wander, but he'd always had difficulty concentrating on mundane tasks. He liked to do math problems in his head when he was running for PE, and he often worked on rote memorization in the weight room.

After an arduous night and exhausting day, his brain was mush. It traveled the path of least resistance, to an oft-visited, infinitely pleasurable place.

Angel Martinez, naked.

He squeezed his eyes shut in an attempt to dispel the image, sunspots swimming behind his lids. Damn her. She'd wanted him to kiss her last night. He knew by the way she'd kissed him back. Maybe he'd gone for it with a little too much gusto, but what the hell? All she had to do was say no.

Her schizo sexuality was driving him crazy.

It occurred to him that he should call and give her a heads-up about his interview with Luke Meza. The idea of talking to her again excited him more than it should have. He tried to stay focused on the work he was doing, but pictures from the past and sensations from last night melded together, swirling in his head. He wondered what it would be like to join her in the shower, to cup the soft weight of her breasts in his palms and feel them against his bare chest. To lift her up against the shower wall . . .

The tool he was cleaning slipped from his hands, gliding along the base of his thumb. Flaying his flesh.

"Motherfucker," he swore, startled by the intense flash of pain. Blood dripped from the cut, splashing into the grimy pan of water below him. He looked around for help, and for something to staunch the flow of blood, but there was nothing, no one.

The site was deserted.

Cursing, he yanked his shirt over his head and wrapped it around his hand. When he didn't see any red stains blossoming through the fabric, he figured the wound was minor. Still, there was no way he was putting his hand back into that grainy, disgusting water.

He wandered out to the parking lot and found Pedro with three other guys, hunkered down in the shade next to a heavy-duty work truck, drinking ice cold Coronas. Dylan's mouth watered for the taste of beer, but nobody offered him one.

He cleared his dry throat. "Uh . . . I think I need a Band-Aid. I'm bleeding."

They all laughed. One of the men said something in rapid-fire Spanish, too fast for Dylan to catch a single word, and they kept laughing.

"He said his wife keeps some tampons in his truck," Pedro translated with a smile. "If you're on your period."

Dylan felt his face flame. "I cut myself," he said through clenched teeth.

"*Ay, muchacho,*" Pedro said, rising. "Let's go take a look."

Pedro didn't bother with a first aid kit. He glanced at the cut, which had already stopped bleeding, and wrapped Dylan's hand with a piece of clean cloth and duct tape. "Have your mom put a real bandage on it when you get home," he recommended.

Dylan felt the humiliating press of tears behind his eyes, and could only nod.

Pedro examined his face, missing nothing. "*Vamanos,*" he said, returning to the black tubs of tools Dylan already loathed. "No scratches," he said, inspecting the clean, shiny surfaces. "You can come back tomorrow."

He didn't know whether to feel relieved or depressed. "Will I be doing this every day?"

Pedro laughed. "No, *chacho*. Some days you will have to work hard."

Dylan hoped he was joking. Getting blood on his hands hadn't made him feel tough, and the other guys had practically called him a pussy. But he nodded, because he wasn't a quitter, and no one ever said it was easy to be a man.

On his way out, Dylan decided to stop by Bull's office. It couldn't hurt to thank him for the job. When he got close to the office door, he heard two men arguing. Not wanting to interrupt, he leaned against the side of the trailer and waited for them to finish.

"Come on, Dad," one of the voices said. "Are you really going to sit there and lecture me about women? Clay's mama would find that highly ironic."

Dylan knew immediately that the man speaking was Jesse Ryan. His ears strained for Bull's response.

"We aren't talking about Clay's mama, we're talking about your wife. I heard Clay was paying her court. While you've been out tomcatting, pissing away my money, the mother of your child has been entertaining other men."

Jesse made a snort of disbelief. "Tammy Lee wouldn't know how to entertain a man if she took lessons."

"Maybe he's giving her lessons."

"Over my dead body," Jesse said in a growl.

"You do this one more time and I'll kill you myself," Bull warned. "I'm tired of paying for your mistakes. You don't take care of your business. You can't even take care of your wife. When are you going to grow up?"

Jesse wisely remained silent.

"This is the last time I bail you out. And you better come in and work for me tomorrow. Fixing cars is obviously not keeping you occupied."

"Yessir," he said in a sulky voice.

Aware that the conversation was winding down, Dylan backed up and moved away from the door, leaving as quietly as possible.

After Luke sent Garrett home, he sat behind a strange desk in an office that didn't feel like his, thinking about the case while the last rays of the sun eked away.

Darkness closed in on him, but he didn't bother to get up or turn on any lights. He still had more than an hour before he had to meet Shay, and he wasn't looking forward to facing her again. She would surely make him pay for the callous way he'd treated her.

He knew he'd screwed up. He just didn't know how to fix it.

If only he hadn't gotten so close to her last night. He'd been freezing his ass off in damp pants and no shirt, the embers of the dying fire barely penetrating the chill in the air. He never should have taken her up on her offer to get warm.

He'd known what it would lead to.

"Damn it," he muttered, rubbing a hand over his face. Now more than ever, he wished he had a place to call home. There was nothing remotely comfortable, or comforting, about his cot in the barracks at the firehouse. Sure, there was a couch, a giant TV, and a stocked fridge, the staples of every bachelor pad, but there was no privacy.

There was no . . . peace.

Tenaja Falls was supposed to be a kind of retreat for him, a few months of rest and relaxation. He was burned-out and he needed to regroup. That was all. While he was here, he planned on charting his future course.

Going back to Vegas was out, but it wasn't as if he had no other options. He had an excellent record, an extensive education in criminal justice, and plenty of experience with investigating organized crime. He could get a job anywhere there was gang activity.

For some reason, working in a big city didn't hold the appeal it once had. Ten years ago, he'd wanted to make a difference. Now he was jaded enough to question whether hitting the mean streets and shaking down gun-toting teenagers was the best way to do it.

On impulse, he picked up the phone and dialed a number he knew by heart. "Mom," he said as soon as she answered, feeling an odd tightening in his throat at the sound of her voice.

"What's wrong?" she asked.

He laughed, feeling some of his tension ease away. "Don't I ever call you just to say hello?"

"Of course, but you sounded funny."

He felt funny, too, but he didn't tell her that. "How's Lauren?"

After they left Pala, his mother had met the love of her life, and she'd been happily remarried for thirty years. Now his stepsister, Lauren, was happily married, too, with a three-year-old daughter and another baby on the way.

His mom chatted about her favorite subject for a few moments, offering him a welcome distraction. And after she was finished catching him up on the latest news, she didn't even ask him when he was going to settle down and have children of his own.

Maybe she'd given up.

She didn't mention the mountain lion mauling, and neither did he. He didn't want her to worry.

"Do you like it there?" she asked, sounding hopeful.

"Yes," he lied.

"Are the people nice?"

He knew where this was going. Straight to finding a small-town girl and hanging up his hat, Andy Griffith–style. "I miss you," he said to change the subject, and because it was true.

She sucked in a little breath of pleasure. "Well, I miss you, too, Luke. We all do."

"I know. I just wanted to tell you. I sort of promised someone I'd tell you"—he swallowed back another laugh at his expense, because he was getting ridiculously sentimental—"that you have a great smile."

She was silent for a moment. "Are you sure you're okay?"

"I'm fine," he said, and suddenly he was.

Since everything had fallen apart in Vegas, he'd been searching for something worthwhile to hold on to. A deeper understanding of himself, and a more meaningful connection to others. Tenaja Falls didn't have much flash, but it had substance. He didn't know if this town was the right place for him, but he *did* know he could make a difference here. Unlike Vegas, where his efforts had seemed like a drop in the bucket.

He wasn't ready to start house-shopping yet, but the idea of staying here brightened his outlook rather than dampening it.

After Luke hung up with his mother, he called Clay Trujillo. The short conversation had revived him, and reminded him of another mother he'd yet to talk to. "Do you know Tamara Ryan?"

"Yeah. Why?"

Luke was reluctant to tell Clay about the blood evidence found at the scene. Sometime before the body was dumped, an unknown female had bled on her. Perhaps Yesenia had been confronted by a jealous wife. Maybe Tamara fit the bill.

"I wanted to ask her a few questions about Jesse. He was the last person to see Yesenia Montes alive."

There was a short pause. "I'll go with you."

It was the response Luke had been fishing for, so he agreed without a qualm. He wanted to find out what was going on between Shay, Jesse, Tamara, and whoever else had been dipping into Tenaja Falls' shallow dating pool.

Clay met him at the station and Luke drove from there, heading toward the outskirts of town. Tamara Ryan lived on the southwestern edge of Tenaja, in a lonely cluster of trailer homes situated near a convenience store just off the main drag.

The place made the quaint little houses in Shay's neighborhood seem prosperous. An older model red Ford Escort sat in the driveway, covered in a fine coat of dust, its cooling system still ticking. Inside, there was the sound of a baby crying.

Luke glanced at Clay, who was striding toward the front door, concern etched on his handsome face.

A young woman opened the door before he got the chance to knock. She was just over five feet tall and slightly built, a pretty brunette with big brown eyes.

Luke thought Shay Phillips looked young, but this girl appeared no older than a teenager. His opinion of Jesse Ryan slipped down another notch. The guy had been robbing the hell out of the cradle.

Her eyes slid from Clay to him and back again. The baby in her arms wailed.

"Can I help?" Clay asked.

"Yeah. I need to change Grace and Mama's . . ." she trailed off, wincing as the baby let out another loud cry, and gesturing toward the couch behind her. "I just got home," she added, obviously exasperated.

She disappeared inside and Clay followed. As soon as his eyes adjusted to the lack of light, Luke saw a slender woman reclined on the sofa, arms akimbo, her bleached blond hair in disarray. There was an empty liquor bottle on the coffee table.

"Darlene," Clay said gently, bending down and wrapping those thin arms around his neck. "Let's get you to your room."

She roused a bit, but didn't fight him. "Clayton? Is that you?"

"Yes, ma'am. Deputy Clayton Trujillo, at your service." He lifted her off the couch as if she weighed nothing.

"I want to dance."

"Sure thing, honey. Let's dance this way."

Luke waited alone in the living room, thinking he couldn't have imagined a more awkward scene. Why was Jesse's child bride living like a pauper, and leaving her baby in the care of a falling-down drunk?

He wasn't here to evaluate anyone's parenting skills, but he did give his surroundings a cursory examination. As a state employee, he was under a legal and ethical obligation to report any evidence of child abuse.

Other than the bottle on the table, and an empty glass next to it, the place was tidy. The carpet was worn but clean, the space free of clutter, and the air smelled faintly of pine-scented furniture polish. On the entertainment center, above the TV, there was one framed photo, a close-up of Tamara cradling a newborn Grace.

The young woman came back into the hallway, baby on her hip, at the same time Clay returned from the bedroom. He sidestepped to let her pass, but she stopped in her tracks, as if his proximity flustered her. The near-collision was so emotionally charged that even Luke felt uncomfortable, and he was ten feet away.

"Thanks," she muttered, as if she was grateful for Clay's assistance but resented its necessity.

Clay shoved his hands into the pockets of his jeans. "It's no big deal."

The baby in her arms continued to cry. "She's hungry," Tamara explained, casting another worried glance at Luke.

He introduced himself quickly. "I need to ask some questions about Jesse. It will only take a few minutes."

"Fine," she said, lifting her chin. It had a decidedly stubborn tilt. "Have a seat."

Luke waited for her to settle in on the couch, Clay at her side, before he took the only other chair, a sturdy oak rocker with a faded blue seat cushion.

Tamara Ryan wasn't at all what he'd expected. She had a silky cap of brown hair, cut bluntly across her forehead, and a slight overbite that gave her a cute, mousy look. With her heart-shaped face and velvety brown eyes, she was attractive, but hardly a femme fatale.

Jesse had thrown Shay over for this mere girl? Or had he been caught with this sweet young thing and made to pay the price?

Having little choice in the matter, for the baby was still fussing, Tamara reached beneath her shirt and unfastened the cup of her bra. Although she tried to stay modestly covered, little Grace wanted a clear shot at her target. The baby gripped the edge of her mother's shirt in her chubby fist, revealing the inner curve of one pale, milk-swollen breast.

Luke averted his eyes respectfully, turning his attention toward Clay while she got the baby situated. The deputy was also looking in the opposite direction, his jaw set in anger, a dull stain coloring his cheekbones. Public breast-feeding was much more common among Indian women, so it didn't faze Luke, and it shouldn't be fazing Clay.

Maybe he felt as though Luke should have offered to wait while she fed the baby in the other room.

Having been raised by his mother, off-reservation, Luke would understand if Tamara was reluctant to nurse her baby in front of a stranger. What he didn't get was how anyone, especially a man, could be offended by the sight. He was baffled by the Anglo hang-up about breasts, although he could certainly relate to their masculine fascination for them.

As Grace snuggled in and began to suckle in earnest, some of the tension eased from Tamara's face. She still looked tired, and far too young for motherhood, despite her body's apparent readiness for the task, but now she also appeared serene, like an underage Madonna.

"How old are you?" he couldn't help but ask.

When Clay flinched at the question, Luke had to wonder if he had a hankering for very young girls, too. Perhaps this one in particular.

"Twenty-three," she answered, glancing at Clay, reading his discomfort.

Surprised, because she looked about seventeen, Luke did some quick math. Maybe the girl had actually been legal when Jesse had started messing around with her. "How long have you and Jesse been married?"

"Five years. Separated for most of it."

He guessed that Grace had come into the picture during a period of time they weren't separated. "When's the last time you saw him?"

Her mouth twisted wryly. "A month ago. At least."

"He doesn't visit Grace?"

"Sometimes he comes when I'm not here. We don't get along."

"Why's that?"

"Because he's a lying, cheating bastard."

Luke couldn't argue that point. And yet, he'd come here to ask invasive questions, not to agree with her. "Do you have proof of his infidelities?"

"Proof?" She let out a harsh laugh, blowing the hair off her forehead. "No. But I'd have to be blind, and an idiot, not to know about his other women."

"Shay Phillips?" he asked, struggling to maintain an aura of nonchalance.

When her eyes darkened, he knew she harbored a slew of ill feelings. He had to admit he had some of those himself. Although Luke didn't consider Jesse his rival, or his equal, he didn't like picturing Shay with another man. "Yes," she said. "And more besides."

"Yesenia Montes?"

Her brows rose. Then the implications of his question sank in. "What, exactly, are you investigating?"

"The accident. Jesse was the last person to see her alive." *That we know of,* he added silently.

Tamara returned her attention to Grace, who had finished feeding on one side. She lifted the baby and began to pat her on the back. "I don't know anything about him and Yesenia. To tell you the truth, I'd be surprised to hear he was with her."

"Why's that?"

"Because although she's a cheap whore, she comes at a price. And Jesse never had to pay for anything in his life."

Luke glanced at Clay, who seemed to not only agree with that description, but to burn with resentment over it. On the way over, he hadn't asked about Clay's relationship with Tamara, because he wasn't sure it was relevant.

He still wasn't sure. But it was pretty damned interesting.

Luke leaned back in his chair, averting his gaze once

again as Tamara finished burping Grace and settled her in to nurse on the other side.

"Do you need anything?" Clay asked her quietly.

"You've done enough."

"I can do more."

"I don't want your money."

Clay cast an annoyed glance toward Luke, probably wishing he would leave them alone for a minute. He didn't. "You gonna let your mom look after Grace while you're in class again?"

"No," she whispered, her eyes wet. "I'll have to drop out."

"Don't. I'll watch her."

Her head jerked toward him. "You would do that?"

"Of course," he said in a stiff voice. "I'm off work at three every day. That will give me plenty of time to get here before you have to leave."

She moistened her lips, hesitant. "I'll think about it."

He nodded curtly and dropped the subject.

"I—I'm not a bad mother," she said after a long pause, pleading with Luke, meeting his gaze. "Grace is in a good day care while I'm at work, but she stays with Mama when I have a late-afternoon class. I'd never have left her if I'd known . . ." She shook her head helplessly. "She usually doesn't start drinking this early."

Luke told her he believed her, because he did, and not to worry. Grace was asleep now, safe and cozy in her arms. He wondered if times had been this hard for his own mother, and guessed that they had.

There was no way he would come between them.

Clay said good-bye and they both left in somber moods, contemplating the situation in shared silence.

Luke wasn't a meddler, but he had a case to solve, and like it or not, Clay was wrapped up in it.

"You have some kind of claim on her?" he asked, meaning Tamara.

Clay's blue eyes narrowed. "No. Why?"

"A man doesn't usually offer that kind of assistance without . . ." He tried to think of a way to put it delicately, because Clay looked like he wanted to punch him, ". . . a return on his investment."

Clay's lips thinned. "Some men."

Luke shrugged, dividing his concentration between Clay and the road. "You always take care of Jesse's leftovers?" he asked, prodding harder.

"She's my niece," he said between clenched teeth.

"Tamara Ryan is your niece?"

"No. Grace is. Jesse and I are brothers."

Luke searched his face for the resemblance, but he didn't see it. As the town rebel, Jesse had the requisite dark good looks and bad-boy attitude. With his light eyes and sun-streaked ponytail, Clay was Jesse's polar opposite in appearance and demeanor.

"We have different mothers," he muttered.

Ah. Everything became very clear. Jesse was legitimate and Clay had been born on the wrong side of the blanket. Literally.

Were the half brothers the best of friends or the worst of enemies? If Luke wasn't mistaken, Clay was infatuated with Jesse's wife. Had Tamara Ryan played up their rivalry, pitting one brother against the other, or was she just another innocent bystander?

Luke could say one thing for Tenaja Falls: it wasn't boring.

16

Just before 8:00 P.M., Shay stood in front of the mirror in the bathroom, adding volume to her hair and applying another layer of mascara. From the confines of Dylan's bedroom, where he'd been holed up since dinner, System of a Down was blaring. Every time the bass line picked up, the shelves rattled.

Home sweet home.

She stepped back from the sink and studied her appearance, wanting to make sure she'd nailed the look she was going for. Tousled blond hair, check. Rock 'n' roll T-shirt, short denim miniskirt, check. Smoky eyes and cinnamon lip gloss, check.

Yep. She looked like trailer trash.

Even her bruised knee, which any lady with class would have the sense to cover up, was on proud display. If anything ruined the ensemble it was her shoes. The black suede Steve Madden pumps had been an indulgence, but they were still kind of wild.

Coco Chanel, she wasn't.

Shay flashed her reflection a bitter smile. When the

doorbell rang ten minutes later, she grabbed her silver metallic purse and rapped a quick good-bye to Dylan on his bedroom door.

Instead of Clay, she was met by Angel Martinez. "Wow," the girl said, taking in Shay's skyscraper heels and short skirt. "You look . . ."

"Like a hooker?"

Angel's eyes jumped up. "No! Are you kidding me? You look hot."

Shay smiled, accepting the teenager's compliment with a grain of salt. Angel was wearing an alarming number of hoop earrings, a scarred leather wristband, and a black tank top cut low enough to show off the kind of cleavage Shay had always longed for.

"You want Dylan?" she asked, stepping aside to let the girl in.

Angel flushed. "Well, yeah. I mean, I just wanted to talk to him, if that's all right—"

Shay lifted a hand to ward off her stammering. "I'll get him for you."

Pounding on the door was useless when Dylan was blasting the stereo, so Shay just walked inside, resigning herself to his wrath. He was sitting at his desk, math book open, scrawling numbers on lined notepaper.

How anyone could study with all that racket was beyond her.

When she put her hand on his shoulder, he startled. He looked past her, to where Angel was standing in the doorway, and came to his feet so fast the chair fell over. He was wearing his usual attire for hanging around the house, basketball shorts and nothing else. Judging by the stricken expression on his face, and Angel's renewed flush, he may as well have been standing there naked.

Horrified, he rushed to put on a T-shirt and turn down the music.

Good grief. Shay would have laughed if the exchange hadn't been so painful to watch. Although Dylan and Angel had looked pretty cozy the last time they'd been in his bedroom together, they were obviously uncomfortable now.

Post-hookup awkwardness. Shay recognized it well.

When the doorbell rang again, she excused herself, leaving her brother and Angel to their own devices. This time it was Luke on her doorstep, and unlike Angel, he didn't miss the nuances of her eye-popping outfit.

"Nice," he said sarcastically, tearing his gaze from her bare legs.

"Clay said he was going to pick me up," she said.

"I told him I would."

She let out a frustrated breath, annoyed with Luke's high-handed behavior. She also couldn't help but notice how delicious he looked in plainclothes. His gray T-shirt accented his broad shoulders and clung to his flat belly, and his faded blue Levi's fit him to perfection. There was nothing more flattering to a man's body, in her opinion, than button-fly jeans.

With her heels on, she only had to look up a few inches to meet his eyes. If he was feeling the effects of a sleepless night or having second thoughts about giving her the brush-off, it didn't show on his face. His expression was guarded, his jaw freshly shaved.

"Are you ready?"

She hesitated, all of the emotions she'd been carrying around inside her threatening to rise to the surface. Post-hookup awkwardness, to the nth degree. "I'm ready," she said, taking a deep breath and stepping out into the night.

Luke knew exactly what Shay was doing.

Her outfit, her eyes, her body, her attitude; everything about her screamed *easy*. He'd never been more certain that she wasn't.

Luke wasn't much of a drinker, but being from Vegas, he was familiar with singles bar dynamics. There was a way men acted around women they'd already had, women they knew they could have again through very little effort. None of the men at the Round-Up treated Shay with disrespect or nonchalance. If anything, they seemed afraid to approach her, like she might incinerate them if they got too close.

Well, she did look hot.

The first thing she'd done, after telling him he wouldn't get anywhere with the locals if he didn't sit down and order a beer, was engage Clay Trujillo in a game of pool. Yes, it was provocative, to show up with one man and flirt with another, and it was naughty to stretch across the pool table in a skirt that short. But she and Clay, Luke finally realized, had about as much chemistry as siblings. Every time she bent forward, Clay looked around the bar warily, daring the patrons to ogle her tush.

They still did, just not as openly as they wanted to.

There were only two other women in the bar, a

raspy-voiced cougar who'd already propositioned him, and a busy, busty waitress. Both had seen Yesenia Montes leave with Jesse Ryan on Friday night.

Lots of the men had seen her, too. Yesenia got around in more ways than one, and she'd been spotted several times over the course of the evening, standing outside the bar, strolling along Tenaja's main drag, and waiting in front of the café. No one had admitted to picking her up or seeing her get picked up, so Luke made a mental log of the sightings and moved on.

He was no closer to solving the case, no more able to control the intensity of his attraction to Shay, no less conflicted by his feelings for her.

As he watched her lean across the table to hit the eight ball into the corner pocket, calves flexing, tattoo on her lower back flashing, he had to admit he was no longer concerned about her sexual history. He didn't really care how many men she'd been with in the past. He just wanted to be the only man in her future.

Luke almost sputtered out a mouthful of beer at the untoward thought.

This morning seemed like a hundred years ago, but he'd been very clear about not wanting to repeat the mistake they'd made. They were all wrong for each other. Christ, she was ten years younger than he was, and ten times more wild. He wasn't sure he was going to stay in Tenaja Falls, and she was a hometown girl through and through.

Even if he wanted to settle down, he wouldn't choose a woman like her to do it with. She was too hot to handle.

Wasn't she?

Shay made her shot and looked up, her laser blue eyes zeroing in on Luke. With some difficulty, he swallowed, replacing the bottle of Bud on the top of the bar because his hands were shaking. As if sensing his sudden vulnerability, she straightened, handing off her cue to Clay and moving in for the kill.

Luke watched her approach, unable to tear his eyes away from her body. Her faded black T-shirt was vintage Stones, the infamous image of the wagging tongue. He knew by the way her breasts moved beneath it that she wasn't wearing a bra.

When she maneuvered onto the bar stool next to him, he had to wonder if she was similarly bare under that tiny skirt.

Sweat broke out on his forehead.

With a knowing smile, she grabbed his bottle of Bud and took a sip. Her hair was loose tonight, falling in sexy waves to the middle of her back. He wanted to stick his hands in it. Her mouth was plump and moist and red, and when he thought about what he wanted to do to it, his skin overheated and his jeans got tight.

She let her lips linger on the rim of the brown bottle, torturing him. "You want to dance?"

Dance? He couldn't even stand. "No."

"Why are you here?" she asked suddenly.

"Here, in this bar?"

"In this town."

He took the bottle away from her, plagued by dirty fantasies in which she ran her tongue up and down the neck. "I needed a job."

"Did you get fired?"

Luke hesitated, caught off guard by her question.

"Las Vegas is the city of vice," she murmured, studying his face. "What's yours? You don't strike me as a gambler. Too uptight. And it can't be alcohol. You've been nursing the same drink for an hour."

"Maybe it was drugs," he said glibly.

"Please. You're so in love with being in control, I bet you've never even tried pot."

He shrugged, too proud to admit she was right.

She lowered her voice. "Was it women? There are plenty of those in Sin City. Exotic dancers, professional escorts . . ."

"Whores," he finished for her, getting annoyed.

"So that's it? You were fired for being a sex addict?" She shook her head, the lights above the bar making the golden strands in her hair shimmer. "I can't say I'm surprised. I mean, every time I turn around you're staring at my—"

"I didn't get fired," he ground out. "I got shot."

Her eyes rounded with dismay.

Luke pulled his gaze away from her, smothering a groan. He hadn't meant to say that. There was no admission guaranteed to soften a woman up more, and he needed Shay to stay mad at him. If she didn't, he wouldn't be able to keep his hands off her. He was a hair's breadth from hauling her out of here and giving in to his baser instincts right now.

"Where?"

"Nowhere," he said, cursing his own stupidity. "Never mind."

"Where?" she repeated.

"In the back," he admitted, feeling a phantom ache

between his shoulder blades. "But I was wearing a bulletproof vest at the time."

Her gaze wandered over him. She looked as though she wanted to pull up his shirt and rain kisses along the length of his spine. He remembered her fingernails digging into his skin last night and tightened his hand around the bottle, so wound up he felt like he might explode.

"It didn't leave a mark?"

"Nothing permanent."

"So that's why you left?"

"No," he admitted. "I'd been investigating some high-profile criminals. Casino guys with deep pockets. There was a hit out on me, I guess. The shooter was never caught, and the department decided I was a liability."

"Oh, Luke," she said.

He shrugged off her pity. "I was transferred to a 'safer, less visible position,' as they put it, so I tendered my resignation."

She bit down on her lush lower lip, obviously feeling sorry for him.

Grinding his teeth, Luke downed the rest of his beer. "I think I'm done here. Are you going to catch a ride with Clay?"

Her soft expression and boo-hoo eyes hardened instantly. "Sure."

Luke hated himself for hurting her, even though it was for her own good. If they slept together again, he wouldn't be able to remain emotionally uninvolved. Hell, he was *already* stuck on her, and the intensity of his feelings rattled him more than he cared to admit.

Besides, he couldn't do right by her unless he decided to stay.

Feeling like a lowlife, a user, and a jerk, he stood to leave, walking away from her at the same time Jesse Ryan came through the door.

Whenever Shay thought a situation couldn't get any worse, her ex-boyfriend showed up to prove her wrong.

Jesse stopped in his tracks at the front entrance, feet braced wide. He looked from her to Luke, nostrils flaring, dark hair falling over one eye. The belligerent, combative expression on his face was one Shay knew all too well.

He was the last person she wanted to see right now, the last man she would use to make Luke jealous, and the last human being on earth she felt like putting her arms around. Even so, that was exactly what she did, for the alternative would have surely involved bloodshed.

"How've you been?" she whispered in Jesse's ear, giving him a tight hug. This close, she could smell the alcohol on his breath. For a moment, she thought the ruse had worked, that he'd been placated by her embrace, but then he looked down at her feet and frowned, noticing something amiss.

In heels, she was taller than him.

Jesse moved his bleary gaze from her bare legs to Luke's face. "I heard you'd been giving the new sheriff a helluva warm welcome."

It was none of his business, and it hadn't been for a long time, but Shay didn't say that. She placed her hand on Jesse's cheek, turning his head back toward her. "Don't worry about him. He was just leaving."

But Luke wouldn't leave, and Jesse wouldn't listen. He'd come to the Round-Up looking for trouble, and wouldn't be satisfied until he found it. Annoyed with her for getting in his way, Jesse pushed her aside with more force than was necessary. Shay stumbled backward, none too steady on high heels and a bruised knee.

Jesse had never hurt her physically, and he probably hadn't intended to this time, but if Clay hadn't been standing right there, Shay would have fallen down hard.

Luke had seen enough. "That's it," he said, grabbing Jesse by the back of the shirt. Collaring him like a wayward schoolboy, Luke shoved him out the door. "You're under arrest for being drunk in public, assaulting a woman . . ."

From the dark parking lot, she could hear the sound of shuffling feet on loose gravel, followed by a sharp knock and a heavy thud.

Shay and Clay, along with a few others, rushed out to see what had happened. Jesse was laid out on the ground, dead to the world. Luke stood over him, rubbing the knuckles on his right hand. He glanced up at the growing crowd. "He was resisting."

Clay smiled, and everyone formed a circle around Jesse. Shay let out the breath she'd been holding, feeling shaky.

"Are you all right?" Luke asked, taking her by the elbow.

"Yeah, I was just . . . worried."

Luke shrugged, looking down at Jesse's prone form. "He'll be fine."

"Not about him, you idiot."

Luke gave her an incredulous stare. "You were worried about me? He was drunk. And I'm bigger than he is."

"He doesn't always fight fair," she murmured.

"So you thought you'd help me out by putting yourself between us? That was stupid, Shay. You could have been hurt."

"I was trying to defuse the situation," she said through clenched teeth. "Next time I'll just let him have at you."

"Good," he said, as if he was looking forward to it.

Shay rolled her eyes heavenward.

The waitress brought Jesse an ice pack, cradling it against his jaw, and the rest of the patrons wandered back inside, deciding the show was over.

"You still want to arrest him?" Clay asked.

Luke deliberated, probably thinking Jesse wasn't worth the trouble.

"We have a drunk tank on the rez," Clay offered. "I could take him there for the night."

"Thanks," Luke said, nodding his agreement. "I'd like to ask him a few questions when he sobers up."

They loaded him up in the passenger seat of Clay's pickup, which took a lot of effort because Jesse was like a ton of bricks. When Clay pulled out of the parking lot, Luke said, "Come on. I'll take you home."

Shay snapped out of the daze she'd been in since Luke had knocked Jesse's lights out. Situations like this often made her feel . . . disconnected. "No thanks," she said, heart thumping with fresh indignation. "I don't need you."

Freudian slip. She'd meant to say, I don't need you *to*.

Luke's eyes darkened. "Don't be ridiculous."

In the space of five minutes, he'd rejected her, called her stupid, and told her she was ridiculous. If Shay wanted to be treated like this, she could have stayed with Jesse. Too furious to utter another word, she turned on her heel and stomped away.

When she heard him coming after her, Shay made a fist with her right hand. She'd been pushed far enough for one evening. If he grabbed her arm, she was going to deck him.

He caught up with her easily, because her shoes weren't made for wading through gravel, but he had the sense not to touch her. "What are you going to do now? Strut down Main Street like a—"

"Whore?" she said, throwing the ugly word back in his face. "Why not? That's what you think I am."

His mouth made an angry line, but he didn't dispute her.

"You sanctimonious son of a bitch," she said, stopping in her tracks. They were standing between parked cars now, his truck on her left side. "Haven't you ever heard of saying no? If you didn't want me—"

He moved so fast she didn't have time to react. "Not want you?" he growled, wrapping his arm around her waist and bringing her body flush against his. "You know goddamned well how much I want you."

Her hands, one clutching her silver purse, the other

still clenched into a fist, rested on his shoulder, ready to push him away. Any second now.

"I've wanted you from the first moment I saw you. I just wasn't interested in waiting in line to get to you."

She gasped, shoving at his chest, but he brought her even closer to him, refusing to give her room to maneuver.

"You're right," he said, struggling to keep his hold on her. "I *am* a sanctimonious son of a bitch. I've judged you unfairly from the start, and I'm sorry." His gaze moved from her trembling lips to her tousled hair. "I never thought you were a whore, but that first morning, you looked so . . . sexual. I assumed you'd been with a man the night before."

Hot color flooded her cheeks. "You're such a jerk. The only man I've been with in the past year is you."

That statement gave him pause. "Really?"

"Yes. And I'm this close to kneeing you in the groin." She held her thumb and forefinger an inch apart to demonstrate.

He loosened his grip by a margin, never taking his attention from her face. "At the time, I guess I was projecting my own thoughts onto you. Blaming you, because I wanted you so much I couldn't control myself."

Shay stared back at him, wavering.

"I still can't," he said, his eyes locked on her mouth. "I can't stop thinking about the way you feel. I can't stop remembering the way you taste."

Tears blurred her vision, because she was in the same boat. How she wanted to hate him! But every time she looked at him, she felt . . . something else. "Damn you," she whispered, lifting her lips to his.

With a low groan, he pressed her back against the side of the truck and covered her mouth with his, kissing her senseless. She dropped her purse and threw her arms around his neck. Their tongues met and tangled, hearts pounding, hands seeking. She threaded her fingers through the short hair at the nape of his neck and held on tight. It was the least graceful kiss of her life, and the most exciting. There was a lot of panting and groping and straining. Their bodies slammed into the passenger door. At one point, she may have bitten him.

When his hands found her bare bottom beneath her skirt and his button fly met the front of her thong panties, she whimpered. A little more friction and she'd explode. He put his lips to her throat and she moaned, wanting to wrap her legs around his waist and forget who she was, where they were . . . how he'd treated her.

The parking lot at the Round-Up had seen this kind of action before, but she hadn't. Although Shay had made a lot of bad choices in her life, screwing a guy up against the side of a pickup truck in a public place wasn't one of them.

"Stop," she gasped, bracing her palms on his chest.

He paused, breathing hard against her neck. Slowly, reluctantly, he let his hands fall away from her.

Pushing her hair off her forehead, she bent down, retrieving her discarded, discount-quality metallic purse from the gravel at her feet. When she straightened, he was watching her, awaiting her decision. Feeling torn, she twisted the cheap fabric in her hands, wanting to tell him to go to hell.

"Take me to Dark Canyon," she whispered instead, squaring her shoulders, meeting his eyes.

17

Dylan sat across from Angel, who was perched on the edge of his rumpled, unmade bed, and tried not to think about what they'd been doing the last time they were here together.

He was punchy from too little sleep and too much Mountain Dew, the muscles in his forearms ached from cleaning tools, and his brain was overloaded with the calc problems he would have to finish during lunch tomorrow. But his hormones were on full alert, proving he was never too tired to think about sex.

"My dad said you called."

Oh. Right. Her reason for being here had nothing to do with jumping his bones. "Yeah," he said, giving himself a mental shake. "It's kind of important."

"There's no privacy at my house. I hope you don't mind that I stopped by."

"Of course not." Clearing his throat, he told her about his interview with Luke Meza. Angel already knew about Yesenia Montes. Apparently, her dad had found the body.

"You told him I was there?" she asked, her eyes widening.

"No. Travis did."

A crease formed between her brows. "That's weird. You'd think he would want to keep that part quiet."

Dylan shrugged. "I thought you should know, in case the sheriff came to question you."

She studied him from beneath lowered lashes. "There's another reason I came over."

His heart rate kicked into overdrive. "Yeah?"

As she reached in her front pocket, he tried not to notice how snugly her jeans fit, or the way her tank top molded to her chest. Why was she wearing such figure-revealing clothes? Did she *like* torturing him?

"I was going to ask you something . . . and you can tell me to get lost, if you want to, but . . ." She let out a frustrated breath, running a hand through her hair. It was down around her shoulders tonight, a cascade of black silk. "Will you help me?"

He glanced down at the crumpled piece of paper in her other hand.

"If I ever summon up the nerve to send my song lyrics to a record label, no one will take me seriously."

Dylan felt a stab of disappointment. He wanted to be her boyfriend, not her tutor. Although he'd looked up some information about learning disabilities at school today, he wasn't all that interested in helping her. He was sick of being treated like a brain. Nor could he ignore the fact that she'd put him out like a wet dog last night, after moaning in his mouth and tangling her fingers through his hair.

"What about your brothers? Can't they read?"

Her mouth thinned with hurt, which made him feel better and worse at the same time. "Juan Carlos used to help me out a lot," she admitted, a faraway look on her face. "School was so easy for him."

Dylan nodded, remembering her brother's devious mind all too well. Juan Carlos had been almost too smart to get caught. Or perhaps getting caught had been his plan all along. He'd always wanted to leave Tenaja Falls. Right now he was probably running cons at juvenile hall, treating his counselors like marks.

"Daniel is a good student, but he's only eight. And Ricardo can't sit still to save his life. He's almost as hopeless as I am." When she ducked her head in embarrassment, her shame cut through him like a blade.

"Give it to me," he said, holding out his hand.

Unable to meet his gaze, she shoved the paper at him. "I looked up some of the words in the dictionary, but I couldn't find them all . . ."

Her handwriting was careful and deliberate, each letter painstakingly formed. She'd obviously put a lot of effort into refining her work, and although it was an improvement over the unintelligible jumble of symbols he'd seen last night, the lyrics still didn't make sense. She'd switched some words and letters around, and omitted others altogether.

"Do you know what an article is?"

She frowned. "Like, in a newspaper?"

"No, like before a noun." He pointed to the page. "Here you wrote 'She took trip to no were.' Do you mean 'She took *a* trip to *nowhere*'?"

Her lips trembled, but she nodded.

He couldn't bear to go over every mistake. There

were too many. "Just sing it to me," he said, getting out a new sheet of paper. "I'll rewrite it for you."

She took a deep, shuddering breath. "Fine."

"Haven't you ever been tested?"

"For what?"

"Learning disabilities. Dyslexia."

Her shoulders stiffened. "You think I have that?"

"I don't know."

She deliberated for a moment, and said, "I started school late, and I was . . . very quiet. The teachers thought I was having trouble learning English as a second language. They kept me in ESL for five years."

Dylan couldn't hide his surprise, because he hadn't known. They'd gone to the same elementary school, but she was a year ahead of him and they'd never had the same teachers.

"By the time I moved on to regular classes, Mama needed a lot of help at home. I was absent more and more, and able to follow along less and less. In high school, I couldn't do anything without Juan Carlos. I never turned in my homework unless he rewrote it for me."

He was floored by her admission. "That's—crazy," he sputtered. "You should have told someone. They could have helped you."

Storm clouds gathered in her dark eyes. "Who could have helped me? The teachers who assumed I couldn't speak English because of the way I look? The ones who kept passing me into the next grade even though I wasn't ready? Or the ones who didn't care if I got a good education because I'm just another poor Mexican girl, destined to end up barefoot and pregnant?"

He wasn't indifferent to her plight, nor was he naïve enough to think teachers treated all of their students equally. Tenaja Falls was no Mecca of enlightenment.

And yet, her willingness to play the martyr rankled.

"But you do speak English," he countered, "and you could have said so. If you didn't get a decent education, you have only yourself to blame."

Glaring at him, she crossed her arms over her chest, which made her breasts swell enticingly above the neckline of her top. If she hadn't continued, he might have forgotten what they were discussing altogether. "I made *sacrifices*," she hissed, "for my family. I wouldn't expect you to understand."

He pulled his gaze up to her face, too pissed off now to be distracted. "Why not? Because I have such an awesome home life?"

"No, because you're incapable of thinking about anyone besides yourself."

His jaw dropped. "That's not tr—"

"Yes it is," she said, jumping to her feet. He stood also, not about to let a short girl tower over him on his own turf. "You're so angry about your mother dying and your father leaving that you can't appreciate what you have."

"I have nothing!" he protested, throwing his arms out at his sides. She need only look around his disaster area of a room to see the proof.

"You have everything," she said, startling him with her vehemence. "You have the potential to be anything. You can leave this town and go wherever you want, do whatever you want, become whoever you want." Her voice softened once again, growing irresistibly husky.

"Do you know what I would give to have that, just for a moment? To be able to look at words and numbers and just . . . understand?"

He stared back at her in silence, thinking his intellect was as much a curse as a gift. There was so much pressure on him to live up to his "potential." What if he didn't want to be all he could be? What if he'd rather blow up the world than make it a better place?

Sometimes he wished he was normal. A high IQ and straight-A average had never won him a date, or earned him any friends at school. Everyone treated him like a leper. Even his own family.

"Do you know what I would give to have what you have?" he asked.

"What do I have?"

"A dad who cares enough to stick around," he said, swallowing past the lump in his throat. "And three brothers who would give their lives for you."

She let out a flustered breath. "Please. My brothers treat me like a maid."

"No. Juan Carlos jumped me once just for looking at you."

His statement gave her pause. "Really? I don't remember that."

He laughed and rubbed the bridge of his nose, not about to elaborate on the incident. "It's true. I had to be very careful about checking you out after that."

The corner of her mouth tipped up. "You weren't that careful."

"You're wrong," he said, disagreeing quietly. "If I'd stared at you as often as I wanted to, I'd have been beaten down on a daily basis. And if he knew what I was imagining . . . he'd have killed me."

Her smile disappeared. He didn't think she was offended by his admission, but he didn't fool himself into believing she was flattered. She'd hate him if she found out he'd seen her naked, and be disgusted by how many times he'd pleasured himself to that mental image. Dylan knew next to nothing about girls, but he was pretty sure they didn't want to be jerked off to and treated like sex objects.

Feeling heat creep up his neck, he sat back down at his desk, taking a paper and pen in hand. "What's the first line?"

She took a deep breath and sang the song again, her sexy, raspy voice vibrating down his spine like a silken caress, all the more effective a cappella. Her songwriting skills were impressive, but it was her singing that blew him away. The hairs on his arms stood up and every fiber of his being was aware of her, awakened by her, aroused by her.

As she finished the last verse, he gripped the pen so tightly that blood welled up from the fresh cut on his hand.

"What did you do to yourself?" she asked, wrapping her slender fingers around his wrist. Bringing his hand toward her, she laid it across her lap, palm up.

"Nothing," he said, sounding hoarse. "It happened at work."

"Work?"

"I got a job on the rez. Casino construction."

Her lips parted in astonishment. "You didn't."

"I did," he asserted, annoyed by her reaction.

"Oh, Dylan," she murmured, making the same face Shay had. Concern and confusion, like he'd signed up for the front line in Iraq. "You'll ruin your hands."

"I'll ruin my hands?" he repeated, angry and incredulous. "Who the fuck do you think I am, Itzhak Perlman?"

She flinched. "Who's that?"

"Never mind," he muttered, pulling away from her.

"You need a bandage."

"I can take care of myself."

"Where's the stuff? I'll do it." Undaunted by his attitude, she sashayed out of his room and into the bathroom, rifling through the medicine cabinet like she owned the place. "Ooh," she said, examining a small spray canister. "Man perfume. Where do you put this?"

He shifted in his chair. "Come here and I'll show you."

She laughed and kept looking until she found some rubbing alcohol and a liquid bandage. Intent on coddling him as if he were one of her kid brothers, she sat down on his bed and brought his hand toward her once again. "I didn't mean to imply that your hands are feminine," she murmured, cleaning the cut with a square of moistened gauze.

He sucked in a sharp breath.

"They aren't." Leaning forward slightly, she lifted his hand to her mouth and blew, drying his skin.

If she'd put her face in his lap, his reaction couldn't have been stronger. Who knew his palm was connected directly to his groin? One touch, and he was totally turned on.

"Does that hurt?" she said, lifting her head in surprise.

He realized he'd just groaned. "No," he said, clearing his throat. "Are you kidding? It feels good."

She rolled her eyes, thinking he was lying. "Don't move," she warned, applying a thin line of blue adhesive to the cut. When she lowered her head again, her soft breath fanning his skin, he held himself motionless, caught between exquisite pleasure and mild pain.

Dude. What a time to find out he was a masochist.

His excitement was impossible to miss; and the sudden tension in the room, difficult to ignore. She straightened abruptly, her gaze flying to his face. "I'm— sorry," she stuttered, dropping his hand like it was hot.

He clenched his jaw, disinclined to apologize for something he had so little control over. She knew he wanted her. If she was shocked that *blowing* on him got him all worked up, that was just too damned bad. He hadn't asked her to come over here and tease him.

But she didn't look shocked, any more than she'd looked offended when he admitted to entertaining impure thoughts about her. If anything, she seemed kind of . . . curious.

"Do you enjoy this?" he asked, an edge in his voice.

She moistened her lips. Her eyes had this smoky glaze to them, a dark heat he wanted to sink into. "Enjoy what?"

"Getting me hard? Having me lust after you?"

"No, I . . ." She trailed off, an almost indiscernible blush tainting her cheeks. On her, embarrassment looked delicious. "I enjoy being . . . desired. But I don't like your anger."

He wondered, and not for the first time, if her past experiences had caused her to be confused about her sexuality. Hell, he was confused about his, and he didn't even have any past experiences. Maybe she was afraid of him. Maybe she just wasn't ready.

He was more than ready, so ready he was about to explode. Even so, if she'd hinted that she wanted to pursue something romantic, rather than sexual, he'd have given her all the time she needed. Instead, she was gazing up at him with those sultry black eyes and "kiss me" lips, sending signals even the horniest kid in the world couldn't misinterpret.

With a Herculean effort, he tore his gaze away from her, because he was in no mood to be jerked around—encouraged and rejected—yet again.

If she'd waited another minute, he'd have walked her home, but she rushed out of his room before he'd recovered well enough to follow. And she left both copies of her lyrics on the top of his desk.

He stared at the pages for a long time, comparing his slanted scrawl to her awkward, meticulous letters until the pages blurred.

Making a strangled, furious sound, he swept his arm across the surface of his desk, clearing it. When that failed to satisfy, he stood and upended the son of a bitch, sending it careening across the room. One sharp corner tore a jagged edge in the drywall before it landed on its side, contents spilling from the drawers, littering the floor.

Angel ran blindly, tears stinging her eyes, the cool night air biting her cheeks and upper arms. She stumbled over a rock on the side of the road and almost went sprawling, but she didn't slow down until she reached the edge of her father's property.

Cutting across the yard in silence, she approached her tiny studio, tiptoeing in the dark, panting lightly.

As she put the key in the lock, someone laid a hand on her shoulder.

"*Madre de Dios,*" she blurted, almost jumping out of her skin.

Her father chuckled at her skittishness. "*Lo siento,*" he said, putting his hands up. "You are very nervous these days, *mi angelita.*"

Angelita. Little angel. She was hardly that. "No, Papá," she protested, dragging her fingers through her hair. "I was just—"

"Visiting the neighbor boy? Dylan Phillips?"

She moistened her lips, tasting salt from the tears she'd already forgotten.

"Let's talk," he said, frowning at her closed door. He'd installed the lock himself, saying a girl her age needed some privacy, and had rarely visited her here. "Do you want to go to the kitchen?"

As surreptitiously as possible, she wiped her cheeks with the back of her hand. "My room is fine." She opened the door and turned on the lamp, glad she'd had the foresight to put her bus schedules away. Gesturing toward the only chair, she took a seat on the edge of her bed, her heart pounding with trepidation.

Her dad was quiet, steady, reliable. He worked his fingers to the bone for their family and had never asked her to do the same. She couldn't imagine what he wanted to speak to her about, because he wasn't one for long, meaningful discussions. A nod or a smile was the most encouragement he gave, a simple reprimand the most punishment.

"*Qué honda?*" she murmured. What's up?

He hesitated, the corner of his mouth twitching, as if searching for the right words. Deep grooves etched into his forehead, making him appear far older than he was. "I know you have had a hard time since your mother left."

"I've been okay," she mumbled.

"Your brothers have done well. Except for Juan Carlos, of course. And Yoli hardly remembers. But you . . ." He placed his fist against the center of his chest. "*Te dueles.*"

She hurt. Fresh tears sprang into her eyes, much too easily.

"Do you know that when I saw the dead woman lying there, I thought it was you?"

She shook her head, astounded by his words.

"I knew you had gone out the night before, and when I left before dawn the next morning, you had not yet returned. I was very worried."

"I'm sorry," she whispered, hanging her head in shame.

"Do not be. You are entitled to have fun with your friends. To live a life of your own. To make your own mistakes."

When he said "mistakes," he looked into her eyes, and she knew he understood what she'd been going through better than he let on.

"I know what happens at the Graveyard, and I will not tell you what to do. But I hate to see you going with boys to fill an empty place in your heart. They will only take from you, and leave you emptier than before."

She stared down at her pointy-toed boots, unable to claim she didn't know firsthand how true his words were.

"What happened with Tony? Did he mistreat you?"

Sniffling, she shrugged her shoulders. "Not really." Tony Duran had been her boyfriend for almost three years, and in that time he'd never once raised his voice to her. He might not have ever really *noticed* her. They'd certainly never engaged in a passionate argument like she and Dylan. Nor a passionate anything else.

They'd broken up after Christmas, after Chad. She hadn't told him what she'd done, or given any reason for her decision, but he'd accepted it the way he did everything else, with neither question nor complaint. If she'd proposed marriage, his reaction might have been the same, so she didn't waste any time crying over him. It was kind of hard to feel upset about ending your relationship with a robot.

"I will buy you a car," her father decided. "I know you want to get out of the house. Now that Yoli is in school, you could get a job, or take classes at the community college."

"You can't afford to buy me a car," she protested. "The boys need new shoes, and the dryer's busted, and the hot water heater's going out. If you didn't send money to Mamá—"

His face darkened with anger, and she knew she'd gone too far. She clamped her mouth shut, but she couldn't take back those impulsive words.

"One of my customers has an old car for sale," he

continued in a tone that brooked no argument. "I will see if he is interested in trading for services."

Angel wasn't a perfect, dutiful daughter, but neither was she openly defiant. She didn't talk back to her father. Showing disrespect, in her family, wasn't an option. Although she knew he couldn't buy her a car, not even an old junker, without cutting corners elsewhere, literally taking food from her siblings' mouths, she didn't say anything more.

Nor could she tell him of her plans, because it would break his spirit, and he would never agree to let her go.

Ending the discussion, he stood slowly and shuffled out the door, moving the way he always did when his back was hurting. Like a man who'd suffered several lifetimes' worth.

Wishing circumstances were different, and that she had any other choice to make, Angel went to her wardrobe, took out her only suitcase, and began to pack.

18

Shay couldn't invite Luke back to her bedroom while her brother was home, and he couldn't sneak her into the firehouse. Booking a hotel room wasn't an option in a town as small as Tenaja Falls either, so they were going to the Visitors' Center at Dark Canyon.

It was risky, but not as risky as tearing each other's clothes off in a public parking lot.

She knew Luke only wanted her for sex, and that she was allowing him to treat her like the kind of woman he thought she was. If it was any consolation, she only wanted one thing from him, too. For the first time in a long while, she was willing to give up the standards nobody believed she had, and enjoy a man solely for his body.

And what a body it was.

She studied him as he drove along the deserted road toward Dark Canyon, eyes trailing over his flat stomach and sinewy arms, admiring the contrast between his pale gray T-shirt and bronzed skin. He handled a truck the way men did, leaning back as far as the space allowed, thighs braced wide, his right arm fully extended and his hand resting lightly on top of the wheel. After meeting up with Jesse's square-shaped face, his knuckles must be throbbing, but he didn't complain. His position was deceptively relaxed, belied only by the tenseness in his jaw and the hard line of his triceps.

Not to mention the ridge of his erection beneath his button fly.

She pulled her gaze away from the front of his jeans, uncomfortably aware of her own arousal. Her nipples strained against the soft cotton T-shirt, and between her legs she felt achy and swollen. In her heightened state of consciousness, the lacy fabric of her panties against her sensitive flesh was both pleasurable and abrasive.

She squirmed in her seat, wishing he would put his hand there. Wishing she had the nerve to put *her* hand there.

A few moments before they arrived, she unlatched her seat belt.

"You stay over there," he growled, proving he was attuned to her every move.

Smiling, she toyed with the frayed edge of her skirt, which was almost short enough to be called indecent. His eyes traveled down the length of her legs, then jerked back to the road.

Heart racing with anticipation, she reached underneath her skirt and took off her panties, careful to avoid getting the stretchy lace snagged on her high heels. He glanced at her again, eyes black with lust, nostrils flaring as if he could smell her.

Well, maybe he could. Her panties were very wet.

Scarcely able to believe her audacity, she opened her purse and dropped the lacy red thong inside, stashing it with a smart click.

He turned his attention back to driving, his expression promising he would make her pay later for taunting him.

She couldn't wait.

As soon as they pulled into the parking lot, she got out of the truck and strode toward the front entrance, keys in hand. While he stood behind her, heat coming off of him in waves, she unlocked the door to the Visitors' Center.

Dark Canyon State Preserve headquarters wasn't an ideal location for a tryst. There were shelves of informational brochures, examples of taxidermy that were as creepy as ghosts in the moonlight, and glass cases of biological items such as owl barf and coyote scat.

A romantic getaway, it was not.

Bypassing the scientific displays, she took Luke by the hand and led him back to her office. There was nothing in there but her computer desk, a couple of office chairs, and an old wool love seat, but at least they were alone.

Ignoring the overhead light, she clicked on her desk lamp, illuminating the small space with a cozy glow. When she snuck a glance at him, the look on his face was priceless. He obviously found the room lacking in sexual possibilities, and she couldn't blame him, but he was so out of his element the situation struck her as comical.

"You think too much," she decided, grabbing him by the front of the shirt. Instead of kissing him senseless, she played a bit coy, nibbling her way across his jaw. When he tried to capture her mouth with his, she pulled her head away, teasing him. His eyes flashed with pique. And arousal.

With no panties on, she could feel moisture slicking her inner thighs. Wanting more freedom, more reaction, more sensation, she stepped back and took off her shirt, dragging the soft cotton over her aching nipples as she bared her breasts.

He didn't blink once.

Smiling, she wiggled her tiny skirt down her hips and stood brazenly before him, clad in high heels and her birthday suit.

His gaze seared her skin, lingering on her breasts and between her legs, making her body throb in response. But he must have known intuitively that she wanted to be in control, because instead of reaching for her, he curled his hands into fists.

She circled him slowly, watching his throat work as she made her perusal. She liked this. Driving him crazy. Making him sweat. Standing directly behind him, she pulled up the back of his shirt, stripping it over his head and tossing it aside.

He arched a glance over his shoulder, obviously uncomfortable with the position. Even so, he held himself motionless while she slid her hands up the length of his spine, her fingertips playing over taut muscle and smooth skin. His body was a study in strength and definition, every inch of it lean and powerful and perfectly toned. He had these sexy indentations at his lower back, and a very cute, very tight butt.

Murmuring her approval, she sank her hands into

his back pockets and kissed the spot between his shoulder blades.

Feeling a rough place beneath her lips, she frowned. "What's this?" she asked, taking her hands out of his pockets and running her fingertips over the scratches.

"You did that."

"Oh." She had a vague recollection of sinking her nails into his hard flesh. "Sorry."

He shrugged, making all those gorgeous muscles dance. "Don't be. I enjoyed it."

Her throat went dry. Heart thumping, she slid her arms around his waist, flattening her breasts against his back and letting her hands drift down his front. "Do you have a condom this time?"

"In my pocket."

Rather than looking for it, she found his erection, surging under the flat of her palm. Her breath hitching, she released the buttons on his fly one by one. Unable to resist, she nipped at his shoulder and moved her hands from front to back once again, burying them in the waistband of his shorts and giving his bare butt an exploratory squeeze.

With a low growl, he turned on her, grabbing her hands by the wrists and jerking them out of his pants. She thought he was going to lift her up against the nearest flat surface and have at her, a move she would have gone along with enthusiastically. Instead, he dipped his head to kiss her, holding her arms behind her back and tangling his tongue with hers, making love to her mouth rather than her body.

After a long moment, he raised his head, his gaze raking over her flushed face as if he wanted to commit every line and curve to memory. Startled by his intensity, she stared back at him in confusion, moistening her throbbing lips.

He was doing this wrong. This was supposed to be about casual sex, pure pleasure, a simple physical connection. But the way he was looking at her . . .

Covering her mouth with his once again, he backed her toward the love seat in the far corner. She smiled against his lips as he perched her on the edge and settled himself between her legs, his knees sinking into the seat cushions at her feet.

This was more like it.

When he released her wrists, she arched against him, desperate for him to suit up and get on with the show. But his eyes slid down her body and his hands took a leisurely path over her hips, setting a different pace.

Shay had never begged a man for anything in her life, but she found herself saying, "Please," in this embarrassingly high-pitched whimper.

Smiling, he bent his head to her, wetting one nipple with his tongue, then the other.

Her inner muscles clenched with longing. "Please, Luke," she panted. "I'm going to ruin the couch."

His gaze lingered on her nipples for another moment before lowering to the other place, where she was wet and pulsing with sensation. "It isn't worth saving," he murmured, moving his mouth down her belly.

"Oh, no," she moaned, bracing her hands by her sides. She couldn't maintain a semblance of control if he kissed her there. She was hanging on by a thread already . . .

He parted her slippery folds with his fingertips,

exposing the taut pink bud of her clitoris and tasting her hungrily.

She cried out, gripping the edge of the love seat and spreading her legs wide, beyond decorum, beyond shame. "Luke," she pleaded, watching his tongue flick hotly against her. At the same time, he sank two fingers deep inside her.

It was good. It was way too good. It was so good she couldn't hang on a moment longer. "Oh, *yes*," she gasped, moving her hands from her sides to bury them in his short hair, holding him there, holding him *right there* while she dissolved in pleasure.

When the world wavered back into focus, Luke was in front of her, stretching a condom over his jutting erection.

Shay blinked a few times, studying him unabashedly. She'd seen him in the dark and felt him in her hand, among other places, but she hadn't really looked her fill. "Hello there," she murmured, reacquainting herself with his manliest of parts.

With a chuckle that sounded pained, he placed the blunt tip of his penis against her, reacquainting her further. She was swollen and slick, still in the flush of orgasm as he slid into her, and so sensitive she felt every inch.

He caught her gaze and held it, gauging her response.

"More," she said, winding her arms around his neck. "More," she said, brushing her lips over his.

His control broke. This time, he took her mouth and her body, thrusting deep and plunging in, filling her everywhere at once. His hands knew all of her feminine secrets and his lips tasted of her musk. He wasn't tender, driving her hard against the wall behind her back and angling her hips up to meet his thrusts, but he was thorough. And he felt so good that tears leaked from the corners of her eyes.

The pegs underneath the love seat scraped along the tile floor and the couch springs groaned in protest.

She thought their first time together had been phenomenal, but this was better. He was still doing it wrong, making too much eye contact, as if he wanted to see the ecstasy on her face while he worshipped her with his cock. He was still too demanding, wringing every drop of pleasure from her, owning her response. There was too much mouth to mouth and skin on skin. But, oh, God, did he make doing it wrong feel right.

She clung to him, pressing her lips to his neck to muffle her scream as she climaxed again. With a muttered curse, he cupped her buttocks and jerked her toward him, penetrating her so deeply she felt as though he wanted to pierce her soul. His body convulsed as he spent himself inside her. Shoulders trembling, he collapsed against her, a bead of sweat trickling down his well-muscled back.

Shay never imagined she would enjoy having a man pant and heave and sweat all over her. After Jesse finished, she'd always wanted him to leave. Immediately, if not sooner. With Luke, she was struck by the urge to stroke his hair and talk drowsy nonsense. She wouldn't mind if he fell asleep on top of her. She wanted him to stay inside her forever.

Realizing her feelings for him went deeper than she'd thought, she panicked, squirming underneath him, pushing at his shoulders. He lifted himself up at once and withdrew from her carefully. She scrambled away from him, gathering up her discarded clothes and hurrying to the ladies' room, hoping to wash away her sullied emotions.

She put on her clothes and stood before the mirror in the darkened room, feeling raw and naked and over-exposed. Studying her reflection was a mistake. Her eyes sparkled with intensity and her cheeks were bright with color.

Taking a deep breath, she returned to the office, preparing to hurt him before he could do the same to her.

One glance at his conflicted face calmed her as nothing else could have. She wasn't going to have to do anything. He was about to ruin it all on his own.

Adding a swagger to her walk, which was difficult on unsteady legs, she tossed her hair over her shoulder and bent to pick up her purse, giving him a sexy show that was part bravado, part façade. On the inside, she was crying.

He ran his fingers through his short hair, and she was struck by the impression that he wanted to apologize for the way he'd taken her. Deep down, he was a gentleman, one who didn't lose his inhibitions any more often than he lost his self-control.

"This morning, in the cave . . . I acted like an ass, and I'm sorry."

She crossed her arms over her chest, accepting his apology with a terse nod. Then she glanced at the clock above his head and manufactured a short yawn.

His eyes narrowed. "I know I said I wasn't looking for a relationship—"

"Neither am I," she interrupted. "Don't worry about it."

"I don't have the best track record with women."

She almost choked on her surprise. Luke Meza was admitting he'd made mistakes *and* that he had relationship issues? Wonders would never cease. Leaning her hip against the desk, she plucked at an invisible piece of lint on her skirt, trying to look bored. "Let me guess. Some bad girl broke your heart."

"She wasn't bad," he admitted, studying her face. "More like troubled."

It didn't take a genius to figure out he thought the same of her, and she didn't want to hear any more. She didn't need him psychoanalyzing her. And her blood boiled with jealousy at the thought of him with another woman, this sultry siren who'd done him wrong.

"She worked at a strip club."

Her mouth fell open.

"As a waitress," he clarified, smiling a little. "And no, I didn't approve. She kept it from me. I didn't find out until after we moved in together."

A liar and a slut, a catty voice inside her head whispered. "Hmm," she said aloud.

"She also did drugs. I didn't know about that until too late, either."

"Too late?"

"After we broke up."

Judging by his expression, his girlfriend's drug habit was something he felt responsible for. "So you found out she worked at a strip club and kicked her out on the streets?"

"Of course not," he said with a frown. "I didn't like

that she'd lied to me about her job, but the tips were good and she was putting herself through college. We argued about it, sure, and then we . . . made up."

In bed. She felt a sharp tug in the middle of her chest, like a twisting knife.

"I bought her a ring. I thought she'd let me pay for her classes if we got married."

"You were in love with her?" she asked, her voice steady.

He shrugged, as if the question didn't bother him. "I thought so. But I was young and stupid and unrealistic. I wanted her to fit an ideal." His eyes met hers, and Shay knew he was comparing her with his ex again. "She wouldn't have."

"Did you propose?"

"No. The night I planned to, she called and said she had to work late. I was pissed off and spoiling for a fight. I went to the club and found one."

"With her?"

"Not exactly. She was waiting on a group of college kids. I'd been watching her all night, counting every drink she peddled, every smile she gave, every tip she collected. Acting like a jealous fool. When one of the guys copped a feel, I lost it."

"You hurt him?"

"Nah. The bouncer pulled me away from him before I did any permanent damage. But she . . . we . . . it was never the same between us. She thought I didn't trust her and she was right. I didn't ask her to marry me, but I did ask her to quit. She refused." He rubbed a hand over his shadowed jaw, looking every bit as drained as Shay felt. "After that, she was home less and less. She started staying out all night and skipping her classes, sleeping all day. Eventually, she moved out . . . and I moved on."

"How long ago was this?"

"Ten years."

"You feel responsible for a girl who lied to you and left you *ten years ago*?"

"She died of a drug overdose last year. I was called in to identify the body." He swallowed hard, his eyes bleak. "They found my name in her emergency contact info. Yeah, it was ten years ago, but I was the only person who cared about her. It was ten years ago, but I was the only one she ever trusted."

Tears burned in her own eyes. "Why are you telling me this?"

"Because I knew you'd understand. Sometimes we feel responsible for things that are beyond our control."

He was talking about her mother. Not fair.

Giving her another pointed glance, he added, "And sometimes we have to let go in order to move on."

She sputtered, incredulous. "You haven't moved on!"

"You're right," he admitted. "I've dated other women, but I haven't put much effort into making it last. In fact, I've actively avoided anyone who seemed . . . needy."

She felt the color drain from her cheeks. "Is that what you think I am?"

He had the nerve to laugh. And the wherewithal to step out of striking range. "No," he said, sobering. "You're the first one who's made me feel like moving on."

She gripped the purse in her hands until her knuckles went white. It was appalling how much she wanted to believe him, to let go of her hang-ups and throw herself into his arms. Being this vulnerable terrified her, however, and she'd been hurt by men far too often. "Let's not make this more complicated than it is," she urged. "You're lots of fun when you take your clothes off, but I never said I wanted to get serious. And the only moving on you'll be doing is when you leave town."

A muscle in his jaw ticked as he weighed her words. "I won't share you," he said quietly, looking into her eyes.

His possessiveness warmed her, scared her, confused her. She shook the feeling away, struggling to remain aloof.

"Are you still in love with Jesse?"

"That's none of your business," she said, her heart racing with anxiety. "This morning you said you didn't want me! You can't just—change your mind about us, and notify me afterward. I'm not your doormat, Luke. And I'm not your girlfriend."

He shoved his hands into his front pockets, a scowl darkening his face. "What if I said I would stay?"

The center dropped out of her stomach. It took her a moment to compose herself, to push aside her emotions and reassemble her defenses. "Don't bother to make empty promises," she said, a thousand past disappointments making her voice gritty. "This is Tenaja Falls. No one with a lick of sense ever stays."

19

Luke was back at Dark Canyon with Shay, lost in sensation once again, gritting his teeth in pleasure at the feel of her slick heat around him, her cushiony hips in his hands, and her soft, wet mouth under his.

When he lifted his gaze to her face, he saw Leticia instead of Shay, her head listing to one side, eyes hollow, skin gray. He pulled away from her in dismay.

That disturbing scene dissolved into another.

He was walking down a long, dark hallway, his footsteps echoing loudly. Urged forward against his will, he opened the door to the morgue and approached a shrouded form on a stainless steel exam table. Reaching out with a shaking hand, he uncovered her face. The dead woman on the table wasn't Leticia, or even Yesenia Montes. It was Shay. Bloody and broken, her slender neck gouged by monster teeth.

He jerked awake with a start.

Wilson Dawes, one of the rookie firemen Luke had been sharing quarters with, was hovering over him, cordless phone in hand. "It's for you."

He sat up and took the receiver, remembering that

his cell phone was still out of order. Wilson had caught him in an awkward moment, sweating, panting . . . and fully aroused.

Jesus Christ. This was great fodder for his next psych eval. His cock didn't know the difference between a sex dream and a nightmare.

"Thanks," he said in a hoarse voice, adjusting the blanket around his waist. Either Dawes didn't notice or wasn't fazed, because he lumbered away with a sleepy yawn, unself-conscious in his own underwear.

Luke lifted the phone to his ear. "Meza."

"We have another body." It was Clay Trujillo.

He straightened, shaking off the remnants of the dream. "Attacked by a lion?"

Pause. "No."

His heart jumped into his throat. "Who is it?"

"Bull Ryan."

Holy hell. Luke hadn't been in town long, but he knew Bull was the owner of Tenaja Building Company. He was also Jesse Ryan's father. And Clay's.

The deputy wouldn't have woken him up unless the circumstances were suspicious. This was a wrongful death investigation.

"You shouldn't be there," Luke said cautiously.

"I know."

"Where is it?"

"On the new construction site."

That was reservation land, out of his jurisdiction. "You call in the FBI?"

"Yeah, but they won't get here for a while and . . . we thought you should see this."

He was already on his feet. "I'll be there in ten minutes."

It took him more like fifteen, but he drove as fast as he dared along the deserted dirt road. By the time he arrived at the site, the morning sun was peeking over the edge of the horizon. A small group of construction workers was gathered around a collection of beat-up trucks in the gravel parking lot.

Two tribal police SUVs blocked the exit. Samson Mortero stood guard next to them, his rifle turned up toward the pink-blue sky.

Luke parked alongside the other vehicles and nodded at Samson, who allowed him to walk past without a word. There was a definite advantage to working with other Indians on a sensitive case. They weren't likely to run their mouths about the details.

A group of construction workers waited on the sidelines, shifting their feet restlessly and talking amongst themselves in Spanish. Luke continued on to the office trailers, where Clay and Chief Mortero were waiting for him.

The chief greeted him somberly, as expressionless as ever. Clay looked as though he was trying to remain calm, but he was a young man in a grueling situation. He wasn't able to keep the anger, or the suspicion, off his face.

"Go take a look," he bit out, jerking his chin toward the open trailer door.

Luke did, stepping into the small office lightly, careful not to touch or disturb any of the evidence. There was a lot of it. Papers strewn across the room. Files ransacked. Chairs overturned.

Bull Ryan lay facedown in the middle of the floor. He couldn't have been there long, probably since quitting time the day before, but the smell of death was overwhelming and would only get worse as the day grew warmer.

There was no blood, no gunshot wound, no knife sticking out of his back.

The only injury, as far as Luke could tell, was at the top of his head. His scalp had been lacerated and was hanging at an odd angle, like a misplaced flap.

Now Luke understood Clay's fury. It flowed through him as well, cold and deliberate, hardening his heart and icing his veins.

Bull Ryan had been *scalped*.

Luke knew immediately that his people were not responsible for this. The Luiseño had never practiced scalping. None of the California Indians had.

Nor did Bull appear to have died from the injury. There was almost no blood, indicating that the wound had been inflicted postmortem. Whoever did this scalped Bull Ryan after they killed him.

The idea that someone would defile a corpse this way chilled and disgusted him. The fact that they had done so with the clear intention to cast suspicion upon, and aspersions toward, his own culture, enraged him.

It was difficult to stay in the room without flying off the handle, to continue his silent examination when he wanted to shout in anger, but Luke kept a quiet front. The evidence would have to be gone over with a fine-tooth comb, and he was sure the FBI would be meticulous. They might be condescending and culturally insensitive, but they were always meticulous.

For now, Luke limited himself to studying the piece of paper clasped in Bull's dead hand. It appeared to be an employment application. Crouching down, he nudged the top of the page with his penlight, revealing a young man's slanted scrawl:

Dylan Phillips.

"Fuck," he muttered, standing abruptly. Shit piled on top of shit.

Outside the trailer, Chief Mortero studied him dispassionately and Clay looked as though he was ready to throw down.

Luke had a flash of intuition. Clay Trujillo didn't think one of his own people was responsible for this . . . cultural mutilation. He thought *Luke* had done it.

"You got something to say to me?" he asked Clay.

Chief Mortero raised his dark brows. "This is a conversation . . ." he trailed off, nodding toward the group of workers in the near distance, ". . . not meant to carry on the wind."

Luke agreed one hundred percent. He pointed at Clay. "Let's take a walk."

Clay followed him readily but Chief Mortero stayed behind, which was even better. Luke didn't want anyone to come between his fists and Clay's face.

"You can't think I had anything to do with that," he said as soon as they were out of earshot, standing on a clearing of sandy, hard-packed dirt.

"You're an outsider. And an Indian." He squinted at Luke's neatly pressed clothes and close-cropped hair. "Sort of."

Luke saw red. It was the same kind of insult he'd heard throughout his childhood. *You're not Indian enough. You act too white.* Coming from a guy with blue eyes, it smarted hard. "I have more Native blood than you ever will."

Clay lifted his chin. "At least I'm proud of who I am."

Luke grabbed him by the front of his uniform. "And I'm not? Why, because I have short hair? That ponytail might have gotten you a lot of pussy in college, pretty boy, but it doesn't make you any more Indian than me."

Clay shoved him backward. "You brought this trouble, *Chief.* It followed you here."

"I didn't bring shit," he returned, standing his ground. "This town was already fucked up when I came."

"Oh, yeah? I heard there was a hit on you."

Luke's blood ran cold. "Who told you that?"

"Mike Shepherd."

Christ. There truly were no secrets in Tenaja Falls. "The guys in Vegas wouldn't mess around with fires or cryptic signs. They'd just shoot me in the head and be done with it."

"Why didn't they do that the first time?"

Luke had considered this question before. A bullet-proof vest was not an inconspicuous accessory. "Maybe they wanted me gone, not necessarily dead."

"Mission accomplished."

"Yeah," he said dismissively, no longer bitter about the turn of events.

"We don't want you here, either. Take your bad vibes somewhere else."

This community didn't want him? How ironic. But Luke was damned if he was going to let anyone tell him he couldn't stay. "I have no motive to harm Bull Ryan. You, on the other hand, are his estranged son."

"I prefer the term *unacknowledged*," he said, his voice dripping sarcasm.

Luke studied his tense face, knowing Clay was struggling to hide how much being illegitimate bothered him. "Does Jesse know you're in love with his wife?"

Clay's mouth twisted bitterly, but he made no reply.

"Maybe I'll ask him myself."

"You do that."

Luke felt some of his anger seep away, because he could empathize with Clay. Although Bull hadn't treated him like a son, Clay mourned the loss all the same. Luke knew how that was. He missed his own father, a man who'd never really been there for him and still wasn't.

"Is Jesse at the station?"

Clay nodded. "Sleeping like a baby."

"I'll meet you over there," Luke said. "But first, I'm going to send Garrett out to pick up someone. A person of interest."

"Who?"

"Dylan Phillips."

Dylan arrived at school dead tired. He hadn't slept well last night, after Angel left, and he hadn't slept at all the night before.

As soon as he got home from work tonight, he was going straight to bed.

He stopped by the vending machines on the way to his locker and bought a twenty-ounce bottle of Mountain Dew. Chugging it, because he needed the caffeine rush before his first-period class, he made his way through the teeming masses, shouldering past giggling cheerleaders and raccoon-eyed Goths.

He entered his locker combination and opened it automatically, going through the motions. The sugary soft drink was already kicking in, rousing him from his zombielike state. When he saw what was pasted inside his locker, the green plastic bottle slipped from his hand, hitting the ground at his feet and spraying sticky yellow liquid all over his Vans.

Ignoring the mess, he reached out to grab the picture.

It was a graphic, full-color shot, totally Not Safe for School, obviously printed out from a porn site on the Internet. The woman in the photo had her hand between her splayed legs, fingers spreading herself open, showing everything she had to offer.

Her body was that of a stranger, but her head, obviously applied by Photoshop, belonged to Shay.

Rage swept through him at the sight. Although the cut-and-paste job was good, he recognized the photo of Shay that had been superimposed over the porn star's face. It had been taken during a backyard BBQ at the Pinter residence on Chad's seventeenth birthday.

"Motherfucker," he muttered, crushing the printout in his hands.

Down the hall, there was a burst of male laughter. Dylan looked their way, only to see Chad with a group of his football buddies, all holding copies of the same picture. When Chad was sure he had Dylan's attention, he leaned forward and licked the page.

"Motherfucker," he said again, through clenched teeth.

Chad laughed and disappeared down the hall with his friends, who were making rude jokes and clapping him on the back.

By the time the bell rang, Dylan still hadn't moved. He was standing at his open locker door, shaking with anger, the fake picture of his sister crumpled in his fist.

He felt like he was going to explode.

He wanted to blow something apart.

There were no incendiary devices in his locker, because he wasn't that stupid, but there were plenty of dangerous materials in the chemistry lab. He pictured breaking the glass case in Mr. Richards' office, stealing a shitload of stuff, and rigging a homemade bomb to put inside Chad's locker.

In this fantasy, severed limbs and general mayhem ensued. Followed immediately by his arrest, expulsion, and incarceration.

"Damn it," he breathed, knowing he couldn't go that route.

He couldn't even fight Chad the old-fashioned way, mano a mano, at least not on school grounds, without getting into trouble with the law.

After taking a few deep breaths to calm his fury, it occurred to him that he didn't need to use chemical warfare or even his fists. He didn't have any explosives on him, but he did have a buck knife. He'd thought it might come in handy at the job site this afternoon, or he wouldn't have brought the contraband item to school.

Now he would use it to exact some revenge.

Going to class was out of the question in his volatile state of mind, so he shut his locker and picked up his soda. It was still half full. Lifting the bottle to his mouth with one hand, he shoved the picture into his pocket with the other, continuing down the hall and across the quad, making his way out to the parking lot and walking off school grounds.

After breakfast, Angel sent Yoli and Daniel out to wait for the school bus. "I want to talk to you for a minute," she said, putting her hand on Ricardo's shoulder before he could follow them.

Ricky was twelve, much too young for the burden she was about to put on him. His brown eyes darted back and forth as the wheels in his mind turned, considering what kind of trouble he'd gotten into lately.

It must have been bad, because his shoulders slumped forward and he nodded, taking a seat on the couch, resigned to his fate.

She smiled at his antics, although her heart was breaking. "Now that Juan Carlos is gone, you're the man of the house. Besides Dad, I mean."

He narrowed his eyes. Ricky wasn't good in school, but he was street smart and sharp. "I guess so," he said. He probably didn't want the role, or to take on any new responsibilities.

Too bad.

"I need you to take care of Daniel and Yoli."

He leapt to his feet. "*Ya los cuido!*" he protested, tapping his thin chest. *I already do.*

She glanced out the window, making sure her brother and sister hadn't overheard. Daniel was a quiet, sensitive boy, and he wouldn't take the news of her leaving well. Ricky was more like Juan Carlos, fiercely independent and ready to take on the world.

Yoli, in particular, would be devastated.

She hated the thought of her sister crying herself to sleep at night, like Angel had done so often after her mother left. Yoli had shared a bed with Angel for the first four years of her life, and had been more like a daughter to her than a sister. Angel's arms ached at the thought of not being there to comfort her, to hold her when she got hurt, to hug her close and smell her hair, to kiss the curls on top of her sweet head. Tears spilled down her cheeks.

She brushed them away impatiently.

"You're leaving," Ricky accused.

"I'm getting a job."

"You can get a job here."

Sure she could. Waiting tables at Esperanza's until she was twenty-one and serving drinks at the Round-Up after that. Or she could skip those middle steps and move right into the position Yesenia Montes had just vacated.

The job she planned on doing in Las Vegas wasn't much better, but at least she wouldn't be shaming her family while living under her father's roof. And what other options were available for an uneducated girl with no job skills? She could work in a fast food restaurant or as a maid, and only make enough money to cover her own expenses.

If she could do it any other way, she would.

She took her brother by the hand. "I'm doing this for you guys. The money I send back will help Dad pay the bills."

He glowered at her, trying to jerk his hand away.

"I have to go today," she said, almost choking on the words. "Tell Yoli and Daniel I love them. And know that I love you."

His face darkened with resentment. "If you loved us, you would stay."

Agony washed over her. "Please," she whispered, holding his hand, squeezing it tight. "Don't say anything until tonight."

He nodded once and she released him. Without another word, he ran out the door and across the front yard, meeting Yoli and Daniel by the side of the road. Angel went to stand at the window, waiting there until the bus came, like she always did.

When Yoli turned and waved, like she always did, flashing her gap-toothed smile, Angel felt her heart tear in two. She lifted her hand and waved back, like she always did, and as soon as the bus pulled away, she sank to the floor in the living room and cried.

She cried for her mother, who'd brought a new baby into the world even though she couldn't take care of her other five children. She cried for her father, who'd never gotten over her mother, even though she wasn't worthy of his love. She cried for Juan Carlos, whose criminal career was probably flourishing in juvenile hall, and for Ricky, who rarely had good days at school and wouldn't have one today.

And finally, she cried for her little sister, who needed her most.

When she was done she felt worse instead of better, but she deserved that. She chased down an aspirin with a Coke and spent a few moments resting with a wet washcloth over her swollen eyes. After some of the tightness in her chest eased, she got up and started cleaning. She wanted the house to be perfect before she left.

Soon the breakfast dishes were put away, the laundry was done, the floors were swept and the counters cleared. Her ride wouldn't come for a few more hours, and she was too antsy to sit still. To kill some more time, she went to her studio to get ready.

She showered and dressed and applied her makeup with shaking hands. Nothing too heavy, just a little mascara and a touch of lip gloss. She wanted to get hired, but she wasn't a tramp. Not yet. Besides, men liked young, innocent-looking women, did they not?

Unable to meet her eyes in the mirror, she left the bathroom. For the third time in four days, someone startled her on her own turf. Dylan Phillips burst through the front door of her bedroom and pulled it shut behind him.

"Snell's after me," he panted, bracing his back against the door. A pulse beat rapidly at the base of his throat. "He just stopped at my house."

"What did you do?"

He gulped and shook his head, refusing to tell her.

"Oh, Dylan," she said in an admonishing tone, moving toward the window. If he got arrested again he'd be leaving Tenaja Falls the same way Juan Carlos had, in the back of a police car. Sure enough, Deputy Snell was driving his black-and-white cruiser along Calle Remolino, slowing down in front of her house. He must not have seen Dylan come this way, because instead of parking at the curb, he floored the engine and took off.

"He's gone," she said, turning back to Dylan.

He sank to a sitting position against the door, relief washing over his fine features. He was kind of sweaty, and his thin cotton T-shirt clung to the lean muscles in his chest. "Sorry. I didn't mean to bust in on you like that."

It was her turn to shrug.

His eyes cruised over her. "Where are you going?"

"Nowhere," she said quickly.

"You look pretty."

She warmed at the compliment. "Thanks." Nice clothes were a luxury the Martinez clan couldn't afford, but she was wearing her newest jeans and a slinky purple top. It was cut lower than her usual style, revealing the V between her breasts. His gaze lingered there, and she went from warm to hot.

Suddenly, she knew exactly what she wanted to do to kill the time.

Dylan was a convenient distraction, but he was also the only boy she'd ever really wanted to sleep with. Her experience with Chad had been more about punishment than pleasure, and her embraces with Tony had never ventured beyond a chaste kiss.

Her pulse pounded at the thought of being with Dylan before she left. This was her last chance. Her last choice.

Although she was far from worldly, she knew that taking off her clothes for strange men would change her as a person. The idea of letting them ogle her naked body made her feel dirty.

Dylan made her feel . . . sexy. Wanted. Beautiful.

This might be her last opportunity to be with him,

or anyone, before she became jaded. She might not ever see him again. She might not ever see herself.

The misery she felt a few short hours ago didn't disappear, but it receded into the background, replaced by a weighty feeling of power and a comforting physical excitement. Her chest rose and fell with every breath, holding his attention.

Unlike her oblivious ex-boyfriend, Dylan Phillips was easily captivated.

There was also something different about him today. Normally, he kept his eyes on her face, only letting them drop to her chest when he thought she wasn't looking. She didn't know what he'd done to get in trouble with the law, and she didn't really care, but it must have been pretty bad. It seemed as though his wild, defiant side had taken over, and he was staring at her openly, not bothering to hide his desire.

She moistened her lips slowly and fidgeted with the spaghetti strap of her tank top, tracing the bodice with one fingertip. "Do you want to sit on my bed?"

His gaze jumped back up to hers. Although it was obvious he wanted her, he was tired of getting jerked around. The sexual glaze in his eyes didn't clear; it just took on a more predatory edge. "Only if I get to fuck you on it."

A thrill raced through her at his words. She knew he was insulting her, repaying her for toying with him one too many times. The last thing he expected was for her to agree to his terms. "Okay," she said anyway, doing exactly that.

20

Dylan regretted the words the instant they flew out of his stupid mouth. He liked Angel, he respected her, and he was maybe even halfway in love with her. Instead of letting her know he had real feelings for her, he blurted out that sex-crazed crap?

And she said . . . okay? He must be losing his mind. "Okay?" he repeated, thinking he'd fantasized her response.

She nibbled on her lush lower lip, torturing him. "Yeah. But just this once."

He was already up and across the room, shrugging out of his backpack. "Why?"

She sat down on the bed, stretching her arms out behind her and bracing her palms on the surface. The position lifted her breasts, causing the impressive swells to strain against the edge of her top. "Because I want to."

His throat went dry and his hands itched to touch her. Rubbing his sweaty palms against his jeans, he took a seat beside her. "I mean, why only once?"

"I have my reasons."

Call him insane, but he was kind of reluctant. He'd

been obsessing about this moment for the past four years. Dirty-dream sequences and *Penthouse Forum* scenarios aside, he'd always figured he'd have to talk her into it. "Is it because you're ashamed to be seen with me?"

Her eyes softened. "No. I'd be proud to be your girl."

"Then why—"

"Shh," she said, putting her fingertip against his lips. "I don't want to talk."

He didn't understand her, or even really believe her, but when she continued to touch his lips, tracing them lightly and staring at his mouth as if there was something interesting about it, all of the blood in his head went south, robbing him of the ability to think. And when she leaned toward him, brushing her thoroughly delicious lips over his completely unremarkable ones, any second thoughts he'd been entertaining fled.

By the way she plastered herself against him, clutching the front of his shirt, he was pretty sure she didn't want to take it slow. He did, so he put his hands on her hips and held her back a little. Using one of the techniques she taught him, he tugged her lower lip into his mouth, sucking gently.

She made a low, urgent sound, somewhere between a growl and a moan, and shoved at his shoulders.

He released her immediately.

She pushed him down on the bed and climbed on top of him, straddling his hips. The proof of his arousal was right there, pulsing against her, and he knew she could feel it, because she rubbed herself along him, her dark eyes burning into his.

And as if that weren't enough to send him over the edge, she lifted her shirt and tossed it aside.

"Oh my God," he groaned. Her bra was black as sin and twice as sexy, her pinup model breasts threatening to spill over the lacy cups. Not sure if he wanted to stop her or encourage her to keep moving, he gripped her slim hips. "You're killing me."

She smiled and tugged on his T-shirt. He leaned forward, helping her take it off, and when his bare chest met her luscious breasts, he knew he'd died and gone to heaven.

His mouth sought hers, and he was no longer interested in, or capable of, taking it slow. He deepened the kiss and thrust his lower body against hers, intent on penetrating every part of her he could get access to. He wanted to touch every part of her, and taste it, too, so he reached for her breasts. "Oh, God," he repeated, enraptured by the feel of all that soft, lace-encased flesh in his hands. Her nipples burned into the centers of his palms.

"Dylan," she said, covering his hands with hers and squeezing harder.

He didn't know how to take her bra off, and he wasn't even going to try. Instead he touched his lips to her bare shoulder, delighting in the way she shivered, and nudged the silky black strap aside. It slipped down, hanging in a sexy loop on her upper arm. He pushed the other strap off her shoulder, but the cups of her bra stayed up.

He frowned, trying to make it disappear with his eyes.

With a breathy laugh, she threaded her fingers

through his short hair and brought his mouth back to hers. They tangled together, tongues and hands and bodies. For a moment, he was lost in a round of frantic kissing and fervent groping, reveling in the heat of her mouth and the soft weight of her body flexing against his. Her bra didn't disintegrate, but he was able to get the lacy cup down far enough that her nipple popped free. Mesmerized by the sight, he leaned forward and wet the dusky tip with his tongue.

She moaned, tightening her grip on his hair.

It hurt. And he loved it.

Panting, he pushed down the fabric covering her other nipple and repeated the action, looking for the same response. He got it. Moaning and hair-pulling.

Jesus God.

She smelled so . . . womanly, like rose-scented soap and freshly washed hair, and her skin was so . . . warm. He buried his face between her breasts and tightened his hands on her hips, praying for strength, patience, and longevity.

"Do you have a condom?" she asked, stroking the back of his neck.

He tried to reel his brain back in. It was a monumental task. "I think so," he rasped. "I mean, yeah. It's in my wallet."

"Is it old?"

He blinked up at her. "A couple months, maybe."

She sat back and held out her palm. "Let's see it."

He kept his wallet in his front pocket because he didn't like sitting on it at school all day, so she had to lift up a little to give him access. Taking the square package out, he handed it to her, trying not to feel embarrassed about the no-frills, "one size fits all" option. Not to mention the straining erection it would soon cover. Right now his dick felt big enough to burst, but he wasn't so warped he thought he needed Magnums.

She inspected the package and nodded, apparently satisfied that the latex hadn't been disintegrating in his wallet for the past four years.

They were being responsible, and he was glad, but the short interruption had changed the dynamic between them. She nibbled at her lower lip, appearing shy and uncertain and far more innocent than her sexy body and provocative lingerie suggested.

She looked scared.

He knew exactly how she felt. "We don't have to do this," he said, clearing his throat. "I mean, I want to, obviously, but . . . I'd rather have you forever than just this once."

To his bewilderment, tears filled her eyes. She leaned forward and pressed her lips to his collarbone, her black hair spilling across his chest. "This is all I can give you, Dylan," she whispered. "Make just this once last forever."

No pressure, though.

Desperate not to disappoint her, even though he was confused by her behavior, he rolled her onto her back. He might not know anything about sex, and he would never be an expert on the female brain, but he knew what his own body was begging for. He covered her mouth with his and ground his hips against hers, trying to possess her through layers of denim.

Maddened by the restrictions, he ended the kiss. "Take off your pants."

Her eyes darkened and her breath hitched. Holding his gaze, she undid the top button on her jeans. Unable to help himself, he looked down as she lowered her zipper, revealing a strip of silky-looking skin, the pathway to heaven.

Eager to see more, he moved to the side, giving her room to maneuver.

As if she was afraid she might chicken out, she shucked out of her jeans quickly. Her panties weren't black, like her bra. Nor were they lace. They were hot pink and very sheer, showcasing the shadowy triangle between her legs.

Dylan almost swallowed his tongue. He couldn't believe this was happening. Earlier today he'd barely escaped getting hauled off to jail. And now he was in bed with a girl who looked like a *Playboy* centerfold.

"Thank you, Jesus," he breathed, beholding God's most perfect creation.

She smiled a little but still seemed nervous, so he made no move to take off her panties. He did release the buttons on his fly, because his dick was aching, and then he went ahead and shoved down the front of his boxers, because—well, fuck it.

Her eyes widened and a faint blush crept over her cheeks, but when he stretched out on top of her, she welcomed him, twining her arms around his neck. He kissed her again and let his weight bear down on her, pressing right up against the front of those pretty pink panties.

Touching her with only one gossamer barrier between them was a heady experience, the most tantalizing of his life, and it quickly proved too much for him.

Bringing his penis into play this early had been a mistake. It wanted to tear through her panties and push inside her with no further preliminaries.

Groaning, he rolled away from her.

She murmured a protest. "I was enjoying that."

He grimaced. "So was I." Too much.

When he thought he had control over himself again, he hazarded another glance at her. She was panting lightly, her eyes closed and her nipples pebbled, her breasts erotically framed by black lace.

Maybe he could do something else she enjoyed.

He slid his palm along her inner thigh until he met the edge of her panties. Through the thin fabric, he could feel how hot she was. Moisture dampened his fingertips. Amazed by physiology, high on endorphins, he cupped her gently, learning the graceful swell of her pubic bone and the slight dip of her femininity. "Tell me how to touch you."

Her eyes flew open.

"What do you like?"

"I—I don't know."

He was curious about her past sexual experiences, but he didn't want to ruin the moment by asking her too many questions. Sweat broke out on his forehead, because he wanted to make it good for her and wasn't sure how. Taking the plunge, he slipped his hand down the front of her panties, into wet curls and sleek heat.

Oh, *fuck.* He was going to come just from touching her. How did you tell a girl you couldn't wait a second longer? "I can't—"

"It's okay."

"I want to—"

"Yes."

Heart racing, pumping more blood to his already raging hard-on, he pulled away from her, fumbling with the condom as she took off her panties. As he positioned himself over her, it occurred to him that he must be dreaming. He'd never had anything but tough luck, and here he was, getting lucky with the most beautiful girl in Tenaja Falls.

Angel was splayed beneath him, eyes like black jewels, breasts provocatively displayed, her body revealed to him. Offered to him. Open to him.

He wanted to savor the moment, but he couldn't focus on anything but getting inside her. Lack of experience had him faltering a few times before he was there, sliding home inch by inch, going all the way. She felt . . . indescribable, like nothing he'd ever imagined.

"Oh, God," he moaned, knowing he was lost.

He tried to make it last forever, he really did. But natural instinct took over and he could only thrust. She wrapped her legs around his hips and her arms around his neck, digging her fingernails into his shoulders and making sexy panting sounds in his ear. Everything fell away but this moment, her body beneath his, his body inside hers. In a burst of heat and light and energy, he exploded.

Dylan wasn't sure how long he lay there, sweating all over her, smothering her, before he returned to reality.

He lifted his head to look at her. She met his gaze levelly.

It struck him that the pleasure had been completely one-sided. She didn't come. She didn't even come close.

Head spinning, he heaved himself off her and stumbled into her bathroom to get rid of the condom. He avoided glancing in the mirror, knowing he was damp-haired and red-faced, while she lay on the bed, unruffled and unaffected.

What a loser he was! A two-pump chump.

Cursing silently, he buttoned his pants and went back out to her bedroom. She'd wrapped the edge of a blanket around herself and was studying him with timid eyes, appearing far from unaffected by their encounter.

"I'm sorry," he said, feeling sick to his stomach. Sitting down on the bed beside her, he shoved his hand through his disheveled hair. "That was terrible. Worse than Chad." To his chagrin, his eyes watered and his throat closed up.

"No," she insisted, snuggling up behind him and resting her head on his bare shoulder. "It wasn't terrible. I liked it."

"All fifteen seconds?"

She smiled against his back. "Yes."

Turning, he put his arms around her and held her for a while, desperate for a chance to make it up to her. Inexplicably, he did the opposite of redeeming himself, and like the miserable excuse for a man he was, he curled up beside her and fell asleep.

When Shay arrived at Dark Canyon, there was a package waiting for her on the front step.

The post office usually delivered during regular working hours, but she hadn't been around much lately.

With a frown, she noticed there was no name or address on the top. Maybe Mike had left something for her.

She hadn't noticed it during last night's rendezvous.

Blushing, she tossed the box on the exam table inside and vowed to put Luke out of her mind. Although Mike had dropped in the day before, it wasn't his job to take care of the minor duties running a wildlife preserve entailed, and she had a lot of work to do. After a wildfire, there were dozens of routine tasks to be performed, data to compile, tests to run.

Not to mention the procedures to follow in the event of a human fatality, most of which she was unfamiliar with. Right now Mike was handling the press and the state investigation, but Shay knew she'd be asked to take on some additional responsibilities.

The story of her life.

On some weekends she had extra staff, college kids and park rangers, but for the most part, Dark Canyon was a one-woman show. Her first order of business was to clean and inspect the tranquilizer guns she and Luke had inadvertently gotten wet. If they couldn't be salvaged, she'd have to write up an extensive damage report.

Before tackling the tranquilizer guns, which would require more concentration than she was currently capable of, she went back to her office and logged on to her e-mail account, trying not to think about last night. Trying not to replay every hot, endless moment.

She'd returned home sexually satisfied but emotionally wrecked.

When Luke asked if she was still in love with Jesse, she was floored by the realization that she never had been. If anything, she'd loved him as a friend. She hadn't continued their affair because he was irresistible; she'd done it because he was easy to resist. Like her father, Jesse was a restless dreamer, handsome and charming and very sweet when he wanted to be. His inability to remain faithful to one woman was actually part of his appeal. By tying herself to him, she'd kept her heart safe. No one could hurt her, not even Jesse, because she hadn't invested anything in their relationship.

Then Luke Meza came along and shattered her defenses.

Making a sound of frustration, she clicked off the computer and jumped to her feet, slamming the chair against the desk. At least her little brother hadn't done anything crazy lately. When she got home last night, he hadn't been debauching the neighbor's daughter in his bedroom. He'd been sound asleep.

Shay contemplated the mysterious package on the exam table, thinking she should swear off relationships with men for good. God knew she was a total failure at them.

Just as she was about to tear open the box, the office phone rang. "Dark Canyon State Preserve," she answered, holding the receiver between her shoulder and her ear.

"It's Mike."

"Oh. Hi." It was the most enthusiastic greeting she could manage. "What's up?"

"There's been some trouble on Los Coyotes this morning."

"Really? What kind of trouble?"

"This is just between us, but they found Bull Ryan in his office. Dead."

She gasped and placed a hand over the middle of her chest. "Heart attack?" she guessed, knowing Bull had watched his blood pressure.

"I haven't seen him yet, and with the way the feds run things I doubt if I will, but I heard he was . . . scalped."

"Scalped?" she repeated, shocked. "By what?"

"A person with a sharp knife, I imagine. And his scalp was lacerated, not cut completely off, but it looks bad, according to your sheriff."

"Oh, Mike," she breathed, saddened for him, and for everyone in the community. "I'm so sorry. Who would do such a thing?"

"I don't know," he said, sounding more forlorn than she'd ever heard him.

Her mind reeled, not with possibilities, but with repercussions. Tenaja Falls would be up in arms over this. Yesenia Montes's accidental death had caused a stir, but Bull Ryan was a respected businessman. To find him scalped? The whole thing was bizarre.

Jesse would be devastated. And Dylan had just started his new job yesterday.

Shay felt a twinge of nerves. Her brother couldn't have been on the construction site during the time of the attack. Could he?

"Be careful out there," Mike warned. "The lion attack, the fire, and now this . . . it just doesn't add up."

"Of course," she murmured.

"We've been working on tracking some untagged lions in the area," he continued. "There aren't a lot of big males within range, as far as we know, so we'll just have to keep our fingers crossed." He paused, collecting his thoughts. "How are you feeling?"

She supposed he meant her knee. "I'm fine." The swelling was gone and the bruises were fading fast. "Ready to hike, climb, track, whatever."

"Take it easy for a few days," he advised gruffly.

It was nice to have someone fuss over her every once in a while. "Did you leave a box here?" she asked, wondering if it was a gift.

"Huh?"

"I found a small package out front. Is it yours?"

"No," he replied. "I don't know anything about it."

"Hmm," she said, eyeing the mysterious object.

Mike cleared his throat. "Listen, we had Hamlet cremated, and I thought you might like to do something with the remains. I mean, they're yours, if you want them."

Shay was touched by the gesture. "Yes," she said, blinking rapidly. "Thank you. Really. It's nice of you to offer."

Mike mumbled that she was welcome and said a quick good-bye, as uncomfortable with sentimental interactions as she was.

She hung up the phone and ran her hand over the surface of the cardboard box, sniffling back a few tears. Maybe someone had dropped off a late birthday present. Maybe a secret admirer—Luke, her foolish heart ventured—had brought her a romantic gift.

As she started opening the top, a faint noise sent her tumbling back in time. It sounded like the rain stick her mama had given her when she was a little girl. She hadn't thought of it in years. The arm-length section of bamboo had been hand-painted and filled with stones. It made a rattling noise, like rain hitting an aluminum rooftop, when it was turned upside down.

Shay saw her mother's face in her mind, the way she'd looked before she got sick. She had been so vibrant, so joyous, so full of love and life and light.

After Dylan was born, her light dimmed. As a child, Shay didn't know about postpartum depression or any of the other maladies her mother suffered from, but she'd learned quite a bit about how to take care of a baby.

How many nights had she fed Dylan, and bathed him, and rocked him to sleep? She couldn't remember. He'd liked the rain stick, too. Sometimes she turned it up and down, over and over, its soothing sound calming him when nothing else would.

So lost in the memory, she didn't see the snake in the box until it bit her.

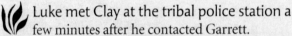 Luke met Clay at the tribal police station a few minutes after he contacted Garrett.

Apparently, Dylan Phillips hadn't shown up to his first class this morning. Not an uncommon occurrence, according to Principal Fischer, especially for a kid with Dylan's track record, but Luke was worried. He tried to reach Shay at home and at Dark Canyon. She must have been between the two places, because he couldn't get ahold of her at either.

Garrett promised he'd find Dylan, and Luke was almost afraid he'd be successful. Luke would go after the boy himself, but he had another dead body to worry about, and a whole mess of suspicious circumstances.

Not that the case was his to solve.

He was out of his jurisdiction, out of his element, and way out of his comfort zone. Small town politics and race relations were complex issues on their own. A suspicious death with bizarre cultural implications, on top of a mountain lion attack, would put Tenaja Falls on the national map and generate the kind of media circus Luke didn't want to deal with.

Being new in town and new on the job left him at a distinct disadvantage. He felt like the stranger on the reservation again, the kid who got hard looks and took hard hits, the one who kept his mouth shut because he didn't know what to say, the one who'd learned that acting aloof was an excellent defense mechanism.

Something about Tenaja Falls stripped away those artifices, like the desert wind laying a man down to his bare bones. Vegas was a place of flattery and falsehoods. Here, everyone seemed like a straight shooter, but Luke still had to watch his back.

His last conversation with Shay had also left him feeling uneasy. He knew he'd mishandled almost every interaction between them so far, from his casual dismissal of her on the sun-warmed rock that first afternoon to his mangled apology attempt in the fertility cave after a round of bone-melting sex.

He'd gotten off on the wrong foot with her from day one, and he could only hope she'd give him a chance to make it up to her.

Trying to roll the tension out of his shoulders, he followed Clay down the hall to the drunk tank, thinking he was lucky that their earlier confrontation hadn't come to blows. The younger man was lanky but strong, quick of mind and light on his feet. Unlike Jesse Ryan, Luke figured Clay wouldn't go down on the first hit.

Instead of throwing punches, Clay led him back to the holding tank. The cell was large enough to accommodate a half-dozen detainees, but Jesse Ryan was the only soul inside. With its concrete benches, aluminum toilet, and stainless steel sink, it was a dreary, uncomfortable-looking space.

Jesse didn't appear bothered by the lack of ambience. He was flat on his back, snoring.

Clay was understandably upset, but he didn't need to be told not to mention Bull Ryan's death. He and Luke exchanged a weighted glance, by tacit agreement promising not to give away any information.

"Rise and shine, bro," Clay said.

Jesse lifted his head, opened one eye, and groaned.

He shoved a lined paper cup through the bars. "I brought you some coffee."

Luke didn't think it was a good idea to give a disgruntled detainee a cup of hot liquid, but that was Clay's business. He hoped Jesse wouldn't throw it in his half-brother's face.

Jesse stood, rubbing a hand over his shadowed jaw. "Which one of y'all hit me?"

Clay hooked his thumb in Luke's direction.

"Remind me not to mess with you again," Jesse said amiably, staggering forward and taking the coffee from Clay's hand.

"The sheriff's here to ask you a few questions."

"I don't remember anything," Jesse announced. "What the hell happened?"

"You stormed into the Round-Up, drunk off your ass, and shoved Shay so hard she fell backward," Clay replied. "If I hadn't been there to catch her, she'd have been hurt."

For a moment, Jesse looked as though he not only remembered, but regretted his actions. Then disdain soured his handsome features and he only appeared surly. "Yeah, you're always there to help out the ladies, aren't you?" He took a sip of coffee and made a bitter face. "Clayton Trueheart. Mr. Chivalrous."

"That's me," Clay responded, giving him a humorless smile.

"Why did you go to the bar last night?" Luke asked.

"I heard this no-good Indian was cozyin' up to my woman," Jesse said.

Luke bristled, taking instant offense.

So did Clay. "That's a goddamned lie," he growled. "I only went over there to see the baby. Tammy needed money for diapers."

Luke realized they weren't talking about Shay, and the slur wasn't intended for him. Jesse hadn't gone to the bar last night to confront Luke; he'd been there to fight with Clay over Tamara.

"If my wife needs anything, she can get it from me," Jesse said, squinting at Clay. "And I mean *anything*. You hear?"

A dull flush crept up Clay's neck, but he didn't respond to the provocation. Again, Luke suspected Clay's interest in Tamara Ryan went beyond chivalry, and he would give the lady whatever she asked for.

It seemed as though Jesse knew it, too. Reluctantly, he turned his attention to Luke. "Is Shay all right?"

Luke thought about his encounter with her at the Visitors' Center and started to feel a little hot under the collar. Last night; she'd been ridiculed, manhandled, and pushed around. Jesse hadn't been very nice to her, either.

"She's fine," he said, clearing his throat.

Jesse studied his face. "I wouldn't want to see her get hurt."

It amazed him how quickly the man could transition from one female to the next. "Shay isn't your concern, slick. And from what I gather, she hasn't been for quite some time."

"Shay will *always* be my concern. If you treat her wrong, I'll tear you apart."

Luke rubbed his thumb over his itching knuckles, tempted to let Jesse out and give him his best shot. But he recognized that Jesse's attitude was more protective than proprietary, the reaction of a friend, not a lover. Although their relationship was over, Jesse still cared about her, and Luke couldn't fault him for that.

He also felt a surge of possessiveness. Shay was *his*.

"Like Yesenia Montes was torn apart?" he asked after a moment, not ready to let Jesse off the hook.

Jesse blanched. "I didn't have anything to do with that."

Luke surveyed their surroundings. "You look pretty comfortable in there. Have you done time?"

Jesse's mouth twisted with resentment as he pushed away from the bars. Placing his cup down on the concrete bench, he stood in front of the urinal and unzipped his pants, showing Luke exactly how he felt about the question.

"What do you drive?" Luke asked, unconcerned by Jesse's bad attitude.

"I have an old Monte Carlo," he said over his shoulder. "But I usually ride my bike."

A car and a motorcycle. Neither of those had bed liners, last time Luke checked. "You have any trucks in the garage?"

"Nope," he said, hitching up his pants when he finished. "Am I free to go, or what?"

Crossing his arms over his chest, Luke arched a glance at Clay.

"Did you see Dad after work yesterday?" Clay asked.

Before that moment, Jesse's behavior had been belligerent, but predictable. Now his expression changed, and a hint of guilt flickered across his face. "Yeah," he said, hiding the reaction behind more bluster. "So?"

"What did you talk about?"

"None of your goddamned business," he sneered.

"Did he tell you I'd been over at Tamara's?"

"Maybe." An uncomfortable silence stretched between them.

Jesse finally seemed to realize this visit wasn't about the minor brawl at the Round-Up last night, and he turned a little green. He swallowed a few times, fighting with his hangover. "What are y'all here for?" he asked. "Is Tammy . . . is something wrong?"

Clay stared at his brother, his expression full of disdain. And pity.

Jesse reached through the bars, grasping the front of Clay's shirt. "Is something wrong with Grace?"

Clay disentangled himself coolly. "Nothing's wrong with Grace. But I can't let you go just yet. I've got some paperwork to finish first."

Jesse nodded, but he appeared shaken. "Sure, man," he said, sitting back down on the bench and putting his head in his hands. "Do whatever you have to."

Luke and Clay walked away from the holding cell, heading down the gleaming hallway together. Before they reached the exit, Clay stopped short, as if he had something to get off his chest. "Jesse wouldn't hurt our dad," he said, giving Luke a warning glance. Daring him to dispute the words.

Luke just shrugged. "But?"

"He owes people money."

"Indians?" he interpreted.

A muscle in his jaw ticked. "Some guys at Wild Rivers. Loan sharks."

Luke was familiar with Wild Rivers Casinos. It was a multimillion-dollar corporation, and co-investors in the current project on Los Coyotes. But surely Clay wasn't suggesting a loan manager would try to collect Jesse's debt from Bull Ryan, and scalp him in the process. "You don't suspect them of—"

"No," Clay said with a scowl. "I'm just getting it out in the open. Jesse can be irresponsible and selfish. But he's not a killer."

Luke appreciated his honesty. He also found it telling that Clay seemed genuinely worried for his half brother. What was it about Jesse Ryan that everyone found so goddamned loveable? His utter lack of integrity, or his puppy dog eyes?

"Let him stew in there. The feds will make him cry like a baby."

The corner of Clay's mouth turned up. "They'll want to interview me, too."

"Were you and Bull close?"

Some of the light drained from Clay's eyes. "No. He acted like he didn't know I was his. But he did know. He had to have."

Luke was saddened, but not particularly surprised, by the admission. During his summers on the rez, he'd seen other men like Bull Ryan, married men who treated Indian women like conveniences and fathered children they never acknowledged. It was only natural that Clay resented the situation. Jesse had been born under the sanctity of wedlock, and he was accepted by his family despite his multiple screwups. Clay was the brother who had done well for himself, but due to the circumstance of his birth, was unable to gain his father's respect.

The radio on Luke's belt kicked on, emitting garbled language and a slew of static. Hearing the words, "Dark Canyon," he turned up the volume.

"Twenty-six-year-old female, five-ten approximately 150 pounds," the operator said. "Possible venomous snakebite. Patient is being admitted to Palomar Medical Center."

Holy Christ. They were talking about Shay.

"You know where that is?" he asked Clay.

The younger man was already moving toward his truck. "I'll drive."

"I'll follow you," Luke decided.

The next thirty minutes were the longest of his life. Palomar Medical Center was the closest hospital in the Tenaja Falls area, but it wasn't nearly close enough. Luke computed the time it would have taken an ambulance to reach Shay and get her to the hospital.

Over an hour. An eternity.

With the miracles of modern medicine, very few people in the United States died from snakebites. As a public servant, Luke knew this was partly due to fast medical treatment and the availability of antivenom. If there wasn't any on hand, she'd be in trouble.

He communicated via CB radio with the emergency services operator and the EMT who responded to the scene, neither of whom were able to give him any detailed information. All he knew was that Shay had been bitten by a rattlesnake, and was in stable condition.

Luke wrapped his fingers around the steering wheel, maneuvering past cars that had pulled to the side of the road. Both he and Clay had their lights flashing, and although it wouldn't be safe to go any faster around the curves, Luke wanted to. For the first time in his career, he wasn't the least bit concerned about public safety.

Some of the damned fools on the road wouldn't even pull over. Luke gritted his teeth, suppressing the urge to fire off a few warning shots.

Finally they were in the parking lot outside the ER. Luke didn't bother to find an open space. He jerked to a stop beside the curb, yanked his keys from the ignition, and hopped out, not waiting to see if Clay would do the same.

At the front desk, there was a blue-haired old lady with wire-rimmed glasses. Luke did a quick survey of the waiting room and didn't see anyone who looked more helpful. "Shay Phillips," he said, surprised he wasn't short of breath. His heart was hammering in his chest as if he'd been running for miles.

The lady smiled placidly. "Are you a blood relation?"

Luke left her sitting there. Ignoring the protests of a couple of nurses in colorful scrub outfits, he stormed through the double doors leading to the emergency room. Growing frantic, he searched the beds, jerking back curtains and calling her name. He startled a gray-faced older gentleman and a boy with a crooked wrist before he found her.

She was reclining in a hospital bed, wearing a faded blue gown, eyes closed, dark lashes fanning her pale cheeks. Tubes were coming out of her nose and she had an IV and a blood pressure monitor attached to her left arm.

She looked so goddamned frail.

Luke's heart felt too heavy for his chest. For a moment, he thought he was having some kind of stress-related attack. Then she opened her eyes, and he realized it was something far more serious.

Shay blinked at Luke groggily.

She hadn't been comfortable, with her injured hand elevated and her body strapped to a bed, attached to a bunch of medical gadgets, but she must have drifted off to sleep.

Before the ambulance picked her up, she'd been a little manic. While she waited for emergency services, she'd recaptured the Red Diamondback Rattlesnake and transferred it to a safer place, trying to remain calm. The cardboard box the snake had been in didn't provide enough oxygen, and she didn't wish the rattler any ill will.

It wasn't his fault she'd stuck her hand in the box.

Luckily, she didn't seem to be having any reaction to the venom. The doctor wanted to keep her here all day in case she began to show symptoms, but he didn't think she required aggressive treatment.

Shay was relieved, because she'd heard of men who'd

gone through the agony of anaphylactic shock, and even those who had lost limbs from severe bites.

Luke yanked the curtain open farther and stood at the side of the bed, gaping at her. The look on his face was so disturbing she sat up and frowned. "What is it?" she asked, her mind flitting from one worst-case scenario to the next.

He made a strange wheezing sound, gripping the curtain so hard several rings popped from the rod overhead.

"Is it Dylan?"

"Dylan?" he choked.

"My brother, Dylan," she explained, wondering what the hell was wrong with him. "Did something happen to him?"

"No," he said, swallowing. "I don't think so."

"Then what is it? You look like you just saw a ghost."

"I thought I had."

She looked around in confusion. "Where?"

"Right here."

Shay wanted to smack some sense into him. Then it dawned on her that he was talking about her. He'd obviously heard she'd been bitten. The crazed look in his eye, the labored breathing, the curtain-ripping . . . it was all for her.

A strange sensation coursed through her, dancing in her belly. She tried to shake it off, but it refused to go. She tried to deny his feelings, too, but concern was written all over his face, and in the way he clutched the nylon curtain like a lifeline.

"Sit down before you pop a blood vessel," she said in a hoarse voice, gesturing to the chair beside her bed.

He remained standing. "Are you going to be all right?"

"Probably. They think it was a dry bite."

"A dry bite?"

"Just a warning nip. Little or no venom."

He closed his eyes and took a deep breath, placing a hand over his chest. Her own heart bounced like a giddy schoolgirl's, swelling with love for him.

The realization that she was in love with him came with a lot of excess baggage, fear and anxiety and disillusionment. For one fleeting, absurdly sentimental moment, she imagined what it would be like to have him love her back.

"How the fuck did you manage to get bit by a rattlesnake?" he said, his brows slashing downward. "On the fucking hand, no less!"

A cold, hard ball settled in the pit of her stomach. Luke Meza wasn't in love with her. He was just at the end of his rope, frazzled by the events of the past few days and so angry that he couldn't keep his emotions, or his mouth, in check. "Language like that will get you kicked off the troop, Eagle Scout."

His jaw clenched. "Do you have any idea what I just went through?"

Laughter bubbled up from within, tearing through her chest. "What you just went through? Are you serious?"

"A few hours ago, I saw Bull Ryan facedown on the ground with his scalp hanging to the side like a loose toupee," he said in a low, furious voice. "And last night I dreamed—" He broke off with another curse, raking a hand through his hair.

She stared at him in wonder. "Dreamed what?"

"That you were dead," he bit out. "I dreamed you were dead."

Judging by his reaction to seeing her in the hospital bed, the idea of her dying disturbed him greatly. She frowned, worried that her brother would hear rumors about the incident and have the same reaction. "I should call Dylan at school," she murmured, reaching for the phone beside the bed.

"Don't bother. He's not there."

Her stomach clenched with dread. "Where is he?"

"I don't know. I sent Garrett out looking for him."

"Why?"

After a moment's hesitation, he leveled with her. "Because his application for employment was in Bull's hand."

She felt the blood drain from her face. "He just started working there yesterday. It doesn't mean anything."

"Maybe not," Luke agreed.

"I have to get out of here," she said, pulling the oxygen tube away from her nose. "I have to go find him."

"Stop." He reached out and stilled her hand. "What did the doctor say?"

She glared at him. "That I'm fine."

"Then why haven't you been discharged?"

"Because some patients have a delayed reaction to rattlesnake venom," she said, lying back against the pillows. "Symptoms can develop up to eight hours later."

He held her gaze. "Promise me you'll stay here. I'll go after Dylan."

Tears flooded her eyes, but she nodded, feeling defeated.

"Tell me what happened with the snake."

Brushing the hair away from her forehead with trembling fingers, she told him about the strange box with the rattler inside.

"You could have been killed." His voice was tight.

"I admit I was careless, opening a rattling box, but—"

"Someone tried to kill you."

"No," she protested. "I get drop-offs sometimes. People mistake a wildlife preserve for an animal rescue. It's irresponsible, of course, to leave a rattlesnake in an unmarked container, especially one without proper ventilation—"

"You could have died, and you're worried about the goddamned snake!"

She flinched at his vehemence.

"Where's the box? Did you bring it?"

Shaking her head, she said, "It's still at Dark Canyon."

"And the snake?"

"In a safe place," she hedged.

He nodded, but his mouth had this hard look about it. It was the way a man held his face before he threw a punch. "I'm going to find whoever did this."

She felt a shiver of unease. "Find Dylan first."

22

Luke met up with Clay on his way out to the lobby. He wanted to go straight to Dark Canyon and tear the place apart looking for clues, but he had a missing Dylan Phillips to deal with and a loan shark to interview.

"False alarm," he said as they walked toward the exit together. "Guess it was a dry bite."

Clay recognized the term and relaxed his shoulders. "Hardly anyone dies from a real bite these days, anyhow. Not with treatment."

"Someone left the snake in an unmarked box on her doorstep at Dark Canyon."

"Son of a bitch," he muttered. "What kind of idiot would do that?"

"It couldn't have been Jesse," Luke admitted grudgingly. "He was locked up all night, and the box wasn't there when we—" He broke off, feeling heat creep up his neck. "It wasn't there last night."

Clay smirked, guessing what they'd been up to. "Jesse might not want to see Shay with another man, but he wouldn't deliberately try to hurt her."

Luke didn't bother to dispute him. It seemed as though the people of Tenaja Falls had difficulty believing any of its residents were capable of wrongdoing, and that attitude was real sweet, but not particularly helpful to his investigation. "What about these guys at Wild Rivers? Are they harmless, too?"

Clay was optimistic, not naïve. "No, they aren't. But I expect you already know that."

Luke's response was noncommittal. Moses Rivers, the man behind the casino chain, had a dangerous reputation. If some of his bookies had roughed up Bull Ryan, Rivers would know about it. He also had ties to Sin City. "I doubt Rivers had anything to do with the hit on me," he said, thinking aloud. "His holdings are all outside of Vegas."

Clay shrugged. "If you want to talk to him, he's been hanging out in Pala, keeping his eye on construction."

"Call the casino and let Rivers know we're coming," Luke said.

"I'll follow you over there," he added, getting into his truck. Before he started the engine, he picked up his radio. "Deputy Snell, come back."

Garrett didn't always answer, but this time he did. "Snell here, over."

"What's the status on our BOLO?" He'd put out a "be on the lookout" alert for Dylan this morning.

"Nothing yet. I checked his house and the Martinez place."

Luke asked him to drive by the basketball courts and signed off, growing increasingly frustrated with the lack of progress, wishing he could be a dozen places at once. He didn't want to leave Shay alone and unprotected, and he didn't trust Garrett at all.

"There's *way* too much going on in this town," he muttered to himself, looking forward to some hard-won monotony.

Luke had never been to the Wild Rivers Casino at Pala Reservation. Construction had started about ten years ago, well after his last visit with his father. He met Clay outside, near the wide automated doors. As they walked in together, all of Luke's thoughts were washed away by casino madness. The garble of voices and whir of slot machines, once music to his ears, now sounded like unnecessary noise.

The lights were too bright, the cigarette smoke too thick. Underneath that, there was a faint metallic odor, the smell of spent coins, stale sweat, and desperation.

He blinked a few times, ignoring the sensory overload and letting the superfluous details fade into the background, an old Vegas trick that didn't come as easily as it once had. A stunning, dark-haired woman came forward to greet them. Her voice was cool and impersonal, but not unpleasant. "Sheriff Meza? I'm Willow Rivers."

He shook her slender hand, noting that she had the figure of a showgirl, encased in a slim-fitting skirt and elegant silk blouse. With her perfect makeup, flawless skin, and seductive smile, she was a very pretty package, but one that left him cold.

Luke pictured Shay's flyaway hair and casual style, her frankness and transparency. Every thought, every emotion was reflected on her face. The woman before him didn't appear to have emotions.

"Deputy Trujillo," she said, nodding as if they'd met before.

"Clay," he corrected, shaking her hand.

She led them toward the elevators, making small talk with Clay as they rode up to her father's apartments. Although Willow Rivers reminded him of a Miss USA contestant, with her smooth responses and carefully crafted persona, he couldn't say he disliked her.

Her presence obviously made Clay uncomfortable, however, and he resisted her attempts to put him at ease. Wielding hospitality like a weapon, she seated them in a plush office inside a penthouse suite and poured them each cold drinks. Her blouse gaped open a little as she placed Clay's drink before him, but he averted his gaze.

"He'll be with you in a moment," she said, leaving the room in a swish of long hair and a whisper of silk.

"You seem nervous," Luke said to Clay, hiding a smile.

"She freaks me out," he admitted under his breath, taking a sip of his 7-Up. "If her father asked her to, she'd probably offer complimentary blow jobs."

Luke almost choked on his own drink. He was still trying to recover when Moses Rivers strode into the room. How a lovely creature like Willow could have sprung from this man's loins was a complete mystery. He was a large, intimidating-looking brute with harsh features, clubbed-back hair, and severely pockmarked skin.

"Do you want anything, Daddy?" Willow asked. Her affection for him seemed genuine, unlike the rest of her. "A cold drink?"

When he looked at his daughter, Moses' face went from ugly to merely homely. "No thanks."

Smiling, she shut the door.

Moses' placid expression disappeared. "*Sheriff* Meza now, is it? How is your health?"

Luke knew the man was referring to his brush with death in Vegas. "My health has always been excellent," he said, hoping Rivers hadn't heard Clay's last comment. "But I can't say the same for everyone in Tenaja Falls."

"I heard about Bull," Moses said, his eyes flat. "It's a shame."

Luke shouldn't have been surprised. This man had friends in very high places, and they kept him well informed. "When did you last see him?"

"Last week. Friday."

"Did you argue?"

"Nothing to argue about. Everything on the site has been running smoothly."

"Do you know anyone who would want to make trouble for him?"

He leaned back in his chair. "No."

"What about his son Jesse? Does he owe you money?"

He folded his hands on top of his desk. "My finances are confidential. If you want to look into them, I suggest you obtain a warrant."

"I'll do that," Luke promised, although he doubted he could get one. Rivers was powerful, connected, and filthy rich. Worse, he was meticulous. Anything illegal this man had done would be buried so deep a hundred investigators couldn't find it.

Rivers studied him cannily. "Do you have family here, Sheriff Meza?"

Luke disliked the question, but in an interview situation, sometimes a little give-and-take was unavoidable. "My father lives in Pala."

"Lawrence Meza? Is that him?"

"Yes."

His brows lifted. "I didn't know he had a son."

Luke stared back at Rivers in uneasy silence, wondering how well the two men knew each other. His father had actually tried to contact Luke about a year ago. Apparently, he'd quit drinking and wanted to make amends. He'd called and left a message less than a week after Leticia's funeral. A lonely affair Luke had paid for, and attended, all by himself.

Luke had never called back. It was too late to repair a relationship that had never really existed. Wasn't it?

"We don't see each other very often," he murmured. The understatement of his life. He shrugged off the subject, aware that Rivers was enjoying his discomfort. "Did you know Yesenia Montes?"

Something in his dark eyes flickered. "We were acquainted."

"How so?"

"The usual way a man who looks like me would be acquainted with a woman who is paid for her time."

Well. That was clear enough. "When did you see her last?"

"I don't remember the exact date. Perhaps you should ask your deputy."

Luke tensed. "Deputy Snell? Why?"

"He was with her the last time I saw her. And he frequently gave her rides to and from the casino." His pockmarked face stretched into an unpleasant smile. "In his squad car."

Dylan sat up and looked around, momentarily disoriented by his surroundings. This wasn't his bedroom. It was Angel's.

And she wasn't here.

"Fuck," he groaned, rubbing a hand over his face. He couldn't believe he'd fallen asleep. What a lame move.

Shaking off the grogginess, he got up and went to the bathroom, catching a glimpse of his reflection in the mirror over the sink while he took a piss.

Did he look different?

He turned his head to one side and examined the line of his jaw, as if losing his virginity might have resulted in the sudden growth of a full beard. Nope. Looking down, he noted that nothing else had changed, either.

But he smiled to himself, puffing out his chest as he zipped up his pants. He felt pretty manly. He just wished he'd been able to make it good for Angel. Maybe he could talk her into letting him try again.

Wildly excited by the prospect, he cleaned up a little and took a swig of her mouthwash before he left the bathroom. As he looked around for his T-shirt, finding it draped over the only chair, it occurred to him that something was missing.

Her room was . . . empty.

Pulse racing, he pulled his shirt over his head and opened her clothes armoire, the only large piece of furniture in the room. There was nothing in it. No clothes, no miscellaneous junk, no extra blankets. And no guitar.

He couldn't believe his eyes, although the evidence was right there in front of him. Angel Martinez had moved out while he was sleeping. And she'd taken everything she owned, so it wasn't as if she'd gone on a short vacation.

Whirling around, he searched the room for signs of her. On the top of her desk, there was a single sheet of paper. He snatched it up and began to read.

> Dylan,
> I'm so sorry leave this way. Pleaz dont regret been with me. I'm glad it happend.
> I wish I cloud stay but I cant. Goodby.
> Angel

"I wish I *cloud* stay?" he sputtered, staring at the words incredulously. She'd written him a kiss-off letter, and she didn't even know how to spell the word *goodbye.*

This was total bullshit.

Muttering a string of curses, he grabbed his backpack and flew out the door, not bothering to shut it behind him. A quick check through the windows of the main house confirmed that she'd really left.

Not just left. She'd run away.

In that moment, Dylan hated her with a passion. More than he hated his mom, whose death he'd mourned bitterly. More than he hated his dad, whose absence Dylan felt acutely. More than he hated Shay, whose abandonment had destroyed him.

It seemed as though Angel had slept with him before she left on purpose, just to make certain he was crushed.

He'd lost his virginity, and now he'd been royally fucked.

Smashing her letter in his hand, he shoved it into his front pocket. There was only one place she could have gone if she was planning on hightailing it out of town.

The bus station.

Dylan had hitched a ride from Palomar High to Calle Remolino and he'd have to do it again to get back to the main drag. Shay didn't like him getting into cars with strangers, but hitching was an accepted mode of transportation in Tenaja Falls. He knew the dangers and only stuck his thumb out for certain types of drivers. Perhaps it was a stereotype, but he'd discovered that Mexican people were often friendly and generous, and didn't associate any stigma with offering someone a ride.

The last person he wanted to get picked up by was Garrett Snell, so Dylan kept his head low as he jogged by the side of the road. Adrenaline propelled him all the way to the nearest cross street, and catching a lift from there was easy.

He stuck his thumb out at the first jalopy. It pulled to a stop a few feet away, music blaring from the open windows, its inhabitants weighing down the chassis.

"*A dónde vas?*" the driver asked.

"*Al estación de autobuses.*"

"*Súbate.*"

Dylan hopped in, as ordered, nodding hello at the

other passengers. The sound of Cumbia filled his ears, pleasant and upbeat, with its carnival bass line and lively accordion. The music didn't assuage his anger, but it affected his outlook, and by the time they arrived he was no longer sure what he would say to Angel if he found her.

Frowning, he dug out a dollar and some change for the driver.

He accepted it easily. *"No tienes equipaje."*

"No," he agreed, looking down at his empty hands. He didn't have any luggage. *"Estoy buscando a mi chica,"* he explained. *I'm looking for my girl.*

The men nodded to each other in understanding. *"Buena suerte."* *Good luck.*

"Grácias," he muttered, getting out and waving good-bye. The little car took off again, leaving a cloud of dust and a lingering tune in its wake.

There was only one bus parked in front of the station, an exhaust-coated contraption with "Sunset Tours" written beneath the windows. Passengers were boarding, stowing their belongings in the storage area along the side.

Angel was last in line, carefully stashing her prized guitar and one sturdy duffel bag.

His heart leapt into his throat and he could only stare at her, assaulted by memories of her on top of him, underneath him, around him. As if sensing his perusal, she looked up, her eyes meeting his, and the moment stretched into an eternity.

He knew then that her voice would haunt him more than anything else. Years from now, he might forget how her body responded to his or how her skin felt beneath his hands, but he would never forget the sound of her voice, husky-sweet, like a hot summer night.

"Dylan," she said in a ragged whisper.

The driver began to close the baggage compartment. "Bus leaves in two minutes, miss."

She nodded, hesitating another moment before she approached him. "Please don't tell my dad," she begged.

He glanced at the bus again, seeing now that the small sign above the front window said "Las Vegas."

She twisted her hands together. "I'm going to call him as soon as I get settled, but I don't want him to worry . . ."

"Why are you going there?"

"To look for work."

"What kind of work?"

She tore her gaze from his, her mouth thinning. And then he knew. He knew why she was going and why she'd kept it a secret.

The outrage and confusion he'd felt upon reading her rejection letter came back with a vengeance, flooding his system. "What the hell was that this morning?" he asked, lowering his voice. "Practice?"

Her eyes filled with hurt. "Don't," she said. "Don't make it cheap."

"Okay," he said, nodding. "I'll make it expensive. How much?"

She brushed her tears away angrily. "Fuck you."

"You already did."

Turning on one heel, she walked away from him, but he caught up with her easily, wrapping his hand around her upper arm. "Wait." She jerked her arm out of his grasp and swung at him, surprising him with a glancing slap across the face. It hurt, and he didn't like it, but he took her in his arms and held her tight, his heart pounding with anxiety. "Please don't go," he said. "I'm sorry."

She struggled her way out of his embrace.

"I—I love you," he blurted, desperate to keep her here.

The anger faded from her eyes. In its wake there was only pity, and he realized that he was making a fool of himself. Nothing he could say would convince her to stay.

When she reached out to touch his face, he flinched. "Good-bye," she said, pressing her cool lips to his burning cheek.

With that, she was gone, her high-heeled boots making tracks in the gravel-strewn dirt at his feet, leaving dusty marks on the metal steps leading up to the passenger seats.

The grizzly-looking bus driver squinted in his direction, daring him to feel lucky. Dylan just stared back at him, thinking he'd never feel lucky again. The driver made a harrumphing sound and tossed his cigarette aside. Dylan watched, his heart growing cold and hard, while the bus pulled away.

It hadn't yet cleared the parking lot when he became aware of another car cruising up behind him, a sleek black shadow.

The horn blipped and red lights flashed as the squad car jerked to a halt. Dylan didn't make a conscious decision to run; he just did it. But he must have been moving in slow motion, still stunned from having his heart torn from his chest, because Garrett caught up with him in seconds, tackled him from behind. They both went down hard on the loose gravel.

It ripped his jeans and cut into his palms.

"You have the right to remain silent," Garrett panted, already winded. Wrenching Dylan's arms behind his back, he cuffed his wrists, continuing to recite the Miranda warning as he patted him down.

Dylan lifted his head, straining to see the bus cruising down the main drag. Was Angel watching him? Did she care?

He must have eaten dirt on the way down, because his lips felt numb and there was a tinny, metallic taste in his mouth. Turning his head to the side, he spat out blood and bits of gravel.

"What's this?" Garrett said, pulling the knife out of his back pocket.

Dylan groaned, knowing he was in deep shit.

"Where've you been today?"

"At your mother's," he said, running his tongue over his teeth to make sure they were all in the right place.

Garrett put his knee on Dylan's neck, pressing him facedown in the dirt and giving him an agonizing demonstration of excessive force. Dylan would have protested, but with a noseful of gravel and a crushed windpipe, he couldn't breathe.

Shay meant to follow the doctor's orders, and she'd had every intention of keeping her promise to Luke. But with every passing moment, she became more and more convinced that her brother was in danger, and she could no longer stay idle.

She picked up the phone beside the bed and dialed a number she knew by heart.

"Palomar High School, Rose speaking."

"May I speak with Principal Fischer? This is Shay Phillips."

"Please hold, Mrs. Phillips."

Shay ground her teeth together.

"Miss Phillips?" a man's smooth voice answered. Principal Fischer never forgot her marital status. "What can I do for you?"

"Did Dylan come to school yet?"

"Not according to any of his teachers."

Damn it. "I saw him get on the bus."

He sighed heavily. "I've heard parents say that before. Despite our best security efforts, students sometimes find a way to leave campus."

"What about Chad Pinter and Travis Sanchez? Are they present and accounted for?"

"I can't give out information about other students, Shay. I'm sorry."

"Thanks anyway," she muttered, and hung up.

Feeling helpless, and hating it, she stared at the clock on the wall across from her, watching the seconds tick by. The puncture wound on her hand was barely discernible. There was no discoloration or localized swelling. It looked like a kitten bite.

"Screw this," she said, reaching for the phone again.

Her friend Lori answered on the third ring. "Hello?"

Shay could hear water running and baby Tommy fussing in the background. She didn't want to put her friend out, but she didn't know who else to turn to. "I'm at Palomar Hospital. Can you come pick me up?"

"Sure, but . . ." There was a muffled noise, like she was adjusting the phone and the baby, ". . . What happened?"

"Nothing big," she lied. "I'll be waiting by the tree out front."

"Okay," Lori replied, sounding dubious. "Twenty minutes?"

Shay thanked her and hung up. She didn't think they could keep her here against her will, but she wasn't sure. Dr. Barnes had already gone over the dangers with her and had been adamant that she stay at least eight hours.

Instead of causing a scene, she started working on the tape around her IV. Getting it put in had been the most uncomfortable part of this "near-death" experience, besides the stress, and it wasn't easy to take out. Wincing, she pulled the needle from her arm and slapped some tape back on over the tender spot.

Her blood pressure gauge and pulse monitor were simple to remove, but they started beeping the instant she took them off. Panicking, she jumped up from the bed, realizing with chagrin that she didn't know where her clothes were.

It couldn't be helped, so she clutched the hospital gown's gaping back, holding it shut, and fled the room like a thief in the night.

The dramatic exit was probably unnecessary, and it was definitely foolhardy, but once she committed to it, there was no going back. Ten minutes later, Lori Snell found her loitering behind the tree in front of the hospital, barefoot and loose-haired, like a deranged escapee from an insane asylum.

"Are you crazy?" Lori said through the open window.

"Probably," Shay replied, letting out a shaky laugh as she climbed into the passenger seat of Lori's SUV. She smiled at Tommy over her shoulder, who gurgled with delight. "He's getting so big."

"Um-hmm," Lori said, pulling out into traffic. "What'd you do?"

Shay gave her an abbreviated version, downplaying the snakebite and emphasizing her concern for Dylan. "Take me to Dark Canyon," she said as Lori drove back toward Tenaja Falls. "That's where my car is."

"Yes, ma'am," Lori muttered, giving her a jaunty salute.

"Sorry to be so bossy," Shay said, furrowing a hand through her tangled hair. "It's just been . . . one of those days."

Lori snorted. "Tell me about it."

Shay studied her friend, noting that Lori looked a little the worse for wear herself. Her eyes were puffy and red, as if she'd been crying. "What's wrong?" she asked, glancing back at Tommy. He was drooling happily, chewing on a blue teething ring.

"Garrett is. Same as always."

Shay's heart went out to her, but she knew when to keep her mouth shut. Once, just once, she'd said, "Why don't you divorce him?" and Lori let her have it.

"I think he's seeing other women."

"No," Shay breathed, shocked by the idea. Garrett had always looked at other women, and wasn't shy about getting an eyeful, but he wasn't a toucher. As far as Shay knew, he'd been faithful to Lori. He was a terrible, horrible, faithful husband.

"He gets calls at all hours. And not just from bookies and poker fiends."

"Women call him?" Shay said, her eyes narrowing. "At the house?"

She nodded miserably. "And on his cell."

Shay couldn't believe Garrett would be such a fool. He was damned lucky to have Lori, who was beauty to his beast. "What are you going to do?"

"I don't know. My mom said she would watch Tommy tonight so we can talk."

Stunned into silence, Shay sat back in her seat to contemplate the situation. As big as her problems with Dylan were, and as harrowing as the events of the past few days had been, she couldn't help but feel a twinge of guilt. She'd been so distracted. Had she let her friend down?

"I'm here for you."

Lori smiled through her tears. "I know."

"If you ever need someone to talk to, or even a place to stay . . ."

"Thanks," Lori said, wiping her cheeks. "But I can always move back in with my parents if it comes to that."

When they arrived at Dark Canyon, Shay gave her friend a big, long hug. Tears filled her eyes, because she wanted the best for Lori. Shay also had her own man troubles to deal with, and she wished they had time to talk now. She could use a supportive ear.

Tommy let out a high-pitched wail, and they broke apart.

"I think he needs to go down for a nap," Lori said, apologizing. "Will you be okay?"

"Of course. Will you?"

Instead of answering, Lori promised to call her later, and Shay climbed out of the passenger seat. With Tommy fussing in the backseat, Lori put the car into gear and turned the radio up as she drove away.

This morning, after going outside to wait for the ambulance, Shay had forgotten to lock up the Visitors' Center. Thank goodness her keys were in the purse on top of her desk, where she'd left them. Changing out of the hospital gown was her first order of business, but before she grabbed her extra clothes, she walked through the building warily, almost expecting to see a human assailant. She wasn't sure she believed the snake had been delivered to her with evil intent, but too many weird things had happened lately to call them all co-incidences.

Luke would be so pissed if he knew she was here alone right now.

The cardboard box the rattler had been delivered in was lying on the floor next to the exam table, innocuous and empty. The snake itself was stretched out in a roomy glass enclosure, unaware of the trouble it had caused. Tiptoeing lightly on her bare feet, she searched the office and the back room, even going so far as to look under the stalls in the restrooms.

The place was deserted.

Breathing a sigh of relief, she took the change of clothes from her desk drawer and ducked into the bathroom. Working with wildlife was often messy, so she always kept a backup outfit on hand. The dark brown corduroys hung too low on her hips, and the old blue T-shirt left a strip of her midsection bare, but even the most ill-fitting ensemble was better than a hospital gown. Slipping on the pair of ratty canvas sneakers, she pulled her hair into a quick ponytail and used the facilities before she walked out.

A man locked his arm around her waist as soon as she cleared the door, lifting her off her feet and hauling her against him. Her first instinct was to kick and fight, but she froze the instant she felt the cold barrel of a gun digging into her temple.

If she hadn't just emptied her bladder, she'd have peed her pants.

23

After parting ways with Clay at Wild Rivers Casino, Luke drove out to Dark Canyon.

Via CB radio, Clay informed him that two FBI special agents had arrived at the construction site to process evidence, and the medical examiner had been allowed to transport the body to the morgue to perform the autopsy. Dr. Hoyt confirmed what Luke already suspected. Bull Ryan had no visible injuries besides the laceration to his scalp, which appeared to have been inflicted after his heart stopped beating.

Hoyt couldn't speculate on the cause of death until the autopsy was complete, but he was able to estimate the time it happened: yesterday in the early evening.

Luke thanked Clay for the information and signed off, wondering why the hell anyone would want to mess around with a dead body. Yesenia Montes had been moved after the lion attack, and Bull Ryan's corpse had been given a new hairline.

It didn't make sense.

He arrived at the Visitors' Center a short time later and let himself in. A small cardboard box was lying on the floor next to a stainless steel exam table, just as Shay had described.

She said she hadn't noticed it the night before, and he knew damned well it hadn't been there during their tryst. He might have been hard as nails with only one thing on his mind, but he was still a cop, trained to notice every detail.

Someone had brought this package here early this morning, hours or minutes after he left with Shay. When he found out who, Luke was going to rip him apart with his bare hands. Maybe even shove the fucking snake down his throat.

There was no sign of a break-in, no discernible footprints near the front door or any tire impressions on the dry desert earth outside. After giving the grounds a quick inspection, and scowling at what must be the offending snake, who appeared to be relaxing comfortably in a posh-looking habitat, he took a pen out of his pocket and crouched down next to the box, upending it carefully.

A triangle-shaped object tumbled out, clattering on the tile floor.

Luke couldn't believe his eyes. He wasn't an expert, but this was a cultural artifact anyone could recognize.

It was an arrowhead, knapped from black obsidian.

His mind raced with possibilities. He didn't believe an Indian had left the spear point here any more than he believed one of his people had scalped Bull Ryan.

So what the hell was going on?

The sound of running water in the restroom brought him up short. He drew his weapon, staying low and cursing himself for a fool. There were no cars outside, other than the one Shay left in the parking lot this morning, and he hadn't bothered to do a thorough sweep.

It was a stupid, careless mistake.

Moving fast, he approached the door to the women's restroom and stood beside it, his pulse pounding with adrenaline.

He had his gun to her head and his arm clamped around her waist as soon as she came out. With her body flush against his, he could smell her hair and that tantalizing herbal scent. Luke recognized Shay with all of his senses.

Horrified, he released her. "What the fuck are you doing here?"

She whirled around to look at him, her eyes wide with fear. "What the fuck are *you* doing here?"

He holstered his revolver, noting that his hands were shaking. "I could have killed you," he said, chilled by the thought.

She crossed her arms over her chest. "You almost gave me a heart attack."

"You promised you would stay in the hospital," he said through clenched teeth, struggling to get a grip on his emotions. "Instead I find you here, traipsing around my crime scene like nothing happened. All but begging for someone to come in and finish the job they started this morning!"

Her face paled. "You didn't have to put a gun to my head."

"I didn't know it was you." He took a slow, agonizing breath, trying to recover. A moment ago, when he thought the perpetrator had returned to the scene, rage had flooded his system. He'd drawn his weapon, and for the first time in his life, he'd wanted to use it.

He still did. He would kill anyone who hurt her.

"I'm sorry," he said. "I didn't mean to scare you."

She looked down at her tennis shoes, muttering something about him being quick on the draw.

It stung in more ways than one. "How did you get here?"

"A friend dropped me off."

"I'm taking you back to the hospital right now."

"The hell you are."

He bit off another curse. "I don't want you mixed up in this, Shay," he said, raking a hand through his hair. "I can't stand the thought of you being in danger. And I hate the idea of you putting yourself at risk."

Her gaze wandered over him, lingering on his disheveled hair and the star pinned to his front pocket before settling back on his face.

To his consternation, the corner of her mouth tilted up, as if the signs of his eminent breakdown pleased her. Reaching out, she threaded her own fingers through his hair, adding to the disarray. Her eyes burned into his, smoky blue, and what passed between them was hotter and stronger and scarier than anything he'd ever felt before.

He pressed her back against the wall, cupping his hand around her chin and rubbing his thumb across her soft lips. She parted them and bit him gently, her small white teeth sinking into the pad of his thumb. After soothing the mark with her tongue, she drew him into the heat of her mouth and sucked gently.

He felt an answering tug in the middle of his chest, below the belt, and all the way down to his toes.

Groaning, he withdrew his wet thumb and traced her lips once more before crushing his mouth over hers. There was no artistry to this kiss, no finesse, just hunger and longing and desperation. She responded in kind, tasting his passion and demanding her pleasure, as frank and sexual and unashamed as she'd ever been.

He wanted her more each day, with each passing moment. He wanted her more every time he had her. He wanted her right here, standing up against the wall.

But she took her hands from his hair and placed them on his chest, breaking the contact. "We can't do this right now."

"No," he agreed, although his erection throbbed in protest.

She disentangled herself from his arms. "I have to find my brother."

That brought back a shard of reality. She was supposed to be resting in a hospital bed. And he was supposed to be investigating her attempted murder. "Right," he said, shaking his head. "I mean, wrong. I'm going to find him. You're—"

The radio on his belt sounded, emitting a hash of garbled words.

Luke snatched up his receiver.

Deputy Snell's voice came over the wire, calm and crisp in a sea of static. "I've got Phillips in the back of my squad car. He was found in possession of a hunting knife." He let out a sinister chuckle. "I think what we've got here is a slam dunk, Sheriff."

Luke met Shay's gaze, reading her fear and confusion. "Don't question him without me," he warned, his pulse racing. "I'll be at the station in a few minutes."

"That's affirmative," Garrett said. "Over and out."

The next ten minutes were the longest of her life. On the way to the hospital this morning, she'd imagined what would happen to Dylan if she died, and tears had sprung to her eyes.

Now she sat next to Luke in terrified silence, so worried she felt nauseous. She was furious with her brother for putting her through this kind of turmoil. Why was he so determined to throw his life away?

Luke didn't say anything, but he seemed as tense as she was. He drove too fast on the bumpy dirt road, jostling them inside the cab. When they arrived at the sheriff's station, she jumped out of his truck and hurried toward the front door, her heart pounding with anxiety and her hands clenched into fists.

Inside, her little brother was sitting at a desk across from Garrett Snell, his hands cuffed behind his back and his eyes brimming with defiance. Upon sight of his torn, dirty T-shirt, and the blood smeared across his chin, her anger didn't evaporate.

It just transferred.

Garrett Snell's uniform was also dirty, but his face was unmarred and his expression smug. He was leaning back in his chair with his arms crossed over his barrel chest, a position that emphasized his considerable bulk.

Garrett was a bully as a kid, a husband, and a police

officer. Shay couldn't let him get away with it a second longer.

"You black-hearted bastard," she said in a low growl, advancing on him. She didn't slap at him wildly or unsheathe her claws; she just grabbed him by the shirt collar, drew back her fist, and punched him square in the mouth.

Pain exploded from her knuckles upon impact. Garrett shoved her backward, sending her flying across the room. Dylan rose to his feet and shouted in protest, almost knocking over the table in front of him. Luke caught her around the waist and held her still.

"How dare you put your hands on him!" she said to Garrett, struggling to break free.

Garrett touched his fingertips to his lips, finding blood there. "He was running," he said in a cold voice. "I had to take him down."

When she looked at Dylan, he nodded, corroborating the story. She felt some of the fight leave her body. "Why would you run?"

"Because I'm guilty. Why else?"

"Oh, Dylan," she said, her disbelief tinged with defeat. Luke's grip on her changed, supporting rather than restraining her.

"Keep that crazy bitch away from me," Garrett warned, rubbing his jaw. "I didn't do anything wrong."

"Except grind your knee into my fucking neck," Dylan said.

Shay's vision narrowed, and she made another fist.

"Let's all just settle down for a minute," Luke said. "Shay, if you can't promise to stay calm, I'll have to ask you to leave the room."

She tried to jerk her arm from his grasp, but he held tight. "You're not allowed to interview my brother without my permission!"

"Actually, I am, in this situation."

She glared at him, her chest rising and falling with agitation. He stared back at her. Faced with no other choice, she gave her consent.

"Go on and sit over there by Dylan."

When he released her, she walked slowly around the perimeter of the table, her eyes on Garrett. All but baring her teeth, she sat down next to Dylan.

Luke turned to Garrett. "I would recommend that you consider your words, and your actions, very carefully from now on."

Garrett's dark gaze moved from Luke to Shay, assessing their body language in his cold, calculating way. He knew what was going on between them. "Those FBI guys might want to sit in on this interview," he said. It was a thinly veiled threat.

Luke made a show of considering the idea. "I think you're right," he said, nodding. "They'll probably be interested in that conversation we had about Yesenia Montes the other day, too. Let's call them in."

Whatever dirt Luke had on Garrett, it must have been good, because the stocky deputy shut up and sat down.

Luke took the seat next to him. "Did you read him the Miranda?"

"Yes," Garrett said. "Although I can't be certain a kid with a mouth like that understands the right to remain silent."

Luke kept his focus on Dylan, refusing to let Garrett's

sarcasm affect him. "Did you get a job on the construction site at Los Coyotes?"

Dylan frowned, as if he hadn't anticipated that particular question. "Yeah. I started yesterday."

"How'd that work out?"

"Okay, I guess."

"Did you see Bull Ryan?"

"Only for a second, when I first got there."

"Not before you left?"

He hesitated. "No. I went to the office to say good-bye, but he was already talking to someone else."

"Who?"

He glanced at Shay. "Jesse."

"Did you listen in?"

The corner of his mouth tipped up. "I might've heard some stuff."

"Like what?"

"Money trouble. Woman trouble." He gave an insouciant shrug. "Whatever."

"Was the conversation friendly?"

"Not really. But it wasn't, like, antagonistic. Just your typical Jesse Ryan bullshit."

"What does that mean?"

"That he got what he wanted without much resistance."

Luke's eyes went to Shay's, clearly reading Dylan's implication that she was also something Jesse had had without much resistance. "A loan?"

"I guess," he replied. "Why are we talking about him anyway?"

Instead of answering, Luke looked at Garrett, who slid a clear plastic bag across the surface of the table.

Inside, there was a hunting knife with a blade that folded down, making it easy to carry or conceal in the palm of a hand.

When she saw it, Shay's heart broke for her brother a little bit more.

Their dad hadn't been big on macho gifts, being a consummate pacifist who disdained material things, but he'd given that knife to Dylan on his tenth birthday. He hadn't been big on family vacations either, but damned if he hadn't taken her and Dylan to the Kern River that year, just weeks before she left for college.

"Every man should know how to clean a fish," he'd said, handing Dylan the shiny new knife. He'd been standing on the wet rocks along the riverbank, blond hair glinting in the late-day sun, holding a flopping trout on a short line.

Remembering the look of wonder in Dylan's eyes as he turned the knife in his hands, she now felt tears burn in her own. At the time, she'd been jealous of their easy male camaraderie. What she wouldn't give now for a dozen more moments like that.

Damn you, Daddy. Why'd you leave?

"Any particular reason you were carrying this?" Luke asked.

Dylan rolled his shoulders and winced, straining against the uncomfortable position. "Let's get real. You know what I did. I know what I did. You want me to sign something, fine. Take off these frigging cuffs and I'll sign whatever you want me to."

Luke's brows rose. "You will?"

"No," Shay said, fear twisting her insides. "He won't

sign anything. He doesn't know what he's talking about. Dylan—"

Her brother ignored her. "I'm guilty, okay? I used the knife to commit a crime and I'd do it again. I enjoyed it. And that stupid jock deserved it. I'd rather have blown up his engine, that would have been cool, or busted out the taillights—"

"Hang on," Luke said, holding a hand up. "You would have busted out whose taillights?"

"Chad's," he said, looking at the faces around him in confusion. "That's why you picked me up, right? Because I slashed his tires."

Shay let out a slow, pent-up breath. She wanted to slide under the table and crumple into a little heap of relief.

"You slashed Chad Pinter's tires," Luke repeated, leaning back in his chair.

"Yeah. What'd you think? That I killed somebody?"

"This is crazy," Garrett muttered, standing. "I can't believe you're buying this. The other day I caught him out on the rez with a backpack full of stuff to make pipe bombs. He's a menace to society."

Shay gasped. One glance at Dylan, whose face was pale with guilt, told her Garrett spoke the truth.

"Sit down, Garrett," Luke returned, his tone mild but his eyes intense.

The CB radio at the deputy's thick waist sounded, saving him from having to comply. It was the dispatch operator, phoning in a vandalism complaint from Chuck Pinter. After Garrett responded with a 10–4, the room fell into a charged silence.

"I'll take care of it," Luke said.

Garrett recognized the statement for what it was: a curt dismissal.

The deputy didn't reply to the rebuke, but he was in many ways a devious man, a plotter rather than a protester. Shay knew Luke was going to have nothing but trouble from him for the rest of their working days.

With a stiff nod, Garrett tossed the keys to his handcuffs on the table and left.

Luke watched him go, contemplating Garrett's perversity with narrowed eyes. Once the deputy was out of sight, Luke turned back to Dylan. "You saw him on Los Coyotes?"

"Yeah."

"When?"

Dylan gulped. "Sunday. And that pipe bomb stuff was just an experiment. Like a science project. I wouldn't use it to hurt anyone."

Shay knew her little brother had issues, but she'd never imagined he would put his life in danger by messing around with homemade explosives.

"Did he hit you?" Luke asked.

Dylan rubbed the side of his mouth against the fabric of his T-shirt. "No. He tackled me from behind and the ground said hello to my face."

"Has he ever hit you?"

When he paused, Shay wished a thousand miseries on Garrett Snell. "No," he said, and she knew he was lying.

So did Luke, but he didn't press further. Instead, he opened the evidence bag and let the knife slide out, unfolding the handle and examining the blade. He must have been satisfied with what he saw, because he stood and unlocked the cuffs at Dylan's wrists. "I have to take that vandalism call," he said, excusing himself.

"What the hell happened?" Dylan asked after Luke was out of earshot.

"Somebody scalped Bull Ryan."

His face went white beneath the layers of grime, making the dried blood on his chin stand out in harsh relief. "Is he dead?"

"Yes."

"Holy shit."

If she'd had any doubts about her brother's innocence, they were erased by the stunned expression he wore. Dylan often hid his feelings from her, and he wasn't always honest, but there was no artifice in his reaction to Bull's death.

She rose to her feet, grabbing a tiny plastic cup from the receptacle and filling it from the water cooler. "Here," she said, and he downed it in one gulp.

"More?"

"Yeah."

Shay was relieved that he hadn't been involved in whatever had gone down on the construction site, and thankful that he seemed relatively unharmed, but she was still furious with him for making pipe bombs. And slashing Chad's tires.

How could he pull such a lame-brained stunt? And why now, when he was so close to graduation?

Too angry to speak, she crossed her arms over her chest and waited for Luke to get off the phone. "The Pinters aren't sure they want to press charges," he said. "They'd like to meet us at the café to discuss the situation. I said I would mediate."

Shay almost wilted with relief. She sent Luke a silent thank you, because she knew how lucky Dylan was to get a chance to make amends. "Are you going to confiscate that?" she asked, looking down at the knife on the table.

Luke hesitated. "I wouldn't recommend he bring it to school again. If Chad's car had been in the school parking lot, instead of across the street, your brother would be on his way to juvenile hall right now."

Shay pocketed the knife. "What do you have to say for yourself?"

Dylan ran a hand along the line of his jaw, feeling for tenderness. "Good thing I wasn't on school property?"

24

Shay fumed all the way to the Bighorn. Chad Pinter was a major pain in the ass, and she hated his parents, but she would make nice with them for Dylan's sake.

The Pinters were already inside the café, chowing down on Betty's after-school special: burger, shake, and fries. At least, Chad and his father were. They had their plates piled high with greasy goodies, while the missus picked at a leafy green salad.

Chuck Pinter was the full-time football coach and part-time Driver's Ed teacher at Palomar High School. He had a take-charge attitude, ham-sized fists, and a burly physique. Marianne Pinter was pretty, petite, and very well preserved. Her slim jeans and tight T-shirt showed off her surgically enhanced chest and skinny legs to perfection.

They hadn't met Luke before, so Chuck did the introductions. When Marianne placed her dainty hand in his, she gave him a thorough once-over and fluttered her lashes.

Shay gritted her teeth and smiled.

After everyone was seated, Luke glanced at Shay, letting the mediation begin.

"I'd like to start by apologizing," Shay said. "I'm horrified by Dylan's behavior."

Marianne pursed her lips as if she'd just sucked on a lemon. Chad stared back at Shay with his usual half-lidded gaze, imagining God only knew what kind of disgusting sexual scenarios. Chuck merely grunted and took another bite of his burger.

"Dylan also has something to say," Shay added.

Dylan placed a hand over his heart. "I am truly, deeply, madly sorry."

Keeping her smile firm, Shay kicked him under the table. "I'll pay for any damages. New tires, towing fees, the works."

Marianne's face puckered again. "I'm afraid that won't be good enough," she said, giving Luke a simpering glance. "Dylan won't learn his lesson if you keep bailing him out, Shay. Surely you know that."

Shay arched a brow. If Marianne Pinter wanted to play hardball with her, she was more than willing to engage. "What do you propose?"

Marianne lifted her snooty little nose in her husband's direction. "He can work off what he owes us in our backyard. Chuck has plenty of digging and hauling to keep Dylan busy."

Shay's temper flared. She'd rather give what little cash she had to the Pinters than have her brother doing their dirty work. "Will Chad be doing yard work also?"

Marianne bristled. "Of course not. What's he done?"

With his loud car, expensive clothes, and entitled attitude, Chad Pinter was the most spoiled kid in Tenaja

Falls. "That's what I'd like to know," she said, turning toward her brother. "I don't think Dylan slashed his tires on a whim."

Dylan slouched down in his chair and looked away, refusing to offer an explanation for his actions.

"Perhaps he's jealous," Marianne said. "Chad *is* a star quarterback."

"Dylan is a starting forward," Shay shot back.

Marianne's mouth curled up at the corner. "My son also has a loving family and a stable home life. Have you given Dylan that?"

Shay's jaw dropped. She drew in a breath to tell Marianne where to go, but Dylan beat her to the punch.

"I'll tell you what else Chad has that I don't," he said in a cool voice. "An extensive collection of adult movies, downloaded on that fancy new computer you bought him. He brings printouts of his favorite images to school."

"Shut up," Chad grated, gripping the edge of the table.

"Today he was circulating a picture of a porn star with my sister's face superimposed over her head." After brief consideration, he dug a wadded up piece of paper out of his pocket. "Check it out."

Shay looked down at the image and gasped. "Why, you filthy little—"

When Luke put his hand on her shoulder, she bit off the word she was about to say. After a brief glance at the printout, he passed the page on to Chad's father. "I'm fairly certain that bringing this kind of material to school is against the rules. It may even be illegal."

"You have no proof that my son did this," Marianne sputtered.

"Sure I do," Dylan said. "I know the combination to his locker and the password for his laptop. I'm also familiar with the websites he frequents and the content he prefers."

The Pinters were speechless, and Chad was seething, but Dylan wasn't done. "It's kind of obvious the lady in the picture isn't Shay. You see, in addition to his bondage fetish, Chad collects photos of busty older women. Ladies who are built like you, Mrs. P." He smiled at Marianne's appalled expression. "It's terribly Oedipal, don't you think?"

Luke made a choking sound and reached for his glass of water.

While Chad stuttered excuses and Marianne turned red with humiliation, Chuck dug a few bills out of his wallet and threw them down on the table. "Just keep your brother away from my kid," he said, pointing his finger at Shay. Clamping his hand around Marianne's arm, he led her away, continuing to grumble as they went out the door. "Should have known the sheriff would side with her. She'll probably thank him on her knees."

Over his shoulder, Chad couldn't resist making a crude gesture, thrusting his tongue against the side of his cheek.

Dylan shot to his feet, but Luke held him back.

"Assholes," Shay muttered when they'd settled down in their seats again. They all looked at each other, and perhaps because the day had been so harrowing, the situation struck her as hilarious rather than sad. She started laughing, and once she started, she couldn't stop. Dylan laughed along with her, and it must have been contagious, because even Luke joined in.

"I can't believe you told Marianne Pinter her son had an Oedipus complex," she gasped, wiping tears from her eyes.

"Too bad she doesn't know what that means," Dylan replied, and set them off again.

Her stress level had reached its breaking point, and the laughter relieved some of the tension that had been escalating all week. It also opened the door for another outpouring of emotion, and before Shay knew it, she was crying.

Not crying laughing. Crying period.

Dylan's laughter trailed off and Luke cleared his throat, handing her a tissue. She took it and cried some more, hating that she was breaking down in front of them, the two people she wanted to be strong for, the ones she cared about most.

Pulling herself together, she blew her nose and took a long drink of water.

"Are you okay?" Luke asked, glancing down at her hand.

Her malady was general hysteria, not hemotoxic shock. "I'm fine," she said, offering him a wobbly smile.

"Because I can take you back—"

"No." She darted a nervous glance at Dylan. "Really."

Her brother frowned at Luke. "Take her back where?"

Luke's eyes bored into hers, letting her know that if she didn't tell Dylan what happened, he would. "The hospital," she said, sighing.

Dylan straightened in his chair. "What happened?"

"Someone left a snake at the preserve. I was careless in handling it."

"What kind of snake?"

"A rattler."

"You got bit by a rattlesnake?" he asked, raising his voice.

"It was more of a graze. No venom."

"Jesus Christ! What the hell is wrong with you?"

"What the hell is wrong with you?" she returned, her insides quaking. "I don't need you slashing tires to defend my honor. You could have been kicked out of school!"

Dylan leaned back in his chair and crossed his arms over his chest, reverting into sullen silence.

Shay felt so many conflicting emotions she couldn't sort through them all. She was proud of her brother for standing up for her but disappointed in him for acting so rashly. As usual, she couldn't prevent him from causing trouble.

"I have to go talk to Garrett," Luke said after a moment. "Will you be all right for an hour or so until I get back?"

"Of course," she murmured. "Be careful."

"I will," he promised, rising from his chair and giving her a quick peck on the cheek before he went out the door.

The way he'd said good-bye was so offhand, and felt so natural, that the implications of his actions didn't sink in right away. If Dylan hadn't been staring at her like she'd grown three heads, she might not have realized that she and Luke had just acted like a couple.

She lifted a hand to her cheek, feeling it grow warm. "What?"

"You're in love with the sheriff," he said, awestruck.

"Not even," she lied.

The corner of his mouth tipped up. "Well, he's in love with you."

That was a far more outrageous notion, and one she didn't have the heart to protest. The idea was too painful, and it made the empty place inside her ache to be filled.

Betty appeared beside her with a carafe, ready to fill something else. "Coffee?"

"No thanks," Shay said, covering the rim of her mug. The small red mark on the edge of her thumb was clearly visible under the fluorescent lights.

"What happened there?"

"Nothing." She drew her hand back self-consciously. To take the attention away from herself, she nodded at Betty, who had her forearm wrapped in gauze. Shay had noticed the bandage a few days ago. "How about you?"

"Just a cat scratch," she replied, winking at Dylan. "What'll you have?"

Her brother asked for a burger with the works and a chocolate shake. Shay's appetite was off, for once in her life, so she requested a small order of fries.

"Coming right up," Betty said, whisking away their menus.

Shay picked at her napkin, considering what to say next. They hadn't talked about their parents in longer than she could remember. He always changed the subject. "I know you miss Mom and Dad," she began. "I miss them, too. That hunting knife—"

"You don't know anything," he said, his face darkening with anger.

She threw up her hands in frustration. "Then talk to me! How am I supposed to understand if you won't let me in?"

He looked down at the table, avoiding her eyes.

"I don't know what to do with you," she said, feeling as inadequate as ever. "I can't stop you from getting angry, and I can't keep you from being self-destructive. I've tried to do right by you, but I don't know where else to turn. I don't know anything about being a proper guardian." She leaned toward him, her voice strained. "I'm not your mother, damn it!"

His head jerked up. "You're not my mother," he repeated, studying her face. "Who took care of me when I was little?"

Shay stared back at him in silence, feeling her throat tighten.

"Who walked me to the bus stop? Who cooked me dinner? Who tucked me in at night?"

Tears welled in her eyes. She hadn't known he remembered.

"I didn't give a damn when Dad left, because I never counted on him," he continued. "He was useless most of the time. I knew better than to expect him to stay. And as for Mom . . . I never knew her at all."

"Oh, Dylan," she whispered, blinking the tears from her eyes.

"The person I counted on was you. As far as I was concerned, you were my mother. I was never mad at them for leaving. They weren't worth it. I was mad at you."

Her heart felt like it was being wrenched from her chest. She pressed a fist to the front of her T-shirt, trying to alleviate the pressure. "You know I had to go to college."

"You left in spirit way before that. Running wild with your loser boyfriend. Sure, you came back to Tenaja Falls, and now you support us financially. But you haven't really been home since Mom killed herself."

The instant the words left his mouth, she knew he was right. She'd been so concerned with maintaining the status quo and ensuring his continued success in school, she'd completely forgotten how to relate to him as a human being.

She hadn't been a mother *or* a sister; she'd been an emotional wasteland.

"I'm sorry," she said, stunned by the realization. "I don't know what to say. Except that you're right. I'm such a screwup."

His expression softened. "No, you're not. Mom and Dad were screwups."

"They loved you."

He shrugged, not bothering to contradict her.

Tears filled her eyes again. "I love you."

"I know," he said, smiling a little. He might have said more, but Betty brought their plates, interrupting the sentimental moment. When forced to decide between making sappy remarks and chowing down on a loaded burger, Dylan made the predictable choice and dug in with his trademark gusto.

Nevertheless, she was pleased with the direction of

the conversation. She hadn't felt this close to her brother in ages. A warm contentment came over her, tempered only slightly by her confusion about her feelings for Luke and a bone-deep weariness.

"I'll try to do better," she said, nibbling on a french fry. "Be home more."

"You do okay," he allowed, taking another huge bite.

Her lips curved as she studied him from across the table. For the first time, her brother looked more like a man than a boy to her, and the sight unsettled her. With his dark blond hair and intense blue eyes, he was the spitting image of their father. And even with blood on his face and a torn T-shirt, he was handsome.

She should be thankful he'd never had any luck with girls.

On the heels of that thought, Angel's father, Fernando Martinez, parked his truck outside the café. Dylan went very still, as if expecting some kind of confrontation, but Fernando merely waved hello as he came through the front door. While he waited for Betty at the register, he took a handkerchief out of his back pocket and wiped his lined forehead. As usual, he looked tired.

Betty reappeared from the kitchen, greeting Fernando with a nervous smile. She handed him some bills from the register.

Their exchange was none of her business, so Shay turned back to Dylan, shoving a few more french fries in her mouth.

"I have to talk to Fernando," Dylan said in a low voice.

"Why?"

A flush crept up his neck. "I was with Angel earlier, and she . . . she left town. She ran away to Vegas. I watched her get on the bus."

"Why would she go there?"

His mouth turned grim. "I think she's planning on doing something stupid. Like getting a job at a strip club."

Uh-oh. With her face and body, Angel wouldn't have any trouble finding work in Vegas. "When did the bus leave?"

He glanced at the clock. "Over an hour ago."

Shay didn't need to hear any more. "Go tell him now," she said, urging him to his feet. "Maybe he can catch up with her."

25

As soon as Luke got in his truck, his radio crackled with distortion. "Domestic disturbance. Reported by a female resident at 420 Larkspur Lane."

A chill raced down Luke's spine. That was Garrett's address.

"Please be advised that the suspect is an off-duty police officer. He should be considered armed and dangerous."

Luke responded to the call, driving as fast as he dared down Tenaja Falls's main drag. He knew from experience that this type of situation had to be handled carefully. Violent acts against women were usually perpetrated by a husband or boyfriend, and a man at home could be extremely defensive.

Being on his own turf, he also had a hell of an advantage.

When Luke pulled up to the driveway, he saw that Garrett wasn't holed up inside his house, pointing a rifle through the mini-blinds. He was sitting in his police car in the front drive, holding his service revolver to his right temple.

Staving off a rush of panic, Luke picked up his radio and called in the details. Talking down a suicidal officer was way out of his area of expertise, but he might not have time to wait for backup.

Had Garrett done something to Lori? Men who committed suicide often did so after harming someone else.

Another feeling came over him, one of almost uncontrollable fury. Garrett had a connection to Yesenia Montes and a well-known gambling problem. According to Dylan, he'd also been on the reservation the day of the fire. It wouldn't surprise Luke if he'd borrowed money from Bull Ryan to pay off Moses Rivers.

Garrett had been quick to point his finger at the rez, after all. He'd probably planted the arrowhead with the snake at Dark Canyon. In addition to his other crimes, if he was indeed guilty, Garrett had tried to kill Shay.

At that moment, Luke didn't give a damn about duty, and he wasn't the least bit concerned about his deputy's future.

Garrett only had to live long enough to suffer.

Luke got out of his truck, surveying the scene. Lori Snell was pacing the front lawn, tears streaming down her face, a cordless phone in her hand. Although she appeared unhurt, she was about a hundred feet from the driveway, well within Garrett's range.

Keeping a visual on Garrett, his hand on his holster, he approached Lori. Her eyes were dark with misery and her cheeks ashen. He'd never seen her before, but despite her frantic state she was pretty, and his disdain for Garrett deepened.

"Where's the baby?" he asked, remembering she had a young child.

She hugged her arms around herself. "With my m-m-mother."

"Good. Why's he doing this?"

Shaking her head, she said, "W-we had a fight, but— I don't think that's it. Something else is bothering him."

Keeping his hand on his gun, he surveyed the neighborhood. Two doors down, there was an older woman looking through the window. "You know the lady in the blue house?"

Her head bobbed up and down. "Yes."

"Go over there and let her make you a cup of tea." He knew it sounded condescending, but he needed to know she was safe. "I can't do my job if I'm worried about you running out here and getting in the way."

She moistened her lips. "Okay. But just—don't shoot him. Please?"

Luke snuck another glance at Garrett. Even from this distance, he could see that the deputy's entire body was trembling, and his gun hand was none too steady.

Damn.

"I won't," he promised, and hoped he could keep it. Garrett would have to pay for what he'd done, and although shooting him sounded tempting, he wouldn't do it unless he had to. He'd never killed a man before. He'd never wanted to.

After one last pleading look, Lori hurried across the lawns and into her neighbor's house. As soon as she was out of sight, Luke turned and walked back toward the driveway, making a wide circle around Garrett's cruiser. The black-and-white squad car looked shiny and sleek in the twilight, a lurking shark in troubled waters.

Flexing his fingers, Luke approached slowly, his heart in his throat, sweat stinging his eyes. Forty feet. Thirty.

"Don't come any closer," Garrett warned.

Luke stopped twenty feet away from the driver's side, staying in Garrett's line of sight but keeping his body at an angle. If Garrett decided to turn his gun on Luke, it would be awkward for him to shoot over his left shoulder. "I just want to talk."

"Stay away!"

Luke came closer. Ten feet. Close enough to see the sheen of perspiration on Garrett's brow. "Tell me what happened."

Garrett let out a strangled sound, somewhere between a sob and a laugh.

"I just want to talk," Luke repeated, hearing the strain in his own voice.

Garrett's gun hand wobbled precariously. "Get away from me!"

"I'll take off my gun belt. Watch." With steady movements, he unfastened his belt and laid it down on the concrete, straightening and holding his arms high.

"Stay back!"

Luke took a deep breath and stepped forward. "I'm unarmed, Garrett. I couldn't grab your gun from here even if I wanted to. If you're going to pull the trigger, I can't stop you. But first tell me why. Tell me what happened."

Garrett's eyes darted back toward the front of the house, looking for Lori.

"You owe it to your wife," he said, struck by a flash of inspiration. "You want her to think you've done this because of her?"

Garrett's face crumpled. "N-no."

Luke wasn't sure he understood the belated concern for Lori. Garrett certainly hadn't been thinking about his wife while he was fooling around with Yesenia Montes.

"There is one thing I'd like you to tell her."

"Name it."

"I lied about having sex with Yesenia. I used that as an excuse because I knew people had seen us together."

Luke hadn't expected this particular confession. "What were you doing with her?"

Garrett made a sniffling noise. "I set her up on dates sometimes. Introduced her to people. Drove her around."

Luke was baffled. "Why?"

"She gave me a cut."

Realization dawned. His sheriff's deputy was a *pimp*. And here Luke thought Tenaja Falls would be less tawdry than Las Vegas.

"I have a gambling problem, in case you didn't know," Garrett continued in a self-deprecating tone. "I needed the extra income."

"You've overextended yourself?"

"And then some. We're going to lose the house. Lori will be better off without me."

"She won't get a dime of insurance money if you pull the trigger," Luke said, relaxing his stance a little.

He was pretty sure Garrett wasn't going to shoot him, or anyone else. "You know, I've never really liked guns," he added, offhand.

Garrett blinked a few times. "You—you haven't?"

"Nah. That was one of the reasons I accepted this position in Tenaja Falls. I didn't think I'd have to wear my gun all the time."

"That's . . . stupid," Garrett decided. "You can't make a routine traffic stop these days without worrying you'll catch some psycho behind the wheel."

Luke found that statement pretty ironic, considering the current situation. "Yeah, I guess. I think I'll quit wearing it anyway. I don't like shooting them. I certainly didn't like getting shot. And the mess they make!" Grimacing, he surveyed the Vic's interior. "You ever seen a man take a hit to the head at close range?"

Garrett swallowed a few times, looking queasy.

"What am I saying? Of course you have. Must've been brains all over in Iraq."

Garrett's lips curled back in distaste, but he couldn't deny it.

"You don't want your wife to see that, man. Lori will be upset about the house. But she'd be more upset about losing her house and the father of her baby." Luke put his hand near the open window. "Give me the gun."

"No."

"Give me the gun, Garrett. Don't wait until the whole neighborhood comes out. This place will be swarming with squad cars from the Palomar substation in a few minutes."

After another moment of indecision, Garrett capitulated, placing his revolver in the palm of Luke's hand.

As Luke wrapped his fingers around the sweaty, skin-warmed steel, he experienced a powerful surge of rage. The temptation to shove the barrel against Garrett's skull and demand some answers was overwhelming. Now he knew why cops sometimes lost control with suspects. "Get out," he said, engaging the safety and tucking the gun into the back of his pants.

"Wh—what? Why?"

"You know procedure as well as I do, Garrett. I'll be sure to mention that I had your full cooperation when I file my report. Now get the fuck out of the car."

Garrett opened the driver's-side door and stepped out, groaning as he considered the ramifications of his actions. Luke had him sprawled over the hood, his hands cuffed behind his back, before he could change his mind.

"Tell me what you did with Yesenia," he demanded, kicking his feet apart.

"Nothing," Garrett said. "Nothing, I swear."

Luke patted him down roughly, every muscle in his body poised to fight. Following instinct instead of procedure, he jerked the cuffs up and shoved Garrett's head down on the hood, applying what he knew to be a painful amount of pressure. "If you don't start talking I'll smear your face all over this driveway."

"I didn't touch her. I swear to God I didn't."

"Did you plant the snake at Dark Canyon?"

He hesitated. "Confessions made under duress are inadmissible."

"I'll show you some duress," Luke muttered, lifting

Garrett from the hood of the car and slamming him facedown again. "Did you plant the snake?"

Garrett made a gurgling noise. Luke lifted him up again.

"Yes," Garrett cried. "I owe Moses Rivers a lot of money. I thought if I implicated him I could use it as a bargaining chip. Reduce my debt, in exchange for taking the heat off."

Desperate times called for desperate measures, Luke supposed.

"I never meant to hurt Shay," Garrett insisted. "I've seen her handle snakes before. She's a pro."

"Did you set the fire?"

Garrett didn't answer. He didn't have to.

"Goddamn you, Garrett! Don't tell me you didn't mean to hurt anyone then, either."

"The wind was stronger than I thought—"

Luke drove his elbow into the middle of Garrett's back, shutting him up. "Is that why you killed Bull Ryan, you lying sack of shit? To cast suspicion on Rivers? Or were you just trying to implicate me?"

"I didn't kill him," he rasped, struggling for breath. "We . . . scuffled, over some money I owed him, and he . . . clutched at his chest. He was dead before he hit the floor. I swear."

"So instead of calling 911, or performing CPR, you cut the top of his head off? You are a sick motherfucker, Snell. They're going to lock you up and throw away the key. And you know how law enforcement officers get treated in prison." He twisted the cuffs. "I hope your cellmate is some big guy named Bubba."

"Please," Garrett gasped.

"Why did you move Yesenia?"

"I didn't," he insisted.

"The fuck you didn't!" Jerking the gun from the waistband of his pants, Luke shoved the barrel against the back of Garrett's thick neck. He still didn't like guns, but he had to admit he liked making his deputy sorry.

"Okay!" Garrett screamed. "Okay, I'll talk. Point that thing somewhere else. Please."

Luke ignored his request. "What did you do to her?"

"She was cheating me out of my cut, keeping all of her earnings. And telling the other girls to do the same."

Other girls? Jesus. It got worse every second. "So you fed her to the lions?"

"I only meant to scare her," he panted. "I didn't think the lion would really attack."

"What lion?" He jammed the barrel into the back of Garrett's neck. "Where?"

"At Betty Louis's ranch," he said, his big body shuddering with stress. "Betty was in on it. She sees girls at the café sometimes, and she does some . . . recruiting for me. It was all her fault, I swear! She's the one with the crazy-ass lion."

"Fernando," Dylan called out, running across the parking lot to catch up with him.

Angel's dad stopped and turned, his face showing surprise.

"I mean, uh, Mr. Martinez," Dylan corrected, faltering. It was a sticky situation, talking to the father of the girl he'd just slept with. "I need to tell you something," he said in a rush. "Angel went to Vegas."

"My daughter went to Las Vegas?"

"Yessir."

"Oh. Well, I hope she has fun." With an uncertain smile, he reached for his door handle.

"No, wait," Dylan said. "I don't mean she went there for a few days. I mean she left town for good."

The smile slid off his face. "How do you know this?"

"I saw her get on the bus." Realizing this wasn't proof enough, he dug into his pocket for the note she left. "She wrote me this," he said, handing it over. "I tried to stop her from leaving but she wouldn't listen."

Fernando inspected the note, his brows raised. He didn't say anything about Angel's odd style of writing, or the content, but Dylan's face burned with embarrassment.

"Angelita is a grown woman, *mijo*," he said sadly, handing the paper back to him. "She makes her own decisions. I'm sorry if you feel let down."

"You don't understand," Dylan said, trying not to panic. "She went to Vegas to sell her body or something. She thinks she's dumb. She thinks she has no future!"

Fernando's dark eyes narrowed with suspicion. "You were with my daughter this afternoon, no? Did you pay her . . . for her body?"

"Of course not," he said, starting to sweat. He'd offered to pay her, but that had been his bruised ego talking. "Maybe she's going to be an exotic dancer," he conceded, picturing her sexy lingerie. "All I know is that she went to find work, and she wouldn't tell me more. Whatever her plan is, it's really bad."

"What is this exotic dancing? Taking off clothes?"

"Yes," Dylan exclaimed, finally getting through to him.

Unlike prostitution, which he didn't seem to believe his daughter capable of, Fernando was visibly upset by the idea of Angel stripping. "When did she leave?"

"At least an hour ago."

"You know this bus, if you see again?"

Dylan nodded.

Fernando jerked his chin toward the passenger side. "*Ándale, pues.*"

Shay waved good-bye to Dylan in the parking lot and promised Fernando she would check in on his kids. He didn't know how long they'd be out looking for Angel.

She wasn't sure she approved of her brother going off on a wild goose chase to Las Vegas, but he was almost an adult now and she had to let him grow up. Although she'd like to continue sheltering him, that time had come and gone.

Luke's absence also worried her. Like most bullies, Garrett was a coward at heart, but such men were dangerous when cornered, and he seemed to have his back to the wall. His marriage was crumbling, and as far as Shay knew, his career was in jeopardy.

The way Garrett treated Lori was none of Shay's business, she supposed, but he had no right to get physical with Dylan. She might file a formal complaint with the county.

"You need a ride home?" Betty asked. Not one to miss out on any Tenaja Falls action, she'd been standing right beside Shay, watching the drama unfold.

"To the Martinez place," she corrected. "If it's no trouble." Shay would have waited for Luke, but with Angel and Fernando both gone, no telling what the Martinez kids were up to. They were too young to fend for themselves.

"Grill's still hot. I'll whip them up some cheese sandwiches."

"Thanks, Betty." Shay crossed her arms in front of her chest and blinked at the last sliver of sunset, feeling fatigue settle over her. "That would be great."

Betty had the sandwiches ready in a snap. She handed them to Shay, piping hot in a large paper bag, and locked the front door. Rubbing her tired eyes, Shay followed her through the kitchen and out the back exit. Betty's shiny new pickup was right behind the building, facing outward, its rear bumper almost kissing the stucco.

Lying on a corrugated liner in the back of the truck, there were a half-dozen fresh rabbit carcasses, tied together with straw-colored twine.

Betty had probably bought the rabbits from Fernando, who'd tossed them in the back of her truck before he came inside. People around here ate plenty of wild game, especially when money was tight, so the sight wasn't unusual.

Shay's reaction to the dead animals was strange, however. While Betty locked the back door, she stared at the stiff legs and beady eyes. Rabbits were typical mountain lion prey. In a flash of intuition, she replayed Betty's explanation of the bandage covering her forearm.

Cat scratch? Must have been a hell of a big cat.

A creepy feeling came over her, dancing along the nape of her neck. Shay didn't know why this scenario had never occurred to her before. It was tragic, but not all that uncommon, for ignorant fools to keep mountain lions as pets.

Don't look back.

Her mother's warning echoed in her ears, and a jumble of nightmare images danced through her head. She saw the hanging tree at the Graveyard. Her mother's dead hand. A yowling lion, his muzzle dripping blood.

But of course, looking back was exactly what she did, turning to question Betty instead of ducking down.

And saw only the cold glint of metal as she was struck.

The ride toward Vegas was tense and silent, but that was to be expected. Dylan felt somewhat responsible for Angel's sudden departure, almost as if he'd instigated her decision to go, and Fernando was none too pleased about the turn of events.

Dylan also knew Angel would resent his interference. She didn't want him now any more than she'd wanted him before; their time together had been an aberration. The best aberration of his life, to be sure, but it meant nothing to her. Like Chad, he'd been a vehicle in her quest for self-destruction.

Dylan didn't have to be a genius to figure Angel's scarred relationship with her mother had taken her down this path, and he could relate to what she was going through. When your own mother didn't love you enough to stick around, it was difficult to believe you were capable of being loved.

Even though he understood Angel's actions on an intellectual level, he couldn't deal with them on an emotional one. And physically, he was a wreck. Fantasizing about his afternoon with Angel while her dad was in the seat next to him was a bad idea, but his mind kept replaying their encounter, no matter how hard he tried to repress it.

"My daughter," Fernando began, startling Dylan out of his inappropriate thoughts, "she told you she thinks she is dumb? That she has no future?"

"Not in those exact words."

"Then in which ones?"

He hesitated, feeling guilty, and a little fearful of Fernando's wrath. "She said, 'I know I'm stupid' once after I saw her handwriting."

Fernando was quiet for another moment. "My father never learned to read. He was the smartest man I knew. My mother could not write her own name, but she told entire stories from memory. She was very wise." He glanced at Dylan, as if expecting an argument. "There is more to intelligence than book learning."

"Yessir," he replied, not having to pretend he agreed.

"I know Angel struggled in school. She never said it bothered her."

Dylan shrugged. Obviously, it had bothered her. But he didn't say that.

"She isn't stupid."

"No sir."

"You are very good in school, *verdád?*"

"*Sí,*" he muttered, smart enough to know where this was going.

Fernando studied Dylan's swollen cheek. "And yet you can't seem to stay out of the way of moving fists. Who did that to your face?"

"Deputy Snell."

"Ah." He turned his attention back to the road. "Even I know it is better to avoid a man like him, and I have only an eighth-grade education."

Dylan felt a smile tug at his lips. Fernando made a good point. Dylan couldn't always dodge Snell, but he could learn how to keep his stupid mouth shut.

"With my daughter . . . *usaste condón?*"

That wiped the smile off his face. "Yes," he said, his neck growing hot.

Fernando glanced into the rearview mirror. "Good. You are much too young to be a father. In fact," he weaved through traffic, "You should not touch Angel again."

Dylan recognized the threat for what it was and didn't respond. If they didn't find Angel, the point was moot, and even if they did, she would probably rather die than sleep with him again. But that was up to her, and nothing Fernando said would stop him.

If she gave him the go-ahead, he would touch her anywhere, anytime, and any way she wished.

Fernando's 4-runner was built for reliability, not speed. Even so, he was punching it down the highway, passing most cars like they were standing still. The time of day also worked to their advantage. At dusk, there was a lot of traffic, enough to slow down a tour bus, but not so much that Fernando couldn't get through.

The preferred route to Vegas was pretty much a straight shot. The last convenient stop along the way, and the most likely place to catch up with Angel, was in Midway, an appropriately named town halfway between Vegas and LA.

Dylan knew without having to be told that this was

their only chance to find her. It was getting dark and soon he wouldn't be able to recognize the bus she'd taken among the others on the crowded freeway. The transit station in Vegas would be huge and chaotic. As soon as she stepped onto the causeway, she would disappear.

After they took the Midway exit and pulled into the rest area, Dylan saw one dusty tour bus sitting in the back of the lot under the dismal glow of fluorescent streetlights.

"I think that's it," he said, straightening in his seat.

But as they came closer, he saw the insignia painted on the side: "Desert Breeze." Not "Sunset Tours."

"No," he said, his heart sinking. "Wrong one. Sorry."

Fernando pulled into a parking space beside the bus just as the driver started the engine and began to drive away. Curling his hands around the steering wheel, he closed his eyes and rested his forehead against it in absolute defeat.

Dylan tore his eyes away from the man's haggard face, watching helplessly as the wrong bus went by, taking their last hope with it. In the space it vacated, he caught a glimpse of a dark, curvy shape, the outline of a black guitar case.

And the girl sitting next to it, using her duffel bag as a cushion, her elbows resting on her bent knees and her chin propped up in her hands, was Angel.

Shay woke up in the passenger seat of Betty's parked truck, alone and disoriented. She was slumped on her side, stomach roiling with nausea, her head pounding as if she'd been downing shots at the Round-Up all night.

But she hadn't been. Had she?

No. The last thing she remembered was being behind the café . . . with Betty. And now she had a headache from hell.

Groaning, she raised a hand to her hair. It was matted with blood, sticky-wet. And her clothes smelled like . . . *coffee.*

That's right. Betty had clocked her over the head with an aluminum coffeepot. But why?

The world outside was dark, not yet black. It was still early evening. She raised herself up to look around and the interior of the cab went spinning. Moaning, she reached out to grab ahold of the dash and squeezed her eyes shut until the motion stopped.

Luke. She had to tell Luke. She had to find Luke and tell him . . . what? Rabbits. Something about rabbits.

Her eyes flew open. Fuck the rabbits, she had to get out of here. Her clumsy hands lifted the door handle and she almost went tumbling out. Light flooded the cab of the truck. She blinked rapidly, trying to clear her vision as she searched her surroundings and her person. Damn. No cell phone. No keys in the ignition, either. No escape.

Terrified by the idea that Betty would come back to finish her off, she stumbled out of the truck, and fell facedown in the dirt. Her head throbbed as if she'd been struck by lightning. Her stomach rebelled, threatening to send its contents hurling back up.

She was vaguely aware that she was no longer in the parking lot behind the café. The ground beneath her was too soft; earth filled her grasping hands. Panting from fear and nausea, she pushed the passenger door shut and let the night envelop her.

As she lay there, trying to catch her breath, she outlined her choices. Stay here and die. Crawl away and find help.

That last one sounded best. She lifted her head again, moving gingerly, studying the gloom around her. Fuzzy shapes began to take focus. Hills and trees and a dirt road. A long fence and lonely mailbox. It all looked kind of familiar.

Oh, shit. She turned to see Betty's ranch-style house, looming behind her like something from a nightmare.

They were out in the middle of nowhere. She could crawl for hours before she found a friendly neighbor in this neck of the woods.

Woods. That was it! She could hide in the woods until the pain in her head subsided. There wasn't much around here but sagebrush and rocks, but the nearby hills offered plenty of cover for a person lying down. At the very least, she should get away from the front yard, and out of sight of the road.

Betty hadn't brought her home for a game of Monopoly, after all. And any moment, she'd be back looking for her.

Decision made, Shay pushed herself up onto her hands and knees. When no vomiting or head-exploding pain ensued, she struggled to her feet, holding on to the side of the truck for balance.

The wild rabbits were still there, dead, bodies stiff, eyes black in the moonlight.

Everything came rushing back to her. Her strange,

foreboding dream. The suspicion that Betty had a pet lion. The blackout blow.

In the close distance, an ear-splitting shriek rang out, shrill and high-pitched, as haunting as a woman's scream. It was the unmistakable sound of an angered lion.

"Oh, God," she whispered, feeling her knees shake. What was Betty doing? Letting the lion out to hunt?

She shrank away from the truck, worried that the scent of rabbit would call the lion closer. Then she lifted her hand to her head in horror, aware that the smell of her own blood also filled the air. She couldn't hide from a hungry lion. And if it came after her, there was no way she could outrun it.

For a moment, she was tempted to crawl back inside the cab of the truck and lock the doors. Betty could still get to her, but the lion couldn't.

Another set of screams filled the night, causing goose bumps to break out on her skin. This time, the yowl didn't merely sound like a woman. It *was* a woman. What if Betty wasn't letting the lion loose? What if she was . . . offering it a victim?

Shay shuddered where she stood, chilled to the bone. Then, still reeling from the blow to her head, she staggered forward, toward the sound.

Along the side of the main house there was an old red barn, open and filled with rusty farming equipment. If Betty had a caged enclosure, it would be out back. On unsteady legs, she passed the barn, moving quietly over the dry earth.

As soon as she rounded the corner, she saw it. A

large chain-link enclosure, bathed in the glow of fluorescent light.

The enclosure stretched from the back of the house
all the way to the fence line. Camouflaged netting covered the links on top and wooden slats added privacy
along the sides. To a casual observer, the enclosure
might appear to be nothing more sinister than an extra-
large dog run, but Shay recognized the signs of a big cat.

The concrete floors looked clean but smelled of territorial markings. An intact male lion definitely lived
here. There was a kiddie pool filled with fresh water in
one corner and she could see a number of "toys" scattered about. A couple of scarred wooden logs, some
sturdy rubber balls, and a few old tires were visible
through the slats.

Pulse racing, mouth dry, Shay crept along the edge
of the enclosure, trying to catch a glimpse of its inhab-
itant. Her eyes were drawn to a square-shaped flap covering the lower half of the house's back door.

Good God. The beast had the run of the house, too!

When the cat came into her line of sight, Shay froze
in place, the hairs on the back of her neck prickling in
awareness. He was at least as big as Hamlet, if not bigger. Muscles bunched beneath his dun-colored coat.
The cage seemed to shrink in his presence.

Betty was standing on the other side of the chain-
link fence. The entrance to the enclosure and the back
gate were both wide open. "Run, you stupid cat!"
Screaming her frustration, she prodded him with a
steel bar while he spat and hissed. "Run!"

Holy *hell*. Betty *was* trying to free him. Shay studied
the barren landscape beyond the fence line, seeing

nothing but dark underbrush and pale rocks the size of headstones.

"Don't," she said, finding her voice. "Don't do this, Betty!"

With another sinister howl, the lion turned his massive head in Shay's direction. When his gray-green eyes met hers, she gulped and took a step back, her heart beating so fast she could hear it thundering in her ears.

"I won't let you take him," Betty said, her face ravaged by grief. "He didn't mean to kill Yesenia. We were only trying to scare her, but Kato got too excited. She started screaming and he pounced. By the time I pried his jaw open, it was too late."

Shay didn't know what to say. Betty seemed on the cusp of madness. She had, after all, just bashed her over the head.

"He's never hurt anyone before," Betty said. "He was only playing."

Shay realized that the woman was trying to save the lion's life, not send him out on another rampage, and she felt a pang of sympathy for her. Shay knew what it was like to lose a beloved friend. Hamlet had been sacrificed unnecessarily, and now Kato would have to be put down as well.

She hated it when animals suffered because of human carelessness.

The circumstances were sad, but Shay couldn't let Betty free a killer lion. "He can go to a rescue facility," she lied. Kato wouldn't be allowed to live, not even in captivity. "He'll be put somewhere safe and secure."

Betty let out a harsh laugh, shaking her head. "He can take his chances in the desert."

Shay scrambled forward, trying to avert a disaster of epic proportions. "No, Betty," she said. "He'll never survive—"

But she was too late. Betty had already entered the cage.

Gasping, Shay stopped in her tracks. No telling what the lion would do.

When he didn't do anything, Betty pointed at the chaparral-covered hills in the distance and waved her hands in frustration. "Go on," she said, gripping the chain links and rattling the fence. "Be free!"

Shay's eyes darted from the open gate to the stationary lion. She knew better than to make any sudden moves around a predatory cat. But what else could she do?

Betty grabbed the animal by the scruff of his neck, trying to force him out. He roared a protest. She didn't listen.

"Oh, Jesus," Shay whimpered, almost too afraid to watch. The cat was going to attack Betty and there was nothing Shay could do about it. With trembling fingers, she reached into her front pocket, closing her fingers around Dylan's hunting knife.

When Betty yelled and pulled on the cat's scruff again, he snapped. In a flash, Betty was stretched out on the ground with the lion's jaws closed around her neck. There was a sickening sound, like a wet crunch, as he applied pressure. Horrified, Shay stumbled toward the gate. Now that the cat was preoccupied, she had the chance to shut him in.

But if she didn't intervene, Betty would surely die.

It was one of those life-altering moments. Shay had

always wondered what she would do in this kind of situation, if she would risk herself to save someone else. Only for Dylan, she'd have said before. And so it was with no small amount of surprise that she found herself rushing to Betty's aid after a short hesitation.

The lion had a death hold on Betty's neck. His jaws were locked; her body was limp. It might be too late already, but Shay picked up a tire and heaved it at him, her head throbbing with pain. Panting from exertion, she dumped a bucket of cold water over the tangled pair. She tried to knock him loose with a block of wood.

He wouldn't budge.

Betty's blood slicked the concrete beneath them.

With nothing left to do but join the fray, Shay extended the knife, gripping it in her white-knuckled hand. Making a strange, feral sound, she sank the blade into his neck, going for the carotid artery.

She missed.

The lion released Betty and let out an earsplitting howl. Screaming, Shay fell away from him, her hands and feet seeking purchase in the slippery mess.

He turned on her and roared, his jaws wet with blood.

Shay's entire life flashed before her eyes. And the world exploded into chaos.

27

Getting on that bus was probably the stupidest thing Angel had ever done. Getting off it in favor of being stranded at a deserted rest stop wasn't too smart, either.

At the bus station, she'd watched Deputy Snell tackle Dylan and wrestle him to the ground. She'd wanted to scream Dylan's name, to tell the bus driver to stop and let her out, to pull at Snell's hair and kick him in the ribs. Instead she'd just sat there, frozen to her seat, weeping silently.

That was what she did for the next three hours.

It finally occurred to her that by leaving for Vegas, she wasn't taking charge of her life. She was allowing the past to overwhelm her. Nor was she helping her brothers and sister by abandoning them, just as their mother had done, and perpetuating a vicious cycle.

She couldn't believe she hadn't seen that until now.

The truth was, she'd been going half-mad since Christmas. Finding out about her mother's new baby had brought her to an all-time low, and the horrible experience with Chad had taken her even lower. Instead of dealing with her feelings, she'd repressed them, pretending everything was fine.

Besides Dylan, she hadn't told anyone what happened. Her boy-crazy best friend thought Chad was cute; she'd have squealed with delight and asked for a play-by-play. And how could a girl talk to her own father about sex? That was just . . . unnatural.

So Angel had kept every detail of the encounter to herself, from Chad's whisky-laced breath and sloppy kisses to his rough hands and crude technique.

Dylan may not have known what he was doing in the bedroom, but what he lacked in experience he made up for in sensitivity. And eagerness to learn. She hadn't lied when she'd told him he'd been way better than Chad. With Dylan, she'd wanted it to last forever. With Chad, she'd prayed it would be over as soon as possible.

Dylan had tried to take his time. He'd attempted to make it good for her.

Chad hadn't cared. In fact, he seemed to take pleasure in hurting her, and after it was over, he couldn't wait to be rid of her. He'd used her and discarded her like trash. Like a wadded-up Kleenex he'd ejaculated into. It wasn't as if she wanted to spend any more time with him, but coming on the heels of her mother's latest rejection, his casual disposal of her virginity had been devastating.

Angel had vowed not to waste any tears on Chad, who was a bad kisser, a poor student, and a miserable excuse for a human being. And she hadn't. She'd refused to think about their hookup altogether until she saw him again at the Graveyard. When he first spotted her, a sly look had passed over his face. He was stinking drunk by the time he approached her, his manner as rude and arrogant as ever.

She knew he'd goaded Travis into hitting on her. She also suspected he'd enjoyed watching his friend hold her down. Seeing Chad again had released a flood of painful memories, and struggling with Travis in the backseat of Chad's stupid car had been her breaking point.

This whole Vegas scheme, the confusing sexual game she'd been playing with Dylan, and every ridiculous thing she'd done over the past few days had been more about her acting out than taking control. A cry for help, rather than a quest for independence.

She wasn't a martyr for her family or the savior of her siblings. She was just another pathetic cliché, the girl who believed she was worthless because her flighty mother left her and a dumb jock used her like a whore.

Brushing away her angry tears, she watched while the last bus cleared out of the parking lot. She was dead alone at a deserted truck stop, vulnerable to the kinds of perverts she thought she'd be tough enough to perform for in Las Vegas.

Alone . . . but for one small pickup truck. Her father's rusty white 4-runner. And, *Santa Maria,* was it a sight for sore eyes.

Her dad came out of the driver's side and she was up on her feet in a flash, launching herself into his open arms.

More tears streamed out of the corners of her eyes, tears of hope and joy and relief. Her mother might not love her, but this man did, so much he'd dropped everything to come after her. He must have driven like a maniac to get here so fast.

She was aware that Dylan was with him, standing in the background. The side of his face was scraped raw. He hung back, obviously pleased to see her but reluctant to interrupt the touching scene.

Her father pushed her back by the shoulders and searched her face. "What are you doing here, *mi hijita*? Were you really going to Las Vegas to . . . dance naked?"

In the background, Dylan shoved his hands into his pockets and glanced away, watching the blur of headlights on the freeway.

Angel tore her gaze from him, feeling betrayed, and looked her father in the eye. He was a stern man, solid and strong. As much as she wanted to, she was unable to lie.

"What were you thinking?" he asked. "Are you *loca*?"

"I thought I could make money. Enough to send some back."

His befuddlement hardened into anger. "You thought I would take money from you? Money you earned—" he gestured to her chest "—*enseñando las tetas*?"

She flushed at his crude language.

"I would rather die than take money from you," he growled, gripping her upper arms and shaking her a little.

Dylan tried to intervene. "Mr. Martinez—"

"*Callate la boca!*" he roared.

He shut up.

"I always wanted the best for you," her father continued, his voice heavy with emotion. "Why do you think we came to America? I grew up in a house with a dirt floor, and never once did I complain." He placed a hand over his heart. "I work very hard for the things we have. And you shame me by suggesting what I've given you isn't good enough? *Desgráciada!*"

"Hey," Dylan said. "She already feels bad—"

She ignored the interruption. "You're right. I was foolish." Her throat tightened. "Disgraceful. I'm sorry."

Her father sighed and he released her arm. "I know I've expected too much from you since your mother left. It was not fair for you to take care of your brothers and sister when you were just a child yourself." His eyes met hers. "I . . . I also am sorry."

Unable to speak, she only nodded, more tears spilling onto her cheeks. He brought her close and kissed the top of her head, murmuring soft words of comfort.

Sniffling, she let his T-shirt absorb her tears. "Let's go home."

He patted her back. "No."

She frowned up at him. "No?"

"I will take you to your aunt Espe."

"I have an aunt Espe?"

"*Sí.* Your mother's sister. Esperanza. She wrote me a letter a few months ago. You've never heard of her because she and your mother didn't get along."

"Where does she live?"

"LA."

"Is she married?"

"No. She lives alone."

"Have you met her?"

"Yes."

"What is she like?"

"Different from your mother," he said, choosing his words with care. "Quiet. Kind."

Angel felt a flutter of nervous energy. "Well, I can't just . . . barge in on her. What if she's not home? What if she . . . doesn't want me?"

He looked guilty. "She wants you. In her letter, she offered to put you in her extra room while you went to one of the local colleges. I didn't think—" He broke off, swearing in Spanish. "I didn't know you were so miserable."

Her breath hitched painfully. "Oh, Papa. It wasn't your fault."

"I have her address in my truck." He studied her in a way that made her sad and happy at the same time. "It is better if you go now."

She knew what he meant. If she went back home first, Yoli would cry and cling to her legs and make it twice as difficult for her to leave. Her gaze skipped over to Dylan, who was watching her face, awaiting her decision.

"Yes," she said, a strange lightness spreading through her chest. "I will go."

Luke threw Garrett into the back of his squad car and got behind the wheel. "Trujillo," he barked into the receiver as he pulled out of the driveway, tires squealing.

"Deputy Trujillo here, over."

"Where the fuck are you?"

"On my way to back you up. Where the fuck are you, sir? Over."

Luke met Garrett's glowering visage through the

rearview mirror. "Where does Betty live?" he asked, hitting the lights.

"Arroyo Drive," he mumbled. "Number 331."

Luke quickly entered it in the navigation system and turned his attention back to the CB. "Go to the Bighorn," he told Clay. "I want you to pick up Shay." When this request was met with silence, Luke realized he was ordering an officer who didn't work for him to pick up his girlfriend at a café. "She might be in danger," he added belatedly. "Over and out."

A few minutes later, Clay communicated with him again. "The café is empty, Sheriff. No one here. And no answer at Shay's house. Over."

He swore offline, raking a hand through his hair. Betty lived on the outskirts of town, and although he was driving fast, he was still several miles away. "Meet me at 331 Arroyo Drive. And call for more backup. We have another lion situation."

Signing off, he focused on the road in front of him, pressing down hard on the gas and taking the corners at a speed that was borderline suicidal. Garrett, handcuffed and unsecured in the backseat, went flying, slamming his head against the door.

Luke didn't slow down.

After what seemed like an eternity, he was there, pulling into the driveway beside a new-model gray pickup, noting the custom bed-liner and a passel of dead rabbits as he drew Garrett's revolver and exited the vehicle.

Somewhere close by, a lion roared, sending a hard chill down his spine. Abandoning stealth, Luke started flat-out running, both hands on his weapon and his eyes sharp. He went around the back of the house, drawn to the light, and was met with the goriest, most frightening scene he'd ever witnessed.

Two women lay in a pool of blood in the middle of a chain-link enclosure, like slave warriors in a gladiator arena. One was facedown, the same way Yesenia Montes had been, her lifeless arms flung out by her sides. The other was still moving, trying to creep backwards, her shoes slipping all over the wet ground.

Between them, the lion. A *big* fucking lion, jaws dripping blood. His muscles bunched in readiness, his odd green eyes alight with deadly intention as he leapt, sailing through the air in a flash of teeth and extended claws, graceful and terrifying, 250 pounds of poetry in motion.

Luke lifted his arm and aimed, squeezing off three shots in rapid succession. Hit mid-air, the lion's body jerked from the impact. He fell as suddenly as he'd jumped, collapsing on top of the scrambling woman in a clumsy, boneless heap.

Hands shaking, because he'd never shot and killed a living thing before, Luke rushed forward, setting the gun on the ground and kneeling by the slain animal. It was unmoving, unseeing, unbreathing. Dead.

With a powerful heave, he shoved the lion's body aside. Beneath it was Shay, her blue eyes wide with fright, face covered in blood.

"Oh my God," he said, gathering her in his arms. She was hurt, maybe badly, but she was alive, and she was hugging him back. He knew he shouldn't move her, but he was so relieved he couldn't let her go. "I wasn't sure it was you under there."

She pressed her face to his neck and sobbed, clinging to him desperately, her entire body trembling. Or maybe that was his body. After a moment, he lifted his head to examine her, running his hands over her throat, searching for injuries. Her hair was hanging in ropy red strands down her back and her clothes were wet.

"Where did he get you?" he asked, tugging at the neck of her T-shirt.

"Nowhere."

"Are you sure?"

"I'm fine." Her eyes darted to the other woman, who was clearly not fine.

Letting his emergency training take over, Luke went to Betty, assessing the damage. The wound on her nape was still seeping blood, and he found a pulse. It was weak, but it was there. She was alive.

In the near-distance, a police siren rang out and then quieted. His backup had arrived. Footsteps thundered along the side of the house.

"Holy Christ, what a mess."

Luke turned to see Clay Trujillo standing at the entrance to the enclosure, flanked by two EMTs. Shay straightened self-consciously, running a trembling hand over her straggly hair. Both of the technicians kneeled next to Betty and started working to save her life. In a few moments, they had her body on a stretcher and were wheeling her away.

"I'm going to call Mike Shepherd," Clay muttered, shaking his head. "This is the wildest shit I've ever seen."

Luke turned his attention back to Shay, thinking she seemed a little shell-shocked, sitting quiet as a mouse next to the body of the fallen lion. He lifted her in his arms and carried her away from the grisly scene, setting her down on a garden bench near an outdoor light. Garrett was probably hollering in the back of the squad car and Luke had a lot of other responsibilities to attend to, but right now he needed to be with Shay.

"I should check on Fernando's kids," she said. "He and Dylan went looking for Angel, and I promised."

"I'll send someone over there in a minute," he said, running his palm over her red-smeared cheek. "Are you sure you're not hurt?"

"Yes," she whispered, inspecting her arms and legs. She was soaked in blood and covered with cat hair. "None of this is mine. But I must look a fright."

He smiled. She was almost unrecognizable, and without a doubt the loveliest woman he'd ever seen. "You look beautiful," he said, feeling his throat close up.

Her eyes filled with tears. "I'm glad you came."

"So am I."

Luke couldn't bear to think about what would have happened if he'd arrived too late. The idea of losing her was excruciating. He'd finally found what he was looking for: permanence. And he'd figured out where he belonged: with Shay.

In her, and Tenaja Falls, he'd found home.

"I love you," he said, more sure of that than he'd ever been of anything.

"You—you what?"

"I love you," he repeated, and nodded to himself. It felt good to be right.

"You can't love me. We've only known each other four days."

"It seems like forever."

"You're overexcited," she insisted. "Under too much stress. It will pass."

"I hope not."

"You want to stay crazy?"

"Why not? Everyone else around here is."

"In a few weeks, you'll be bored."

"Bored," he repeated with relish. "I can't wait."

She smiled at him. Her teeth, and the whites of her eyes, were very bright against her blood-streaked face. "I've been feeling a little stressed-out myself."

"I don't blame you," he said, taking a handkerchief from his pocket. Moistening it with water from a fountain behind her, he began to clean the grime off her face.

"I might even be suffering from overexcitement."

He stilled. "Really?"

"Yes," she whispered, covering his hand with hers. "But as long as we're both crazy, I guess I . . . I love you, too."

Luke was glad he'd cleared most of the blood from her face. Because, overexcited as he was, he couldn't help but kiss her. She kissed him back with matching enthusiasm, twining her arms around his neck and threading her fingers through his hair.

He laughed against her mouth, holding her close and savoring her abandon, deliriously happy, crazy in love.

28

After the uproar settled down, and life in Tenaja Falls went back to normal, Luke took her to his father's neighborhood on the Pala reservation. He paused in front of a small, one-story house with whitewashed adobe walls and a red tile roof. Instead of stopping, he drove on, parking in the shade of an oak tree at the end of the cul-de-sac.

He didn't say anything, and she couldn't guess what he was thinking, but the day was hot and Shay wanted to feel the wind on her face. Sighing with contentment, she got out of the truck and stood at the edge of the scenic overlook, watching the sunny yellow grass on the hillside below sway in the breeze.

He came up behind her, wrapping his arms around her waist. A warm shiver traveled down her spine as he pressed his lips to the side of her neck and smoothed his hands over her lower abdomen.

At first, she thought he was merely resting his hands in a convenient place. It took her a moment to realize the significance of the position. She turned her head to look at him, reading the question in his eyes.

"Oh," she said, not sure why she was blushing. "I'm not."

It had been about three weeks since the night Luke shot Betty's lion. Betty was still in critical condition, not expected to live much longer. Garrett Snell was in jail awaiting trial, and Lori had filed for divorce.

Angel had also left town. She was staying with her aunt in LA, working at a local coffeehouse and singing there on open mike night. Dylan had been moping since she'd gone, listening to dreary music and finding very little joy in life. Basketball season was over and he already had a new job working for Bull's replacement on the construction site.

Shay didn't know if he enjoyed the work, but he always came home exhausted and went straight to bed. He slept so deeply she felt compelled to check on him. He never woke up when she placed her palm over his forehead, making sure he wasn't feverish, like she'd done so many times when he was a baby.

Speaking of babies, she and Luke hadn't made one that night in the fertility cave. He'd been coming over every morning as soon as Dylan left for school, and some evenings, too. She wouldn't let him spend the night, so they made the most of their stolen moments together.

Today was Saturday, and although Dylan wasn't home, she'd been coy with Luke this morning, shying away from his touch instead of tearing his clothes off.

And now he knew why.

To her amazement, he seemed disappointed. "I dreamed that you had a round belly," he said, smiling against her neck.

She relaxed a little, laughing. "I *do* have a round belly."

"No you don't," he insisted, flattening his palm over her. "This is barely a curve. And it's very sexy."

"You think my armpits are sexy," she said in a husky voice. "You're obviously deranged."

Chuckling, he buried his face in her hair. "Mmm. It's not my fault you smell so good."

One of their more leisurely mornings together, he'd worshipped every inch of her body with his mouth, nuzzling the sensitive skin under her arms and finding the ticklish place behind her knees, kissing the tattoo on the nape of her neck and placing his open mouth over the one at her lower back.

He must have been thinking about that, too, because he swelled against her. "I guess it's better this way," he said, his breath hot on her ear. "When I ask you to marry me, I don't want you to feel as though you have to say yes."

She let out a yelp of surprise and turned around to face him, her eyes wide with disbelief.

Perhaps astonishment was the reaction he'd been hoping for, because he smiled in satisfaction. And maybe there was something more in her expression, a hint that she wasn't averse to the idea, because she saw a flicker of intent in his eyes.

"Don't you dare," she gasped, casting a nervous glance around them. If Luke Meza got down on one knee right here by the side of the road, she would have a heart attack.

"Okay," he agreed, laughing out loud. "I'll buy you a ring first."

She gaped at him incredulously. Then, realizing she was acting as though she couldn't believe anyone would want to marry her, she snapped her mouth shut.

"You'd have said yes." He seemed almost as shocked as she was.

"Dream on," she retorted.

He kissed her then, quieting her sassy mouth, and she knew there was no escaping this. She would say yes. Always and forever.

"I love you," he said, holding her close.

He must have spoken those words a hundred times now, and they never failed to make her heart skip a beat. "I love you, too," she murmured, returning the favor.

Still smiling, he took her by the hand, dropping a kiss on her bare knuckles before he led her into the neighborhood where he grew up.

It was Luke's father they were visiting, not her own, but she was struck by a pang of nervousness all the same. "What if he doesn't like me?"

"Then we'll leave," he said, as simple as that.

She smiled back at him, and they walked together, hand in hand, toward the past and into the future, moving forward, moving on.

About the Author

Jill Sorenson's family moved from a small town in Kansas to a suburb of San Diego when she was twelve. In the past twenty years, she hasn't lost her appreciation for sunny weather, her fascination with the Pacific Ocean, or her love for Southern California culture. She still lives in San Diego with her husband, Chris, and their two children. Jill is happily working on her next novel.

Can't get enough of Sorenson's sexy suspense?

Turn the page for a sneak peek inside

THE EDGE
OF NIGHT

BY
JILL SORENSON

The Edge of Night
BY JILL SORENSON

1

Daniela Flores tightened her grip on the cold, wet aluminum railing, keeping her eyes on the horizon as she took slow, deep breaths.

She wasn't seasick. She'd been on smaller boats in rougher water than this more times than she could count. San Francisco Bay wasn't known for smooth sailing, and many of the other passengers were feeling poorly, but Daniela's discomfort had nothing to do with a rollicking hull, an unsteady surface, or brisk salt spray.

Her ailment was more mental than physical. Since the accident, she disliked cramped quarters and confined spaces.

Across the crowded cabin, past whey-faced day-trippers and sturdy-legged sailors, the open sea beckoned, mocking her with its infinite expanse. Although a boat this size wasn't the same as a shrinking box or the crushed cab of a car, it didn't offer a convenient escape route.

The water here was a chilly 50 degrees.

She much preferred the sunny beaches of San Diego,

her hometown, where ocean temps hovered at an agreeable 70 degrees this time of year, or southern Mexico, her birthplace, where the sea was as warm and sultry as a hot summer night.

In this particular area, the cold wasn't the greatest deterrent for swimmers. Her destination, twenty-seven miles off the coast of San Francisco, was a seldom visited place called the Farallones. The islands were home to many endangered animals, including the subject of her current research project, the Steller sea lion.

They were also surrounded by great white sharks.

The captain's intercom crackled with distortion as he made an announcement. "Devil's Teeth, dead ahead."

The Farallones had earned this moniker a hundred years ago from the fishermen and egg collectors who dared eke out a living here. With no docking facilities, the rocky crags were inhospitable in the extreme, rising from the sea in a jumble of sharp, serrated edges. Although teeming with animal life, every nook and cranny filled with birds and seals and sea lions, the surface area was devoid of greenery.

During the spring the islands were grassy and lush, dotted with small shrubs and speckled with wildflowers. Now, in late September, the salt-sprayed granite was noticeably bare, picked as clean as old bones.

Daniela watched the godforsaken place materialize before her with a mixture of dread and anticipation. On this cold, gray day, the islands were shrouded by fog, cloaked in mystery. If anything, the landscape was even less appealing than the pictures she'd seen. And yet, she could make out the pale brown coat of a Steller sea lion, reclining near the top of a cliff like a king lording over his realm.

Her heart began to race with excitement, thudding in her chest. The Farallones were a wildlife researcher's dream come true. Surely she could set aside her phobia and enjoy her stay here. Six weeks of uninterrupted study were almost impossible to come by, and she'd been waiting over a year for this unique opportunity.

Whenever she was feeling closed in, she would do her breathing exercises. She would stay focused on the present rather than letting the trauma of the past overwhelm her, blurring the edges of her vision and squeezing the air from her lungs. She would keep her eyes on the horizon and her feet planted firmly on the ground.

As they drew closer to the main island, she noticed a single house. It was a large, ramshackle dwelling, built over a century ago for light keepers and their families. The old Victorian stood stark and lonely on the only flat stretch of terrain, an ordinary structure on alien landscape. Like a gas station on the moon.

"Looks cozy, don't it?"

The deckhand's voice startled her. She dragged her gaze from the whitewashed house to his wind-chafed face. "Cozier than a tent in Antarctica," she replied, reminding herself that she'd braved fiercer conditions before.

He gave her another once-over and grunted, jerking his chin toward the shore. "They'll be coming for you now."

She caught a glimpse of two dark figures walking along a footpath etched into the side of the cliff, a few hundred yards from the house. With no docking facilities, setting foot on the island was a tricky process. The research biologists had access to a beat-up Boston whaler, which was hoisted above the surface of the water by a formidable-looking crane.

At a mere fifteen feet, the boat was shorter than a full-grown great white.

While she watched, one of the figures boarded the whaler, and the other lowered it to the pounding surf below. In a few efficient moments, the boat was speeding out to pick her up.

"Don't panic now," she whispered, squaring her shoulders.

The man driving the boat brought it alongside the charter and killed the engine, exchanging a friendly greeting with another crew member.

When he stood, throwing the deckhand a rope to tie off the whaler, she studied him with unabashed curiosity. His legs were covered by dark, waterproof trousers and knee-high rubber boots, same as hers. Unlike her immaculate, just-purchased ensemble, his clothes were well-used and far from spotless. His black windbreaker was splotched with what might have been bird droppings, and his face was shadowed by a week's worth of stubble.

"Seen any sharks today?" the deckhand asked.

The man grinned. "Day ain't over yet."

She guessed, based on his dark good looks, that this was Jason Ruiz, the Filipino oceanographer she'd been communicating with via email. She'd seen a grainy photo of him once and it hadn't done him justice.

The deckhand lobbed her duffel in his direction. After catching it deftly, he motioned with his gloved fingers. "Toss her to me. I'm ready."

The deckhand's eyes were merry, full of mischief. Daniela took a step back. "I'd rather not—"

"We're just messing with you," Jason said, patting the aluminum seat beside him. "Give 'er a jump."

She moistened her dry lips, measuring the distance between the boats with trepidation. The expanse across was less than two feet, but the drop went quite a ways down. And, although the whaler was tied off, it was still a moving target.

Her stomach churned as she watched it pitch and sway. "Jump?"

"Yep. And try not to hit water. Just because we haven't seen them today doesn't mean they aren't there."

The deckhand laughed, as if this were a joke. It wasn't. This time of year, the sharks were most definitely there. They came to the Farallones every fall to dine on a rich assortment of seals and sea lions.

Daniela stared at the surface of the water, feeling faint.

She'd been debriefed about the boat situation, of course. But reading a matter-of-fact description about what she needed to do to access the island was different than actually going through with it. Leaping from a charter to an aluminum boat in shark-infested waters . . . it was madness. One false move, one tiny miscalculation, and . . .

Gulp.

Jason gave the deckhand a knowing smirk. "Just throw her over here, Jackie. She can't weigh much more than that bag."

"No," she protested, scrambling up on the edge of the railing. She was pretty sure they were teasing again, but she also didn't want to give herself time to reconsider. Chickening out before she'd begun was not an option.

She took a deep breath, braced her hands behind her on the rail, and pushed off, flailing toward the whaler with arms and legs akimbo.

She didn't fall into the water. She didn't hit the aluminum seat, either. She collided with Jason Ruiz, almost knocking them both off balance. He threw his arms around her and braced his legs wide, holding her steady until the boat stopped rocking.

Daniela clung to him for a prolonged moment, her heart racing. She hadn't been this close to a man in a long time, and it felt good. Strange, but good. He was quite a bit taller than she was, and a whole lot stronger. She could feel the muscles in his arms and the flatness of his chest against her breasts.

He smelled good, too. Like salt and ocean and hard work. But even while she registered these sensations, there was one irrational, overriding thought: Not Sean.

"I'm sorry," she said, clearing her throat.

"Don't mention it," he murmured, making sure she was ready to stand on her own before he released her. "I never get tired of beautiful women throwing themselves at me. I only wish I'd showered in recent memory." The corner of his mouth tipped up. "There's a shortage of hot water on the island, and we're all a bit rank."

She couldn't help but smile. "You don't smell bad."

"Really? I thought I smelled like bird crap and BO."

Laughing, she shook her head. "Bird crap, maybe." The faint odor of ammonia filled her nostrils, but it was coming from the island not him.

"I'm Jason."

"Daniela," she said, grasping his hand. As quickly as it cropped up, the sexual tension between them dissolved. He was still smiling at her in an appreciative, masculine way, and she was smiling back at him, unable to deny his considerable appeal, but there was no intensity to their admiration for each other.

He was just a handsome charmer with an easy line, and she'd known men like him before. Her ex-husband, for one. Women had always dropped at Sean's feet, and he'd done little to discourage them.

Feeling her smile slip, she pulled her hand away.

If he noticed her change of mood, he didn't remark upon it. "Ready?" he asked, catching the rope the deckhand threw at him and tucking it away.

Nodding, she perched on the edge of the aluminum seat, paralyzed by self-consciousness. She was so far out of her element here. The past two years, she'd been in virtual seclusion, working from her desk at home and putting in late hours at the research facility. She'd interacted with more spreadsheets than animals. This trip was, in part, an attempt to get her life back. A return to her roots.

She hadn't chosen conservation biology to spend all her time indoors.

Rubbing elbows with other scientists, most of whom were men, was nothing new, and she was no stranger to roughing it, but she hadn't socialized, much less dated, in ages. The close proximity of a hot guy rattled her more than she'd like to admit.

And she couldn't stop comparing him to Sean.

The two men probably knew each other. There weren't that many shark experts in the world, let alone the West Coast, and Jason was from San Diego. They were close in age, although Sean was about five years older. Both of them were tall and fit and remarkably good-looking. They were also consummate outdoorsmen and staunch environmentalists, more comfortable on a surfboard than in a boardroom.

Upon closer inspection, Jason was the more striking of the two, with his exotic eyes and sensual mouth. But Sean's all-American ruggedness had always hit her in the right spot.

Daniela turned her gaze back to the calm-inducing horizon. She hadn't seen Sean in over a year, and he still managed to monopolize her thoughts.

Maneuvering the whaler back into position beneath the boom was a task that required concentration and dexterity. When Jason found the proper place, he stood and hitched the heavy metal hook to the hull with no assistance from her. She did her best to hang onto her seat and stay out of his way.

Once connected, the whaler was lifted high into the air by the crane, and this ride was no less nerve-wracking than the two-hour boat trip to the islands or the precarious jump she'd taken a few moments ago. Heart racing with anxiety, she gripped the aluminum bench until her knuckles went white. When the boat shuddered to a stop over dry land, she breathed a sigh of relief and flexed her icy hands.

She couldn't believe she was actually here. Southeast Farallon Island was an odd place, like no other on earth, and the first thing that struck her was the noise. It was nature in chaos. The sound of crashing surf and cawing birds reverberated in her ears, and wind whipped at her clothes like children vying for attention.

Jason grinned at the boom operator, clearly at home in this wild place. "Thanks, Liz," he shouted, raising his voice to be heard above the cacophony.

The woman at the controls watched while Jason helped Daniela climb from the dangling boat, her expression cool.

Daniela stepped forward to introduce herself. "Liz? I'm Daniela Flores."

"Elizabeth Winters," she said, extending a slender, black-gloved hand.

Daniela accepted her handshake with an uncertain smile.

"I'm the only one allowed to call her Liz," Jason explained, hefting her duffel bag over his shoulder. "Because we're special friends."

Elizabeth regarded him like he was something unpleasant stuck to the bottom of her shoe. Daniela didn't know what to make of her. She was tall and slim, dressed in Gore-Tex from head to toe, with a gray-blue windbreaker that matched the color of her eyes. A thick auburn braid trailed over one shoulder, and she had the delicate skin of a redhead. Her face was pale and freckled and very lovely.

"I'll refrain from sharing my pet name for you," she said dryly.

He laughed, delighted to have irked her. Elizabeth seemed more annoyed than amused. Perhaps she was immune to charming men.

Daniela decided that she liked her. "How is your conservation project coming along?" she asked as they followed Jason down the steep, pebble-strewn path toward the houses. "I was fascinated by the study you published recently on the black-feathered cormorant."

Elizabeth's cheeks flushed with pleasure. "Thank you. The islands get so much attention for their sharks." She made a face at Jason's well-formed back, as if he were responsible for the Farallones' notoriety. "Many of the birds here are in far greater need of protection, but the majority of funds are spent on shark research. Investors with deep pockets love to see red water and flashing teeth."

"Watch your step," Jason warned them, turning toward Elizabeth and placing his hand on her slim waist.

She tensed at his touch. "I'm fine."

Nodding, he released her and continued on.

Daniela traversed the slope with caution, feeling rocks crumble and roll like ball bearings beneath her booted feet.

"Where was I?" Elizabeth asked.

" 'Flashing teeth,' " Daniela supplied, eyes cast downward.

"Oh, right. The tourists come for the sharks as well. Boatloads of gawkers cruise by every weekend. I mean, this is supposed to be an animal sanctuary. Last Sunday they all but ruined my chances at seeing two blue-crested warblers mate—"

Her rising voice shut off like a switch as she lost her footing. Quick as lightning, Jason caught her by both arms and hauled her against him, saving her from a nasty tumble down the side of the cliff.

She stared up at him, wide-eyed and short of breath.

"Like I said," he murmured, letting her go. "Watch your step."

"Sorry." With a trilling laugh, she glanced back at Daniela. "I tend to get overexcited, talking about my causes."

"No need to apologize for being passionate," Daniela said, intrigued by the subject matter. Not to mention the byplay between Elizabeth and Jason. "How close do the tourists get?" she asked as they started down the hill again. "I thought the waters here were too treacherous for recreational boaters."

"Oh, they are," Jason replied. "But a cage-diving operation comes during shark season. They dock a couple of hundred feet offshore, drop the cages, and throw out chum."

Daniela was shocked. "They *chum*? Near the islands?" The practice of luring sharks with chum, a noxious mixture of blood and fish parts, was looked down on by scientists. It changed the animals' natural behavior and made them less wary of humans.

"Yeah. Unfortunately, it's not illegal."

She arrived at the base of the slope, where the ground was more stable. "I can't imagine getting in the water here. Even with a steel cage for protection."

"Crazy thrill seekers," Jason said, winking at Elizabeth. Obviously, his profession as a shark researcher put him in the same category. "Daniela is here to observe the Steller sea lion. She's from the Scripps Institute in San Diego."

Elizabeth's brows rose. "Excellent. That's a topnotch organization."

"Oh, yes," Daniela said, unable to contain her own excitement. "We're collecting the necessary data to keep the Steller on the endangered list. I hope my work here makes a difference."

"So do I," Elizabeth said kindly.

"We've got an awesome crew this season." Jason shifted the weight of her duffel as he approached the front door of the house. "Brent Masterson is here, filming some footage for his documentary. Taryn is one of the most enthusiastic interns I've ever met. And although Dr. Fitzwilliam had to back out at the last minute, his replacement is a name I'm sure you'll recognize. We've nabbed the leading shark expert in the Western Hemisphere—"

Daniela's stomach dropped as soon as he opened the door. For standing behind it was a man she recognized very well, indeed. The leading shark expert of the Western Hemisphere had his hands all over a gorgeous blonde, laughing as he tried to wrestle her to the ground.

"—Sean Carmichael," Jason finished, gazing upon Daniela's ex-husband with hero-worship in his eyes.

Available from *Rouge Romance*:

Tessa Dare's 'Stud Club' Trilogy:

ONE DANCE WITH A DUKE
Spencer Dumarque, the fourth Duke of Morland, has a reputation as the dashing "Duke of Midnight." Each evening he selects one lady for a scandalous midnight waltz. But none of the ladies of the ton catch his interest for long, until Lady Amelia d'Orsay tries her luck.

TWICE TEMPTED BY A ROUGE
Brooding war hero, Rhys St. Maur, returns to his ancestral home on the Devonshire moors following the murder of his friend in the elite gentlemen's society known as the Stud Club. There, he is offered a chance at redemption in the arms of beautiful innkeeper, Meredith Maddox, who dares him to face the demons of his past.

THREE NIGHTS WITH A SCOUNDREL
The bastard son of a nobleman, Julian Bellamy plotted to have the last laugh on a society that once spurned him. But meeting Leo Chatwick, founder of the exclusive Stud Club, and Lily, his enchanting sister, made Julian reconsider his wild ways. When Leo is murdered Julian vows to see the woman he secretly loves married to a man of her own class. Lily, however, has a very different husband in mind.

* * *

THE CLUB by Sharon Page
Lady Jane Beaumont's friend Delphinia has vanished and Jane must enter into a dangerous charade to find her. In London's most secretive gentlemen's club, Jane awaits the lover she has procured for the evening. But the man who enters her bedchamber is no stranger. He is Delphinia's brother and London's most notorious rake – a man on a rescue mission of his own.

Tracy Anne Warren's *Trap* Trilogy:

THE HUSBAND TRAP
Violet Brantford has always longed for Adrian Winter, the
wealthy Duke of Raeburn, who is set to marry Violet's vivacious
twin sister, Jeannette. However, when Jeannette refuses to go
through with the ceremony, Violet finds herself walking down
the aisle in her sister's place in order to avoid a scandal. But
keeping up the pretence with a man as divine as the Duke will
take all of Violet's skills…

THE WIFE TRAP
After orchestrating a scandalous high-society ruse, Lady
Jeannette Brantford is banished from her family's estate in
England and sent to live in the Irish countryside. But en route to
her dreaded destination, she encounters Darragh O'Brien, a
devilishly handsome architect who transforms Jeannette's
punishment into a delicious whirlwind of wits, words, and
undeniable passion.

THE WEDDING TRAP
Lord Christopher Winter has volunteered to transform quiet,
reserved heiress Eliza into a stunning belle. There's just one
problem: Eliza has always been head over heels in love with the
very man who is trying to find her a husband!

THE WARRIOR by Nicole Jordan
Ariane is betrothed to the feared Norman knight Ranulf de
Vernay. But cruel circumstance has branded Ariane's father a
traitor to the crown and Ranulf is returning home, not as
bridegroom… but as conqueror. But though he has come to
claim her lands and body as his prize, it is the mighty warrior
who must surrender to Ariane's passion and her remarkable
healing love.